Fridrikh Neznansky is a graduate of the Moscow Institute of Law and spent fifteen years as a Criminal Investigator in Moscow. He now lives in West Germany. He wrote (with Edward Topol) the best-selling *Red Square* and *Deadly Games*. *The Fair at Sokolniki* reflects his deep knowledge of the elite and the underworld in the Soviet Union.

By *Fridrikh Neznansky and Edward Topol*

RED SQUARE
DEADLY GAMES

and published by Corgi Books

THE FAIR
AT SOKOLNIKI

Fridrikh Neznansky

Translated from the Russian by
Robert Porter

CORGI BOOKS

THE FAIR AT SOKOLNIKI

A CORGI BOOK   0 552 12855 4

Originally published in Great Britain by Bantam Press, a division of
Transworld Publishers Ltd

PRINTING HISTORY

Bantam Press edition published 1986
Corgi edition published 1987

Copyright © Possev Verlag, V. Gorachek K.G. 1984
Translation copyright © Robert Porter 1986

Conditions of sale:
1. This book is sold subject to the condition that it shall
not, by way of trade *or otherwise*, be lent, re-sold, hired
out or otherwise circulated in any form of binding or cover
other than that in which it is published *and without a similar
condition including this condition being imposed on the
subsequent purchaser.*
2. This book is sold subject to the Standard Conditions
of Sale of Net Books and may not be re-sold in the U.K.
below the net price fixed by the publishers for the book.

Corgi Books are published by Transworld Publishers Ltd.,
61–63 Uxbridge Road, Ealing, London W5 5SA,
in Australia by Transworld Publishers (Aust.) Pty. Ltd.,
15–23 Helles Avenue, Moorebank, NSW 2170, and in New
Zealand by Transworld Publishers (N.Z.) Ltd., Cnr. Moselle
and Waipareira Avenues, Henderson, Auckland.

Reproduced, printed and bound in Great Britain by
Hazell Watson & Viney Limited,
Member of the BPCC Group,
Aylesbury, Bucks

To my wife, Lida

Main Characters

TURETSKY, Alexander Borisovich (Sasha, Shurik). Junior Investigator at the Moscow Prosecutor's Office

SHCHASTLIVAYA, Margarita Nikolayevna (Rita). Forensic pathologist

MERKULOV, Konstantin Dmitriyevich. Serious Crimes Investigator, Moscow Prosecutor's Office

PARKHOMENKO, Leonid Vasilyevich (Lyona). Chief of Investigations Section, Moscow Prosecutor's Office

ROMANOVA, Alexandra Ivanovna (Shura). Chief of the second section of Moscow CID; lieutenant-colonel in the Militia

GRYAZNOV, Vyacheslav (Slava). Inspector in Moscow CID; captain in the Militia

ANDROPOV, Yuri Vladimirovich. General Secretary of the Central Committee of the Communist Party of the USSR

GEORGADZE, Mikhail Porfiryevich. Secretary to the Praesidium of the Supreme Soviet of the USSR

YEMELYANOV, Sergei Andreyevich (Seryosha). Instructor of the Central Committee of the Communist Party of the USSR, later Chief Prosecutor of Moscow

RAKITIN, Viktor Nikolayevich (Vitya). Senior employee in the Ministry of Foreign Trade of the USSR

RAKITINA, Viktoria Ippolitovna (Vika). His wife

RAKITIN, Alexei (Lyosha). His son.

TSAPKO, Ippolit Alexeyevich. His father-in-law; previously Deputy Chief of Intelligence at Soviet GHQ

KUPRIYANOVA, Valeria Sergeyevna (Lera, Valya). Ballet dancer; Rakitin's mistress.

KASSARIN, Vasily Vasilyevich. Head of Special Investigations, Main Adminsitration 'T' Committee of the KGB of the USSR; major-general in Security

KAZAKOV (KRAMARENKO), Vladimir Georgiyevich (Volodya). Deputy Manager of the Elisei Food Store; long criminal record; 'King' of the Hippodrome racetrack; KGB agent

SOYA-SERKO, Alla Alexandrovna. Widow of the professor at the Conservatory; gymnastics coach

VOLIN, Igor. Coach at the NAUKA sports club; expert in unarmed combat

The wolf-hunt's on, the wolf-hunt's on
For the grey full-grown predators and the pups alike.

V. VYSOTSKY

PROLOGUE

The train from St Moritz was almost empty when it reached Zurich, its passengers quickly melting into the milling crowd of travellers at the station. A tall suntanned man of about forty left the train and made straight for the escalator which led down to the shopping centre under Bahnhofplatz. But the subterranean domain of countless shops did not attract his attention. With an athlete's quick light stride he passed them by and took the stairs up from the precinct to the Bahnhofstrasse at the other side of the square, heading towards Lake Zurich.

Three hundred metres or so later, he slackened his pace as he approached a shabby café, glancing back over his shoulder and pretending to check his watch against the clock of the old church on the other side of the street, which had just started to strike midday.

The street looked clear enough. The man with the tan went into the café and sat at a table by the window. He lit a cigarette and leant back in his chair, easing the stiff set of his shoulders and his clenched jaw. The bus from Brunau should have arrived ten minutes before. . . .

A young waitress wearing Alpine national dress flitted over to his table, and he ordered coffee. When she brought it over on a little tray a minute later, he gulped it down greedily and then caught sight of the person he was waiting for. A fat old man in a tartan jacket was almost running along the Bahnhofstrasse, the speed with which he was ducking and weaving to avoid collisions with passers-by surprising in view of his obvious age and florid hypertensive complexion. The sun-tanned man breathed out softly, his feeling of taut expectancy ebbing away. He

9

stubbed out his cigarette. Then, casually, he looked at his watch again, put some money on the table and walked out of the café.

His timing was accurate to a fraction of a second. Two blocks down the road he could have caught up with the fat man, who, having negotiated the huge revolving doors of the Röntgen Bank, was obviously making for Lake Zurich. Hanging back in the crowd, however, the sun-tanned man followed at a distance. The fat man chose an unobtrusive bench in the shade in the lakeside park, sat down and waited.

The watcher circled the bench before moving in. There were plenty of people about – but no one who counted, he was sure. The man in the tartan jacket jumped to his feet and just checked himself from embracing the other man. 'Hello, Vasenka,' he said instead in pure Russian. For reply, 'Vasenka' patted the old man on the hand, almost patronisingly, and smiled. The change of expression altered his face beyond recognition: the corners of the green eyes seemed to slant downwards, and his long teeth were bared for an instant.

With an odd jerking movement, he passed his hand across his face to flick a strand of hair. By the time his hand reached his side again, the grimacing smile had disappeared. Meanwhile, the old man was fumbling with the inside pocket of his jacket, struggling to withdraw a small but obviously heavy package. He offered it deferentially to 'Vasenka', who unwrapped the paper slowly and deliberately, then froze in satisfaction as his experienced eye evaluated the contents: a sapphire necklace, diamond brooches, pearls, emeralds, antique coins. . . .

'That's the lot, Vasya. The last instalment.'

He nodded his head and picked out an emerald ring from the pile of valuables. He folded the package carefully and put it into his jacket pocket, the ring still in the palm of his hand. Absently, almost shyly, he toyed with the fountain pen in his breast pocket while extending the hand which held the emerald.

'And this one is just for you, Andrei Yemelyanovich. A wedding present for your granddaughter.'

Hesitantly, the old man stretched out his hand. His face had suddenly puckered as if he was about to burst into tears of gratitude, but he never had the chance. The man with the tan seemed about to sneeze. He slipped out his handkerchief and at the same instant pressed a little spring in the fountain pen. . . .

A few moments later he melted inconspicuously into the crowd of citizens and tourists in the sunny lakeside park.

Several hours afterwards some passers-by discovered the body of the old man on the park bench, his hand out-stretched as if begging. An autopsy established that Andrei Yemelyanovich Zotov, artist, eighty-one years old, of Russian origin, had died of a heart-attack.

PART ONE
Duty Investigator, Call Out!

1

His first waking thought was of Rita. Today, for sure, he would see her. Today he wouldn't mind leaving the warmth of his bed for the icy morning chill of the squalid shared apartment. . . . Shivering, he pulled the covers closer round him while fumbling automatically for the switch of the bedside lamp. What the hell time was it anyway? It was still dark outside, but that didn't mean a thing. And then the pounding on the door began.

Irka Frolovskaya, the visiting niece of one of the ancient dames who lived in his block, tentatively opened his door and called round it in alarm: 'Shurik! Shurik! Quick, look what's happened to your jeans!'

Jesus Christ! Like a scalded cat, Alexander Borisovich Turetsky, pride and joy of the Law Faculty of Moscow University from which he had just graduated *summa cum laude*, bolted from his room, wearing nothing but a moth-eaten pair of knee-length rayon boxer shorts. His Wranglers, put to air overnight on the long radiator in the communal kitchen, had dried rigid and board-like. For once, the radiator seemed to have been working over-time. The blue jeans for which he had paid a black-marketeer a hundred and fifty roubles were done to a crisp. Sasha was horrified. All he needed was to be late for his first day at work.

'Have you got an iron?' he yelled.

Irka got an antediluvian flat iron from her aunt's room and stood it to heat on the hotplate of the range while she and Sasha sprinkled, dampened and finally doused the crackling denim. While Irka battled to iron the jeans,

Sasha splashed ice-cold water over himself behind the makeshift curtain in the kitchen extension, cursing for the millionth time the minimal amenities in the overcrowded apartment. He had a scratchy shave, then swallowed two cold hard-boiled eggs washed down with some buttermilk.

With a smile at Irka, who wasn't a bad kid when she wasn't taking up too much space, he took the jeans back to his room. Though they were still damp around the waistband, he struggled into them and put on his red and black check shirt. A glance in the mirror revealed a good-looking, brown-haired twenty-five-year-old, pale-faced against a background of bright pink wallpaper – though perhaps he was pale at the thought of his first day of real work in the office of the Moscow District Prosecutor.

He grabbed his jacket, shouted his thanks to Irka, and dived down the stairs. Twenty to ten! The hell with wet jeans, pink wallpaper and cold eggs. Today he was going to see Rita!

He ran across the apartment block's forecourt, then past the Fillipov church, leapt over the wrought-iron fence on to Gogol Boulevard and sprinted for the bus-stop. Getting on to a packed trolley-bus was an art he had long since mastered. With one foot on the bottom step, he grabbed the strap on a long-legged colonel's greatcoat, and allowed himself to be towed blindly behind. Once inside, he put himself gladly into the hands of two pretty little students, who pushed him into the depths of a number 13 going as far as Trubnaya Street.

The driver braked sharply. Some degenerate, or else one of those hundred-year-old crones from the Arbat, was jaywalking. The passengers standing in the aisle went sprawling *en masse* towards the driver's cab. Alexander Borisovich Turetsky, Junior Investigator, couldn't keep his feet and ended up in the lap of a large lady wearing a fox-fur coat. She didn't seem to mind.

'Sasha.'

Glancing quickly to one side, he saw sitting next to

them none other than his new boss, Konstantin Dmitriye-vich Merkulov, Judicial Counsellor and Serious Crimes Investigator of the Moscow Public Prosecutor's Office.

Struggling to his feet, Sasha Turetsky, super-sleuth, deduced: 'You're not on your way from home, are you?' He knew that Merkulov lived on the other side of Moscow.

'That's right, I'm not coming from home,' said Merku-lov, deadpan.

'Where have you come from, then?' Sasha asked tact-lessly, before remembering that official business should never be discussed in a public place.

'From Pirogovskaya Street,' Merkulov announced to the interested lady in fox-fur and all the other passengers.

'The morgue?' Had Investigator Merkulov been, bright and early, to a post-mortem in one of the two morgues on Great Pirogovskaya Street?

'No, kid, not the morgue. Lelya's sick again. She's had to go back to hospital. I managed to get my hands on some Altai honey – don't ask me how – and I've just taken it to her. It's the best thing for her complaint, better than any antibiotic!'

Meathead! How could he have forgotten? Merkulov was the star of the Public Prosecutor's Office and there were dozens of stories about him, including the tale of the crusty confirmed bachelor, Konstantin Dmitriyevich Merkulov, falling in love like a first-year student with a quiet woman by the name of Lelya who suffered from tuberculosis and, as if that wasn't enough, the added drawback of a delicate, fair-haired daughter. It was like *La Dame aux Camélias* all over again – with an added touch of socialist realism. But Kostya had been determined to marry her, despite many loaded warnings. Now, every morning, Merkulov took Lidochka to school and, from time to time, Lelya to the TB clinic. The poor fool seemed to believe that one day she would finally be cured.

The trolley-bus reached the Nikita Gates where most of

the passengers – obviously employees of the Telegraph Agency – got out. Sasha sat down on the warm seat recently vacated by the fat woman. The much-reviled new Moscow Arts Theatre flashed past the window as the bus got under way again. Then the Pushkin monument, then the Novosti Press Agency. The bus was coming up to Petrovka. They jumped from the platform at the back and, ignoring the red light of the pedestrian crossing, made for the GUVD building, the Ministry of Internal Affairs, at Petrovka 38. Five minutes later, Sasha's first day officially working, instead of observing, had begun.

That morning in Moscow workers tended their machines, raising productivity as the new General Secretary, Comrade Andropov, had called on them to do. Civil servants in ministries and government departments skilfully shuffled incoming and outgoing memoranda, bringing further confusion and delay to the business of building communism. Housewives stood for long hours in queues, cursing and swearing – not so much at the lack of productivity as at the lack of meat. They seemed not to realise that the two were connected.

Merkulov and Turetsky couldn't have cared less. They had the task of fighting crime in Moscow, the indices of which were rising with an unbelievable rapidity to which the press turned a blind eye. Russia had already caught up with the American *per capita* production of coal and cement. It seemed it would be only a matter of time before the Moscow murder rate of four a day caught up, then overtook, New York's five homicides every twenty-four hours.

The duty section of the GUVD – to give it its correct name – was a daunting combination of modern technology and barrack-room boorishness. Three floors of the ancient former private residence in Sredne-Karetny Lane housed the latest electronic computer equipment, bought – or, if rumours were to be believed, stolen – from Japan and America. However, the benefits of such dearly (or cheaply) obtained technology were being reaped by a bunch of the biggest idiots imaginable, all relegated to the duty section for a variety of misdemeanours – drunkenness, petty extortion, bedding other men's wives. As a rule, they were ex-political workers, passport officials, anti-corruption squad.

Potashev, the duty section chief, was a shining exception – he seemed to have a head on his shoulders. He brought Merkulov and Turetsky up to date on the operations situation.

'Murders in the last twenty-four hours – five,' he boomed. 'Suicides – nine. Rapes – seventeen. Robberies – seventy-five. Incidents of hooliganism, serious – two hundred and fifty. Incidents of hooliganism, minor – two thousand and four. Drunks picked up on the street – five thousand, two hundred and eighty-three. . . .'

At that moment a crackling sound came over the loudspeaker, and someone said in a heavy Tartar accent: 'Dooty Investigator, call out!'

The duty section was filled with spontaneous hoots and jeers, and Potashev bellowed angrily: 'Sabirov! Are you off your head or something?'

Major Sabirov of the Moscow CID sat directly opposite Potashev's desk, at the other side of the room. He was probably too lazy to get off his fat backside and amble across. Colonel Potashev flicked off his desk speaker and took the call-out phone call. Replacing the receiver, he told Merkulov matter-of-factly: 'The Commandant's office in the Kremlin has rung. You'll have to go over to Red Square. There's a self-immolation there – or, at least, an attempt.' He lit a cigarette and went on lazily: 'A lot of them about these days – this is the third this month. Don't pussy-foot with him, men. If he's still alive, wrap a canvas round him and get him to Sklifosovksy Emergencies Institute. If he's had it, take him to Nikolskoye Crematorium. They can finish the job there!'

'What would we do without his quick thinking?' Sasha murmured from the corner of his mouth.

Merkulov's team creaked into action. It wasn't until

19

they were outside in the yard, getting into the blue Mercedes which was a gift to his Moscow friends from the West Berlin chief of police, that the tall red-haired CID man, Inspector Gryaznov, said pointedly: 'We're short-handed, Konstantin Dmitriyevich.'

'Huh?' said Merkulov, preoccupied with checking through his scene-of-the-crime kit in its shabby cardboard briefcase, and not really registering Gryaznov's words. But at least one other member of the team knew exactly who was missing. . . .

'I said, the team's short-handed,' Gryaznov repeated slowly and clearly. 'There's clearly you and junior officer, there's me, and here's Kozlov from forensics. Rex and Lieutenant Panyushkin are already asleep in the Mercedes, but the pathologist's not here.'

It was news to Merkulov. 'No doctor?' he yelled. 'We have to deal with a human torch with no doctor present? Whose duty day is it, for Christ's sake?'

Turetksy watched Gryaznov run keenly upstairs to check the duty roster and discover – surprise, surprise – that it was none other than Margarita Nikolayevna Shchastlivaya, a specialist from the City Hospital No. 1, who was supposed to be on duty with them today.

Merkulov slumped against the wine-coloured upholstery of the Mercedes and sighed dramatically.

'Makes no difference if we wait for ten or fifteen minutes more. Our friend in Red Square's probably a heap of ashes by now. No sweat, men.'

'There must be a good reason why she hasn't showed?' Turetsky began. 'Margarita Shchastlivaya is never late.'

'I obviously haven't studied her as closely as you, kid,' Merkulov said with a sly wink.

The blush spread to the tips of Turetsky's ears, but fortunately everybody's attention had switched to the gateman, who was opening up for a smart export-model red Lada. For any ordinary employee the car would have seemed suspiciously affluent, but not for Rita Shchastlivaya, the most beautiful, accomplished and well-connected woman Sasha Turetsky had ever met. Her husband was a major-general, currently stationed in Afghanistan.

At the approach road into Red Square by the History Museum was a bus full of police militiamen, carrying Kalashnikov automatics and wearing bullet-proof vests. A detachment of Kremlin guardsmen was marching from the direction of the Spassky Tower towards the Mausoleum, and the Mercedes, as if leading the parade, drove on to the cobbled stones of the Kremlin to the mellow chimes of the Kremlin bells carried on the wind from the other side of the square.

Traces of public mourning for the late Brezhnev were everywhere. Along the grey granite tribunes stood thousands of drooping wreaths – from fraternal communist parties, from hostile states, from peoples struggling for their liberation, from the Soviet republics which had already achieved liberation, and also from countless ministries and government departments.

Passing the wreaths and duplicated portraits of Brezhnev, the Mercedes came right up to Lenin's Mausoleum before stopping at a signal from a thunder-faced captain standing by a row of militiamen.

'What's going on, Captain?' Merkulov asked the red-faced officer.

'You'll see,' he said in a strangled voice, and let them through the police cordon.

Turetsky had already drawn a nightmarish picture in his mind – a charred, half-recognizable corpse on the steps of Lenin's Mausoleum. Instead, ten yards from the entrance, stood a camp-bed: an ordinary, khaki-coloured, ex-army camp-bed. On it squatted an old man in a black padded jacket with a green canvas cape. He had a can of petrol by his side and was holding on grimly with both hands to a scrawled placard which read:

21

Andropov! I have been on the waiting list for an apartment for thirty years. Khrushchev and Brezhnev made promises but they didn't give me anywhere to live. If you don't, either, I'm going to set light to myself now on Red Square. I've got nothing to lose. Signed: a working man, Ivan Chekharin.

The call-out team was incredulous. Rita Shchastlivaya could hardly stop herself from laughing. For once, Merkulov was caught on the hop.

'Why is he still here?' he finally asked the captain accusingly.

'And where would you like him to be?'

'What do you mean, where? Anywhere but here!'

Merkulov nodded in the direction of the GUM department store. Opposite it was the 117th police precinct under whose jurisdiction the Red Square area came.

'Oh, no,' drawled the captain, narrowing his eyes. 'Oh, no, friend. You don't catch me that way! I'm not ready for retirement yet. Haven't you heard, they only buried Brezhnev the other day – and what will Comrade Yuri Vladimirovich Andropov's line on Comrade Chekharin be? You haven't got the faintest idea, I haven't, even the Kremlin commandant, General-Lieutenant Shornikov, doesn't know! This is a problem for the District Prosecutor's Office; it's all yours!'

'All right, all right. We get the picture.' Bristling, Merkulov strode over to the car radio. It took him just quarter of an hour to settle a problem of thirty years' standing. First, he got in touch with Dianov of the administrative section of the Moscow City Communist Party. He in turn tracked down Promyslov, the Mayor of Moscow, who happened to be in the Kremlin. In a matter of minutes, the Moscow Soviet passed an extraordinary resolution allocating a three-roomed flat on the newly built Brezhnev housing estate to the family of one Ivan Kuzmich Chekharin, born 1917, fitter and sanitary technician.

Folding his camp-bed and his placard (the police confiscated the can of petrol), Chekharin trotted meekly behind the distinctly relieved-looking captain to the busfull of cops, with their bullet-proof vests and Kalashnikovs, which had drawn up close by.

The 'dissident' said goodbye to the team in lugubrious tones. He seemed to have made his point but he still wasn't sure where they were taking him. Was it really to show him his new flat on the Brezhnev housing estate, or was it to Butyrki Prison?

2

At 11.45 the team left Red Square, not for Petrovka 38 but along Gorky Street towards Leningradsky Prospekt. The wailing of the car's siren forced the traffic over to the right, away from the Mercedes.

Merkulov was on the car radio to headquarters. The whole operations team, including the inquisitive Rex, his long ears pricked up, was listening intently. What could possibly top that diplomatic triumph? A familiar chuckle came over the radio.

'Did I put the wind up you men! You've got to believe me – I had no idea myself! Those lying buck-passers in the Kremlin will catch it, I swear to you. I've already made a report to the General, and he'll blast them! Trushin is talking to the Deputy Minister, Zabotin, right now, and he—'

'Forget it,' Merkulov said, interrupting. 'Let's just forget all about it, Colonel. So what's new? Where to next?'

The Duty Officer's voice grew serious. 'Leningradsky Prospekt, no. 145, block 5, apartment 93. According to a report from the 129th, half an hour ago, there's been a family row. A truck-driver – Mokridin's his name – with his five-year-old daughter watching, slit open his wife's

23

belly with a bayonet. Seems she wouldn't give him the money for a few vodkas.'

'Is she alive?' Merkulov broke in.

'No chance.'

'And what about him, Mokritsyn?'

'*Mokridin*. He's dead too. When the local boys on the beat started to break in, he stuck the bayonet in his heart. Seems like quite a tidy one, this time.'

'What about the girl?'

'They've taken her into care already. Danilovskaya Street. The local education department is seeing to that; it's not our problem.'

There was a moment's respectful silence, then Merkulov confirmed: 'So there's no need to rush, Nikolai Viktorovich?'

'No point, Konstantin Dmitriyevich.'

The sergeant at the wheel needed no further cue. He switched off the siren and slipped into the stream of traffic behind a green Zhiguli. It was just another routine callout.

3

The Kremlin bells must have been chiming twelve when he came out of the Metro and set off along the broad alleyway towards the park. He stopped at a tobacco-kiosk at the start of his walk, bought some Prima cigarettes, opened the pack and took one out. He broke it in two. One half he put back in the pack, the other half he stuck in a brown wooden cigarette-holder. He lit it with an imported gas-lighter.

While he was going through this standard procedure, his newish bright russet-coloured briefcase rested on a bench littered with handbills, newspapers and bottles. When he'd lit his cigarette, the man picked up his brief-

24

case and strode off along the alleyway, towards the central gates of Sokolniki Park.

It was still fine weather but, according to the long-range forecast, winter was due to start tomorrow.

At the first entrance to the park, he showed his pass for the exhibition then slackened his pace. His heart was thumping painfully, and his breathing was harsh and irregular. If only he'd thought to bring his heart tablets with him.

The main pavilion was at the other side of a small paved square with a cluster of flagpoles at its centre. He did not make for the pavilion's entrance but retreated to a green-painted bench where he sat down under a clump of dead-looking leafless trees. He shivered, not from infirmity but from fear.

He took out his black spectacle-case and cleaned his glasses with a piece of velvet. Long-sighted, he usually wore them only to work, but perhaps they might disguise the top half of his face just a little. He took off his grey hat and mopped his brow with a handkerchief. Then he put the hat back on, pulled it lower over his brow, and started carefully wiping his damp palms with the handkerchief. A quick look at his Japanese wristwatch – eighteen minutes past twelve – confirmed that he had a few more minutes to pull himself together.

At twenty-past twelve, he snapped open the metal clasps of his briefcase and took out a square greenish package about the size of a deck of cards. He slipped it under his coat and into the breast pocket of his jacket. Then he stood up, picked up his briefcase and headed for the main pavilion of the international electronics trade fair, which should now be open. He moved calmly and unhurriedly towards the pavilion's entrance.

The fair, in which firms from thirty-three different countries were taking part, should have opened on the previous Friday. But the death of the Leader, Leonid Brezhnev, had upset the organisers' plans, and after hasty consultation with the Central Committee they had taken the bold decision to open the fair immediately after Leonid Ilyich's funeral. The tickets and passes for 12 November were now valid for Wednesday, 17 November 1982.

There seemed to be some confusion in front of the main pavilion. Ambassadors' and foreign correspondents' cars were rolling up, one after the other. And at any minute now the 'unscheduled' visit of the General Secretary, Yuri Andropov, and the Chairman of the Council of Ministers, Nikolai Tikhonov, was to take place.

The man with the briefcase strolled along by the flagpoles, pretending to be deeply interested in the various national flags of the participating countries. Carefully observing the arrival of the foreign guests, he did not notice that he himself was being tailed. Concealed in the crowd about them, two men were watching him: a tall, fair-haired, fit-looking man wearing a hooded windcheater, and a brown-haired man of medium build in a short chequered coat.

At one o'clock the sleek official car of the American ambassador drew up at the main pavilion, followed by several new limousines containing American correspondents.

The man with the briefcase walked rapidly towards the barrier which blocked the entrance to the pavilion. Someone touched him smartly on the shoulder, and he spun round. It was a swarthy-looking lieutenant from the Dzerzhinsky division. The military section of the Ministry of Internal Affairs always took charge of security at the trade fairs and exhibitions in Sokolniki Park.

'Stand back, dad!' said the boyish lieutenant.

'What for? I've got a pass!'

'And I've got my instructions,' said the lieutenant, stepping between him and the barrier. 'We've had orders from the top not to let anyone in for the time being, whether they've got tickets and passes or not. Look, it's not just you; I'm not letting anyone in.' He gestured towards the crowd at the turnstiles.

'On your way, citizen, move along. Have a beer in the

Prague. Come back in half an hour when the government's left, and I'll let you in.'

The cheerful lieutenant's smile was wry but determined. It would be pointless to argue. The man snapped his fingers in irritation and strode off down the alleyway the lieutenant had indicated. It could be worse. The person he had arranged to meet would wait, he was sure. In half an hour's time he would hand over the dark red briefcase that smelt of new leather.

The tall blond athlete in the windcheater with the hood up, and the brown-haired man in the short chequered coat followed on behind him relentlessly.

Confidential

To the Senior Duty Officer
GUVD (Chief Ministry of Administration of
Internal Affairs)
Moscow City Executive Committee
Colonel N. V. Potashev

Official Telephone Report

Today, 17 November 1982, at 14.10 between the main pavilion of the international trade fair at Sokolniki Park and the Prague beer-hall in a wooded area of the park, police car patrolmen Sergeants Glazkov and Cherednichenko discovered the body of an unidentified male, aged 40–50 years, hanging from an aspen tree by a wire noose.

The location has been cordoned off by the police and a unit of the Dzerzhinsky division.

Given that the body was discovered at the very moment Comrade Andropov and the diplomatic corps in Moscow were visiting the fair, and that the circumstances surrounding the death are unclarified, I urgently request that an operations team from Moscow CID be despatched to the scene to conduct investigations.

Deputy Chief of Sokolniki District
Administration of Internal Affairs
Lieutenant-Colonel of Police
G. Bratishka

The local CID men were swarming all over the wooded parkland of Sokolniki under the guidance of their boss, Bratishka, a shrimp of a man. But Merkulov's team were making most headway, thanks to Rex and his burly handler, Panyushkin. Having sniffed the soles of the victim's reddish shoes with their rubber tread, Rex dragged his handler first towards the beer-hall, and then back into the clearing, and then towards the pavilions of the fair.

About fifteen minutes later, both man and dog came back foaming at the mouth. The dog's teeth were bared, and the man was swearing. A quarter of an hour after that, Panyushkin handed Merkulov a 'Report on the Use of the Police Dog', written in indelible pencil on squared paper, from which it emerged that the dog had picked up a scent and taken its handler across the clearing to the Prague where it had gone for a drunk at one of the tables by the door. Then it had left the bar, gone back to the corpse, and then led them to the main pavilion of the fair where it had lost the scent because of the great number of people there.

While this was going on, the rest of the team examined the scene of the incident. At first sight, it seemed a typical case of hanging or strangulation. All the signs pointed to suicide: the fissure, the knot at the back of the neck, the head twisted unnaturally to one side, the swollen tongue sticking out, the eyes bulging. On the ground were four bricks, stacked neatly, and a grey hat.

Not far from the clearing where the body was found, the customary crowd of sightseers had gathered. One of the sergeants who had found the corpse pushed them roughly away and then turned to Merkulov.

'Comrad Investigator, I've got a couple for you here, a boy and a girl. They say they saw something, so I've been holding them. What shall I do with them?'

'Turn them over to the Captain here,' said Merkulov, nodding in Gryaznov's direction. 'And it would be best to disperse the rest. Tell them all politely to go away. Remember, we've a lot of important visitors in the park today.'

The sergeant saluted, and Gryaznov promptly sat down on a tree stump and started taking statements from the two witnesses – a frightened youth and a nervously giggling girl.

It looked so much like an open-and-shut case that something, somewhere, had to be wrong, Merkulov instinctively knew.

'Konstantin Dmitriyevich,' said Rita in an undertone. 'It looks like murder to me.'

'Don't let's jump to conclusions, Comrade Rita.'

The routine of the scene began. Merkulov searched the trunk, the branches, and crawled about under the tree. Then he stood up and moved away from the hanged man, widening the radius of his search. He called over the forensic specialist from the scientific and technical section, Kozlov, and together they examined and then charted the first set of footprints that Merkulov had discovered.

Kozlov photographed them to scale after they squatted down on their haunches and carefully removed from the prints every tiny twig, blade of grass and leaf. Then they made the soil form by spraying on it a special acetone in celluloid solution. When these preliminaries were completed, Kozlov poured plaster of Paris into the footprints. The plaster casts were removed twenty minutes later, wrapped in cellophane, and then packed into a box of wood shavings. Merkulov and Kozlov went over the second run of footprints – which were especially prominent in the thick sticky mud. From later examination of these, they might well discover not only a person's way of walking but also their build, sex, and state of health.

After all the rigmarole with the footprints, Kozlov started on his photography act: lying on the ground, getting up again, standing up on tiptoe to snap the corpse from every angle with his Zenith. Only when this was done did Merkulov give the order to take down the body from the tree. While he carefully packed away the wire in a box, Rita set about her external examination of the body.

'Who's going to conduct the operational work on this case – the Moscow CID or you local boys?' Merkulov demanded.

'I suppose we will,' sighed Bratishka. 'Seeing as it's our patch, it's up to us at first – even if Moscow CID do get involved later. Tell me, Comrade Merkulov, is it murder or suicide?'

'Looks like murder. The facial cyanosis was well advanced. Do you know what I'm talking about?'

Bratishka stayed ambiguously silent.

'Cyanosis,' Merkulov continued patiently, 'that is, violet discolouration of the skin, is a posthumous development that occurs owing to the gradual closing of the blood vessels.'

'So?' snapped Bratishka. 'Isn't that what happened in this case?'

'If we assume he hanged himself,' chipped in Rita, 'given the classic position of the body with the feet not touching the ground, that death would have had to have happened suddenly, wouldn't it? There would be a *sudden* closing of the vessels in his neck, in which case cyanosis could not take place. Our pigeon has very pronounced cyanosis, extensive pointed, haemorrhaging in the facial skin and conjuctiva. . . .'

Rita explained a bit more to Bratishka. Sasha Turetsky was lost in admiration. She was amazing. He liked everything about her. The stern grey eyes, high forehead and flaxen hair; her low, rather husky voice; the way she smoked and what she wore; her lean, elegant, aristocratic figure. . . .

He suddenly realised that this was neither the time nor the place to be admiring a beautiful woman. They were

31

standing in a tight circle in the middle of which was the dead man, lying on his back, his arms outstretched, fists clenched, right leg bent at the knee.

At Merkulov's order, Turetsky examined the contents of his pockets. Nothing worthwhile there: a comb, keys, a book of Metro tickets, seventy copecks in small change. Not even a notebook, let alone money or documents!

There remained one last straightforward task. With Rita's help, Kozlov set about taking the deceased's fingerprints. The forensic expert bent over the corpse and began to straighten the fingers of its right hand.

'Hey, look here!' he exclaimed. Merkulov and Turetsky bent over the corpse. From the unclenched right fist the forensic expert had extracted a scrap of paper. In the poor light of the dying November day, the crumpled remnant of an American hundred-dollar bill was clearly visible. Merkulov sucked in his breath noisily. The 'suicide' in Sokolniki Park was taking on a rather different slant.

But, for now, he was going by the book. Merkulov gave instructions for the body to be taken to the morgue. Two red-faced ambulancemen in dirty grey coats casually dumped the body on to a wheeled stretcher and shoved it summarily into the meat-wagon – a minibus with a red cross. The ambulance, which had been sent an hour before by the super-efficient Potashev, had stood there the whole time, engine running, while its guardians breathed beer and defiance over Merkulov, beefing that he should let them go home to their cosy morgue: 'Since we ain't had a bite or a drop all day.'

Gryaznov came up and reported to Merkulov. 'Witnesses state that they saw the deceased with two other people: a tall, athletic-looking blond man and a brown-haired man of medium build. The first was wearing a windcheater with a hood, and the other was in a chequered coat. Apparently they looked pretty tough. No one knows anything else about them.'

In addition to the youth and the girl, Gryaznov, with

the help of the local Sokolniki CID, had questioned everyone in the vicinity. The result was a blank. True, there was the evidence of the old kiosk-holder, the lieutenant and another youngster from his unit, but that was only relevant to the corpse.

'The witnesses say,' said Gryaznov, continuing his report, 'that the man was anxious to get into the fair. He seemed very nervous and kept switching his briefcase from one hand to the other. It was a fat one, with locks, tan-coloured. Imported, probably Hungarian, new-looking. . . .'

Merkulov froze like a hound before the kill. The brief-case was missing. He had his motive.

According to the science of criminology, you need the answers to eight categories of question before solving a murder. For the time being, there was only a complete answer to the first, the place and the time of death; Moscow, Sokolniki, 17 November, 1.30 p.m.

Night was falling and a sudden wind sprang up. The weather had broken as sharply as a boy's voice. Merkulov had his winter clothes on already, just like an old man: a dark blue padded official-issue greatcoat, a lamb's-wool hat with earflaps, official badge on the front of it, and fur-lined boots. The rest of the team were beginning to freeze.

Sizing up the situation, Merkulov said briskly: 'All right, men, go over to the Prague. Comrade Bratishka will go with you. Mix a little business with pleasure, as they say. Question the drunk the dog went for, and get yourselves a meal. And that includes Rex.' He scratched the dog behind one ear.

'What about you? Aren't you coming with us?' asked Rita. Turetsky felt a sudden stab of jealousy, sharper than the evening chill.

'I'll give it a miss.'

Merkulov strolled slowly across the clearing, eyes to the ground. Anyone who did not know differently might easily have taken him for a retired military man, out picking late mushrooms in Sokolniki Park.

The dinner laid out in the manager's office was a feast: fish soup, sizzling pork with stewed cabbage, amber Pilsner lager. Between the first and second courses, Gryaznov and Turetsky interrogated Kondratenko, a typical vagrant.

He couldn't remember a damn thing about a man with a briefcase. He could only recall that he had been drinking and eating – that is, that he had been finishing off other people's leftovers. God only knew who had been sitting next to him.

Half an hour later, Merkulov was still 'picking mushrooms' – walking round the clearing, studying the ground beneath his feet. He took the sandwich Rita handed him, sat down on a tree stump and began eating hungrily. Turetsky held the paper cup of coffee for him till it almost burnt his hand. When Merkulov had polished off the coffee as well, he asked the junior investigator to go over to the rubbish-bin and throw the litter away. Aristocratic shit, Turetsky thought moodily. Why can't he chuck it in the bushes like everyone else!

When he came back, Merkulov was smoking a Dymok cigarette, still sitting on the stump.

'Well, then, Konstantin Dmitriyevich, did you find any decent mushrooms – or only toadstools?' Turetsky asked with a smirk.

Merkulov looked up in surprise, his grey-blue eyes mild and unwavering. He took a shiny object out of his greatcoat pocket. On a square silver disc, enamelled in bright red, were the words 'Master of sport of the USSR'. Merkulov turned the medal over; the fastening pin was broken. Flatly, he asked: 'Would you say this was a toadstool or a decent mushroom?'

'Cyanosis, you said. But apart from the cyanosis there are two other facts which suggest a violent death.'

'What are they?'

'He had two fissures on his neck, not just one.'

The police Mercedes ran through Komsomol Square, home of Moscow's three famous railway stations, then past Yaroslavsky which looked like an ancient Boyar tower. Half-dozing, Turetsky had some difficulty in following the conversation at the front of the car. Beside him, Panyushkin was crooning to Rex, who was panting noisily, and Kozlov seemed to be asleep.

'The first one, the horizontal one, was caused by the noose,' Rita was saying. 'The second fissure is perpendicular and was caused later, when the body was strung up.'

'OK,' said Merkulov. 'And what's your other lead?'

'The noose itself. It was too small for a man acting alone to get his head through while balancing on a pile of bricks.'

'OK, maybe. The small noose would more or less rule out suicide?'

'So, Konstantin Dmitriyevich,' Rita asked, 'who do you think our pigeon is?'

Merkulov did not answer immediately. Finally, he said consideringly: 'By his physical appearance, you'd say he was a typical Muscovite. But his clothing's wrong somehow. You know what I mean? His clothes and especially – no offence! – his underwear suggest a certain touch of class. The underwear was obviously imported. After all, what does an ordinary Soviet citizen wear? Mass-produced black knee-length sateen pants or long johns. This man's been doing business abroad, it's obvious. You just can't get underwear like that here, not even in the hard-currency shops.

'And where did he get that hard currency from? He doesn't look like a black-marketeer – too respectable-looking. There's only one thing he can be – a top VIP, an executive-grade functionary from the Ministry of Foreign Affairs or the Foreign Trade Department. Give it an hour or so, you'll see, we'll be hearing about some big cheese who's gone missing. I told Bratishka to check out the cadre appointments in the main government departments.'

'What the hell's the point?' Turetsky wondered through a haze of sleep. 'It's not our business anyway. We should make tracks for downtown.'

Every Moscow Investigator has to do a twenty-four-hour duty downtown once every two or three months. Homicide investigations, as a rule, are carried out by men from the District Prosecutor's office in whichever precinct the crime has been committed.

Turetsky heard Merkulov mumbling to Rita something about this not being an open-and-shut case: if it was an ordinary homicide motivated by theft – after all, they'd lifted his cash and briefcase – why did the villains hang about and lug the body all over the place to hang it from a tree? Why all the theatricals? Dimly, he heard Rita asking why they hadn't let the old man into the fair, but didn't catch the reply. . . .

For suddenly he was on the sun-drenched dance-terrace of Sokolniki Park, wearing only his underwear and carrying his old school briefcase under his arm. The dancers kept trying to snatch it from him. A warm breeze was ruffling his hair. Suddenly, a sharp pain was biting into his neck – he struggled to turn round and there was Lieutenant-Colonel Bratishka with a hood over his head, strangling Sasha with some chest-expanders.

There was a burst of submachine-gun fire. The dancers were mown down, sprawling on the boards of the dance-floor. The vague outline of a woman appeared. She was coming closer and closer. She had a Kalashnikov automatic in her hands, and smiled a Mona Lisa smile as she squeezed the trigger. Horrified, he recognised Rita and fell down, down. . . . In the background, someone laughed crazily.

Turetsky opened his eyes blearily. Rex was barking in his ear as he recognised familiar haunts: the Mercedes was rolling into the forecourt of good old Petrovka 38. After less than a day, it was beginning to feel like home.

*　　*　　*

The room behind the door marked 'Investigator' was neat and tidy. The carafe on the table was full of fresh water, and a clean chequered towel hung by the mirror. A round table covered with a green cloth was surrounded by two sofas and two armchairs. The connecting door into the forensic scientists' room was wide open, and Rita was on the phone.

'I've been busy, Sergei. Anyway, it's very difficult to get a line to Kabul.'

That meant she was talking to her husband. Turetsky's heart sank. Rita never talked about her husband; it was as if he didn't exist. But, of course, everyone knew that Sergei Ivanovich Shchastlivy, major-general in the Red Army, was a hero of the Soviet Republic, serving in Afghanistan.

There were times when he thought he'd caught her looking at him half-mockingly, half-enquiringly. Maybe she was just waiting for him to make the first move. Maybe . . . and then she'd get a call from Kabul and he had to pretend she was just a colleague. There was nothing between them, and never could be.

Merkulov sat at the table filling a leatherette notebook, his 'Duty Investigator's Diary', with minute handwriting. There was a stock of similar brown books on the table – twelve in all, one for each month. What a wonderful basis for a series of detective stories they would make. Turetsky had even thought up a title: *Duty Investigator, Call Out!* But the idea was a dead duck from the word go, for who was going to give permission for the ulcers of the socialist society to be exposed? There were no such ulcers, and there could never be.

Turetsky was beginning to feel left out, so abandoned Merkulov's office for the dubious attractions of the smokeroom. The motley support crew of the police force gathered there – drivers, lab technicians, dog-handlers; they always knew what was going on. One minute there could tell you more than a month of news bulletins on the radio or television.

Through the click of dominoes and the filthy language of the players he could hear someone saying in a hoarse voice: 'So we went into the cellar of Beria's house, and the skeletons there – pitch dark it was, but there must have been a hundred of them, cross my heart, on the word of a party member! The forensic expert, Zhivoderov, said: "They look like women to me." '

'You know, when Beria had done all he wanted to with some girl, the guards would take her into the cellar and finish her off.'

Someone else was more precise. 'That's right. My son-in-law's old man was telling me yesterday that when Beria was in power he screwed about five hundred girls. He knows, because in 1953 he was a stoker in the Ministry of State Security in Furkasovsky Street. . . .'

When he saw Turetsky, their usual driver – a down-to-earth, white-haired sergeant – said: 'Sit down, Comrade Investigator, and play my dominoes for me. I'm snatching a few hours' sleep.' But it was too hot and fume-ridden in the smokeroom. As Turetsky left, the hoarse-voiced man was finishing off his story. 'The bosses really put the screws on for a cover-up: the Ministry of Internal Affairs, the KGB, the Central Committee. They fart-arsed about for a bit, and then they gave orders for all the bones to be buried deeper, so that no one could ever dig them up again.'

Merkulov was still sitting at the table, thoughtfully sketching in his investigator's diary the profile of a woman. He didn't seem to notice Turetsky returning to the office. Suddenly the voice of the Assistant Duty Officer came over the loudspeaker above the door.

'Comrade Merkulov, telephone – the head of the City Prosecutor's Office wants you.'

He picked up the receiver with a sigh. His immediate boss, the Head of Investigations, Parkhomenko, was a real pain in the arse. Merkulov was sitting half-turned away from the Junior Investigator, who studied the web of wrinkles around his eyes and the prematurely greying hair at his temples as he made his report.

'OK, OK. Of course I've notified the KGB, Moscow CID and the Anti-Corruption Squad. . . . We'll know everything about him in an hour. . . . Yes, we can trace the dollars through the hard-currency section of the KGB and the Anti-Corruption Squad. But the real teaser is that briefcase. I'm not ruling out connections with foreigners, not at all. . . . Yes, with the Inspectors, the Central Committee and the City Committee. As soon as anything breaks, I'll let you know, Leonid Vasilyevich. . . . Yes, he's been of great assistance.'

At this point the conversation finally caught Turetsky's attention. 'Yes, he's very keen. Shows a lot of promise. I'll keep you informed. . . .'

The Junior Investigator didn't know whether he should be surprised or flattered.

Gryaznov came into the office and said in an assumed Tartar accent, in clear imitation of Major Sabirov: 'Dooty Investigator, call out!'

'Are you kidding, Gryaznov?' He wasn't. At exactly midnight, as the strains of the national anthem crackled over the loudspeaker, the full team set off for the Central Hotel.

5

18 November 1982 – 4 a.m.

'Come on, men, let's go over the whole thing again from the top,' said Merkulov. 'Let's try to find the link between these two cases. I know we're all tired, but at nine o'clock tomorrow – what am I saying? – today – I'll be laying it on the line, making a report about two murders.'

They had just got back to Petrovka from the Central Hotel and were once again sitting round the table in the Investigator's office. Merkulov, Kozlov, Rita and

Turetsky. Panyushkin and Rex were no longer needed, and the others were waiting for Gryaznov who had been called away to the phone.

'Do you want to start, Alexander Borisovich?' Merkulov prompted.

'OK.' Turetsky cleared his throat and put on the desk the barely legible fourth copy of the report which had been compiled to Merkulov's dictation at the hotel. Perhaps he should read it in the dry businesslike tones of their boss, Parkhomenko.

'About twelve o'clock last night, the chambermaid on the fifth floor of the Central Hotel told the manageress on duty that there had been a murder in room 547. The young athletic-looking woman who was found dead was not a guest in the hotel. The room was permanently booked in the name of Viktor Nikolayevich Rakitin, and a woman would visit him there. Captain Gryaznov obtained this information from the manager's records.'

Gryaznov arrived then, entering the room with a worried expression on his face. He sat down at the table without interrupting.

'The chambermaid,' Turetsky went on, 'didn't see the woman go into the room; she probably had her own key. But when the chambermaid was going down the corridor she heard voices coming from the room. A woman's voice talking fast – trying to justify herself, it sounded like – and a rougher man's voice which kept asking her about some duplicate copies. The maid thought they were just guests talking and didn't attach any significance to the conversation.

'Some time later, when she was sitting at her table at the end of the corridor, she heard a strange noise like a window banging in the wind. Alarmed and vaguely suspicious, the maid ran towards the room. A couple of men burst out of it. She didn't see their faces too clearly: the corridor wasn't very well lit, and one of them had the hood of his jacket up. She described him as of athletic build, and the other was no weakling but smaller, with brown hair, and wearing a short chequered coat. They didn't wait for the lift, just ran down the stairs. She did notice, though, that the brown-haired one was holding a green bag with flaps, the sort you get from a hard-currency shop.

'Alarmed by the two strangers running off like that, the chambermaid went into room 547. A woman was lying on the big double bed, the same woman who often visited Rakitin. She didn't move. The chambermaid thought she was ill and touched her, but pulled her hand away immediately – there was a bloodstain on her white blouse, just under the heart.'

Turetsky paused and lit a cigarette.

'The death of the woman was the result of a gunshot wound in the heart. The shot was most probably fired from a pistol with a silencer. We found the cartridge-case, but the bullet is almost certainly still in the body. We carried out an examination and interrogated the witnesses: the chambermaid, the manageress, the hall porter. The last saw the murderers clearly and gave an accurate description of them. The descriptions coincide down to the last detail with the descriptions taken down in statements in Sokolniki Park: a big blond man with a hooded coat, and a brown-haired man in a short chequered coat.

'There's one other interesting detail. The resident of room 547, Rakitin, left a note for this woman with the porter, which because of the usual mix-ups that occur in hotels never got passed on to the addressee. This is what is says: "Lera, I've gone to meet Biggy. Wait for me in the room. Viktor."

Turetsky's style of delivery was obviously getting on Gryaznov's nerves. He kept trying to interrupt, but Merkulov stopped him each time with a wave of his hand. Ignoring Gryaznov, Turetsky went on: 'The porter thought that a car was waiting for the two men outside; he heard the noise of a vehicle driving off, but he wasn't sure if they were the people in it. The state of the hotel room suggested that there had been an illegal search there: the table and armchairs were overturned, drawers were pulled out and lying on the floor, the wardrobe was wide open. I suppose this woman and the occupant of the room were . . . having an affair.'

The brilliant deduction had them all hooting with laughter. Even Kozlov, who had fallen asleep again, woke up.

'What are you laughing at?' Turetsky objected. 'That's what the chambermaid said, and you should pay attention to the voice of the people! I submit that this woman was killed by men working for her lover, Rakitin, about whom so far we know nothing. Find him and we find the killer.'

'Oh, no!' said Gryaznov brusquely. 'I've been trying to get a word in, but you wouldn't let me. Bratishka's just rung from Sokolniki to report that the corpse has been identified. The dead man's name is Rakitin – Viktor Niko-layevich Rakitin – the occupant of the hotel room where the woman was found murdered.'

There was a stunned pause. Finally, Merkulov broke the spell. 'It is now quite obvious, dear comrades, that these two crimes were carried out by the same people. I propose we put the two together and turn them over to the Sokolniki District Prosecutor for further investigation. In view of the late – or, rather, early – hour, I declare this conference closed. Let's turn in.'

Turetsky went off to his own room and settled down to sleep, but tossed and turned on his hard leatherette couch for a whole hour. Finally, waves of sleep started to roll over him, one after another. During his lucid moments he remembered that he had two free days ahead. . . .

There were no more call-outs that night.

PART TWO
The Routine of Investigation

Top Secret
To the General Public Prosecutor of the USSR
State Counsellor of Justice
Comrade A. M. Rekunkov

As you know, on the personal instructions of the General Secretary of the Central Committee of the Communist Party, Comrade Yu. V. Andropov, we are carrying out an operation code-named 'Export', the purpose of which is to expose corruption in our system of foreign trade.

Links have been established between separate executive workers of the USSR Foreign Trade Department (Vneshtorg) and the directors of large firms in Western countries. The former first deputy minister, Yu. Brezhnev, the head of the central directorate, V. Pavlov, the chairman of Technical and Industrial Export, Yu. Smelyakov, and others have been systematically accepting substantial bribes in Soviet and foreign currency, and also in the form of valuables and antiques; and in return have been handing over to foreigners state secrets, mainly in the field of economics, and offering conditions when concluding contracts which are exceptionally advantageous to these firms and detrimental to our own country. Although our data are incomplete, we estimate the material damage to the Soviet Union caused by these people to be one and a half billion American dollars.

Yesterday the corpse of the head of the central directorate of Vneshtorg, V. N. Rakitin, was found in Sokolniki Park. According to the information at present available to us, Rakitin was the victim of common criminals, identity unknown, but most likely Soviet citizens.

However, according to one account, the brief-case which was stolen from Rakitin contained secret documents, and this gives us grounds for handing the case over to the organs of state security.

Taking into consideration the above-mentioned facts, we request that the Moscow State Prosecutor's Office be relieved of the matter and the case of the murder of V. N. Rakitin be referred for further investigations to the Department of Special Investigations of the KGB of the USSR.

Head of the third Main Administration 'T'
Committee
(Scientific–Technical Strategic Investigators),
KGB, USSR
Colonel-General of State Security
A. N. SEREBROVSKY

Head of Department of Special Investigations
in the third Main Administration 'T'
Committee
Major-General of State Security
V. V. KASSARIN

To Colonel-General of State Security
Comrade A. N. Serebrovsky

Major-General of State Security
Comrade V. V. Kassarin

By the constitution and the legislature, the Public Prosecutor's Office of the USSR is empowered to ensure that the law is enforced with precision and uniformity throughout the territory of the country, and also to undertake the investigation of all especially dangerous crimes through the forces of the apparatus of the Public Prosecutor's Office of the USSR, so that the organs of state security may be free to concentrate their efforts on enemies abroad.

In compliance with these requirements of the Politburo of the Central Committee of the Communist Party of the Soviet Union, and of the General Secretary of the Central Committee of the CPSU, Yu. V. Andropov himself, the present case must be investigated by my apparatus since, as you yourself point out, V. N. Rakitin was most probably murdered by common criminals, citizens of the USSR, not by foreigners or Western intelligence agents. The point about the stolen briefcase containing secret documents has not yet been proven. However, even this circumstance gives no ground for relieving the Public Prosecutor's Office of the USSR in this case.

The Main Administration 'T' Committee of the KGB of the USSR may liaise with Investigator K. D. Merkulov, to whom I have referred the investigation of the aforementioned case. The case will only be passed to you should it transpire that any Western intelligence agencies played any part in the murder.

General Public Prosecutor of the USSR
State Counsellor of Justice
A. M. REKUNKOV

1

The lavatory in Sasha Turetsky's apartment didn't work. Or, rather, it was so blocked up that the shit was spilling over the edge of the bowl whenever they flushed it. Everyone in the apartment was annoyed with it. The women took the line that it was his job, as the only man available, to repair the lavatory. (The other member of the stronger sex was snoring his head off in the corner room after yet another drinking bout.) Sasha had done what he could – he'd been ringing the maintenance men for an hour, but all the plumbers had disappeared for the day.

Between the phone calls he'd been trying to read *Izvestiya*. Deepest condolences on the occasion of Brezhnev's death . . . Talks between Andropov and Castro . . . Production rising . . . An interview with General Jaruzelski . . . Successful operations by the insurrectionary forces in the south of Guatemala . . . Gloomy statistics on a direct link between crime and unemployment in America: 'One per cent rise in unemployment causes an additional 318 murders, say American sociologists.'

The newspapers only ever mentioned the American and Australian crime figures, and yet at a conference he had attended last year Sasha Turetsky was told that the number of murders in the Soviet republic had jumped to sixteen thousand, and the suicides totalled thirty-five thousand. But, according to the newspapers, Russian citizens were the most law-abiding in the world!

He put down the paper on the kitchen table. They split the cost of it between the apartment's inhabitants, so it was a case of first come first served and then pass it on.

The kitchen was suddenly invaded by what looked like some sort of deputation, with old man Grisha bringing up the rear. He was a self-styled toilet engineer. The deputation was headed by a red-nosed woman from the housing office who immediately told everyone to stand in line to attention.

Then she began to interrogate them. What exactly had they been putting down the lavatory, and when? She kept looking knowingly at Sasha, far more often that she did at the others, though he had not had anything at all to do with blocking up the lavatory – he hadn't been home for the last twenty-four hours. The women all stood in a circle, with their plump arms tucked under their jutting bosoms, and delivered their versions of events. Finally, Sasha had had just about all he could take. He yelled at the woman with the red nose that she could find the culprits later, but at this moment the shit was seeping through on to the floor below.

'Don't use language like that to me – and you a policeman, too!' she bawled. Apparently the phrase he should have used was 'faecal waste'. He promised to remember that next time. Then the people who lived on the floor below came running upstairs. 'Faecal waste' had started falling on to their gas-rings.

In the general hubbub, Sasha managed to slip away to his own room. It was small and badly furnished, but he loved the old Arbat and so put up with its lack of amenities and abundance of neighbours. The old women he shared with lived in hope of a better life in the next world when all he wanted was a room in a new apartment block. Maybe it would take as long.

Anyhow, he was not doing too badly on Leninsky Prospekt. But two years earlier his mother had married a man called Satin, the manager of some trade trust, and they had promptly thrown him out of the house, after managing to fiddle him this dark, plainly furnished little room, a sort of cross between a goods wagon and a cell in Presnya Transit Prison.

There really was nothing to do. That is, he could do what he liked – either go to the cinema or ring up some girl he knew – but he couldn't summon up any enthusiasm.

Sasha sat on the divan and stared at the pink wallpaper. He was lonely. Just lately, he'd felt increasingly lonely. It wasn't the apartment. He didn't think he would have been any happier in, say, a plush self-contained place in 'Zavety Ilyicha', where members of the Politburo lived. Even on the teeming streets of Moscow he felt lonely. Maybe one person – one woman – could make him happier. But only in the realms of fantasy. . . .

He was very hungry, and there was no food in his kitchen cupboard and they were still going on about the lavatory outside. Should he go out to a little café on the Arbat, have a cheese omelette and a Turkish coffee?

Sasha put on his blue blazer and even a tie. He wasn't so well off for trousers, but it didn't matter – his jeans would do.

The phone rang. He didn't think it could be for him. He had two clear days ahead.

'Alex, would you be so good as to come to the telephone,' said Polina Vasilyevna, rapping on the door with her knuckles. She had once run a finishing school for young ladies.

It was Merkulov on the phone. He thought Sasha might like to come over to the Prosecutor's Office – right away. So much for the Turkish coffee.

Sasha walked through the biting south-east wind and falling sleet to the new Metro station on the Arbat. Despite the filthy weather, he felt suddenly clear-headed and elated. The feeling of loneliness had slipped away, and the thrill of the chase was on him again.

In the hallway of the Prosecutor's Office, he shook the sleet from his padded coat and breathed in the appetising smell of hot pies from the basement canteen. He couldn't resist it, and hurried down to the canteen to buy two: a cabbage one, which he swallowed then and there at the checkout, and the other one, a meat pie, he finished chewing as he went upstairs to the second floor. He turned the handle of the door to Merkulov's office.

'Don't play the fucking innocent with me, Colonel!' said a furious voice.

Sasha stepped hesitantly into the office. A KGB colonel was strutting round the room like a farmyard rooster.

A thickset general, wearing the insignia of the home forces on his greatcoat lapel, was lounging on the divan, making no secret of the fact that he was pissed off. Merkulov waved vaguely to Sasha as if to say 'Sit down somewhere, if you can find yourself a seat'. He sat on the window-sill. The general glanced at him as if he was part of the furniture and carried on yelling.

'How come you knew nothing about your superiors' decision to restrict access to the fair, fuckerwit? My men were acting properly, in accordance with instructions!'

'Comrade General, I don't know under what instructions your goons were acting, but they blew our operation to catch Rakitin,' said the Colonel. After a pause, he added: 'Fuck you, too.'

The general turned even redder. He leapt from the divan and really let fly. The air turned blue. Though on the defensive, the colonel swore back uninhibitedly. Sasha creased up, barely able to stop himself from laughing out loud. So sometimes the comrades from the security organs really did go over the top! Whatever happened to the much-praised self-restraint of the secret service?

Merkulov sat at his desk, gloomily shifting his gaze from one to the other. He was leaning his head against his left hand, and his right was playing with his writing set. Finally he had had enough. He slammed the marble inkstand against his desk.

'Take it easy, comrades! I get the picture. You, Comrade Pavlov,' he said, turning to the KGB man, 'were after your American – without knowing anything about Rakitin. And you, Comrade Flyagin, were carrying out orders received from the regular KGB, and so you delayed spectators going into the pavilions by one hour, didn't you? And now the American, who is possibly a professional spy, will slip happily away tomorrow, back to the capitalist sharks. The briefcase he was after has disappeared; Rakitin has been murdered and his fancy woman, too; our murderers are happily walking the streets of Moscow, if they haven't already cleared off for a well-earned vacation to Gagry or Nice! And so, Comrade Colonel – to use the language of the security boys – the shit is really hitting the fan.'

The colonel exploded again when he heard this; but Merkulov, as if losing interest in the whole business, started rummaging around in his desk drawer and pulling out various bits of paper. A tense silence reigned by the time he finally found the forms used for witnesses' statements and handed them to the security men, saying brusquely: 'Make your depositions in writing, please.'

The general and the colonel bent over the desk like schoolboys. They wrote slowly and at length. Sasha sat on the window-sill like a tailor's dummy.

He hadn't a clue what was going on. What American spy? What were 'our' murderers to do with him? Hadn't Merkulov referred the case to the Sokolniki District Prosecutor because it was his patch?

And then he noticed there had been some changes in the boss's office: the table with the carafe had been shifted to the far corner, and the potted plant – which he, personally, couldn't stand – now occupied a central position by the window. He whistled aloud, alarming the comrades from the security organs even further. Whenever Merkulov got the urge to start moving things around, it meant he'd just been given a serious new case to solve. The new layout of the office was clear proof that Merkulov (and, naturally, his assistant) were now in charge of investigating the double murder of Viktor Rakitin and his lady-friend.

The two men finally completed their scribbling, slapped the sheets of paper down in front of Merkulov, saluted smartly and, with measured tread, left the office. At that moment, the intercom burst into life and the voice of the City Prosecutor's secretary said: 'Investigator Merkulov, have you asked for the Rakitin business to be classified? Also, the Moscow City Prosecutor, Comrade Malkov, and the head of the section supervising the organs of state security, Comrade Funtov, want to see you.'

Merkulov tapped the microphone against the intercom a few times with his pencil, shorthand for 'I'll be over right away.' He glanced over the statements, put one in a file, dropped the other one in front of Sasha and left the office quickly. Then, just as fast, he came back, pulled some sheets of paper from the typewriter and threw one of these copies towards Sasha. Evidently, while he was messing around with Malkov, no time was to be wasted. Sasha read the typed page first.

Resolution
(On combining of criminal cases)
I, Merkulov, Investigator of Serious Crimes, Moscow City Prosecutor's Office, having examined the evidence relating to the criminal cases arising from the murder of citizen Rakitin and an unidentified woman, in accordance with article 26 of the Criminal Code of the RSFSR,

HAVE RESOLVED:

1. Bearing in mind the instructions of the General Prosecutor of the USSR, who referred to me personally the investigation of the murders, that both cases be pursued by me, that they be classified as 'top secret', that the investigation be conducted in accordance with the special regulations relating to secret cases.
2. In view of the fact that both crimes are linked, that they be combined under one operation.
3. In so far as the investigation of the aforementioned crimes presents significant difficulties, that an investigation squad comprising K. D. Merkulov (Chief), V. S. Gryaznov (officer of Moscow CID) and A. B. Turetsky (Junior Investigator) be formed.

Serious Crimes Investigator
Judicial Counsellor
K. MERKULOV

53

So the General Prosecutor, Rekunkov, had summoned Merkulov earlier that morning, and several pairs of toes had been trodden on already. Though, usually, prosecutors and investigators were in no rush to take on classified murder cases. Usually it was the job of the CID to hunt down murderers, and the prosecutor's task was to collect evidence, expose criminals and get the case through court. This case was obviously different. It could be dynamite.

The KGB colonel had written:

I am the head of the third section of the Crimes section of the KGB for the city of Moscow and Moscow district. Our section deals with foreigners who make contact with Muscovites.

An American journalist, Zbigniew Podgursky (known to his friends as Biggy), stayed in the Belgrade Hotel for three weeks, having ostensibly come to collect material about life in Soviet society. From the moment he landed my section had contrived and controlled his schedule. Without knowing it, Podgursky did just what we wanted him to: he met people with whom we had planted information for his book, he ate at tables we had bugged, he slept with one of our girls. It was she who informed me that on 17 November Podgursky was to have a meeting at the Sokolniki fair.

We did not know the man who had contacted the American, so we hoped to get to him through Podgursky. We decided to monitor this meeting, though we did not attach too much significance to it – many Moscow black-marketeers try to sell their wares to foreigners and what better place for this purpose than the Sokolniki fair?

We would have cleared up the whole thing if this person had got to Podgursky, but they never met. Only today did we learn that this person was

54

an executive functionary of the Foreign Trade Department, Rakitin. Of course, this is a mystery – why should a man like Rakitin go to meet Podgursky? Unforeseen circumstances stacked the cards against us: we were waiting for this man inside, that is, at the fair, and we did not know that KGB Centre would issue a sudden instruction to the head of the Dzerzhinsky division to delay the entry of the public to the fair by one hour. This meant that we not only lost track of Rakitin and his briefcase, but that we also allowed him to be murdered.

Tomorrow, 19 November, Podgursky is to leave the territory of the USSR. We agreed on this with the Ministry of Foreign Affairs. Until then we will continue to follow his every movement: in addition to microphones and tele-cameras in his hotel room, we have also placed infra-red cameras which can record all his actions, even in complete darkness.

Statement signed
PAVLOV

There was something about this explanation Sasha did not like. In fact, he did not like any of it, though it sounded as if it would make a good movie. Five thousand questions were spinning round in his head, but he knew Merkulov wouldn't stand for any amateurish whys and wherefores now. They were in the big league now. Merkulov came back into the office, made Sasha sign a pass, and struggled into his coat.

'We're going to the morgue.'

'But. . . .' Sasha opened his mouth without knowing what he was going to ask.

Merkulov laughed. 'That's right, kid. Let's keep all our options open.' He pulled out a cigarette, sat on the edge of his desk, and lit up. 'Comrade Turetsky, it looks like you and I have stepped straight into the shit'

'Say that again, Konstantin Dmitriyevich. I didn't hear you the first time,' Sasha said with a grin.

2

City Hospital No. 1 was situated right at the end of Leninsky Prospekt, between Neskuchny Garden and the Ministry of Higher Education. The morgue was in the basement of the sixth wing. As you walked towards it, you wouldn't notice anything out of the ordinary apart from the three meat-wagons parked in the courtyard outside. Sometimes you might see a hearse, a stately black bus taking some dear departed on their final journey. Today, the rear doors of all three ambulances were open. The crew were fond of the open air.

Despite the bad weather, two people were waiting outside – a woman in her forties and a youth of about eighteen – standing by a door marked 'No unauthorised personnel.' Sasha realised immediately that these must be the Rakitins. They bore a remarkable resemblance to one another – both tall and bright-eyed. She had obviously been a beautiful woman in her day and was still not bad, just a bit dried-up with layers of make-up failing to conceal her deep wrinkles. The black hat with the half-veil, though elegant, was distinctly old-fashioned.

Mrs Rakitin took a step forward. 'Hello, Kostya. I recognised you immediately, even after all these years. God, what a way to meet again!'

'Hello, Viktoria Ippolitovna – Vika!' Merkulov kissed the hand stretched out to him.

What was going on? How did he know her? He hadn't said anything to Sasha.

'Kostya, is it true, has Vitya really been killed? As soon as you rang, Lyosha and I rushed over here. The car's waiting for us on Leninsky Prospekt.' Mrs Rakitin spoke

56

in a rather mannered way, Sasha noted. 'Let's go, please. I have to see him!'

Her son took her arm gently and squeezed her hand. Merkulov seemed to size her up before saying sympathetically: 'Will you be able to stand it, Viktoria Ippolitovna?'

Her son answered for her. 'Mum will stand it. She can stand anything!'

They walked along an echoing corridor which led into the anatomy hall. Though it was late in the day, pathologists were working at their benches. One of them, a six-foot bald man who looked more like a hammerthrower than a doctor, left his bench and came over, wearing a bloodied apron and rubber gloves.

'I am Dr Zhivoderov, head of the morgue,' he said. 'What can I do for you?'

Sasha started feverishly trying to recall where he had recently heard that name. . . . That was it! The man with the hoarse voice in the smokeroom the day before – he'd been talking about an expert called Zhivoderov examining skeletons in Beria's 'castle'.

The pathologist screwed up his short-sighted eyes and said: 'Kostya, it must be years! I'm sorry, I didn't recognise you at first. That means you'll get rich, they say.'

Sasha thought he was going to chew the fat with Merkulov about the old days, but Merkulov nodded towards the Rakitins and interrupted in his official tone.

'Oleg Vsevolodovich, show us the man from Sokolniki. He's one of Shchastlivaya's.'

Zhivoderov was not at all offended, and led the way. The procession passed into the next room where the corpses were lying on zinc tables. They were covered with tattered old bedsheets marked in black letters 'Hosp. No. 1'. There were about twenty tables.

Sasha looked sideways at Mrs Rakitin, who seemed to be doing well so far. When he reached the middle of the second row, Zhivoderov – who obviously knew his stock – took hold of one corner of a sheet and pulled it back in a

57

smooth practised movement. White-faced, the Rakitins looked down at the corpse. Without moving a muscle, Viktoria Ippolitovna whispered through bloodless lips: 'It's him.' Her eyes were dry.

Zhivoderov gestured the younger Rakitin to come forward. He took a few steps and crumpled to the floor.

'Sasha,' said Merkulov breathlessly as he tried to support the boy's gangling body. 'Take them through to the Doctor's room and give them a few minutes to recover.'

3

The Rakitins lived in a well-known high-rise block on Vostaniye Square. Their tower block and another six were built on Stalin's personal orders on the seven hills of Moscow and were, according to the dictator, intended to immortalise his epoch.

The Rakitin family occupied a huge five-bedroomed apartment, the last word in residential luxury. Not bad at all, Sasha thought. I've only seen places like this in the movies before.

'You won't take offence if we go into the kitchen, will you? Even when times are good, we like sitting and chatting there.'

'Please don't stand on ceremony,' said Merkulov smoothly.

'And there's a little rule we have: no smoking in the apartment! Please forgive my mentioning it.' Viktoria Ippolitovna sounded just the slightest bit coy, and Lyosha gave her a sharp look.

Sasha had never seen a kitchen to compare with it. He'd never seen such furnishings, not even at visiting foreign exhibitions. There was an oval table made of ebony, covered in red glass and surrounded by six chairs of the same wood, with red velvet seats. The huge refrigerator was red and the walls were black-tiled. There were countless gleaming built-in wall-units. What did they keep in them?

Merkulov gingerly pulled out a chair, and Sasha supposed it was all right for him to sit down, too. At least his jeans were clean.

As Viktoria Ippolitovna was setting the table for tea, she and Merkulov recalled the far-off days when his family used to live in a village full of old Bolsheviks, Kratovo, where the Voevodins, Vika's parents, also made their home. Her grandfather was the equivalent of the last of the Mohicans amongst Lenin's old guard. He had died only five years before, and one of the streets of the Old Arbat was named after him.

'So you work in the Prosecutor's Office? I must admit we all thought that you'd take after your grandfather: become an academician like him, doing aerodynamics or physics. And they talk about genes! They're all scientists in your family, aren't they? You're the only one with a humanities degree. Have you got a high rank?'

Mrs Rakitin gestured to the two huge stars in Merkulov's velvet lapel.

'Judicial Counsellor, a kind of lieutenant-colonel,' Merkulov said nonchalantly.

'That's not too bad for thirty-six.'

Mrs Rakitin drank some tea, and there was an awkward silence.

'Well, then, Kostya,' said Viktoria Ippolitovna, rousing herself finally. 'What else is there to say?' "The paths of our youth are overgrown with weeds." '

An iron lady! In the same situation Sasha's mother would have been in a dead faint long since, but here was this woman reciting poetry!

'Konstantin Dmitriyevich, can I ask you a question?' Lyosha spoke at last.

'Alexei, you can ask as many questions as you like. But I'm afraid we don't have many answers as yet.'

59

'So you don't know who killed my father?'

'No, I don't. I don't know who, and I don't know why.'

Rakitin junior was also a little old-fashioned – he was polite, educated and serious for his age – but Sasha instinctively liked him much more than he liked Mrs Rakitin. Lyosha cleared his throat and spoke again.

'If I can be of any assistance to you, Konstantin Dmitriyevich. . . .'

'We'll bear it in mind, Alexei. Keep in touch with Sasha here – that is, Alexander Borisovich Turetsky. Take his phone number.'

'OK.' Lyosha took a notebook and a Parker pen from his pocket. As he did so, he knocked a cup of tea over the table.

Mrs Rakitin hissed: 'Clumsy! Some assistant you've found yourself, Kostya. He'd better go and sit in his room if he can't behave better.'

Lyosha got up from the table, still carrying the notebook.

'I'm sorry. I think I would like to be on my own. Goodbye, gentlemen.' And he added: 'Take it easy, Mum.'

Viktoria Ippolitovna was soon back to her usual self – glacial and serene.

'Vika.' Merkulov approached her. 'Maybe you could tell us a bit about Viktor Nikolayevich – his work, his acquaintances, his interests. You know, it sometimes happens that seemingly insignificant details can give us a clue, tell us what to look for, and where. . . .'

Mrs Rakitin sat in her chair, dry-eyed and stern. The high goffered collar of her white blouse reminded Sasha of a picture of the first Queen Elizabeth of England he had once seen in a history textbook.

'Well, Kostya.' She seemed to be thinking hard. 'I'll start from the very beginning. As an outsider, you might see things more clearly than I did at the time.'

Viktoria Ippolitovna put her elbows on the table and cupped her chin in her palms. She seemed to have chosen to address her remarks directly to Sasha, like an actor zeroing in on one member of a theatre audience.

'Imagine, young man, a family of old Bolsheviks. My grandfather was a Hero of Labour, a party member since before the Revolution. My grandmother worked in Krupskaya's secretariat. All his life, my father served in intelligence; he was Deputy Chief of Military Intelligence before his retirement.

'On my mother's insistence, I became a teacher of English. I am a senior lecturer at the Moscow Institute of International Relations. I met Viktor Rakitin twenty-two years ago. He was a student of mine and, I must say, a very good one. Then he became my husband and, to start with, everything I wanted.

'Viktor was from a simple family, from somewhere outside Maikop. So, at a family conference, it was decided – we decided – that the young man was the wax from which we could model just the person we wanted. In short, we decided to make a career for him. And not just a career, a *great* career. Do you understand what I'm talking about?'

Sasha did not altogether understand, but so as to encourage her flow of words he nodded sharply.

'Rakitin had all the right qualities. One, he was from a working-class family; two, there wasn't the slightest blot on his copybook; and three, he had our connections. Viktor was qualified in two fields – he was a metallurgist and a foreign trade expert. Even Academician Bardin told Daddy that Viktor had a head on his shoulders! He had achieved some success for himself, dealing in bauxite, gold and diamonds. And at the Ministry of Foreign Trade, where Daddy managed to place him, he soon went to the top. Viktor was an achiever from the word go. They made him head of an association, then head of a directorate. He was taken on to the executive staff of the Ministry and then . . . then something went wrong.'

Mrs Rakitin's tone faltered a little, her voice and manner lost their abrasive theatricality. Pressing her hand against her forehead, and fixing her eyes straight ahead, she continued her narrative, flatly, as if dictating into a tape-recorder.

Rakitin was aspiring to be a deputy minister. Then, suddenly, it was decided to send him to Washington as a Soviet trade representative. Viktoria Ippolitovna was overjoyed – who in the Soviet Union would not want to spend some time in America? – especially since she spoke English. However, the appointment was never confirmed, for reasons unknown. The disappointment landed her in hospital – she started having asthma attacks which became more and more frequent.

Viktor would not talk about things, or would give evasive answers to her questions. Then Viktoria approached her father, and he went to his friend, the head of the administration of cadres in the Foreign Trade Ministry, a former KGB general. And what the Voevodin family learnt about Rakitin horrified them.

Ostensibly, there was some query about Rakitin's diamond-dealing. But, in fact, the business went much further than that. Apparently he did not agree with some plans or directives emanating direct from the Central Committee and the Politburo. He had been making speeches against them at various meetings right up to Central Committee and Council of Ministers level. Worse, he kept publicly insisting that it was essential to reform, root and branch, the foreign trade organisations abroad. He kept calling for the conservation and not frittering away of state assets, and so on and so forth. He even had some supporters in the Academy of Sciences and the strategic institutes which were planning foreign trade policy under instruction from the Central Committee and the KGB.

It was fascinating to hear all this, but from Sasha's point of view the story seemed to have no bearing whatsoever on the murder – especially as it had been carried out in such a primitive fashion. Even if Rakitin were a dissident, there were plenty of psychiatric hospitals to deal with him more subtly. Why did he end up strung from a tree?

'It was decided up top' – Viktoria Ippolitovna pointed a red nail towards the ceiling – 'that it was revisionism. They attributed it to Vitya's political shortsightedness and even stuck a label on him – you know how we do these things – he was "an anti-party nationalist"! After that sort of smear, Vitya's career nose-dived, and things could have been even worse if it hadn't been for Daddy's connections.'

She stood up abruptly from the table and, with a note of genuine sorrow in her voice, said: 'This isn't the way for Russians to sit about after a death. Let's drink to my Vitya. May he rest in peace.'

She took down from the top shelf of a cupboard an embossed porcelain bottle of rowanberry liqueur brandy, a rare luxury these days.

'Vitya and I bought this the day we got married. We decided we would drink it on our silver wedding anniversary.'

Mrs Rakitin poured the brandy into crystal glasses, saying: 'May the ground be soft for him.' She swallowed her drink in one go, then poured herself another right away and knocked that back, too. She unbuttoned the high collar of her rustling blouse and sat down in her chair before springing restlessly to her feet.

'Excuse me, I'll just go and change – this straitjacket is too much for me.'

They sat in silence for a moment, then Merkulov picked up the bottle, looked enquiringly at Sasha and without waiting for his answering nod poured out fresh glasses of liqueur.

'To the success of a hopeless case!' Sasha said.

'Let's drink to that,' replied Merkulov thoughtfully, clinking glasses.

When Mrs Rakitin came back into the kitchen, Sasha did not recognise her at first: she was wearing a traditional long dress with a shawl round her shoulders. Her fair hair was loosened and hung low over her forehead. She went over to the table and poured herself another drink. Before them stood an unsophisticated Russian woman, drunk on brandy and grief. Without addressing anyone in particular, her voice catching on her sobs, she finished her monologue.

'I had dedicated my whole life to him, always thinking that one day our time would come, and he just let me down! I used to say to him: "Vitya, forget about the State; that's just fine words! Kids' talk! Look around you. What is 'the people' you talk about? Where is it? Do you really think those numskulls in smelly clothes, going into Moscow on stinking trains to do their shopping, are *your people*? They don't need you! Think of yourself! Or, if you don't want to think of yourself, think about your son!" But he, he just kept on: "In the interests of Russia. . . ." And what thanks did he get! He just kept on and on with his reforms until they wrung his neck!'

Mrs Rakitin went over to the sideboard unsteadily and picked up a pack of Marlboros. She lit one, inhaling greedily, then threw the cigarettes on to the table and said abruptly: 'Help yourselves.' Sasha immediately took an American cigarette, but Merkulov reached for a Dymok.

Sasha went over Viktoria Ippolitovna's story in his mind but could not find any clues in it. She seemed to know nothing about Podgursky – or was she hiding something? Merkulov was not asking the usual questions.

'Why am I telling you all this? What's it all got to do with his death?' Viktoria suddenly bawled aloud. Her tears washed away the last vestiges of make-up. 'They killed him because of a woman. A woman!'

It was so unexpected that Sasha spluttered on his cigarette. Merkulov took her by the arm and asked insistently: 'Because of what woman, Vika?'

'How do I know who his tarts were? Did they really want Viktor? No, just his money and the presents from abroad! But he never shared that last bitch with anyone, that's all I know. He never once bought me even a flower, but he used to send baskets of roses to that ballerina!'

'What ballerina, Vika? Keep calm, Viktoria Ippolitovna. What ballerina?' Merkulov was still holding Mrs
Rakitin's arm, quietly but persistently demanding an
answer.

But Sasha could see it was no good. Viktoria was past
any rational response and could only keep repeating the
same thing, again and again. 'Baskets of roses, and not a
flower or a bouquet for me. But for her baskets of. . . .'

Lyosha peered into the room, alarmed. Merkulov
beckoned to him and said: 'Try to calm your mother,
Alexei. This is a tough time for her just now.'

'Don't worry, Konstantin Dmitriyevich. My mother
can stand anything.' The boy used the same words as in
the morgue. 'Come on, I'll see you out.'

They put on their coats and, quietly closing behind
them the door with the gilded name-plate, 'V. N.
Rakitin', left the apartment. Even outside the door they
could still hear Viktoria Ippolitovna's fading voice.

'You hear, Lyosha? Not even one flower. . . .'

4

It was drizzling miserably in the thickening twilight. They
left the Rakitins' tower block and went past the window of
a foodstore. Behind the thick glass glistened huge joints
of ham, glassy-eyed grouse, a sturgeon the size of a shark
gleaming majestically from an enormous platter – all artificial, of course. It was spooky to see all that window-
dressing when there wasn't even a herring's tail for sale in
the shops.

They went down the steps to the pavement and set off
from the trolley-bus stop for the Sadovoye ring-road.

Suddenly Merkulov stopped and pulled a twist of paper
out of his greatcoat pocket. He stood looking at it for a
moment, then straightened it out and took a few steps

towards a street-lamp. It was a piece of paper torn from a school exercise-book. In a large childlike hand was written: 'Her name is Valeria Kupriyanova.'

Merkulov looked dumbfounded. Sasha said: 'Lyosha!'

Merkulov headed for the phone booth on the corner of the Sadovoye ring-road, next to a shoe-cleaner's stall.

'Put me through to Romanova. . . . Shura, is that you? Hello, yes, it's Merkulov again. I'm coming to see you, with my assistant. Meanwhile, find out all you can about Valeria Kupriyanova. She's a ballet dancer. If you find her, bring her over to Petrovka.'

The head of the second section of Moscow CID, Shura Romanova, greeted them like special guests. She made them drink 'just a drop' as soon as they arrived: a huge tumbler of vodka each, served with some sweets. Merkulov knocked his glass back without a murmur, only his Adam's apple moving. Sasha finished his 'drop' in three goes, gasping as the flaming spirit hit his stomach. Shura obligingly rushed over to the safe for some 'ES' – emergency supplies of Nezhin gherkins in a sealed jar, intended only for the delectation of the head of Moscow CID.

Lieutenant-Colonel Alexandra Ivanovna Romanova was the spitting image of Catherine the Great – in police uniform. She was short and large-boned with a determined chin and astonishingly young, cornflower-blue eyes. She was the only woman in Moscow to be the head of a CID section. And she had been given the task of finding the murderers involved in their case.

'I don't understand this Rakitin. Why should he want to meet an American in full view of everyone at the fair?' Shura spoke in a sing-song voice with a pronounced southern accent, peppering her comments appropriately and inappropriately with emotionless obscenities. 'In the first place, he had access to all the official functions, the receptions, the banquets. He could have just met this Podgursky in a restaurant or at a party. What took him to the fair?'

'He knew as well as you or I do, Shura,' said Merkulov with a shrug of his shoulders, 'that there would be surveillance in all those other places. All the conversation would be bugged. You don't need me to tell you that throughout Moscow there are up to a hundred thousand listening devices, planted in apartments and official residences, even in lavatories. But in Sokolniki, out there in the open, you can't follow everyone – there aren't enough feet and ears. A crowd is the best place for a spy. But was Rakitin one? The KGB have told me that they have no evidence of any spying activity.'

'Kostya! Stop pissing around with those security boys. What exactly did the tart tell you – the one they fitted the American up with. . .?'

Shura never pulled her punches.

Merkulov met Romanova's gaze and held it steadily. 'Yes, I have been pissing around with security, Comrade Lieutenant-Colonel. And the tart told her boss that she knew nothing of substance, only that there would be a meeting. She couldn't get any more out of her john. That's what they told me.'

' "That's what they told me," ' mimicked Shura. 'You're an investigator, aren't you? Couldn't you have questioned her yourself?'

Merkulov laughed hollowly. 'Shura, would you expose one of *your* informers? Come on, they didn't let me near her.'

'Not let you! Let the bastards try that one on me. I'd fix it so that the little whore got caught in the act, drag her out from under some buck nigger and have the bitch singing her head and arse off!'

Shura was well away by now. While they waited for the information on the ballet dancer, Valeria Kupriyanova, Sasha could hardly keep his eyes open. Merkulov and Romanova, meanwhile, carried on in the same vein, summarizing the results obtained in the initial stages of the investigation, and abusing the KGB.

'Oh, we wouldn't be sitting here till midnight if those

children and grandchildren of Felix Dzerzhinsky weren't such shitheads,' concluded Shura. 'No, it's true, Konstantin.' And she popped another sweet into her mouth. 'My boys do similar jobs much more professionally than our so-called security people. And for half the salary, what's more!' Without pausing, she said: 'Why are you standing there like a fart in a trance, Arthur? Come in!'

A tall broad-shouldered giant was standing in the doorway, a brown-haired good-looking man of about thirty-two, wearing a brand-new suit.

'My deputy, Arthur Andreyevich Krasnikovsky,' said Shura, introducing the new arrival. 'Well, where's your ballerina?'

'She's disappeared,' said Krasnikovsky. 'She didn't show up for the morning rehearsal of *The Golden Age*. She wasn't there for the evening performance of *Aibolit*, either. They had to use an understudy – invited in a girl from the Bolshoi Theatre ballet school. But they're really stuck for someone to take the part of Varvara. No one but Kupriyanova can do it, apparently.' And Arthur pulled a glossy theatre leaflet from his breast pocket – the week's programme from the Moscow Associated Theatres Bureau.

Sasha jumped up. Even in his drunken state he recognised the ballerina pictured on the cover. She had been found murdered in the Central Hotel the previous night.

In the photograph taken by the famous theatrical photographer Shapiro, Krupriyanova had her hair in funny curls. She was wearing a coloured pinafore and holding a mop in her hands. . . . But it was the same woman, he was sure.

'It's still got to be proven,' said Merkulov wearily. 'You see to the identification tomorrow. We'll give you a second day off in lieu.'

5

19 November 1982

'Investigators of the Prosecutor's office! As a rule you have to deal with complex cases. But you must realise that the path to THE TRUTH often lies not only in a combination of barely perceptible clues. . . .'

The young investigators were sitting in a dark auditorium of the Moscow Public Prosecutor's Office, watching educational films. Sasha's head was aching a bit, and his stomach still felt queasy from the 'drop' he had had with Shura the night before. The droning voice of the lecturer continued.

'The path to THE TRUTH lies through a ticket of so-called trivia, over a sea of unforgivable oversights and tragic mistakes.'

Any idiot knew that! Tanya Zernova was sitting next to Sasha. The pretty little daughter of the secretary to the Council of Ministers had eyes only for him. He pretended not to notice, especially as the chief was sitting right behind him. He was the one who had been instructed to arrange the screening of this crap – with everything else they had to do.

The first two parts of the film were documentary. The third was a reconstruction of a crime and its investigation; and, though the actors in it were only second-rate, it was well done. Really quite amusing. The bank on Plyush-chikha Street appeared on the screen. A shortish thickset policeman was standing at his post and earnestly picking his fat nose. The camera cut to two masked figures; a shot was fired, and the policeman fell.

Then came the interior of the bank and a close-up of the oxy-acetylene equipment which the masked burglars were using to cut open the safe. Wads of notes disappeared into canvas bags. The job done, the criminals went out into the street, jumped into a waiting taxi, and tore off in the direction of Borodinsky Bridge.

F.A.S.—4

Another group of people appeared: investigators, accompanied by numerous forensic scientists, witnesses, dogs, policemen. They all joined in destroying the evidence left by the criminals: they stamped around the doorway, threw cigarette-ends everywhere and committed other acts of criminal carelessness. One investigator, clearly in imitation of Charlie Chaplin, tried particularly hard. He examined the safe and put his hand in the exact spot where an inky fingerprint had clearly been left. He found a glove on the floor, and carefully picking it up between finger and thumb, dumped it in the ash-can. . . .

A vague feeling of unease was haunting Sasha. It wasn't just his upset stomach, was it? Then he realised what it was. . . .

The investigator on the screen carried on with his work, giving the cleaning woman a string bag containing a water melon which had unaccountably been found by the window, but Sasha was already heading for the exit. He suddenly felt very unwell indeed, and it was nothing to do with the 'drop'.

Jesus Christ! That Charlie Chaplin character was Sherlock Holmes in comparison with the cretinous half-witted goon, Alexander Turetsky! Covered in sweat, he shot along the corridor like a bullet from a gun, slid down the banisters, and dashed out into the street where, arms flapping like a scarecrow, he tried to hail a cab. Spraying him in freezing cold water, a handsome black ZIL pulled up and ruddy-faced driver asked: 'Where you going, fella? If it's the hospital, I'm not taking you!'

The moonlighting cab-driver took him to the Central Hotel for three roubles. On the way he tried to justify the high price, saying that the bosses were getting on to them, wouldn't let them make a bit on the side like they used to. . . . Sasha didn't listen.

Pulling out his identification card as he ran in search of the hotel manager, he found a yellow-haired tailor's dummy of about his own age in the buffet on the first floor, drinking coffee.

Gasping, Sasha explained to him that he had to make a second examination of room 547 where two days before the woman's body had been found. It had just come to light, he confided, strictly between themselves, that she was a famous ballet dancer. That was all that could be divulged. He would need the keys and two witnesses, at the double.

The yellow-haired man got the message right away – this was obviously not the first time he had had dealings with the police. He took a bunch of keys and shouted as he ran: 'Mitrofanova, come on!' He dashed up the stairs two at a time. The diminutive Mitrofanova and Sasha rushed after him like a couple of hounds. For some reason they ignored the existence of the lift.

When the woman on duty on the fifth floor saw them, her face froze. The manager just gestured her to sit tight and turned the key in the lock before bursting into the room.

The first thing they saw, freezing them to the spot in astonishment, was someone's bare backside. For an instant even Sasha forgot why he was there. It belonged to a pretty, scared little creature of about fifteen. She leapt up from the floor, revealing the other scared creature sitting in an armchair before her. He had a black moustache, a gaberdine jacket covered in insignia, and his trousers round his ankles. The further conclusive proof of his masculinity was plain for all to see.

Someone squealed like a piglet – it must have been the manager. The floor manageress was howling and beating her breast, while the imperturtable Mitrofanova had already gone to ring the police.

But Sasha couldn't have cared less about the scene before them. He had seen what he wanted – the black lacquered notebook on the black varnished armrest of the other armchair in the corner of the room. Just where he had left it the night they had been called out to examine the scene of the woman's murder.

He had found the ill-fated book between the seat and

71

the back of the divan – God only knew how it had got there. He had put it by his side on the arm of the chair, intending to enter it in his report, and then he had simply forgotten it.

Trying to hold the book by the edges so as not to leave fingerprints on it, Sasha carefully turned the pages, which were marked alphabetically. There was only one single note in the book, under the letter 'L': 'Lesya – 15 R.' Well, no problem. The ballet dancer had either lent or borrowed fifteen roubles from someone called Lesya, probably Olesya, but that hardly helped the enquiry. However, on the first page was an address: V. S. Kupriyanova, Sretensky St no. 13, apart. 15, tel. 211.44.85.

Sasha did not have the appropriate form with him for a report, so he went to the floorwoman's desk and tore a page from her magazine. Engrossed in his own affairs, he hardly noticed that the room was filling up with police officers of various ranks.

His witnesses were distracted by the – for them – more interesting goings-on in room 547, and he had to wait until they were through with their statements to the police, whose report finally announced that:

> Zhurgaev Ergash, Director of the Agitation and Propaganda Department of the Fergane District Committee of the Communist Party of Uzbekistan, while in Moscow on business to attend the session of the Central Committee of the CPSU to discuss questions of ideology, did conduct himself in an immoral fashion and did commit a minor act of hooliganism, to wit: having bribed the floor manageress, A. M. Silkina, with 50 roubles, he took to a room which was not designated to him a juvenile he had chanced to meet at the Central Telegraph Agency, by name Maya Rozova, fifteen years old, pupil of the eighth grade, School No. 185 in the capital. Having promised to give her a turquoise ring (value 15

72

roubles), he committed an act of sexual perversion with her, but was discovered and apprehended at the scene of the crime thanks to the vigilance of the administration of the Central Hotel.

Sasha left the building and strode along Gorky Street to Pushkin Square. At every telephone booth he tried to get through to Merkulov, who seemed to have disappeared. He didn't bother with the identification of Kupriyanova's body. Who was he supposed to show it to? Usually the father, mother or spouse of the deceased was taken, but he did not even know if her parents were alive or where to find her husband. He finally stopped at a callbox in the Metro and dialled Rita's number on impulse.

'Yes.' Her voice was cool and indifferent. Sasha was tongue-tied. Rita said sharply, 'Idiots,' and hung up.

Of course it was idiotic. The whole day had been idiotic.

A whole day had been lost because of that notebook, maybe two days. If he hadn't forgotten it, perhaps they would have known the name of the ballet dancer on the first day and everything might have turned out differently. He didn't relish the thought of confessing his sins to Merkulov. He'd go bananas naturally but, face it, the notebook had no real value. Just one innocent entry that didn't mean a thing.

Sasha rang Petrovka, just in case.

'Ah, the young star of the Prosecutor's Office!' Gryaznov greeted him. 'What fun and games have you been up to? I haven't been able to get hold of anyone for two hours. You might say we've been cracking your case for you here while you're off sunning yourself somewhere.'

The middle-aged star of the CID Office laid into their conduct of the case at some length and then suddenly suggested: 'Listen, Sasha, I fancy a bite to eat. I've got twenty roubles burning a hole in my pocket, so get over to the Narva and I'll tell you the whole story. As supervising prosecutor. . . .'

6

The day after the murders Captain Gryaznov had a rest period, but the next day he was back on the trail. That morning he had gone to Smolensk Street, to the Foreign Trade Ministry.

At the Cadre Management Office of the Ministry of Foreign Trade of the USSR, the Moscow CID captain was received courteously without any of the usual crap like 'Come back tomorrow; we have a board meeting' or 'Take a seat for a couple of hours; we're receiving a delegation from Bangladesh'! Setting aside all the other business, the Head of Cadres, a retired KGB general by the name of Ryabenky, invited his unexpected guest into his office and stayed closeted with him for a good half-hour.

They each had a glass of export Ararat brandy, and Gryaznov learnt the following: Rakitin was a good worker but he let his bosses down badly over something and there was a chance he might have been dismissed in time. But it was difficult to sack him because for many years he had worked not only for military intelligence but also for 'T' committee, the strategic problems arm of the KGB. . . .

Ryabenky was being crafty. He was not telling all he could and kept referring to the need for secrecy, but in the end he gave Gryaznov an extract from the minutes of an executive meeting of the Ministry from which it was clear that V. N. Rakitin, head of a directorate, had recently received a severe reprimand and been given a final warning.

'I wanted to get to Patolichev,' said Gryaznov hastily, 'but can anyone get to the Minister himself?' Even his assistants didn't want to talk. Apparently in the morning he was receiving Japanese journalists, the president of Armco steel was coming to lunch, and in the evening he was summoned to the international section of the Central Committee.

74

Gryaznov shrugged his shoulders dismissively. Whatever he thought, Sasha knew you couldn't entrust brainwork to the ordinary police. Operational work was another matter. As if to confirm it, Gryaznov described how he had spent the second half of the day.

Captain Gryaznov had an appointment with Major Krasnikovsky for two o'clock. By this time Arthur had found out practically everything about the owner of the badge marked 'Master of Sport of the USSR', no. 10569, which Merkulov had found in Sokolniki Park.

Slava Gryaznov had to spend some time at Skatertny Street in the Sports Committee, and in Moscow State University on the Lenin Hills. Taking in Igor Volin, a trainer in the Voluntary Sports Association, NAUKA, would have to be done gently and tactfully. The 'fish' would have to be played so that it would not take fright or have the chance to prepare an alibi. . . .

Igor Volin, head of the unarmed combat section of the sports club at Moscow University, always organized his day meticulously. In the morning he drove his Volga to the central market for fresh groceries. Towards twelve o'clock, he would look in briefly at the University where his assistants were coaching members of the students' sports club in self-defence. He would stay there for an hour to an hour and a half at most. In the afternoon he would be seen on Fersman Street in the hard-currency shop, and in the evening at the coin-collectors' club at Shabolovka Street. In short, every move he made in his fast-moving, regulated life was being monitored.

There were a lot of cars parked on Fersman Street, but Volin's black Volga with the dent in the right wing wasn't one of them. Krasnikovsky and Gryaznov decided to wait for him here. They had confidence in their informer, who had told them that most afternoons Volin would show up, driving a black Volga with a dent in the right wing. And so the men of Moscow CID watched gloomily as a hefty officer directed the traffic at the crossroads.

It was Friday, a good day for business. Representatives

of the privileged classes – diplomats, senior dignitaries of ministries, scientists who travelled abroad a lot, and also citizens who had received inheritances from relatives abroad – all came to the currency shop from time to time to do their shopping, not with Soviet roubles but with hard currency. They would drive up in their Volgas and Moskviches and Zhigulis, bought for the same kind of currency from the store by Luzhnetsky Bridge.

At three-thirty a black Volga with a dent in the right wing drew up. Two men got out, one a puny red-haired man in a leather jacket and jeans.

At this point in his story, Gryaznov suddenly roared with laughter. 'Christ, Sasha, I'm red-haired myself, I've seen red-haired people before, but I've never seen anything like this one – he even has red eyes!' Gryaznov cut himself some more shaslik and went on.

'The other one was a tall thickset blond man, obviously an athlete. Even though it was five degrees above, he was wearing a hide coat and a deerskin cap. They made for the door of the hard-currency store, and Arthur Krasnikovsky said: "Him in the tanned coat. That's our man!" '

They had a quick discussion, and Gryaznov went over to the traffic policeman.

The puny man and the tall one were gone about twenty minutes. At last they came out. They walked towards their car, taking their time, having made no purchases. The tall one seemed totally calm and at ease. A man who looked as sure of himself as he did made you think twice before you approached him. They were allowed to get into the car, the doors slammed, and then the traffic policeman appeared. The tall blond man got out of the car reluctantly, still looking unperturbed. The policeman started checking his driving licence ponderously. The blond man's licence was in order. At that moment Gryaznov came over, as agreed.

The tall blond man turned his bull neck and stared hard at Gryaznov's CID identification card. He glanced around him. Behind him stood the burly Krasnikovsky, a former light-heavyweight boxer and international bronze medallist.

'Don't get excited,' said the boxer.

'I won't,' said the self-defence expert.

'Your car seems to fit the description of the one we're looking for,' explained Gryaznov. 'We'll have to check it out, so you'd better come over to Petrovka with us.'

'You can check it here, can't you?'

'It's more convenient there.'

Volin fell silent, obviously thinking hard. He looked round at the three of them and nodded.

'I hope it won't take long.'

'No, no, not long!' said all three reassuringly, the traffic policeman and the two CID men. All three armed men were a bit afraid of one self-defence expert. God only knew what he might try. He was a master of sport, after all. And if he put up any resistance it might be embarrassing with so many passers-by around.

Outside Moscow CID headquarters at Petrovka, Volin opened the bonnet of his Volga himself. They also asked him to open the boot. He took his time but did as he was told. Flashes of bright green and red almost dazzled the spectators: there were boxes of scarves, about fifty in each, inside.

'What's this?'

'Presents for relatives.'

'You've got a lot of relatives, haven't you?'

'Yes.'

'And is the document-case yours?'

'Yes.'

'Then take it with you.'

They went up to the fourth floor with some witnesses to make a statement. Romanova suggested that Volin show them what was in the document-case. He hesitated, then finally made up his mind to snap open the locks and lift the lid. There were wads of money, coupons for the hard-currency shops, and an imported handgun and silencer.

'In short, Investigator, I could teach you a thing or

77

two!' said Gryaznov in self-satisfaction as he finished his account of the successes of the Moscow CID's second section. He lit a Belomor cigarette, blew out a long blue stream of smoke, tapped the ash into his empty coffee-cup and gave a satisfied grunt.

'So, pal, me and old Arthur didn't do so bad, did we?'

The small orchestra struck up at the far end of the room. Sasha nodded his head. No, they hadn't done so bad at all. One thought stopped him from feeling over-joyed at their coup. Was Volin, his old unarmed-combat instructor at university, really a murderer?

He pulled on his coat and asked Gryaznov: 'Where is he now?'

Gryaznov narrowed his eyes and said slowly: 'Why? Do you know him?'

Sasha shrugged. 'Slightly. We used to meet at the sports club. So where is he?'

'Where he belongs: in one of our cells at Petrovka.'

'And the little man?'

'He just happened to be with Volin, getting a lift to the hard-currency shop. We let him go.'

And Gryaznov casually tossed down the twenty roubles that were burning a hole in his pocket on to the dish where the bill for dinner lay.

7

20 November 1982
'I was about thirteen then. My mother put some buckwheat porridge on to boil and told me to take it off in half an hour and put it under a cushion to cook through. Then she went to work. It was the winter holidays, and a few minutes later one of my schoolmates came running in and said: "Let's go and see *Carnival Night*!" Of course I forgot all about the porridge right away.'

Merkulov puffed on his Dymok and went on: 'We were sitting in the cinema, watching the newsreel. We weren't all that interested, and kept chatting and making a noise – the place was half-empty anyway. Suddenly I heard the announcer say solemnly: "And also Marshal Porich"! You can imagine how scared I was my porridge had burnt! And it had, too.' Merkulov laughed. 'It was a good job there wasn't a fire. And you feel like Charlie Chaplin all because of a mislaid notebook. Forget it, pal.'

They laughed, but Sasha saw Merkulov glancing at his watch – he was waiting for the results of the forensic tests on Kupriyanova's lost notebook which Sasha had handed to Slava Gryaznov the day before to pass on to the lab boys.

It was what they called a 'black Saturday'. It should have been a day off but they were hard at it, compiling a schedule of the enquiry. They were both bent over their desks: Sasha's old and battered, Merkulov's gleaming with varnish.

This was the first time Sasha had done this sort of work for real – student seminars and practicals were just kids' stuff by comparison. He pulled a face at Merkulov, who pretended not to notice. He knew only too well how to fill in the slots in the monthly calendar, but Sasha must learn for himself.

From time to time, Merkulov dialled a number, obviously trying to reach his wife in hospital, but he kept getting the engaged signal. Between doing this and working out the schedule, he would occasionally open the middle drawer of his desk and try to wind up an old onion-shaped watch.

Sasha felt increasingly irritated. From what he could see the watch was ready for the scrapheap – the glass was broken, and when Merkulov shook it the inner works rattled.

Sighing, Sasha opened the large ruled notebook stamped with the crest of The Public Prosecutor's Office of the USSR. On paper headed 'Schedule of the Investigation', he wrote his possible theories.

First theory: Rakitin and Kupriyanova were murdered on grounds of jealousy: (a) possibly by killers hired by Rakitin's wife, (b) by a man who was jealous of Kupriyanova's relationship with Rakitin.

Second theory: Rakitin and Kupriyanova were murdered in order to conceal crimes committed by people who were afraid that these crimes would otherwise be exposed by their victims.

Third theory: Rakitin and Kupriyanova were murdered in order to acquire certain valuables – Soviet and American hard-currency, articles unknown, and possibly papers of a secret nature.

All very neat and plausible – on paper. But the evidence they had so far did not support any of the theories – or even completely contradicted them. Sasha remembered an exercise from criminology class, took a separate piece of paper and started sketching out a flowchart. In the three big squares he wrote the number of each theory, and drew lines from those to other, smaller, squares which represented possible perpetrators of the crime, with rectangles for the hard evidence obtained so far. The resulting patterns were horrific. The squares seemed to be floating in air, and the rectangles combined to form a closed impenetrable circle. Merkulov looked sceptically across at the doodle.

'Go in for computer-programming in your spare time, Comrade Turetsky?'

He reached over for the chart, studying it inscrutably for several minutes. Sasha felt a light sweat prickle under his arms and between his shoulderblades.

'That's all very well, kid' – Merkulov's tone was unexpectedly mild – 'but there's no logic here, and there can't be any because the murders themselves are all wrong.'

Just like Merkulov! Vague and unscientific as usual. But Sasha knew what he meant. On the basis of the material evidence they had, the murders shouldn't have taken place – there was no motive.

Merkulov put his elbows on his desk and his palms together, as if in prayer. When he did that, it meant he was in deadly earnest.

'Come on, Alexander Borisovich, cut the fancy crap and look at what we do know.

'Viktor Nikolayevich Rakitin, directorate head at the Ministry of Foreign Trade, also working for Chief Intelligence at headquarters of the Ministry of Defence and the KGB strategic board, goes to Sokolniki Park where an electronics trade fair is opening to meet an American journalist called Zbigniev Podgursky. He has a briefcase with him – containing secret papers, valuables, American currency? The purpose of the meeting is unclear. Rakitin is hardly a professional spy – leaving his mistress a message containing the name of the American shows that.

'Two men were tailing Rakitin – just observing him, "minding" him, *after* him? He fails to meet Podgursky and a little later is found brutally murdered. The briefcase has vanished. That evening, in the Central Hotel, Kupriyanova is murdered. The murderers were looking for duplicate copies of something – possibly whatever was in the briefcase. A certain Volin is arrested, the owner of the "Master of Sports" badge that was found at the scene of the crime. A handgun with a silencer is found in the boot of his car. Moscow CID is certain that he is one of the murderers.'

Merkulov obviously did not go for that – or not until the results of the forensic tests and Volin's interrogation convinced him.

'That's it, Sasha. More holes than my granny's colander.'

He stubbed out his cigarette in the ashtray and lit another right away. 'We need more facts. Let's leave Volin and his gang to Moscow CID for the time being. We need to follow up some more contacts, especially Valeria Kupriyanova's.'

Merkulov was trying to follow the criminals' logic. They had gone straight from Rakitin to Kupriyanova, so then they'd go – or had already gone – from her to other people she knew. Sasha had once read somewhere that a criminal had a hundred paths, and is free to take any one of them. But an investigator has only one path – the one the criminal takes. Merkulov and he had to hit on that single path. . . .

Someone knocked politely on the door, and Captain Vyacheslav Gryaznov came into the office. He looked like an Olympic gold medallist in his newly pressed grey greatcoat, his narrow captain's epaulettes shining like silver.

'Comrade Junior Officer, request permission to speak to the Comrade Investigator!' said Gryaznov jokingly. 'On instructions from the Head of Moscow CID, I have come to place myself entirely at your disposal.'

For answer, Merkulov clumsily placed his open hand to the side of his head and grinned. The salute did not come off, and realising it himself, he waved his hand dismissively.

'Skip the formalities, Slava, just carry on here as you would at home – or at Moscow CID anyway.'

Gryaznov took him literally. He shrugged off his greatcoat and sprawled in an armchair opposite his new boss.

'Is that your watch, Konstantin Dmitriyevich?'

Sasha felt his former dull irritation returning. Here they were, working their balls off and this goon turned up just to kid around and pass the time of day. But Merkulov smiled guilelessly and explained: 'My grandfather gave it to me. I forgot to take it out of my trouser pocket and it went through the washing machine. It's just about a hundred years old. . . .'

The phone rang. Merkulov picked up the receiver and gestured the others to be quiet.

Gryaznov busied himself quietly unpacking his briefcase. He got out a round of smoked sausage, a jar of red caviare, two jars of marrow, a half-kilo of sturgeon, a bag of oranges and a box of assorted chocolates.

'I've got this for Kostya,' he whispered to Sasha, 'or, rather, for his better half. We get a special deal for shopping at Petrovka every Friday.'

Merkulov finished talking and feasted his eyes on the riches that Slava had brought.

'Thanks a lot, pal. Lida and I will have a party tonight. And I've got some more good news: Lelya is being discharged from hospital in a few days, so things will be a bit easier for us then. I'm not much of a cook.'

'What can I say, Konstantin Dmitriyevich, except that it's tough without a wife? Though, of course, it depends on the wife. . . .' Gryaznov pursed already-thin lips. Sasha knew that his wife had left him about a year ago, after ten years together. Still, not every woman could put up with a policeman for a husband – with no days off, irregular hours, nothing but work. . . .

'What do I owe you, Slava?'

'Exactly sixteen roubles.' Gryaznov regained his usual easygoing manner and added: 'I can wait till payday.'

'I'd be glad if you would. I've got sixty roubles on me, but. . . .'

'Forget it, Comrade Investigator,' said Gryaznov, and pulled a thin sheaf of paper from the bottom of his case. 'I've got some lab reports for you here. You may find something worthwhile.'

Merkulov turned to the forensic report on the notebook. Sasha read it over his shoulder. In the handwriting expert's opinion, the words 'Lesya – 15 R.' were in Kupriyanova's hand and had been written in the previous forty-eight hours prior to her death. Sasha did not fully understand why Merkulov seemed so pleased that Valeria had made the note. Wasn't it clear before?

Then they looked at the fingerprint expert's conclusions: there were lots of ballet dancer's prints on the lacquered cover of the book, and no one else's. The prints were clear and unsmudged, which suggested that the book had not been in anyone else's hands, even if they had been wearing gloves.

'Incidentally, this ballet dancer had no friend or relative by the name of Lesya. I checked with the people at the theatre and her neighbours,' Gryaznov announced.

'Oh yeah?' said Merkulov aggressively. 'That means that you didn't check properly. Never mind. I'll do it myself. If you'd said you couldn't *find* anyone by that name, I wouldn't mind.'

He was really sore, but Gryaznov just said brightly: 'Calm down, Konstantin Dmitriyevich. I've got a special present for you.' And he handed Merkulov another official document.

Forensic Report
Moscow, 19 November 1982

Acting on instructions from Investigator Comrade Merkulov of the Moscow Prosecutor's Office, I, G. G. Bochan, forensic scientist, conducted forensic tests on a scrap of American currency, a hundred-dollar note, to establish whether it was genuine, and the method by which it was produced.

For purpose of comparison, a genuine hundred-dollar note was provided by the State Treasury of the USSR by special request of the Public Prosecutor of Moscow, Comrade Malkov.

Given the small size of the fragment, the question of the note's authenticity remains open to debate, but spectral analysis of the paper established that the chemical composition of the note used for comparison differed substantially from the chemical composition of the scrap. . . .

Conclusion. The banknote, of which a scrap was the subject of examination, was made by means of a metal plate similar to that used to print the genuine note. The paper of which the fragment was made differed from the sample note as follows:

(*a*) in chemical composition
(*b*) in thickness
(*c*) in weight
(*d*) in cross-section
(*e*) in ash content

   Deduction. On balance of probability, the scrap is from a *forged* banknote. In both physical and chemical composition the paper used is similar to that used in the USSR for the manufacture of fifty-rouble notes by the State Mint.

G. BOCHAN
Forensic scientist

And then something clicked with Merkulov. He got up from behind his desk and strode to the middle of the floor. He looked like a gypsy performer. He clapped his hands and started to sing.

'I used to come home at dawn
Young and drinking vodka. . . .'

Then he began to dance, clicking his heels rhythmically. The performance had Gryaznov and Sasha rooted to the spot. It finished as the Serious Crimes Investigator declaimed:

'I studied at the gypsy faculty
And got an education!'

Then it was Sasha and Gryaznov's turn to rejoice. They whooped and yelled for about ten minutes while Merkulov immersed himself in the other documents, a big grin on his face.

The phone rang, and Merkulov picked it up and listened for about a minute, without saying a word.

Gryaznov whispered: 'He's happy because Lelya's on the mend.'

85

Merkulov hung up. He finished what he was writing and handed it to Sasha. 'Run over to the Duty Prosecutor and have Omelchenko put a stamp and his signature on that.'

'Now?'

'Now!' Merkulov glanced at his watch. 'That was Romanova on the phone. Because it's the weekend, all the bosses are away sunning themselves so she's asked us to get a search warrant for her, and an order to hold Volin for three days. She thinks he is the big blond guy who murdered Rakitin.'

'And the ballet dancer,' said Gryaznov triumphantly.

'And the ballet dancer,' repeated Merkulov indifferently.

'And what do you think, Konstantin Dmitriyevich?' asked Gryaznov insistently. 'Do you think he's the killer?'

Instead of replying, Merkulov said: 'Look, at three o'clock I've got a date with three girls. I'll give two of them to you! Take your pick: Petrovka or Leninsky Prospekt. No, better still' – Merkulov poked a long finger into Sasha's chest – 'you go to Leninsky Prospekt, and you, Slava, go over to Romanova!'

He got over to the main building of the Prosecutor's office and back again with the search warrant and remand order in literally three minutes. Gryaznov was still around, but Merkulov wasn't. The captain explained that he'd dashed off to see his wife at Pirogovskaya Street. The phone went again, and Gryaznov snatched up the receiver.

'Yes, yes, certainly Comrade Lieutenant-Colonel! I have the warrant here. I'm on my way, Alexandra Ivanovna. I've just got to drop Investigator Turetsky at the morgue.'

8

No two ways about it, she was a peach. She should have been making films in Hollywood or, at the very least, draping herself over Kuznestsky Bridge modelling clothes. And here she was cutting up corpses! It was enough to drive a man crazy.

Sasha watched Rita's neat well-adjusted movements. As the autopsy proceeded, she gave a short commentary just like Professor Tumanov in the anatomy department of the Second Medical Institute where, as a student, he had attended classes in forensic medicine.

'The mark on the skin caused by the bullet as it entered the torso or the muscles, we call the point of entry. There it is – take a look: a rounded shape with multiple ragged edges just under the heart.'

Rita adjusted her grip on the body and raised the ballet dancer's head. Then, with one powerful slash of the scalpel, she slit the whole body from neck to groin, impassively exposing all its intestines. Blood splashed over her starched coat. She sighed, took a saw and started to cut through the ribcage. A few minutes later, she pulled out the bullet which had struck down Kupriyanova. Sasha could feel the vomit rising in his throat.

'Did you bring the other bullet?' she asked in a matter-of-fact voice. 'Merkulov rang before you arrived to say that you'd arrested a man with a gun. I want to check the calibre of the bullets in it with the murder weapon's.'

Averting his eyes, Sasha put the bullet Gryaznov had given him into Rita's palm, which was covered in a bloodstained rubber glove.

'No, that's not it.'

'What do you mean?'

'It's not the right calibre,' she said confidently. 'This is 7.62, and she was killed with a .9 calibre.'

Rita dropped the first, red-tinged bullet into a cellophane sample-bag, and then the second into another, and handed them both to Sasha, who shuddered as he touched them. The bags felt sticky. He could barely stop himself from running out to the men's room right away to wash his hands.

Rita used an electric saw to cut open the skull and then, taking a sharp scalpel, set about making small incisions into what looked like a lot of worm-eaten mushrooms – the exposed grey matter of the hemisphere of the brain. She was muttering things to herself, like a witch-doctor. Sasha listened carefully. She seemed to be saying: 'Nice and clean, nice and clean.'

He closed his eyes and thought beautiful thoughts – then became dimly aware that someone had entered the laboratory and was standing behind him.

'You can't come in here. Who do you want, citizen?' Rita asked sharply.

Sasha turned round. A stranger stood resting his hand on the desk where the lab boys wrote up their reports. He was short and skinny with a broad clean-shaven face, thinning hair and large horn-rimmed glasses. He was well dressed in foreign-looking clothes.

With a nervous cough, he said. 'I'm Kupriyanov, Valeria's husband. Well, really, ex-husband. I've just flown in from Warsaw. She had hardly any relatives, just an aunt who's in poor health. She asked me to come over and make the funeral arrangements.'

'Could you tell me your full name?' Sasha asked gently.

'Nikolai Petrovich Kupriyanov.'

'Nikolai Petrovich, does the name "Lesya" or "Olesya" mean anything to you? Did Valeria Sergeyevna have a friend or relative of that name or something similar?'

'Lesya?' said Nikolai Petrovich, shaking his head uncertainly. 'No, I don't recall anyone.'

'Please, Nikolai Petrovich, if you do remember, can you call this number?' Sasha gave him a piece of paper with Merkulov's number on it.

'Yes, of course.'

Rita asked Kupriyanov please to take a seat outside. After standing quite still for a second or two, he went out, wiping his eyes.

So now we have our formal identification, Sasha thought. Though it's a waste of time making out a report. Half the people in Moscow could confirm that the woman was Kupriyanova.

About twenty minutes later, Rita told the orderly to sew up the body. She took off her gloves and washed her hands thoroughly under the tap, then went out into the corridor, Sasha following. Kupriyanov was pacing up and down. Rita sat down gracefully on a folding chair and called him over to her. Kupriyanov lowered himself obediently on to the seat next to her, put his elbows on his knees and covered his face with his hands.

She signalled for Sasha to leave them alone. He went into the doctors' common room. Looking back, he saw Rita patting Kupriyanov's hunched shoulders.

A few minutes later, Rita came into the common room where he was drinking coffee with a nurse and told him she had given Kupriyanov permission to go ahead and bury the woman the next day.

'You might have consulted me first,' Sasha objected.

But what difference did it make? They couldn't put off the funeral indefinitely.

'Do you want a cup of coffee?' he offered. Suddenly it was very important to him that she should stay.

'It's lousy here,' said Rita, going over to an old locker and getting out her coat.

'But I've got a real Armenian copper pot at my place. Let's got and make a decent cup there!'

God! He sounded like a desperate college kid. Time for another of Rita Shchastlivaya's famous putdowns.

She turned round, looked him straight in the eye and said nothing. Then, cradling her coat like a baby, she said after a long pause: 'Well, if you're doing nothing, how about coming with me and visiting some friends of mine?' And then, more animatedly, she added: 'They're kind of crazy, but good people. Only we'll have to take a bottle or two with us.'

The nurse was listening, unabashed, to their conversation. She turned her empty coffee-glass over on to its saucer and said approvingly: 'Well, that's great. Enjoy yourselves while you can. What kind of a life is this for kids like you, up to your elbows in blood and shit all day long. . . ?'

9

Investigations are like life – if you're lucky, you'll get a home run. That's the way the search of Volin's apartment progressed.

While Sasha was watching the autopsy, the operations team took the search warrant and set off for the house in Davydkovo where Volin lived. The sports instructor didn't just possess weights and barbells of every conceivable kind. In his apartment they found packs of hard-to-come-by kerchiefs, a collection of icons, packed for export, and other items from churches together with valuable museum pieces. There were more than a hundred kilos of silver coins alone, and seventy-five medals struck from precious metals. It was more like a museum storeroom than an apartment.

There were several portable radio transmitters of foreign manufacture which could be used to communicate over a distance of several kilometres. And behind the ice-box in the corner were bits of housebreaking equipment: rope-ladders, hacksaws, wire-cutters, bags.

Major Krasnikovsky fairly glowed with delight. Over the previous two months Moscow CID had gathered background information on the activities of one particular gang. Antiques had been stolen from several apartments. One particular coin-collector always came to numismatists' club in a Zhiguli or a Niva or a Volga. One man had been arrested for selling icons to foreigners. And so on.

The operations section had been asked to establish the connection between the various facts. And now they had cracked it!

10

Having queued for half an hour for vodka, they drove down Lyusinovsky Street towards Danilovsky market. There was a sudden flurry of light powdery snow, and Rita turned on the windscreen wipers.

'Any reason for visiting your friends?' Sasha asked.

'No reason. Just for the hell of it. And, anyway, today is Gunners' Day. And I'm a sort of gunner.'

'Not exactly,' Sasha said. It was her husband, the major-general who commanded an artillery division in Afghanistan.

'I had a year of it in Afghanistan, too. After that nightmare, the Sklifosovsky Emergencies Institute is a holiday camp. There were hundreds of dead and wounded every day. Ours and theirs.'

That dying cadence was just like her. Sasha always said she should be in Hollywood. Involuntarily he looked sideways at her smartly gloved hands on the steering wheel. As if reading his thoughts, she continued: 'True, they pay you in hard currency. I earned enough to buy this car, for instance. But that's all in the past now.'

If only your husband was in the past as well, Sasha thought.

Once again, Rita seemed to guess what he was thinking. Softly, almost inaudibly, she said, 'I wasn't very good at being a general's wife,' and put her foot down hard on the accelerator.

The car skidded on a sharp bend and turned on to a

great snow-covered expanse of grass in the middle of which stood a little house embedded in the earth. Rita switched off the engine, and Sasha climbed out of the car awkwardly holding two bottles by the neck.

Her boots slipping and sliding on the wet snow, Rita ran up to the front window and rapped on it, code-like: one-two, one-two-three. Then she came back and took Sasha's arm in both hands and they went up to the front door together.

There was a huge blue Ford alongside the house. It looked incongruous somehow, parked beside the little peasant shack.

The door opened, and from somewhere out of the ground crawled a small bearded man with bright eyes.

'Rita, sweetheart! I haven't seen you for a hundred years. Sasha, isn't it? Come on in. I'm Georgi, owner of this palace.'

So Rita had been talking about him. . . . Sasha's heart skipped a beat. Meanwhile, their host was carefully relieving him of the vodka, kissing each bottle in turn tenderly.

Sounds of rejoicing emanated from the room at the arrival of some hard liquor, and someone struck up on the piano: 'Louder the music, play the victory.' At first Sasha could not see anything for cigarette smoke and subdued lighting. Georgi, or simply Zhora, tried to introduce the other people at the party to him. A beautiful voluptuous girl sat on the window-sill, a sad expression on her face.

'My name's Alyona,' she said, a note of stagey despair in her voice.

'She brought the brawn,' declared someone in a theatrical baritone.

And there, at the piano, was none other than a famous actor from the Contemporary Theatre, Valentin Nikulin.

'You know Valya, of course,' said Zhora, waving a hand in his direction. 'And this is Senya.'

A fat man with round glasses jumped up and rapped

out, military fashion: 'Senya Shteinbock, chemist, attached to Military Intelligence!'

Everyone looked very surprised, as if they had not known it before.

'Let me explain,' said Senya, continuing in the same vein. 'By special government instruction, I am part of an anti-air-attack team whose task is to locate territory infected by bacteria. If there is a bacteriological attack from the air, they dress me up in a special suit and send me up front. If I come back alive, they can send in other military units. If I don't come back, it means the area is infected.'

Everyone laughed, even Alyona. From the far corner of the room two bearded men shouted out in chorus, 'And we're from the FBI!' before continuing their heated discussion.

'They're lying! They're old schoolmates of mine – fellow-daubers,' said Zhora.

Sasha realised that the huge room was actually an artist's studio. Finished and unfinished canvases, all executed in shades of dark brown, lined the walls. Many of them were portraits of Alyona, with and without her clothes. Sasha liked them a lot, despite the gloomy colouring.

The chemist from Military Intelligence distributed the vodka in tumblers and they all sat round the coffee-table on which was a large wooden bowl containing the remains of the brawn and some salad.

'And how do investigators drink – out of tumblers or out of little glasses?' asked Senya pointedly.

So they knew about his job. Sasha looked sideways at Rita, who shrugged innocently.

'Half-tumblers,' he answered.

For some reason they all decided it was a smart answer. Zhora roared with laughter, and even Senya smiled wryly.

Rita settled closer beside him. Her face was still cold from snowy night air as she leant against him and whispered, 'To us,' raising her tumbler with a half-smile. Sasha emptied his at a gulp.

Nikulin stuffed a large piece of brawn into his mouth and went back to the piano stool.

'Ladies and gentlemen, I'm now going to perform for you a delightful little number!' he said with his mouth full. Then, swallowing the brawn, he sang:

> 'Oh, I feel sick inside,
> Someone'll have my hide,
> My clothes don't fit,
> Only got a five-copeck bit.'

Valentin himself seemed most pleased with his performance. He whinnied loudly, displaying horse-like teeth, and then, without any discernible change of expression, began to play some sad slow dance-music. They got to their feet, Sasha with Rita and Zhora with Alyona.

The ground seemed to fall away. Sasha staggered slightly from the vodka, the heat, the nearness of Rita. Wordlessly, he slid his arms round her, and her lips grazed his cheek. That cool, amused, distant expression had gone from her grey eyes, he noticed disbelievingly. But in a moment, he knew, he'd wake up with a start. This had to be a dream.

Suddenly Valentin stopped playing and roared: 'How come we haven't got more women?'

At that very moment, an ear-splitting pounding at the window outside shattered the calm.

Valentin leapt up from his stool as if he had been stung. Shouting 'Inka!' he rushed not to the door but to the table.

'Don't let her in yet!' he yelled in an unexpectedly shrill voice after Zhora, who had gone to open the door for the new arrival. Nikulin poured himself a full tumbler of vodka, gulped it down in one, and dashed round the table in search of something to eat. He had obviously not been thinking of his wife when he had spoken of the shortage of women.

Zhora fumbled with the lock as long as he could, then Inka fairly flew into the room. Nikulin was once again at the piano, obliviously singing one of Okudzhava's songs. His wife threw a suspicious look at him, but for the time being her interest had been caught by something else. Without even saying hello, Inka put her hands on her hips and asked: 'Who came in the Ford?'

Everyone was silent. Then, suddenly, Alyona said in a thin little voice: 'Well, I suppose I did.'

'Where did you get it from?' Inka continued her heavily loaded interrogation.

'Oh, an American,' replied Alyona faintly and, for some reason, burst out crying.

Zhora shook his fist at Inka and went over to comfort the inconsolable-looking Alyona, alternately patting her knee and wiping the tears from her cheeks.

Sasha wanted to laugh, imagining sad fat Alyona sitting disconsolately in a fabulous foreign car.

Inka sat down next to her husband, her beautiful blue eyes fixed on him not in affection but to gauge how much he had had to drink. Sasha sighed. Inka had brought him tumbling back to earth when moments before he'd been in heaven. Swallowing resolutely, he looked down into Rita's amused grey eyes.

'Let's go to my place,' he suggested.

She shook her head dismissively.

'No. We'll go to mine.'

11

In the meantime, Shura Romanova was threshing about in her office. She'd caught Volin like a fish on ice, but the self-defence expert wasn't saying a word. It was as if he were a deaf-mute.

Romanova had worked for Moscow CID for twenty-five years, and for almost fifteen of them she had headed the second section, never knowing a day's peace and quiet. Anyone else in her position would have long since gone off his head and swallowed broken glass, but Shura enjoyed rude good health and a rare zest for life. Lieutenant-Colonel Romanova was a difficult lady to surprise. If a Martian suddenly showed up and pleaded guilty to something, she would take it in her stride and charge him.

Shura contemplated the strong handsome man imperturbably. In a day or two he'd be eating shit in one of their cells where her best agents would really be able to go to work on him. And then this little dicky bird wouldn't be able to stop singing. She had broken braver men than him in her twenty-five years' service. What a waste!

12

21 November 1982

Sasha was woken by a piercing ringing noise. He opened his eyes momentarily and saw a slim hand move towards the alarm-clock. The room fell silent again.

'Sleep a bit more,' she said. 'You've had enough this week.'

He was about to do as he was told, snuggling into Rita's warm shoulder. Then he pulled her towards him instead. She didn't resist.

He could not understand what had woken him the second time. He lay with his eyes closed, trying to remember what he had been dreaming about. The strong smell of coffee assailed him. The bed felt unfamiliar. Somehow. . . .

Jesus Christ! He jumped out of bed stark naked, pulled the sheet around him and went out to the bathroom. A cold shower finally restored him to full glowing consciousness.

Rita came out of the kitchen wearing something incredibly flimsy, her ash-blond hair tied in a demure ponytail at the nape of her neck. She put down the tray of coffee and toast, came over to Sasha and pressed herself to him with a sigh.

'Rita,' he gulped.

They sat on the divan. The toast tasted good, but Sasha ate it with difficulty. There was a sensation of growing alarm in the pit of his stomach.

'What's up, Sasha?'

He wanted to pretend, to say that everything was fine, great! But he looked into Rita's eyes and said: 'You're someone else's wife.'

She snatched up her packet of cigarettes, but it was empty. He didn't have any, either; Rita's friends had smoked them all the night before.

They drank coffee in silence, cup after cup.

The tension was broken by the ringing of the phone. Rita shuddered as if someone had hit her, then took the receiver.

'Yes,' she said, scarcely audibly. Then she listened for a long time, her face gradually betraying more and more embarrassment. She dropped the receiver in her lap and said: 'It's Merkulov. He needs you.'

In his surprise, Sasha knocked the coffee-pot on to the divan, splashing the upholstery with a stream of thick brown liquid. They both bent forward to pick up the coffee-pot and banged foreheads. Sasha grabbed the receiver and yelled: 'What is it, Konstantin Dmitriyevich?'

Merkulov coughed tactfully for a few seconds, allowing Sasha time to calm down a little.

'I've just explained to Ritochka' – *Ritochka!* – 'what the problem is. We have got to take a trip out of town urgently. I need reinforcements – you, Rita and her car. I'm sorry to ask you today, but I have to bring you in.'

*   *   *

They sat silently in the Lada, speeding down the empty Frunzensky Embankment towards the Krymsky Bridge and then on to the Sadovoye ring-road. Sasha had forgotten his initial anger with Merkulov, though he still didn't understand why he, Rita and her car were so vital.

He sensed that Rita was happy about their jaunt with Merkulov. They talked about nothing in particular, and Sasha felt his jangling mood of the morning evaporating – well, almost. Executing a smart turn at Kolkhoz Square, they came on to Prospekt Mir where Rita braked sharply at a tobacconist's kiosk.

'No Stolichny,' said the vendor, gazing into space.

'You can keep the change,' Sasha said, knowing the score. The man immediately produced the cigarettes from under the counter.

For some reason Merkulov had told them to meet him not by the Footwear Store on Prospekt Mir on the seventh floor of which he had his apartment, but in the hustle and bustle of the Exhibition of Economic Achievements.

Even from a distance they could make out his tall figure detaching itself from the crowd around the exhibition turnstiles. He was wearing a thick brown coat. Was it because it was Sunday that he had decided to exchange his prosecutor's blue greatcoat for plain clothes?

'Rita, Sasha, hello. Sorry to spoil your Sunday but this trip is vital,' he said, climbing into the back of the car. Sasha noticed that his coat pocket was bulging suspiciously. Merkulov caught the glance and tried for a jaunty tone.

'Yes, I've brought my "Walther", just in case.'

So it was no joke.

'Ritochka, no turning off. Just keep going, straight along Yaroslavskoe Road. We'll go as far as Bolshevo and then we'll have to start looking. Here's the address – the corner of Turgenev Street and Alley 19, the "Swallow" co-operative. Lucian Germanovich Romadin.'

A sense of anticipation gripped Sasha. He turned round to Merkulov and asked: 'Is he Lesya?'

Merkulov nodded his head and in a few words explained how he had tracked Romadin down. . . .

Nikolai Petrovich Kupriyanov was grief-stricken when he came home from the morgue. Although he had lost Valeria some time before, he could not come to terms with her death. For some hours he just sat on a chair in the hallway of his apartment, his eyes fixed on one spot. All he could see was that terrible picture at the morgue with his Valeria, his only love, lying there dead, mutilated by a doctor's scalpel. Still young, still beautiful. . . .

It was strange. The young man, the investigator, hadn't asked him a single question. 'They' must have known that Colonel Kupriyanov of HQ was abroad in Warsaw when this terrible murder took place. True, the investigator showed an interest in some friend of Valya's with the peculiar name of Lada? No, Lesya. He tried to concentrate. Lesya, Lesya. Yes, that was it, not Lesya, but Lyosya, Lyosik!

That's what Valya used to call her first music teacher, Lucian Germanovich Romadin, now retired and cultivating flowers in his garden in Bolshevo. Kupriyanov dashed about the apartment, wondering what to do. 'They' don't ask questions for nothing. It was probably very important for them to find Lyosik.

He pulled out the piece of paper that the young investigator had given him: 'Konstantin Dmitriyevich Merkulov – tel. 2691132.' But there was no reply when he rang on Saturday night. Then he rang directory enquiries, which was engaged for a whole hour. Finally, he got through. At first the girl refused categorically to try to find the number.

'We don't give the number, citizen, unless you give us the address!'

Kupriyanov begged her to give him the number of all the Merkulovs in Moscow. At last, she took pity on him.

'The most interesting thing is there's only one K. D. Merkulov in the whole of Moscow! Anyway, Kupriyanov finally got me at half-past eleven this morning. I'd been out all morning with Lida at Ostankino for her figure-skating class.'

Yaroslavskoe Road turned into a pot-holed, out-of-town dirt-track. Oncoming vehicles splattered them with slush, and the windscreen-wipers could barely cope. The rear window of the Lada was completely covered.

At last Rita said: 'Bolshevo.'

The scarcely visible sign told them to turn off to the right. They cut across a railway track and ran into the village.

'We must ask as few questions as possible,' warned Merkulov.

Just then a young motorcyclist rode up. Taking off her helmet, she was revealed as a girl with a shock of auburn hair. She gave Rita directions in no time at all, and a few minutes later, having turned right at the end of the street, they found themselves crawling up a steep narrow road. It skirted a wood and then ran parallel to the main road they had left a fair way below. Another sharp turn and the road seemed to leave civilisation far behind. Gently sloping away to one side they had a view of a wide stretch of winter wheat; on the horizon was a grey-blue blur of forest. The road had become no wider than the car.

Sasha turned to Merkulov and said: 'Yes. You couldn't make it on foot from the station to here. It must be about fifteen kilometres.'

Rita looked at the speedometer. 'Thirteen kilometres and six hundred metres.'

They covered about another kilometre before they saw in front of them some arched wooden gates above which was written: 'The Swallow Country Cottage Building Co-operative.'

The scene beyond was like a ghost town – the cottages were obviously summer homes. They skidded down a wide silent street strewn with building materials.

'Now, where do we find Turgenev Street?' mumbled Merkulov.

Rita stopped the car and wound down her window.

'We're in it now. There is only one street.'

Sasha saw a puff of smoke rising from the chimney of a two-storey cottage at the end of the street. 'Is that what we're looking for?'

Rita put the car in gear, but it didn't budge. While the engine roared impotently they climbed out to find the back wheels stuck deep in a slippery hole. Rita threw up her hands. This was adding insult to injury since the road was asphalted about five metres on. Up to their ankles in mud, they trudged over to the asphalt and, in a few minutes, were approaching the house. A board on a post alongside it read 'Alley 19'.

The house was separated from the road by a hedge – the management of the co-operative obviously did not allow fences. There was a gap in the hedge at one point, so they went through it and stepped on to an ornamental path of dressed stone.

Unexpectedly, beauty and tranquility reigned all around them in a solid wall of evergreen shrubs and similar trees which seemed to form an intricate maze. And at its heart stood an old decaying wooden house. They began to walk round it, trying to find a way in.

Suddenly, Rita stood stock still and said quietly: 'Look!'

By the porch, right in front of them on the path, lay a huge Newfoundland dog, its powerful forepaws extended before it and its tongue lolling as it panted noisily. Even Merkulov was thrown.

'So what do we do now, kids?' he asked.

Sasha called, quietly: 'Lucian Germanovich.'

The great dog heaved itself up and, opening its huge mouth, gave a yawn which came out sounding like a lion's roar. From somewhere behind the house there came the sound of squelching footsteps and an old man's voice demanding: 'What is it, Mister?'

Mister barked once and lay down again, wearily closing his basilisk eyes. A very tall, very thin, very old man came round from behind the house. He was wearing rubber boots and a padded jacket but no hat. His long grey hair blew about his skull like down with every step he took.

'What can I do for you, comrades? Have you lost your way?'

'No, I don't think so. Are you Comrade Romadin?'

'That's me, friends. And whom do I have the honour. . . ? But, please come into the house first. There's no electricity in the village today, and I only have a fire in one room, but my house is your house.'

13

Two citizens were calmly standing at the trolley-bus stop on the corner of Kalinin Prospekt and Suvorovsky Boulevard. They had been staking out the House of Journalists since twelve o'clock and so they were getting a little tired.

'There he is, your Gryaznov,' said one of them as a tall figure in a black leather coat and black cap came out of the Arbat pedestrian underpass.

'Good,' answered the other. 'We can have a quick one in the bar to warm up.'

He pulled his hat over his eyes and followed Gryaznov into the foyer of the House of Journalists.

Gryaznov, veteran operations man, completely absorbed in his own thoughts, did not notice that he was being tailed.

In the well-known beer-cellar, no less famous than the House of Journalists, all the benches round the long tables were fully occupied despite the early hour.

Gryaznov got into the beer-queue and waited patiently for several minutes before he found himself at the counter, behind which stood an attractive barmaid wearing a white cap perched on her newly permed hair.

'Good God – Slavik!' said the barmaid cheerfully, flashing her lynx-like eyes at Gryaznov. 'What will it be today? A drop of vodka, or Cognac?'

'Hello, Tonya,' said Gryaznov, leaning over the counter. 'No boozing, I'm afraid. I'm here on official business.'

Smiling a gold-toothed smile, Tonya continued pouring foaming beer into fat beer-mugs. 'Oh, who are you after, then?' asked the green-eyed girl, one of Petrovka's informers of ten years' standing. She gave a conspiratorial wink.

'A man with a beard and a diamond bracelet . . . often changes his car. Sometimes he drives a Zhiguli, sometimes a VW. Know anyone like that?'

'Go and see Vladimirov, our manager. Say I sent you. He'll help you. Next, please!' said Tonya briskly.

Gryaznov went up to the first floor and sat by the counter there, lighting his last cigarette and crumpling up the empty packet.

'What do you want?' asked the barman, a youth of about twenty.

'Get Vladimirov. Tell him I've come from Tonya,' said Gryaznov. Noticing that his neighbour was sipping Cognac, he added: 'And a hundred grams of Cognac – no, make that a hundred and fifty.'

Vladimirov, the manager, appeared a few minutes later, accompanied by the youthful barman. He looked short-sightedly at Gryaznov, took off his glasses and proceeded to wipe them on a grubby handkerchief.

'I'm from Moscow CID,' Gryaznov began.

But Vladimirov interrupted him. 'I know, I've just been talking to Tonya. The man you're after is Volodya Kazakov. He'll be here later. He's usually here by eleven with some of his sidekicks, like Eric Lipa the scriptwriter from Mosfilm. Do you know him?'

Gryaznov shook his head.

'Thank your lucky stars, then,' said Vladimirov. 'You're better off not mixing with villains like them. A real hard case – could run rings round most people.'

'Who, Kazakov?' asked Gryaznov.

'No, that Eric Lipa,' replied the manger. It was obvious that the scriptwriter had really got to him somehow.

'We'll talk about Lipa later,' said Gryaznov quickly. 'I'm interested in Kazakov for now. Where can I find him?'

The manager looked surprised.

'Where? Where he usually is, of course – at the horses!'

Captain Gryaznov sighed deeply and glanced sideways at his neighbour at the bar. The man in the raincoat had finished his Cognac and was engrossed in reading *Soviet Sport*; he obviously had no interest in their conversation.

Gryaznov pulled out his notebook and pencil, ready to note down the address. Then he repeated his question.

'Comrade Vladimirov, I'm asking you in plain Russian – where can I find this Kazakov?'

Vladimirov raised his hands in amazement. 'For Christ's sake, aren't you cops slow on the uptake? Everyone in Moscow knows that on Sundays Kazakov goes to the races. And they, comrade, are held at the Hippodrome. Is that clear enough for you?'

14

The old maestro, Lucian Germanovich Romadin, was sobbing his heart out, gasping and groaning till Sasha feared he might suddenly die on them. Rita tried to get some vodka down Romadin to calm him, while Merkulov stared despondently at the floor.

'Please forgive me, for her sake,' the old man said. 'You see, I've known Valya since she was six. All my family died in the siege of Leningrad, and Valya became a sort of granddaughter to me.' He got up from the wooden bench. 'But I realise you haven't come here just to talk about that. I'll be all right in a minute. Will you excuse me a moment?'

He pulled on his padded jacket and went out. Merkulov and Sasha crossed over to the window to observe Romadin rummaging about in a garden shed. About fifteen minutes later he came back with a full sack of potatoes, a jar of pickled gherkins and a bottle of some bluish liquid. Sasha and Rita did their best to help. He brought in a bucket of coal and tipped it into the stove while she peeled the potatoes for lunch.

Merkulov and Lucian Germanovich began to speak quietly together.

'Valya visited me last Sunday. No, she wasn't alone; she had an admirer with her. She always had a lot of admirers. . . . No, she split up with Nikolai Petrovich because he drank too much, even though he was a colonel in the Soviet Army. . . . Well, what's the point of hiding it? She isn't with us any more. I can't recall his surname, but his first name and patronymic were Viktor Nikolaye-vich. . . . Yes, she sometimes borrowed money from me. . . . I have rather a profitable business – since I retired I have started cultivating flowers.'

Sasha listened closely.

'No, Konstantin Dmitriyevich, the last time she came it was just to drop in. They turned up in a black Volga, stayed here for a couple of hours, and then drove off. Oh, yes, I forgot, they spent a long time looking at my greenhouse.'

'You have a greenhouse!' exclaimed Merkulov.

'Good heavens, yes. Almost everything I have is in that greenhouse! Summer or winter, I can do wonders in there. If you're interested. . . .'

'I'm very, very interested. Alexander Borisovich! Rita!'

Sasha was about to stammer something about their needing impartial witnesses present at a search, but Merkulov was already on his way, almost running towards the greenhouse, overtaking their host. Mister strode along beside him, growling softly.

The greenhouse was screened by some spreading fir-trees. Romadin opened the door, and they went in. It was only a stuffy ramshackle structure covered with plastic sheeting, but Rita clapped her hands in admiration. And there was something to wonder at. By the dim light of the dying November day, the greenhouse was like some subterranean grotto. Little streams of water trickled down man-made hillocks of fresh-smelling earth, butterflies fluttered about in a strange green light.

'This is neat,' Sasha said to Merkulov, but his boss's face registered absolutely nothing. He took the flashlight from their host's hands and began shining it over the floor. There was a stack of boxes in one corner, and Merkulov crossed over to them and asked sharply: 'What's this?'

'Oh, they're my greatest treasure,' said Romadin fearfully. 'They're different kinds of roses: Californias, miniatures, ramblers. Of course, they're just seedlings as yet.'

Merkulov's flashlight flickered over the boxes. On the corners of them were clearly visible pencilled markings – '1 R.', '2 R.'. . . . Merkulov and Sasha dragged out the box marked '15 R.'.

'I'm sorry, Lucian Germanovich, but I'm going to have to mess up these seedlings.'

The old man looked helplessly at Rita, as though seeking her protection. But, scattering the fine soil from around the pathetic shoots, Merkulov was already uncovering a bundle wrapped in oilcloth.

Sasha reminded him again of the need for witnesses at a search, but Merkulov stopped him short.

'To hell with procedure.'

Lucian Germanovich crossed himself.

15

Do you know about the finish of a trotting race? The finish is what they call the last hundred metres before the finishing-line. The harnessed horse has to cover that distance at top speed, even if it kills itself in the process. The finish represents the maximum application of strength and endurance. And sometimes, to squeeze the last ounce out of a trotter over the finish, you whip it till it bleeds. . . .

Gryaznov arrived at the Moscow Hippodrome race-track at half-past three. It was about five degrees centigrade, and the races were in full swing. Topaz, the hot favourite, ridden by the famous jockey, Hadji-murat, was coming up to the finish in the fourth race.

Waving his identification under the nose of the women on the gate, the captain went through to the grandstand and sat down not far from the entrance. He had to find the bookmaker nicknamed Angela Davis.

The Moscow Hippodrome buzzed like a beehive that has been disturbed. The finish of the race was approaching. Topaz, the favourite, was not in the lead; an outsider, a colt called Granite, was in front.

'Only two hundred metres left, with Topaz, Granite and Little Star in the lead,' said the commentator, his voice conveying all the excitement of the race. 'One hundred metres to go. Granite in the lead by half a length, followed by Topaz and then Little Star. And they're at the finish – with ten metres to go it's. . . .'

'Put him out to grass!' 'Turn Topaz into soap!' 'Come on, Murat.' 'Come on, Granite – just a bit more!' shouted the crowd in their excitement. People jumped out of their seats and stood on them, or pressed against the barriers and matched the horse's steps to the finishing-line.

'I told you Granite would come in at ten to one!' a big man kept shouting in a hoarse voice. He had an enormous bush of wiry black hair about his head.

'That must be Angela Davis,' decided Gryaznov.

The black-haired man was standing on some high ground by the entrance, holding a piece of paper in one hand with the odds worked out. The lucky punters swarmed around him.

Before going to the Hippodrome, Gryaznov had done a bit of research at CID headquarters, and he had in his pocket a nice little incriminating dossier from which it emerged that Davis, alias Citizen Avakov, was a swindler and a crook. Gryaznov was hoping to do a quick deal. He would promise to lose all the filth he had on Avakov in return for information about the 'King of the Hippodrome'. Captain Gryaznov was also in possession of some more interesting information.

For more than fifty years the Moscow Hippodrome had subsidised two of the capital's foremost institutions. One of these was the Bolshoi Theatre, which, by royal decree of Alexander III, right to this day is maintained by a subsidy from the Hippodrome. The other was the Moscow Mafia, which not only looked after its own but also gave the Moscow police and security forces an easy life.

It is worth noting that in the fifty-odd years of the Moscow Hippodrome's existence not a single case of fraud on the part of the bookmakers has ever been proved. And this is all due to the efforts of the Mafia – the four families which in effect run the Hippodrome. Each employee of this empire – each bookmaker, that is – knows that if he cheats a punter the bosses will kill him. For didn't they get rid of the Olympic boxing champion, Valery Popenchenko, who had the audacity to take on the Mafia?

In his box, the steward bent over the black and white photographs of the finish, trying to decide which horse was a nose ahead.

A fellow-employee slipped him a scrap of paper torn from a notebook. It read, '1-2, 2-5, 3-3', and bore four signatures. The steward immediately announced over the loudspeaker: 'First, number two: Granite; second, number five: Little Star; third, number three: Topaz.' The big four had spoken and who was the steward to disagree?

Volodya Kazakov, an imposing figure of a man, bearded and wearing an expensive imported overcoat, had his eyes glued to his Zeiss binoculars so as to get a bird's-eye view of his 'employees' – the bookies – taking bets from the gambling population. So far today a hundred of his boys had ruined more than one each of the huge crowd.

The fat-faced Avakov, nicknamed Angela Davis, had been doing especially well. That smart operator barely had the time to collect the punters' money, but he took bets with real style. A maths and physics graduate, he had not so much a brain as a computer. In his job at the Kurchatov Institute he only earned a hundred and fifty roubles a month, but working for Kazakov the Armenian picked up three to five hundred roubles every racing day. Kazakov himself made from thirty to fifty thousand a meet, in envelopes received from his bookies containing only hundred-rouble notes.

Someone touched him lightly on the shoulder. He frowned in annoyance and turned round sharply. A beautiful brunette in a tight-fitting sweater and smoky-coloured jacket, who looked astonishingly like the famous actress Bystritskaya, said with a wide smile: 'Hi, Volodya. Vasily asked me to tell you to be a bit more careful with his goods!'

Recognising the brunette, Kazakov nodded silently and started thinking hard. He did not want to talk openly with Vasily's emissary while his henchmen Lipa and Redkin were around. He didn't trust them.

Half-turning away as if to scan the track, the brunette said out of the corner of her mouth: 'Stash the goods, the money and all the rest somewhere else as soon as you can. But be careful! They've picked up Volin already. And Moscow CID is interested in you, too. Look, one of them is talking to your boy now.' She nodded towards the grandstand.

Kazakov stood up and, taking his binoculars, leant over the rails of his box. A red-haired man in a leather coat, holding a cap in his hand, was talking to Angela Davis. Kazakov thought his face looked familiar. . . .

'Fuck it!' he yelled, thumping his fist against the wooden side of the box. 'That's all I need!' He glowered as he growled: 'So Angela Davis is a squealer, is he?'

The brunette said gently: 'Take it easy, Volodya. Vasily called the White House, and they've agreed to take in everything you bring them – for the usual percentage. You know it's the most reliable bank in the country; not even the KGB can get in. So get a move on! And I've been told to tell you that, if they pull you in for questioning, hang on; don't give in to any of their games. You'll be all right, so don't talk. I'd better get out of here.'

She left the box, nodding to Kazakov's two friends at the back. By the door, she suddenly turned and, with a pearly smile, delivered the final blow.

'Volodya, you've got two days. Volin won't be able to hold out any longer.'

Top Secret

To the Head of Special Investigations
3rd Main Administration of 'T' Committee,
KGB, USSR
Major-General of State Security
V. V. Kassarin

Special Report

In accordance with your directive no. 147 of 18 November of this year, and in compliance with Instruction no. 5, 47, 'Rules governing activities of the KGB of the USSR', the fifth section is continuing its investigation of the murder of V. N. Rakitin.

Today we conducted surveillance of Captain V. S. Gryaznov, a member of the investigation team. The subject left the Arbat Metro station at five to two and went to the House of Journalists where he conducted investigative work and collected information. He then went to Leningradsky Prospekt no. 25 where the Moscow Hippodrome is situated. Our personnel followed the subject and noted his contacts.

We have not been able to tap the home telephones of K. D. Merkulov and his junior officer A. B. Turetsky, as the Moscow telephone network is turned on to automatic on Sundays and the telephone staff are away. None the less, from a conversation we had with Citizen A. G. Fox, one of Turetsky's neighbours, a woman who has worked for the security forces since 1937, it was ascertained that Turetsky did not spend the night at home. His whereabouts are unknown at the moment.

Investigator Merkulov took his stepdaughter Lida, aged ten, to a figure-skating rink at nine o'clock and came home at 11.30 to his address on Prospekt Mir no. 119, apartment 75. Half an hour later, Merkulov again left the house and went from one foodstore to another. One cannot exclude the possibility that, being a professional, he knew he was being shadowed. He left a store through the back way, got on to the Metro, changed several times and eventually escaped surveillance. (Captain Beloshapko, who was responsible for this lapse, has been severely reprimanded.)

At the present time the fifth section is continuing its surveillance of Gryaznov and is undertaking measures to expose Merkulov and Turetsky. You will be informed in full of the results achieved.

Head of 5th Section
Major of State Security
P. SMOLYARCHUK
21 November 1982

16

Rita put her foot on the accelerator and Sasha pushed. Romadin finished putting some brushwood under the rear wheel and feebly joined in. Black smoke poured from the exhaust, and the car wheels splattered mud over their faces, coats and trousers like machine-gun fire.

They had been trying to extricate the stranded Lada for half an hour and they were getting nowhere. Their host trotted off to fetch a shovel and stick it under the wheel. This manoeuvre met with a similar lack of success.

'How do you keep in contact with the outside world?' Sasha asked at last, barely able to catch his breath.

'What? Well, I. . . .' The old man suddenly struck himself on the forehead and said: 'Of all the old fools!' Five minutes later they heard the roar of an engine and an old GAZ fairly flew out on to the road, their host happily ensconced behind the wheel.

They finally managed to tow the car on to firm ground. Rita, snug and clean inside, stepped out daintily and laughed when she saw Sasha's mud-splattered face.

Merkulov had shut himself away in one of the rooms of Romadin's house to assess their discovery. After freeing the car, Rita and Sasha just mooched around the place with nothing much to do. Romadin cleared the table, then vanished into his greenhouse to try to salvage the seedlings that Merkulov had uprooted.

Rita suggested suddenly: 'Do you want to learn to drive, Sasha?'

He sweated blood, trying not to seem a complete idiot.

'Clutch, brake, change gear, accelerator. . . . Clutch, brake, change gear. . . .'

Yipee, the engine hadn't stalled. He was driving!

'Brake,' yelled Rita frantically. The car skidded to a halt a millimetre away from a telegraph pole. They kissed for a long time; then suddenly surprising even himself, Sasha said: 'Marry me.'

Rita turned away for a moment, looking out of the side-window. Then she smiled widely and said: 'OK.'

17

The CID men lost Kazakov at the Hippodrome. While Gryaznov was doing his deal and persuading Angela Davis to co-operate, Kazakov said goodbye to his cronies and quietly left his box in the company of his two boxer bodyguards, giving his staff essential instructions. He got into a VW and made himself scarce. It was seven o'clock in the evening.

Once Gryaznov discovered he had gone, he rang the department, asked the men on duty to go to Kazakov's home and gave them the address. He himself stayed on at the Hippodrome to lean on Lipa and another associate, Redkin, who were sitting in the 'King's' box.

Twenty minutes later an operations team rolled up at the block where Kazakov lived. It was a luxury skyscraper on the Kotelnicheskaya Embankment famed throughout Moscow. There, on the tenth floor of 'B' block in two adjacent three-roomed apartments knocked into one, lived the confirmed bachelor. Naturally, he was not at home.

The detectives could do nothing but stand and observe the huge panelled door with its legion of locks and bolts to keep at bay uninvited guests – in this case, the employees of the Moscow CID. They questioned old Aunty Pasha, the lift-operator, and discovered that 'the manager', as Kazakov was called in the block, had only just come by with his assistants, collected a few suitcases, parcels and packages, and gone off somewhere in a VW. . . .

Meanwhile Gryaznov, infuriated by their statements, was holding Kazakov's two racing cronies. The first of them was Gera Redkin, a hard-bitten man who worked as legal adviser to the Taganka Theatre. Once a police investigator himself, he'd been thrown out for drinking. He seemed disinclined to take the bait Gryaznov was offering and earn an honest crust by co-operating.

But the second man, the Mosfilm scriptwriter Eric Lipa (he was really Erast Lipaprick, according to his passport), needed no persuasion, gentle or otherwise. He asked Gryaznov if they could be left alone together in the police room at the racetrack. Then, coughing intermittently, rolling his eyes towards heaven and swearing on his mother's grave, he confessed to the CID captain that for ten years now, since the time he had moved to Moscow from his native Poltava, he had maintained contact with the KGB.

As one of their informers, he had exposed quite a number of unreliable people among his colleagues, friends and even relatives. Exactly 116 denunciations had been sent to the KGB, the Ministry of Internal Affairs and the People's Inspectorate – Gryaznov could check for himself. Now, with civic courage and the greatest of pleasure, he would give all the necessary evidence regarding his former acquaintance, Vladimir Georgiyevich Kazakov, in whom he had been so grievously mistaken. . . .

The captain learnt a lot of interesting things about Kazakov from Lipaprick – as well as beginning to appreciate how fitting his real name was.

One thing he learnt was that at half-past nine 'the manager' was to meet his bodyguard on a motorcycle on the Moscow ring-road at the Ryazan turn-off, together with another man. By ten to ten-thirty they were to be in Lukhovitsy, the village where most of the members of the Supreme Soviet lived. . . .

Outside, it was drizzling unpleasantly. Sasha, Rita and Romadin were drinking tea in the kitchen with Mister lying under the table. From time to time he would raise his muzzle to check on his master. Merkulov had still not shown himself.

At last Sasha could hold out no longer. He opened the door to the next room to discover Merkulov sitting motionless in a deep armchair in front of a blazing fire in the uncertain light cast by the kerosene-lamp and the flickering flames; his thin face seemed to have aged several years.

What had happened to the Merkulov of the day before? That man could clown around at the sight of a lousy scrap of paper back from the forensic scientist, rejoicing at a tiny success as the riddles of the investigation unfolded before him. Today he looked a tired old warrior who had lost interest in everything around him.

Sasha was burning with curiosity. What the hell was in that bundle of papers to justify two deaths already? What had caused this dramatic change in the boss? But he knew Merkulov too well. Asking him questions in his present mood would be so much wasted breath.

'We'll have to go,'said Merkulov, hauling himself to his feet and coming into the kitchen. 'Listen, everybody. The investigation could be concluded here and now, and yet it continues. For your own sakes, and for the safety of those closest to you, not a word about what we found, or even about our visit here. I don't want to frighten you, but I'm scared shitless myself.'

Shura and her patrol had raced to the ring-road turn-off and now they were kicking their heels at the roadside. She was cursing and swearing richly. No Kazakov, no Gryaznov, and it was nearly ten o'clock already! She had thought she was going to spend Sunday with her husband and her sons, but that red-haired idiot had upset her plans, dragged her away from home and then done a disappearing act.

'The bastard!' she spat. 'If he's wasting my time, I'll. . . .'

Defending his comrade, Krasnikovsky said: 'It looks like Slava's been led a bit of a dance.'

'Bad dancers always get their bollocks in a twist. Kazakov won't show if we give him another day. Fifteen minutes more and then we're off!'

A stream of buses and light vehicles were speeding round the Moscow ring-road. The road traffic in the capital was increasing all the time with more than half a million vehicles registered in Moscow. . . .

A hail of sleet splashed across the windscreen. There was the sharp smell of ammonia in the air from the chemical plant by the South Port.

'Two minutes to ten, and the "King of the Hippodrome" has disappeared into thin air!' said Romanova, leaning back wearily in the seat of the police Volga.

Major Krasnikovsky, Captain Potekhin and the driver said nothing. They knew that when their boss was in a bad mood it was best to let her get on with it or you could find yourself on the wrong end of her foul tongue.

'Comrade Lieutenant-Colonel! Comrade Lieutenant-Colonel! Listen, I think it's them!' exclaimed the driver.

A cavalcade was coming from the direction of Moscow: first a powerful IZH motorcycle, then a red VW – a conspicuous vehicle in Russia. They sped past so quickly that no one got their numbers. Then a blue Zhiguli shot by after the IZH and the VW, no less fast.

The radio crackled into life.

'The front one, the front one! I'm on his tail. Follow me!'

It was Gryaznov's voice distorted through the speaker.

Romanova said hoarsely: 'After him – fast!'

The dark-brown police Volga with the souped-up engine tore off in pursuit.

The road between Alpatevo and Fruktovaya is straight and on a slight incline. To the left, there is an open meadow as far as the skyline. To the right, forest plantation. It was here that Gryaznov's team nearly caught up with Kazakov's VW. A few minutes more and the 'King of the Hippodrome' would be theirs! At first they did not see the motorcyclist ahead who seemed to be adjusting something on his bike.

Gaibov, Gryaznov's driver, registered the rider, slowed down – and ran slap into a hail of bullets! Gryaznov just managed to glimpse out of the corner of his eye that the goddamned motorcyclist was firing from the knee before there was a shower of broken glass and Gaibov slumped across his lap.

'Slava, take over,' shouted Lieutenant Nagorny prostrate on the back seat of the car. Afterwards, Gryaznov could not explain how he managed to grab the wheel, get his foot past Gaibov's body and on to the accelerator while all the time shielding his head under the dashboard. Afterwards, he was amazed at himself.

'Shura, Shura,' he screamed into the transmitter. 'It's a fit-up.'

The radio went dead.

The car swerved sharply, turned over on its right side and skidded to a halt at the roadside. . . .

Romanova did not see the motorcyclist – there was no trace of him when they passed the fatal spot.

'Kuzmich, over to the right. That's Slava's car!' she yelled.

Gryaznov ran over to the open window of the Volga

and said angrily: 'That bastard motorcyclist wounded Gaibov and Nagorny, and the VW got away! Get an ambulance and the traffic police, fast!'

Any hopes of catching Kazakov were over. An ambulance and the traffic police quickly arrived. The ambulancemen took the wounded police officers to the district hospital in Lukhovitsy. The Zhiguli was worst off: both front wheels and the radiator were holed.

Romanova took Gryaznov back in the Volga, squeezed beside Krasnikovsky and Potekhin in the back seat. Nobody felt like talking as they sped down Fruktovaya and flashed past the Grachevo-Gorki State farm estate. And then disaster! The smell of burning oil filled the Volga.

'I don't believe it,' said the driver in a rage. 'The fucking oil-feed's leaking!'

They had to pull in and radio for help from the local police. Romanova turned her head and said: 'A bit fed up, then, are we?'

Looking at Gryaznov, the picture of thwarted misery, she could not help laughing. The rain was still running down the captain's long nose and dripping off the end.

'Oh, very neat!' she exclaimed, taking Gryaznov's trendy cap from his head. There were two holes in it where a bullet had passed straight through. 'Talk about the luck of the devil!' she chuckled.

Slava turned perceptibly paler and put his hands hastily to the back of his head. Shura leant over her seat and slid one hand behind his neck.

'Just grazed you,' she said quietly, and kissed Gryaznov's red wet forelock.

Captain Galkin was on duty that evening in the Lukhovitsy precinct, and Lieutenant Fedosov was doing the shift with him. The communications desk, the teletyper and the radio were all theirs.

At 22.20 one of the phones rang. Fedosov picked up the receiver casually, but from the galvanic movement of his pen-holding hand over the incident-log Galkin realised that something big had happened. He looked over Fedosov's shoulder. An attack on a Moscow CID operations team!

He said briefly: 'Notify Moscow, and send out some cars!' Then he started dialling a number on the other phone – the chief had to be informed right away. Through the window Galkin could see the door of the police station bursting open as officers ran out and jumped into a car which then hurtled off round a bend in the road.

The Duty Officer sat Fedosov at the teletyper and got on the radio himself – he had to notify all neighbouring stations. He booked a call to Moscow to talk to his directorate, hurrying the switchboard operator all the time. 'Come on, darling. Fast!'

By the time Colonel Zhuravlev, their chief, dashed into the duty room and ordered them to raise the alarm, not only the two police directorates – district and city – knew what had happened, but also the Ministry of Internal Affairs. All state traffic units were put on red alert and ordered to set up roadblocks on all routes out of Lukhovitsy. He told the traffic police that they had to look out for both a red VW and an IZH motorcycle.

'The incident took place by Fruktovaya Station. Gaibov, the CID driver, is in hospital having an operation – a gunshot wound in the head. Lieutenant Nagorny is concussed. Moscow CID Lieutenant-Colonel Romanova is pursuing the bandits in one of our cars. . . .'

An overstatement if not a bare-faced lie.

Stopping briefly to ask the locals if anyone had seen a red car of foreign make, Romanova's team headed off at random. Who knew – they might get lucky?

They passed a palatial white three-storey building on a hill, surrounded by a double solid fence and sentry-boxes. One side of the huge estate stretched down to a lake.

'Shall we check it out?' asked the driver, braking by the gravel driveway.

'Kuzmich, are you crazy or something? This is where Georgadze lives, Secretary to the Praesidium of the

Supreme Soviet. I suppose you think *he's* going to be harbouring bandits? If we so much as suggest it, the General will have our hides! Back on the road.'

More than fifty minutes had passed from the moment of the attack to the renewal of the man-hunt, and it had taken some time to cordon off the area. There'd been enough time for Kazakov to bury his loot, or dig it up, several times over, and then make himself scarce. Given his money and connections, it wouldn't be difficult to lose himself in the provinces – Ryazan, Lipetsk, or even Rostov.

20

'See you tomorrow, then?'

'Yes, tomorrow.'

Sasha kissed Rita on the cheek and watched the tail-lights of her car receding. They disappeared at the turn-off to Sivtsev Vrazhek. He made his way up to the fourth floor slowly, and tried not to make a noise as he went down his apartment corridor. There was a note stuck under his door, written in the old-fashioned hand of one of the women in the block.

> Alex, your mother has been ringing – four times
> yesterday and three times today! She asked you
> to call her when you get back. P. V. Korobitsyn.

Something new in the state of Denmark – Sasha's mother needed him. He looked at his watch, but it was too late to call her then.

Kazakov finished stashing the valuables, leaving himself just a tiny bit for expenses. He got rid of his helpers, too. One headed for Lipetsk in the VW; the other, on the motorbike, hid out in the forest, staying in a remote village with a woodsman he knew. Kazakov himself decided to make for the Black Sea, for Novorossiisk, where he would be as secure as the first secretary of the town council.

He changed his appearance quickly, exchanging coats with one of his men and taking off the false beard he habitually wore. Then he bought a ticket for the Moscow–Novorossiisk express and settled into an inconspicuous seat in the station restaurant.

He had the feeling that Ryazan, where he'd previously lived it up, was not for him any more. There was a good chance the police might tail him there. . . . There was his train! He jumped on immediately, brushing past a stopping guard who was helping down a woman with a baby. Kazakov sat down by the window in a compartment at the end of the front car, facing the direction the train was travelling in. That way it was easier to duck out in case of danger. He didn't pay much attention to the other passengers – two black-haired women and a teenager. The doors were what held his gaze. That was where retribution might come from.

But he reckoned on escaping retribution by telling the boss everything. He'd find a way of hushing it all up, sorting the whole mess out, maybe even punishing those who dared to try to track him down.

A casual look at Kazakov would have shown just a tired man, dozing off. As it left the circle of lights around the station, the train began eating up the kilometres.

Sergeants Sukhoyedov and Zamotayev, railway policemen at Ryazan main station, got an instruction to comb all stations and trains. The bosses had arranged to have this section of the railway sealed off. The object of the search was 'to find a brown-haired man, medium height, with a beard, wearing a mouse-coloured coat of foreign make'. This was put out by the Lukhovitsy police who themselves had no clear idea what the hunted criminal really looked like.

Sukhoyedov and Zamotayev promptly forgot their weariness. They were both time-servers, both pathologically afraid of error: if they ever caused a major fuck-up, one would just report on the incompetence of the other. So they both suffered in silence.

On the Novorossiisk express everything was just as it had been on all the other expresses. They opened the door into a compartment, glanced right and left almost without stopping, and then up at the baggage-racks. 'Citizen, smoking forbidden. This car's for non-smokers!' More doors, then the platform at the end of the corridor. The thundering of the tracks beneath them as they stepped over. Another platform; this must be number. . . .

A little after two in the morning Sukhoyedov, followed by Zamotayev, opened the last door and went into the front coach. Sukhoyedov went straight through to the driver's cab, inwardly dismissing the coach's occupants. And then Zamotayev registered the denim suit – American, by the look of it. No, they'd been told he had a beard and this guy was clean-shaven. The communication had also mentioned a mouse-coloured coat, but this passenger didn't have a coat like that, only a half-length jacket. There it was hanging on the hook beside him, khaki-coloured with green buttons. He didn't turn round when Zamotayev knocked on the door of his compartment. He was asleep or maybe looking out of the window. Anyway, he stayed calm, didn't react to the police uniform.

'Where are you travelling to, citizen?'

A routine question, just for the hell of it.

The man looked up but said nothing. There was a rucksack behind him on the seat, but there was nothing special about that. It was a tourist's rucksack, like millions of others. So what?

Zamotayev asked another question, loudly this time, for his partner's benefit and also to buy time.

'Got your papers with you?'

The brown-haired man got up, feeling in his pocket as if for his documents. By now Sukhoyedov was standing next to his partner in the doorway. He had no chance of reacting to sudden movement. The blow caught him under the heart.

Zamotayev was able to deflect the second blow, which was aimed at him. He grabbed the hand that held the knife and threw himself on the man. He started twisting the passenger's wrist, smashing it against the seat, but there was no taking this man the way the police manuals told you. Seeing that his partner was in a bad way, Zamotayev reached for his gun.

The brown-haired man took advantage of that second's pause and leapt towards the door. Another second and he would be on the track! Zamotayev shot into the air. The report sounded artifically loud in the empty corridor of the carriage. The fugitive suddenly jerked in the doorway, and then froze. Zamotayev took aim at his legs but never pulled the trigger. To the sergeant's utter amazement, the fugitive clutched at the air and slumped slowly to the floor.

The co-driver came rushing out when he heard the shot.

'As senior official,' shouted Zamotayev to him, terrified, 'I order you to go on Ryazhsk without stopping! Radio ahead that I've arrested an armed criminal. He and my partner have been wounded!'

'Sergeant, I've no right to go through non-stop. It'll

cost me my job!' shouted the co-driver in reply.

The police officer went white.

'Do as you're told, motherfucker!'

Two minutes later the passengers heard over the train loudspeaker system that 'Because of technical problems, the Moscow–Novorossiisk express would be making no stops until Ryazhsk.' The co-driver repeated the message a good four times.

The Novorossiisk train reached Ryazhsk at 3.16 a.m. A few uniformed policemen, a doctor and four ambulance-men with stretchers boarded the front car. A shaken Zamotayev was waiting for them in the front compartment, standing in the doorway, still with his gun in his hand. They'd been ordered to take the bandit alive, and the sergeant still couldn't figure out how he'd managed to hit him in the head by firing at the ceiling.

The two bleeding men were lying on the bench seats in the compartment. A passport in the name of Vladimir Georgiyevich Kazakov was found in the brown-haired man's green coat, along with an ID card in the same name showing him to be the deputy manager of Food Store No. 1. They also found a loaded pistol, imported, complete with silencer, tucked in the belt of his denim jeans, and the rucksack held unsealed wads of newish hundred-rouble bills. The case officers also found in the rucksack a canvas bag full of huge diamonds which, according to the experts, came from South Africa. . . .

23

Whatever the cost, they now had to locate and arrest Kazakov's henchmen, the one who drove the VW away and the one on the IZH motorcycle. They were the only ones who could now give precise information as to where

Kazakov had hidden his gang's loot. So Romanova's team was divided in two.

Keeping Gryaznov with her, Shura set up base in the Lukhovitsky precinct and continued the search for the motorcyclist. She sent Krasnikovsky and Potekhin off in the Lukhovitsky chief's Volga to the town of Lipetsk. That was where, according to information from Moscow, all trace of the red VW had been lost.

It was twenty kilometres from Lukhovitsy to the forest. The village of Olkhovka, where the woodsman Ryabov lived, stood in a small valley. All around were hills, thickly wooded with pine-trees. There were four ponds which were probably good for fishing.

'And great for mushroom-picking in the summer,' reflected Romanova. 'It would be nice to take my boys here and enjoy the forest.' After a nervous sleepless night she wanted to catch her breath and take a break. At her age – forty-five – there was nothing unnatural about that. But it was only a passing fancy. Her thoughts were working in a different direction. The Moscow CID had sent a message: 'Motorcyclist probably one Georgy Trofimovich Lukashevich, born 1949, two convictions for armed robbery and hooliganism. Paroled six months ago and temporarily registered for residence in Moscow under administrative police surveillance. Capable of anything.' Armed, on a motorcycle, and he had to be taken without bloodshed. . . .

The local police officer told them that the woodsman Ryabov had been seen to have a guest staying with him. He'd arrived on an IZH motorcycle. At five in the morning, Ryabov had gone off with him somewhere deep in the forest. No one knew when they would be back.

This information was useful but didn't answer the basic question: where was Lukashevich now?

The search had been going on for more than seven hours. All the routes out of Olkhovka were being watched. The trap was set, but the quarry hadn't shown himself.

126

Her heart skipped a beat when Captain Gryaznov's tense voice came over the radio.

'I can see Lukashevich. He's in the GAZ, moving off to the right of the woodsman. Shall I move?'

'Leave him,' said Romanova quietly. 'He's mine!'

She stepped out on to the road alone. Just a woman like any other, only a bit better dressed than the locals in Lukhovitsy. She raised her hands as if wanting a lift or directions. The car stopped, and in a flash Romanova was at the driver's door. She wrenched it open, grabbed Lukashevich by the sleeve, and said: 'You're booked; we'll settle the charges after we've had a good long chat.'

Gryaznov and the local policeman suddenly materialised out of nowhere. They pounced on their quarry, spinning him round and pulling a heavy TT automatic and two spare clips out of his belt.

Outwardly, Gely Lukashevich stayed calm. He puffed out his cheeks with a faint sigh, and red blotches appeared on his face and neck.

'Start talking, Lukashevich!' said Lieutenant-Colonel Romanova.

24

Gennady Frolov, once a well-known boxer and the Hippodrome King's bodyguard, was like a hunted animal. Slinking around the streets of a town he barely knew, he had a strong hunch they were on to him.

Two hours earlier he'd abandoned the VW in a nondescript cul-de-sac off Communist Street, and was now travelling on foot, constantly checking whether he was being tailed or not. . . .

Major Krasnikovsky kept his distance and dogged Frolov all the way. He could have taken the boxer long since without a murmur, but he knew that his man had to contact his cronies sooner or later. Why else would he have gone to Lipetsk? They might as well tie up all the loose ends.

This was the Major's first time in Lipetsk and he was keeping a close eye on the geography of the place – he didn't want to lose his way with all this doubling back. Frolov was going round in circles, coming back each time to where he'd left the car. He didn't know that for some time now a police Volga had been parked at the other end of the cul-de-sac, concealing Captain Potekhin, and that there was another police car round the corner with men from the local CID in it.

It was starting to get light and there were more people out in the streets. At last Frolov went into the entrance of a one-storey building on Communist Street, a house converted into an auto repairs station. Krasnikovsky signalled Potekhin to get ready. He himself only just had time to hide behind a stack of cardboard boxes in the yard before he saw Frolov come hurrying out of the entrance and head away from his car. What should he do? There were members of the public everywhere. What if Frolov opened fire? The Major grabbed a carton, hoisted it on to his shoulder and sauntered straight for Frolov. Frolov stepped aside slightly. No danger here, just some crank carting his television set off somewhere first thing in the morning. Krasnikovsky drew level with him, dropped the box, and Frolov felt a gun in the small of his back.

'Hands up!'

As they walked away, Frolov said angrily: 'Another half-hour and I'd have been out of this shit-hole. I would have left my car for the men in the garage to strip for the spares. . . .'

25

'The laws of conservation of substances in nature,' reflected Volin, 'operate in human society, too. And our Soviet society is no exception. When one person has a piece of luck, someone else is heading for a fall. So fortune and misfortune eventually cancel each other out.'

In cell 23 of the remand centre of the City Administration of Internal Affairs of the Moscow Executive Committee, everyone was asleep – except Volin. Only now, as he tossed and turned on his uncomfortable bug-infested top bunk and stared through the iron bars of the black prison window, did he fully realise the tragi-comedy of his position. No doubt he'd been helped along by the advice of his two highly qualified cellmates, both very smart lawyers, by the names of Fishkin and Gubkin, who had been arrested on a serious charge regarding bribes to the Supreme Court of the RSFSR.

What was funny about the whole thing was that he, Volin, a third-rate black-marketeer, currency speculator and petty thief, had been detained on Friday and had been starving on bread and water in this stinking hole for three days without any right to receive parcels of food or anything else. They were fitting him up for killing someone, and the bastard who had dragged him into all this had been released by the cretins of Moscow CID as a 'chance companion'. It was he, Yurochka Leonovich, who owned all that loot, all those goodies, all those valuables they had found both in the car and when they searched the apartments of Volin and his relatives. The very thought of the rat sleeping in a feather bed with some pneumatic blond while he, Volin, was being eaten alive by bedbugs made him sick. The injustice of it!

Volin hardly noticed the pervasive stench anymore: the tobacco smoke, the smell of urine, of shit and unwashed bodies. But no matter how he tried he couldn't get used to the grotesque snoring of his cellmate on the bunk below.

He'd give his soul to the devil not to have to hear that long-drawn-out whistling and grunting ever again.

But the worst of it all was that he had given the prosecutor false evidence the day before. He had told this judicial counsellor when he made his rounds of the cells and asked if 'there were any complaints' that the police had planted all the money, the gun and the lurex kerchiefs in his car when he was in the hard-currency shop with his pal, picking up a suit of clothes for the New Year.

He had insisted that there should be a special enquiry, and that the jerks should be punished for breach of socialist legality. Now maybe he ought to tell the truth – explain in a civilised fashion. That he wasn't their man, that he just chanced to get caught up in the case, that he was just a legman. But he'd made his biggest mistake with that medal. It stuck in his gullet to think how he'd always worn it on the lapel of his jacket, and then he'd lost it. . . .

In July – no, August – he was at the races, placing big bets. He had put everything on Topaz and lost it. He wanted to win it back and so he borrowed money off Kazakov – and lost again. He'd asked again for a loan – of about 10,000 roubles this time. 'The Beard', the cunning bastard, told him that he had a guiding principle: 'Take no one at their word, not even your own mother.' Volin had to give some kind of guarantee. But what can you give if you're cleaned out? So he offered Kazakov all he had at the time – his party membership card and medal.

Volodya returned neither card nor medal, saying: 'When you settle up in full, you little commie, then you'll get your stuff back!' He was a real peach, Volodya, King of the Hippodrome. Because of that debt, he'd had to rob some churches of damned icons – Volodya had knocked five thousand off his debt for them. He still had another five thousand hanging round his goddamned neck.

The Volga was something else again. Volin knew all right that it was stolen, that the serial numbers on the engine and chassis had been scratched out. He knew it, but he'd still bought it. After all, he wasn't the one who had stolen the car!

But that was the way it always was – one man got lucky, another got trouble. At that moment it dawned on Volin: why not tell the truth? To hell with them all, Volodya and Yurochka! They wouldn't try anything with Moscow CID. They wouldn't be able to carry out their threats when Volin was holed up here. . . .

Volin jumped down from his bunk and went to the iron door. He banged on it in desperation. His cellmates started swearing as they were woken up by the noise. On the other side of the judas-hole, which slid open for a second, the warder said with a yawn: 'I'll give you a banging, you bastard. I'll transfer you to the punishment cell. You can bang your head against the wall there all your life, if you like. You'll soon see how good I am at my job, you whoreson. . . .'

But Volin was past caring or fear; half-demented, he yelled so that all Petrovka could hear: 'Open up! I want to see the investigator! Take me to the investigator, now. I'll testify! His name's Merkulov!'

PART THREE
Wolf-Hunt

ENTER KASSARIN

1

22 November 1982

Leonid Vasilyevich Parkhomenko, the Chief of the Investigations Section of the City Prosecutor's Office, had an elongated, scholarly-looking face. He had attentive brown eyes behind thick-lensed spectacles with gold frames, and a good head of thick brown hair streaked with grey. Outwardly and inwardly he bore a powerful resemblance to a mule.

With a sweep of his hand, Parkhomenko invited Sasha to sit down. Bemused, he sank into a soft armchair on the other side of the chief's desk. A minute before, Sasha had bumped into him in the corridor outside the Prosecutor's Office and, as if recalling something, Parkhomenko had said amicably: 'Ah, Turetsky! Just the person I want to see!' So here they sat, Sasha waiting to hear what the chief had to say.

But Leonid Vasilyevich looked at his watch – working hours did not begin until ten o'clock – then struck a match, lit a Belomor, and settled himself more comfortably in his, the boss's, chair, still saying nothing.

'Sasha!' he said at last, man to man and friendly, two comrades on a difficult investigation. 'Sasha,' he repeated, drawing deeply on his cigarette and pulling a grey file marked in ink 'A. B. Turetsky' towards himself. 'Your trainee period will soon be coming to an end and I'd like to get straight a few details about your work with us before the Prosecutor's board. Before your certification.'

Parkhomenko bowed his head and rested his chin on his chest. So he'd been studying Sasha's record on the famous card-index. For many years Parkhomenko had busied

135

himself farting around keeping dossiers on every one of his fellow-employees from the lowest secretary to the top man.

It would be understandable if he'd made notes about, for instance, which member of the collective had what achievements to his credit; or what mistakes he had made; or, when all was said and done, how he reacted to remarks made to him by his chiefs. But the fact was that Parkhomenko spent each day writing out in a fastidious hand on neatly ruled sheets of paper everything that informers told him – how much booze one investigator had drunk at a celebration of the Revolution on 7 November, who had slept with whom after the party, and so on.

Sasha's heart skipped a beat. Had he found out about Rita? But Parkhomenko continued: 'Well, how's the work going? How's Merkulov – not upsetting you, I trust?' He fixed his inquisitive gaze straight at Sasha's face.

'Well, what boss doesn't. . . ?' Sasha was about to reply with some joking remark. But Parkhomenko had no intention of abandoning the topic.

'We consider Konstantin Dmitriyevich an experienced worker, but he does have – how shall I put it? – certain bees in his bonnet.' Parkhomenko tapped his forehead meaningfully. 'Independence in an investigator when he is operating in the line of duty – I have in mind judicial independence as envisaged in article 127 of the judicial code – is a useful thing, but only within certain limits. As long as it does not, so to speak, run counter to the prescribed powers of the Head of Investigations. And what is it that the Head of Investigations exercises? He exercises control over the activities of the individual investigator. And how do you monitor the activities of someone like Merkulov, you may ask, if he keeps slipping through your fingers like an eel? What if his every action says: "I'm as good as the next man, so get off my back."?

'Then, Sasha, you have to be a snake in the grass yourself. Keep a close eye on Merkulov – for his own good, incidentally. Note that. If the situation turned nasty, he could make so much trouble that the Party wouldn't give you or me the time of day. After all, you're in his team. Things can't go on like this, with you trying to get your certification.'

Parkhomenko was talking rubbish. Sasha's certification did not depend on Merkulov's actions. But the boss had obviously decided to recruit Sasha as an informer. Who better to rat on Merkulov?

And he did have a certain canine sense of smell. Had he somehow got wind of the unofficial trip to Bolshevo?

'Do you understand what I'm talking about?' Parkhomenko asked.

'No. Sorry, Leonid Vasilyevich.'

'Well, between friends, I've just been talking to the Moscow Prosecutor, Comrade Malkov, and we've come to a decision. I want you, as a Komsomol man, fully to understand, without any misunderstanding. . . .'

'You and your Malkov,' Sasha wanted to say. 'You and your Malkov aren't worth as much as Merkulov's little finger. I'm lucky I got on his team for my traineeship.'

'So we have decided to ask you,' Parkhomenko droned on, 'as senior comrades ask juniors, as fellow-communists. It's all for the good of the cause, of course. For the good of the common cause which we all serve! You are to bring me a report every day on what your team has been doing on the case, the Rakitin case. In short . . . I cannot stress how important . . . your future in part depends on whether you and we work together or not. . . . Oh, and of course no one is to know about this!'

At last Parkhomenko had got to the point. Sasha wanted to get to his feet and tell the old mule just what he thought of him: that he was a drunk and a parasite who lived off the backs of others, that he didn't know his own people and wasn't fit to do the job they carried out so professionally. But instead he just nodded and said: 'I understand, Comrade Parkhomenko, just as you say.'

There was a lot of truth in the saying that another

man's soul is darkness. His soul was no exception, it seemed.

'I see you're a sensible boy, Sasha. We'll work well together,' said Parkhomenko, not concealing his smile of satisfaction.

Sasha nodded mutely.

Parkhomenko settled back in his armchair more comfortably. He took another dossier from a desk drawer – a rather thick one not at all like Sasha's feeble little affair. Its cover was labelled 'K. D. Merkulov'. Parkhomenko pushed a long sheet of paper towards Sasha and smiled his asinine smile.

'Well, shall we start with what happened yesterday?'

Sometimes the line between truth and lies is as thin as a spider's web.

> To the Head of Investigations Section
> of the Moscow Prosecutor's Office
> Senior Judicial Counsellor
> Comrade L. V. Parkhomenko

Report

In accordance with your requirements of immediate notification to you personally of all activities of our team in its investigation of the murder of Rakitin and Kupriyanova, I report the following:

Yesterday, i.e., 21 November of this year, a Moscow CID operation squad attached to our team arrested several especially dangerous criminals, to wit: Lukashevich, Frolov and Kazakov. The last of these has a severe gunshot wound in the head. In addition, the suspect Volin is being held under guard in the remand centre. The 'Master of Sport' badge which was found in Sokolniki Park where Rakitin was murdered belongs to him.

Yesterday, I was resting. I was engaged in my

own personal affairs and had no contact with Comrade Merkulov.

Signed
Junior Officer
A. B. Turetsky

Sasha handed the report across the table to the Head of Investigations. In silence Parkhomenko read it.

Sasha glanced idly out of the window at some building foundations being dug out. By spring the Moscow Prosecutor's Office would have a new wing.

'Excellent,' said Parkhomenko, after a telling pause. He was probably weighing up how much of the report was truth and how much lies. 'Any questions?'

'No, all quite clear, Leonid Vasilyevich,' Sasha replied. 'And do you have any questions for me?'

'Not at present,' he said with a smile which revealed alternate black tobacco-stained and gold teeth.

'Excellent,' Sasha said in turn.

Parkhomenko frowned and assumed his usual officious expression.

'Then, you can go, Comrade Turetsky.' He glanced at his watch. 'Ten o'clock, so off to work with you. By the way, I've given you and Merkulov a few new cases. Take whichever you like – maybe the stolen antiques, that's straightforward enough. Try to solve it yourself. It'll count towards your certification!'

Going up to his office on the second floor, Sasha wondered if Merkulov was in yet. He could not wait to tell him that Parkhomenko had just 'recruited' him.

2

But Merkulov was late. Sasha sat in his office and read Parkhomenko's orders, seeing that the 'VI' – valuable instruction – concerned him, too.

Written Instruction
(In accordance with article 29 of the law
concerning the Prosecutor's Office)
In view of the fact that Serious Crimes Investigator, E. M. Barkov, has been transferred, on the personal instructions of the General Prosecutor, to the Prosecutor's Office of the USSR to investigate cases involving malpractices in the central administration of the Ministry of Internal Affairs of the USSR, all investigations in his competence are, by order of the Moscow Prosecutor, Comrade M. G. Malkov, transferred to you.

In pursuance of individual investigations you are to utilise more actively your junior officer, Alexander Turetsky, entrusting to him alone the conclusion of the enquiry regarding the theft of citizen Soya-Serko's collection of antiques.

Attached: 5 investigations in 30 volumes

Head of Investigations
Moscow City Prosecutor's Office
Senior Judicial Counsellor
L. PARKHOMENKO

The huge polished surface of Merkulov's desk was already cluttered with brown cardboard-bound tomes. Sasha barely had time to skim through the chief's instructions before Garik, the large curly-haired office secretary, backed through the doorway humping the last armful of files. He dumped them on the divan like a pile of logs.

Garik was a good man; everyone liked him. Because he

'had no stage presence' he had been kicked out of the drama school of the Moscow Arts Theatre, and now he was having to slave away in the Prosecutor's Office in order to get a training post that might lead to a place in law school.

Merkulov chose that moment to appear. He did not look his best. If Sasha had not known that Merkulov was thirty-six, he would have thought him ten years older at least.

'What the hell's all this?' he asked by way of greeting. Still in his snow-covered coat, he went over to his desk and stood there reading Parkhomenko's instruction.

'Konstantin Dmitriyevich,' said Garik soothingly, as if trying to justify the injustices of their bosses, 'in the Union Prosecutor's Office – on Andropov's orders – they're forming a special team – to investigate some crimes that have been committed inside the Ministry of Internal Affairs. The Minister, Shchelokov, is involved! His son has been dealing in Mercedes apparently, and some other big shots have been fiddling really big money – millions of roubles.'

Garik spluttered and spread his arms theatrically wide to express the size of the 'big deals' that the men in the Ministry of Internal Affairs had been doing. 'They've sent Edik over there, and Iodalis, too.'

'How do you know all this, about these "big deals"?' asked Merkulov, calm and quiet, as if he was conducting an interrogation. He shook the snow off his hat right over Garik's feet. 'Been reading secret memoranda on the quiet, have we?'

Garik was not one to take offence. He was far too guileless.

'No, Konstantin Dmitriyevich, I didn't read anything – I heard it. I can hear through the wall all that goes on in Parkhomenko's office. Malkov himself came to see him this morning. He said a lot of very interesting things!'

'What about, exactly?' Sasha asked, unable to restrain himself.

141

'Well, about yesterday's secret meeting of leading party activists in the administrative organs,' said Garik with a very meaningful smile.

'And?'

'Andropov made a speech there. He ordered the screws to be put on – squeeze the workers a bit more and put a few more inside. And no soft options for anyone – even for the bosses and the party men!'

'So he's aiming to wage war on bribery, embezzlement and criminal negligence, is he?' asked Merkulov, casually prompting Garik towards the required phraseology. 'He's ordered them to put on the pressure above and below? Is that it?'

'Exactly!' said Garik, nodding his shaggy head. 'And there's something else I've remembered. In Moscow alone over the last week they've put three hundred people inside. And that's just the bosses! Those men were taking bribes, not only in thousands of roubles but also in kind – clothes, the good life, even women! Can you believe it?' A mask of genuine suffering distorted his ruddy face. They should never have kicked him out of the theatre.

'But why us?' Sasha said indignantly. 'Konstantin Dmitriyevich and I are over our heads with this Sokolniki business, and now they've given us five of Barkov's cases, too! Are we supposed to put them in cold storage or what? Aren't there any other investigators?'

'Malkov told Lyona', interrupted Garik, 'that they're increasing their staff. We work harder than anyone else, but the KGB and the Ministry of Internal Affairs are bursting at the seams apparently.'

'By how many?' said Merkulov, livening up.

'When?' Sasha asked, naturally very interested in the issue of increasing personnel.

His year's traineeship was supposed to finish in July, and the last thing he wanted was to part company with Merkulov and be packed off to a flea-pit like Babushkin or a stinking hole like Perovo.

'By summer,' answered Garik, 'they're going to add

142

fifty, and we'll have ten of them.'

From the moment Sasha had seen the first batch of Barkov's cases on the desk, he had decided that there would definitely be trouble. The boss would be bound to give Parkhomenko and Malkov hell! Was it even possible to carry out fifteen investigations simultaneously?

While Garik was relating the secret communication from the Moscow Prosecutor's Office, Merkulov had put his uniform coat on a hanger, taken out a clothes-brush from his desk drawer and carefully brushed off the melting snowflakes. Once he was satisfied he hung the hanger on the large nail in the wall, loosened his tie and the collar of his cream-coloured regulation shirt, and settled down in his ancient but sturdy armchair with its 'haemorrhoidal' – the additional soft cushion.

Then he lit a cigarette, and asked Garik and Sasha in a matter-of-fact voice: 'Well, boys, shall we take a trip to Luzhniki tonight? I've got two extra tickets for the hockey match!'

Extract from the resolution regarding transfer of case to the Moscow Prosecutor's Office

On 21 August 1982 a robbery was committed at the following address: Taneyevykh Street (formerly B. Vlasyevsky Street) no. 6, apartment 67. Using a variety of keys, unknown criminals entered the apartment belonging to the widow of Professor Soya-Serko of the Moscow Conservatory, a senior coach in gymnastics, Alla Alexandrovna Soya-Serko, and despite the alarm system installed and the complex locks stole a collection of rare antiques which had been assembled by the Soya-Serko family over the course of nearly a hundred years. The approximate value of the collection is 884,469 roubles. The objects stolen include such rare items as the icon by ancient Russian painters of the fifteenth-century 'St Georgy in life', worth 130,000 roubles; a fourteenth-century bronze dish in the shape of an eagle; a seventeenth-century statuette of a ballerina (in gold); a tortoise-shell diamond-studded comb and a gold snuff-box with precious stones, both eighteenth-century – in all 146 items of property.

In view of the failure to locate the culprits after a two-month period the enquiry was closed by the investigations section of the Leninsky District Committee of Internal Affairs. However, at the request of the cosmonaut P. I. Popovich, the enquiry has been reopened by the General Prosecutor's Office of the USSR, which has arranged for the investigation to be transferred to the Investigations Committee of the Moscow Prosecutor's Office with the aim of solving the crime as expeditiously as possible.

3

The first of the secondhand stores to which Merkulov despatched Sasha that morning was a huge affair in Izmailovo. He asked the driver to take the Volga round to the service entrance, then sought out the manager. He introduced himself, thrusting his official identification under the manager's nose while making his request. The manager, obviously a retired soldier, pressed the switch to the shop loudspeaker and made an announcement in a subdued voice. A minute later, the valuers and some of the sales personnel appeared in his office.

'Comrades,' Sasha said, blushing to find himself the centre of interest, 'would you please look at these photographs and try to remember if any of these things has passed through your hands?'

'No, none of these,' said one of the experts. 'We had a statuette similar to this about three weeks ago, but it wasn't this one. I would recognise that straight away. Ours was gold, too.'

'Hang on, hang on! That bronze dish in the shape of an eagle,' recalled another. 'No. No, it wasn't *quite* the same. And candlesticks like these come and go all the time. They find their way to Israel usually; people can't wait to take them off us. Whereas this snuff-box – I've never seen one like it in my life.'

'Neither have I,' said the manager, though no one was asking him.

Sasha had no luck, either, in the next dealer's shop in Presnya. None of 'his' items had come their way in recent months.

But in the third shop, on the Sadovoye ring-road, the picture suddenly changed. The experts immediately recognised two of the items – the diamond-studded tortoise-shell comb and a set of ivory articles.

'Oh, yes. Do you realise,' said an old black-haired woman, 'that these are museum pieces – both the comb and the set? These things should never have been in private hands.' She fluttered her false eyelashes and clasped her hands together dramatically.

'Was this a long time ago?' Sasha asked firmly.

'About a month. Maybe a bit less.'

'Why guess, Emilia Gavrilovna?' intervened the manager, a good-looking young man in a suede jacket. 'We can fix it exactly. We do keep our books in order, you know. I would just like to make one little matter clear, though. We do not handle museum pieces here. Emilia Gavrilovna was rather exaggerating, as usual. Please forgive her; she got rather carried away in her enthusiasm. God only knows what our comrade from the Prosecutor's Office might think goes on here. . . .'

'Ivan Ivanich,' said Emilia, pursing her painted lips, 'you know I can be mistaken about people but never about things. I could swear—'

'You've misunderstood me, love,' said the handsome manager, turning pale, his eyes flickering rapidly beneath sable brows. 'I simply wanted to say, if our friend from the Prosecutor's Office permits, that we can find out immediately from our records just when these goods came to us and when they were sold.'

'If you would be so kind,' Sasha said, using one of Merkulov's more ironic tones. He'd taken an instant dislike to the handsome young man in his smart expensive suede jacket.

The tortoise-shell comb with the diamond inset and the carved ivory set came into the shop and were sold on the same day: 23 October. From what Miss Sorokina, the shop's expert valuer, told Sasha when he questioned her in a room of the local trade union committee, he managed to piece together the facts surrounding a somewhat unusual transaction. Apparently, the deal was struck in the manager's office on 23 October. At about eleven o'clock that morning, a buyer and a vendor came to see him together.

The vendor was Yury Yurevich Leonovich, according

to his passport, a thin, red-haired, middle-aged man; the buyer was a tall thickset blond with an accent that suggested he came from one of the Baltic states. They had not asked for his name, since this is not required by the regulations governing business transacted through secondhand dealers' shops. The Balt was handed these very items, the comb and the set, by the red-haired man. The manager made out a receipt for the purchase and the sale without ever leaving his office.

Sorokina remembered the valuables well. She had assessed them – and they were worth a fortune!

Sasha made one other discovery in the shop. The victim of the crime, Soya-Serko, was often to be seen on the Sadovoye ring-road. When a shop salesman, Popkov, saw the photograph of her which Sasha showed the sales staff, he immediately recognised Alla Alexandrovna and gabbled out a description of Mrs Soya-Serko, obviously from the life. Apparently, Popkov admired her 'languid brown eyes, and the small dark mole on her chin', and he dwelt especially on her 'shapely legs and the curve of her hips'.

Over the last two years, that is, since the death of her husband, she had often dropped in to do a deal of some kind, either to sell something or to buy very valuable items. She was obviously actively renewing the collection she had inherited from her husband. However, when pressed, the store's manager was unable to find her name on any of the several thousand receipts for the previous two years.

Sasha quickly jotted down the witnesses' statements and extracted the original receipt in the name of Leonovich from the shop's accounts. Then he got into the police Volga and told the driver to go over to Novokuznetskaya Street where Soya-Serko had been summoned for questioning at four o'clock.

It seemed that the young widow was connected not only with museum employees and antiques connoisseurs, but also in all probability with black-market dealers. Yet there was not a word about any of these connections in her statements. Anyone who really appreciated things of beauty would give their right arm to aid the investigation, wouldn't they? But supposing this Soya-Serko woman wasn't a collector at all, merely an acquirer? Not interested in the quality so much as in the price? And maybe not too quick to enquire where a piece came from. . . .

And, if Alla hadn't done all she could to help so far, she wasn't going to start helping Sasha wholeheartedly. She'd have to be watched very carefully, as if she was a cunning vixen, leading them on to a false trail.

4

At Petrovka 38 in Shura's office, at Shura's own desk, Merkulov was interrogating Volin.

To begin with, under article 123 of the judicial code, he suggested to the suspect that he should tell all he knew of the crimes and the circumstances surrounding them. Merkulov listened to Volin's saga in silence, neither interrupting nor commenting at any stage. Only afterwards did he start asking questions.

Merkulov only took down 'matters of substance' in the official statement, pretending he didn't give a damn about all the suspect's beefing about the Hippodrome, Kazakov, Leonovich. . . . The method had been tried and tested hundreds of times on human 'guinea-pigs'. It was like a bucket of cold water.

Volin calmed down and answered the Investigator's probing questions without batting an eyelid.

Step by step, event by event. . . . The Investigator forced himself to hold back from time to time, to go over something, think it through, not to hurry. In science they talk about 'slow reading'. When a person reads something he should absorb every detail, every sentence, every word. . . . Merkulov applied the same principles to criminology. A slow reading of Citizen Volin's turbulent life had taken two hours so far, and there was plenty more to come.

It was his desire for the good life that led Volin into Mafia hands. Merkulov knew a bit about the psychology of sportsmen; he knew that the 'disease of stardom' had broken more than one of them. After the honour and glory and the trips abroad came the chilly Calvary of coaching in some secondary school or, worse still, in some third-rate sports club or institute. The crunch had come for self-defence expert Volin, too, when he left competitive sport for the drabness of everyday work.

Then fortune came knocking at his door again. Hanging out at the Sports Committee of the USSR, he realised that all the leading bureaucrats there were mixed up in a huge racket. A rosy-cheeked sports manager in the Komsomol, Seryozha Pavlov, had, in effect, sold Soviet sport down the river to various villains, foreign and home-grown. A band of smooth operators got public money out of the State Treasury, took 70 per cent of it themselves and handed 30 per cent to the Sports Minister, Comrade Pavlov.

Volin tried to get in on this lucrative act, but was squeezed out – born too late, he supposed. Still brooding on the injustice of it, he made the acquaintance of his benefactors, Volodya Kazakov and Yury Leonovich, at the headquarters of the Sports Committee on Sautertny Street. As far as he could see, these big shots weren't really part of Pavlov's organisation, only attached to it. Half a glance told Volin that Volodya Kazakov, an imposing, bearded man with a diamond bracelet on his right wrist, was big-time. Together with another three families, he ran the racket at the Moscow Hippodrome racetrack.

So as to avoid stupid questions from the law-abiding public, the Anti-Corruption Squad, and the People's Inspectorate about his new motor vehicles, his country home, the two apartments knocked into one, or the diamond bracelet, Kazakov had bought himself a 'cover': in name only, he was the deputy director of the Renown Elisei Food Store No. 1.

Twice a month he showed up in the office of the manager there, his bosom pal Yuri Sokolov, and nonchalantly signed for a salary he did not draw. Instead, he handed an envelope to Sokolov with a little something in it – the odd thousand American dollars or so. Sokolov was always in need of some convertible currency to pay for his gifted son's education in the West.

Kazakov had amassed more than one sack of money from his bookmaking activities, and it was the need to convert these eight-kilogram bags (that was how much a million Soviet hundred-rouble notes weighed, Merkulov learnt) into something more worthwhile – gold, diamonds or antiques – that brought him to Leonovich.

The red-head occupied an executive post at the Ministry of Foreign Affairs; he worked in the administrative section which handled the diplomatic corps. He had at his fingertips opportunities for moneymaking that only a fairy godmother could bestow on anyone else. For instance, he could sell imported cars when they were relinquished by diplomats being posted abroad.

But the main event wasn't car-dealing. Leonovich did his really big deals with visiting foreigners, businessmen mostly. They smuggled Western goodies into Moscow, and took Russian antiques back to Paris, London or wherever.

From Volin's testimony it became clear to the Investigator that the operations involving foreign goods in short supply, and the reciprocal smuggling abroad of Russian antiques, were so widespread, and the proceeds so huge, that the sister organs of the CID, the KGB and the Ministry of Internal Affairs ought to be informed immediately. All Merkulov had to do was to pick up the phone, make a call, and then have his secretary make out a copy of Volin's statement for the security men.

But if he pursued his investigation now, and arrested Sokolov and those with him who had stolen more than a million roubles' worth of goods in short supply, also selling off black-market goods through the back door – tons of black and red caviare, chicken delicacies and sides of beef, hundreds of cases of vintage Cognac and vodka intended for export – then immediately all these 'godfathers' and racketeers, well-respected public figures like Shchelokov, Churbanov and Tsinyov, all with their own percentage of Sokolov's business, would come crawling out of the woodwork.

Given a warning, in half an hour they would classify the multi-million racket as 'inadvertent negligence', and before you knew it the whole gang would escape with nothing worse than a scare. No, it was no good handing this case over to the Ministry of Internal Affairs, nor to that other great institution under the jurisdiction of General Tsinyov, the KGB.

New information on that was all too fresh in his mind; information which he had gained from reading Rakitin's notes in front of a roaring fire in the comfortable house of the old musician, Lucian Romadin. . . .

Merkulov concluded his interrogation and handed Volin over to an elderly sergeant. By then the crook looked grey-faced and broken. Merkulov tried to smile reassuringly, but the muscles of his face seemed to have set, stiff and unyielding.

In the doorway, Volin and his escort bumped into Romanova, who came running to the room. She could hardly contain herself until the door had closed behind them.

'Take that, Merkulov, and read it! Gely Lukashevich has just finished squealing. Why couldn't he have kept his mouth shut!'

' "All the suitcases and packets of money, the gold bars and the diamonds were taken by Kazakov, Genka Frolov and me to the 'White House', where Mikhail Porfiryevich Georgadze, Secretary to the Praesidium of the Supreme Soviet, lives," ' Merkulov read aloud.

He put the statement down on the desk.

'That's terrific, Alexandra Ivanovna. It's wonderful how you get your birds to sing.'

'Terrific! Wonderful! What's with you, Konstantin? We need this like a hole in the head!'

Merkulov smiled grimly to see Lieutenant-Colonel Romanova, scourge of all the crooks and hooligans in Moscow, shaking like a jelly.

'Calm down, Shura. I'll think of something,' he said.

He put his hands to his face and sat like that for a minute or so. Then he took a deep breath, picked up the phone and dialled a local number.

'Sergei Andreyevich? This is Konstantin speaking. Long time no see, yes. Listen, Seryosha, have you had lunch? No? How'd you like to be my guest in half an hour at the Budapest? Don't worry, friend, there'll be a table for us.'

He hung up and turned to Romanova, saying: 'Turn this place upside down if you have to, but in five minutes I want a hundred roubles on my desk. No, better make that a hundred and fifty. . . .'

5

In inviting out to lunch his old friend and colleague Sergei Andreyevich Yemelyanov, with whom he had sweated blood at the Prosecutor's Office in Zelyanogradsky district, Merkulov was clutching at straws. But Sergei Andreyevich was a big gun now, Instructor of the Central Committee no less. He might have some new angles on this latest development. Yemelyanov seemed to find the information on Georgadze's activities distinctly exciting.

He listened while walking briskly up and down the private room in the restaurant, his hands behind his back and his head on one side. He looked exactly like Vladimir Ilyich Lenin, and even rolled his *r*'s a little, in the French manner, like the first Soviet leader had done.

'Our country is at a crossroads. One can feel it especially now, today! Brezhnev is dead and a resolute Leninist is at the helm at last. A new historical era is beginning in the life of our state! A new era!' Yemelyanov looked inquisitively at Merkulov, trying to fathom if the latter had understood the full implications of his statement.

A courtly grey-haired waiter took the dirty plates away, set clean ones and polished the already gleaming stainless-steel cutlery with the aplomb of a new conjuror. He cleared the centre of the table, stood a copper dish of delicious-smelling goulash there and withdrew gracefully.

'What you've just said about Georgadze has far-reaching implications,' the Instructor of the Central Committee declared, seating himself at the table. 'You know this is just what Andropov is after now – a clear example. Yuri has decided to introduce iron discipline in the country. It's time, high time, we cleansed our Russia of Brezhnev's toadies, damn them. If we are going to teach the people that crime does not pay, we must come down hard on all the Shchelokovs, Shchivayevs and Medunovs. Damn them, they've drunk away their class conscience, become Rockefellers and Morgans. And, you know yourself, you can't dupe the people. They may know enough to hold their tongues, but they see everything, hear everything, know everything.'

There was a long pause. Yemelyanov drained his glass of Tokay and started on the goulash.

'But, then, of course, Georgadze is not just a run-of-the-mill Medunov. He's the number two in the Praesidium.' Yemelyanov wiped his mouth, red from the rich sauce, with a starched napkin. His hand froze in mid-air as he glanced around and said, almost in a whisper: 'OK, let's get this show on the road. I'll try to get to Andropov today. Give me the papers.'

He put the Prosecutor's file in his own Central Committee briefcase, folded back the corner of the tablecloth and tapped his crossed fingers on the wooden table. He might have been a top party man, but he was still as superstitious as an unlettered peasant.

Then he said unexpectedly: 'Do you want to join me as Deputy?'

Merkulov was lost.

'Do you know what Andropov's historical mission is? It's that he does not want to change everything in the state on his own. We shall do everything – we, the new generation of party men, specialists in our own fields. Andropov is putting us in power, the forty – well, fifty-year-olds. But first we have to get rid of all the rubbish under our feet.

'And if you and I, friend, wring Georgadze's neck tomorrow, then you just see – Yuri Vladimirovich will offer me the post of Prosecutor of Moscow. Not in gratitude – oh, no. As a sign of confidence in me! Old man Malkov will be pensioned off – he's on the way out, it's clear. And when that happens will you join me as Deputy? Will you help me root out all the rubbish?'

Merkulov's eyes narrowed.

'You bet!'

They drank a cup of strong coffee each, Merkulov settled handsomely with the waiter and they made their way outside. On busy Neglinka Street, it had started to rain again.

6

A beautiful – or, rather, striking – brunette appeared at the door. Wearing a light smoky-coloured coat and a snow-white, fine-stitched shawl, carrying a smart black handbag, she smiled a pearly smile and her velvety dark eyes seemed to radiate innocent warmth and friendliness. Sasha took an instinctive dislike to her.

'My name is Soya-Serko. Barkov asked me to come.'

Alla Alexandrovna sat on a chair and began examining the office curiously – Sasha, too, as if he were part of the furniture. 'I was told my case was now with Turetsky,' she continued. 'Is that you?'

Sasha nodded curtly. She could cut all the introductory rubbish so far as he was concerned. He fished sheet no. 13 out of the file, a list of her acquaintances she had made for the investigating officer. All these people, according to Alla Alexandrovna's testimony, had shown interest of one sort or another in her collection.

'This list, Mrs Soya-Serko. Isn't it a little one-dimensional? There are museum employees, scholars and antiques collectors listed here, but I'm sure you know other sorts of people, too. You have had to sell, exchange and buy certain items in your collection after all.' It was not so much a question as an assertion, and Sasha did not wait for an answer but went on: 'You must have come across less Ritzy types, swindlers, people after goods on the side, black-marketeers. Right?'

Soya-Serko sighed loudly and pulled out a packet of Marlboro. She lit one calmly, but Sasha could sense the tension inside her. She did not offer him a cigarette, which meant she was smoking involuntarily.

'You're quite right, Alexander Borisovich. But how does one manage without such people these days? They're the only ones who can get things done, after all. So, yes, Father, I have sinned. . . . So what?'

From her tone, Sasha realised she'd regained her control. He wasn't Merkulov, after all. She offered him a cigarette politely, pulling herself together, getting ready to pull the wool further over an inexperienced investigator's eyes.

'So far as the collection was concerned, I could never have done anything worthwhile with it if I hadn't broken the rules occasionally. Take any enterprise and it's the same. You just can't get anything done in this country for all the rules and regulations. They're always introducing prohibitions, making things more complicated, raising prices. Just you try to get hold of a decent antique. . . .'

How candid and guileless she was being, really shooting her mouth off in the most trusting fashion. But when was she going to say anything of substance?

As he listened to her, Sasha wondered how he could bring the subject round to Leonovich and the man from the Baltic States. He knew nothing concrete about this Yuri Yuryevich – who or what he was. But he took a flyer and asked: 'Why isn't Yuri on your list?'

She wasn't thrown by that, just looked at him with her dark velvet eyes, now slightly more focused, brighter-looking.

'Yuri? Who's he?'

'He's your acquaintance, not mine,' Sasha said, getting to his feet.

'You're talking in riddles,' she said, wrinkling her nose prettily. 'Who on earth is Yuri? I don't recall anyone of that name.'

'Are you saying you don't know anyone called Yuri?'

'No, of course not,' said Soya-Serko with a charming smile. 'I must do, if you say so. I just can't think of anyone at the moment.'

'You really ought to. I'm not insisting, just advising. You stand to benefit most when we crack the case. Look at the valuables they got away with. Real museum pieces, apparently. Nineteenth-century stuff, nearly all of it.'

'Nineteenth and eighteenth,' said the victim with a sad shake of her finely moulded head. 'My father-in-law's father started the collection.'

'Well, then, that's why I'm asking. Do you suspect anyone from among your contacts?'

'You'll have to give me a bit of time to think about it. I'll try to work it out when I get home and sit down quietly.'

'You do that,' Sasha said approvingly. 'Meanwhile we'll check out all the people on your first list. We have to do our stuff. What with Popovich writing complaints at your request.'

'What Popovich? What complaints?' Soya-Serko

started visibly, despite her pose of naïve trust and calm. She wasn't play-acting now. She really didn't know anything about the complaint.

'Yes, Popovich, your friend. You remember the cosmonaut, twice Hero of the Soviet Union? Just take a look at his complaint on sheet 53.' Sasha pulled Popovich's complaint out of the unbound sheaf of documents. His honours and titles took up half the pages: twice Hero of the Soviet Union, Merited Cosmonaut, Deputy to the Supreme Soviet, Chairman of the Federation of the Sports Committee, Head of the Union of Friendship between the USSR and one of the godforsaken African colonies. . . .

'Oh, what a fool I am!' exclaimed Soya-Serko, coquettishly slapping her forehead. 'Pavel, of course! I approached him and asked him to do what he could to help. But that was a long time ago, immediately after the robbery, and I'd almost forgotten. I asked him to help me and now I'm denying it. What an idiot!'

Alla Alexandrovna smiled with all her former candour, but Sasha was unconvinced.

'Well, these things happen, I suppose. So when can I expect a call from you?' he said, trying to maintain good relations with this personal friend of a famous cosmonaut.

'About this Yuri person?' she asked, shaking his hand firmly.

'Not just him – about all his circle.'

'Oh, yes, I see.'

'Good, I'll be waiting to hear from you, then.'

As Soya-Serko went out, Sasha dialled his mother's number. It rang for a long time. He was beginning to get nervous in case there was something the matter when at last his mother's breathless voice came on the line.

'Hello.'

'Mother, it's me.'

'Oh, son, I've been expecting you to call. I've been trying to get you for ages, but you're never home. Can you come over tonight?'

157

Holding the phone, Sasha was simultaneously trying to gather up all the statements on the Soya-Serko case and stuff them into the folder.

'What's this all about?' he asked, knowing very well that his mother wasn't one for dinner-parties. 'Is someone else expected or something?'

'Sasha, it's been so long since we've seen you. . . .'

'And the other reason?'

'Well, Pavel Semyonovich is always going on at me, saying "Your son never visits". And he wants to introduce you to a friend of his. It's to do with your job. The friend is someone big in the same field, you see. He might be able to pull strings, get you a really good posting with prospects and more money. A hundred and forty roubles a month isn't exactly—'

Sasha lost his temper. His mother was always nagging about his career, his salary, the hours he worked. . . .

'Look, Mother, I don't think so. I've got an appointment now, and then another one, I can't promise anything.'

'Sasha, please. Just for me. Please, come over.'

She knew that tragic voice always got to him.

'OK, OK. But I can't promise to be there early. Between nine and ten, all right?'

'All right,' she repeated, and put down the phone.

Fifty years old and still a child at heart! Sasha's mother always did exactly what other people wanted.

He left the office a minute later, and strode out of the new building which housed the Investigations Department of the Moscow Prosecutor's Office. He was in a hurry to meet Merkulov.

The icy rain that had begun to fall that morning still had not stopped. He walked along Novokuznetskaya Street towards Paveletsky Station. The melting snow was forming dangerous pools on the Sadovoye ring-road, and the traffic was moving at a snail's pace. Some men in yellow work-jackets were fixing a tow-rope to a Moskvich that had been in too big a hurry.

7

The follow-up list regarding operations and enquiries to be made as a result of the CID's nocturnal adventures was compiled by Merkulov and then passed to Vyacheslav Gryaznov. The Captain, after only a few hours' sleep, had to run all over town, arranging emergency forensic tests and enquiries. He reached the Central Office of Addresses and turned the files of the Special Section of the Ministry of the Interior upside down. He'd even found time to make out an intelligible report, and now he was sitting in Romanova's office staring blankly at the ceiling. He reacted to Merkulov's greeting with a vacant 'Hi'.

After the delights of Hungarian cuisine and drinking Tokay, Merkulov felt inclined to be generous.

'Look, can I organise some tea for you?'

'No,' said Gryaznov, with an indifferent wave of the hand. The only thing he wanted to do now was to take off his soaking-wet shoes.

'Alexandra Ivanovna,' said Merkulov to Romanova, 'shall we let the Captain go home now?'

Romanova jumped up from her seat.

'Yes, what are you doing hanging around here, Vyacheslav? Go on, clear off home. Get your arse out of here.'

'I'll make tracks, then,' said Gryaznov. He got up and, without saying another word, walked out of the door, his boots squelching miserably.

'How come he's looking so tired?' asked Romanova in a whisper as soon as Gryaznov had closed the door behind him.

Merkulov shrugged his shoulders and picked up the reports Gryaznov had organised. Slava had got a lot done that day! It was all clear-cut with Lukashevich and Frolov, and the police had taken the woodsman and the auto-repair man in for questioning. But Kazakov, that's what he wanted to see. . . .

'Alexandra Ivanovna, just look what he's come up with!'

It was like something out of the extraordinary adventures of Father Brown. When they had checked the contents of Kazakov's pockets, they had discovered a letter he had written but forgotten to post. The letter itself was of no interest – it was just a complaint about bad service at the Moscow auto centre.

Gryaznov's attention was first drawn to it because of the appalling spelling. He almost thought that the crook might have made the mistakes deliberately, maybe as some sort of code. Then he had a feeling that he'd encountered such mistakes as 'deelay', 'somhow', 'fotograffed' once before, a long time ago. It was the 'deelays' especially which bothered him. He could have sworn he had met this Kazakov before, but he knew he had never come across the name. . . .

Mamma mia, how could he have forgotten! He'd pulled in a hardened criminal over the murder of a club manager in Penza ten years ago. At the time Gryaznov was just at the start of his career, working as an ops man with Penza CID. Anyway Kazakov, or whatever his name was then, broke out the day before the trial, cutting the guard's throat with a home-made knife. The evening of the same day they found the body of the manager of a pharmacy at Penza goods station. The shop had been robbed, the pharmacist stripped naked. Nearby were the prison clothes of the same criminal (what was his name?) and a length of wire with which he had strangled the pharmacist, a little Jew. Wait a minute – Kazakov had had a Jewish name, too, then. It began with R. What was it? Rokhman? No – Roshman. No, it was not as obvious as that.

Gryaznov rushed over to the central records room of the CID at the Ministry of the Interior. That was him! Vladimir Yosifovich Rachel, who had written a complaint to the Penza Prosecutor's Office.

'From the rongly akuzed V. I. Rachel. I rekwest you to

stop the deelays wiv the food. And to bring me some hiding.'

Hiding! Gryaznov remembered the laugh they'd had over that one. The fool meant 'iodine'. But what was this?

'Sept. 12th, 1970, sentenced to one year's corrective labour under article 154 of the Criminal Code of the RSFSR for petty black-marketeering. Aug. 15th, 1972, sentenced under article 154 of the Criminal Code of the RSFSR to five years' imprisonment for large-scale black-marketeering. Sentence served in full. At present resides in town of Kerch, at. . . .'

The hardest part was getting through to Kerch on the phone. Gryaznov lost a whole hour trying to get a line. Finally, a voice of indeterminate sex answered: 'This is 22-12.'

The rest went like clockwork. The records at the Penza Office of Internal Affairs were in perfect order. Gryaznov was put through to the head of the CID there, Colonel Torbayev, a man who remembered not just his talented Lieutenant Gryaznov, but everything else in the world as well.

The answer to Gryaznov's question took some time coming. After Rachel's escape from prison, there was an all-Union search for him. Vladimir Yosifovich Rachel was serving a prison sentence from August of 1972 and so could not have committed a crime in the October. Questioned about his documents, Rachel explained that at a bazaar about five years before his wallet had been filched together with money, his passport and driving licence. Some considerable time elapsed before Rachel suddenly 'remembered' that his wallet had not been stolen at a bazaar, but under more serious circumstances, and he gave new evidence. In 1967, just at the May Day celebrations, in the town of Kerch, there was a murder. Volodya Kramarenko, hooligan and thief, renowned throughout the Kerch estuary, killed his cousin Mikhail in a brawl. And, naturally, he disappeared from town, without a trace. About ten days later, in the dead of night, there was a loud knocking on the door of the Rachel's house. A complete stranger was standing on the doorstep. Rachel's wife Mirra stepped back from the door and a scruffy, bearded man came into the hall. He had a knife in his hand.

'Quick, I want some grub, money and a change of clothes.' They realised then that it was Kramarenko.

'Oh, Volodya, no one would ever recognise you with a beard,' Mirra Rachel told him. She dug out an old rucksack from somewhere and started fitting Kramarenko out for the road. Then she took her husband's new jacket off its hanger and put it on Volodya's shoulders.

By way of farewell Kramarenko said: 'I can always rely on the Jews.'

Only on the next day did the Rachels realise that the jacket still had all the husband's documents in the pocket. . . .

Vladimir Yosifovich Rachel was sending in this belated confession in the hope that the 'forces of law and order' would have a change of heart and cut his sentence in half. However, instead of expressing their gratitude they wanted to slap another sentence on him for withholding information about a dangerous criminal. But then they felt sorry for him, did not make out a case against him, and just left him to sit out his original sentence to the end.

Merkulov was slipping on his coat when Shura Romanova suddenly said: 'Don't you go complaining!'

'What? Who to?' Merkulov asked in confusion.

'Kazakov loved making complaints. Rachel and Kramarenko did, too. And that's what cooked his goose.'

8

In the morning Merkulov rang the Red Banner of Labour
Scientific Research Insitute of Neurosurgery, named after
Academician N. N. Burdenko, where the wounded Kazakov had been taken. He asked Academician Glev Ivanovich Solovyov to come to the phone.

They were old acquaintances. Fifteen years earlier,
Merkulov had saved the professor's reputation by proving
he was innocent of negligence in the death of a female
patient. He spent a long time persuading Solovyov to
operate on Kazakov personally – they needed him alive
for their enquiry.

The operation had been going on for over seven hours.
Merkulov sat in the office of the Institute Director, a man
called Konovalov, watching its progress on a closed-
circuit television.

They could not see Kazakov's face, just the contours of
his head beneath the folds of a green sheet. For some
reason it reminded Merkulov of the old photographer in
Kratovo – he, too, used to cover himself up like that, his
rounded head under the covers shrouding the primitive
wooden apparatus, only his hand materialising from
under the black cloth to take the cover off the lens, like
lifting his hat to someone in the street. Merkulov could
only see a hand now. Kazakov's large sleeping hand.

Konovalov called Merkulov over to another screen,
which was linked to a microscope.

'A bird's-eye view, Konstantin Dmitriyevich!'

Merkulov looked through the eye-piece. He could see a
deep wet hole, the bottom of which quickly filled with
blood like a footprint disappearing in a marsh. And then
the suction tube did its work, revealing the yellowish
matter of the brain, the colour of ancient marble. Merkulov shuddered as he watched the pincers move in, barely
quivering, and then they pulled out the deadly mass of the
bullet, deepening the bleeding wound. . . .

Half an hour later, Glev Ivanovich Solovyov came out of the operating theatre and said with his usual pronounced stammer: 'D-d-dear K-K-Konstantin D-D-Dmitriyevich, go-g-good-day!'

Apparently the surgeon only stammered when he was outside the operating theatre.

'F-f-from w-what I know about b-b-bullets, I'd s-s-say this one c-comes f-f-from a foreign g-g-gun.' Solovyov handed the Investigator a little cellophane packet, but Merkulov could see for himself that it was not a nine-millimetre bullet but much smaller. 'R-r-regarding your c-c-client, there's no n-n-need to w-worry. The bullet didn't d-damage the brain t-t-tissue. I think you'll b-b-be able to talk to him in a f-few d-days. . . .'

'Comrade Academicians,' announced Merkulov solemnly, 'as of this minute, Kazakov is a special-category patient of national importance. I must ask you to limit the number of medical staff having access to him, especially nurses and lab specialists. Only allow in outsiders with my written permission. I'm giving instructions now for a round-the-clock guard to be mounted inside and outside the hospital.' Merkulov picked up the phone, and as he dialled Romanova's number added: 'No one is to go near him without my express permission – man or beast.'

9

Four paces forward. Four paces back. He was walking up and down under the narrow awning of the Metro station. Each time he turned he looked intently in the direction of Novokuznetskaya Street where Sasha was coming from.

'Anyone who does not know how to wait should not be in intelligence work' – the phrase from some silly spy-thriller came unbidden to Sasha's mind.

'Lyosha, what a surprise! Been waiting long?'

164

Rakitin junior started guiltily. 'Oh, Alexander Borisovich. I've just been to the museum with some friends. You know, the Bakhrushin Theatre Museum? They're still in there – I'm waiting for them – how good to meet you again.'

'Stop kidding about. You were waiting for me, weren't you?' Sasha knew it wouldn't take much pressure to get Lyosha to come clean.

The boy nodded, shamefaced. 'Well, I suppose so.'

'And you waited for me on Friday. And over the weekend you rang my home number,' Sasha continued.

The gangling boy kept shifting his weight from one foot to the other.

'I must talk to someone. Konstantin Dmitriyevich said that if there were any problems I should get hold of you.'

They went into the hall of the Metro Station and stood by the small-change machines. Crowds of people pushed past them, but there was no time to go to a bar or café, or back to the Prosecutor's Office.

'Take this,' said Lyosha Rakitin, handing Sasha a package. Sasha did not notice whether the boy had just taken it out of his pocket or had held it in his hand all the time.

It was a blue envelope obviously stuffed full of sheets of paper folded into four.

'What's this?' Sasha asked.

'The notes Dad was keeping. I don't want them to fall into other people's hands. When they came I was able to get the package out of the desk drawer and pocket it. . . .'

Sasha was confused, but he noticed that Lyosha was scared. He kept licking his lips as if his mouth had suddenly gone dry.

'Who are "they"?'

'Can't you guess?' said Lyosha, shaking his head vigorously. By some feat of gravity, his woollen hat stayed on.

'There were three of them. A colonel, a major and a plain-clothes man who looked like a rat. He was in charge. He told Mum that my father was an American spy. It's a lie! My father was an honest man, more honest

165

than all of them. He loved his country, I know that. My grandfather will confirm it, and Valery Sergeyevich Ponomaryov, Dad's friend.'

Lyosha was shaking with fear and defiance.

'When was this?'

'The day Dad was killed – Wednesday. The day before you came. They turned our apartment upside down, even looked down the lavatory bowl. But I don't think they found anything. Only they really frightened Mum, threatened her. I heard them. . . . You must forgive her for not saying anything to you. I couldn't, either. The apartment could be bugged, couldn't it?'

Sasha nodded. They could have bugged the apartment. It was even their duty to.

'Lyosha, are you sure those three men were from the KGB?'

'The grandson of a general in the State Intelligence can't be wrong,' said Alexei with some of his mother's arrogance. 'They had blue tabs, and I saw that the colonel had a badge saying "Merited Security Man".'

'Did you get their full names and ranks?'

'Sorry, no, I didn't.' Lyosha stared at the floor once again. 'Maybe Mum knows – but don't say anything to her about our meeting! If you need me, don't ring my home number. Ring Yulya – her number's in there. I've got to go now.'

A second later, Rakitin junior had melted into the crowd as he dashed from an escalator.

Sasha took out a cigarette, struck a match, inhaled and then saw a policeman heading towards him. Smoking on the Moscow Metro was strictly forbidden.

10

'Makarov! You going to put that puck in or not?' roared a red-faced fan on Sasha's right, straight into his ear.

Merkulov and he were sitting way up top – Garik had left them when he met some people he knew from the Moscow Arts Theatre. Below, the game unfolded on the ice. Sasha's side, Spartak, was pushing the Wings into their own half. He'd thought the Spartaks would have been well on their way by now, but somehow it just wasn't working out. Scoring in the first minute of play, the Spartaks had now been charging around their opponents' goal with no result for fifteen minutes.

During this time, Sasha managed to tell his boss about this first day of independent work as an investigator – the brilliant exposure of the secondhand dealers and the inconclusive questioning of Madame Soya-Serko.

'We'll have to take in Leonovich,' said Merkulov thoughtfully. 'And we'll search Madame's place tomorrow – if we have time.'

He spoke softly but distinctly, and Sasha heard him well enough above the roar of the crowd and the scraping of the ice. Merkulov seemed barely interested in the game, kept looking from side to side as if hoping to see someone he knew in the stands.

When Sasha told him about Parkhomenko's recruiting of him, Merkulov just sighed. The comment that time was indistinct but it included the word 'bastard'. When he got to the bit about the 'chance' meeting with Rakitin junior, Merkulov stiffened and started to listen intently to every word. He stopped looking around and concentrated instead on Sasha's nylon coat. Sasha was about to put his hand to his pocket and bring out the blue package when Merkulov said: 'No, don't!'

So he really was scared that they were being watched. Sasha joined in the applause for Spartak as they scored a second time.

'Do you remember me saying we were really in the shit?'

'Yes.'

'I was wrong then. I thought it was just a piece of shit, but now it's an ocean. An ocean of shit!'

Sasha glanced at Merkulov. He was pale-faced and sweaty-looking.

'Konstantin Dmitriyevich. . . .'

'Yes.'

'Tell me about the papers. The ones you found at the musician's place.'

Merkulov looked even more worried, but Sasha kept on at him like a bull terrier.

'Honest, I won't say a word – even under torture!'

Merkulov studied his face, long and seriously. Then he said: 'There are many different kinds of torture.'

Sasha wondered if Merkulov was cracking up, and decided to stop asking questions and watch the game. But he could not concentrate on the hockey for long. Merkulov seemed to be expecting his next sidelong glance, because he started whispering quickly.

'Rakitin had top-secret government information in his briefcase. It was a copy of a plan for taking over all the world markets, primarily the market for raw materials. There were three main facets to the plan. First, obtaining Western electronics developments by means of espionage. Next, taking over the narcotics and armaments markets for the third world countries. But the main thrust was the military seizure of all countries where oil, uranium, bauxite, nickel and other key metals are produced. In all, fifteen designated countries. Complete mastery of the raw materials market would bring the West, and especially America, to its knees before the socialist camp. . . .'

Merkulov rattled off all the information, and then sighed and drew breath. Sasha tried to look horrified but, frankly, couldn't see anything wrong with bringing the West to its knees.

'Rakitin translated this third point, Doctrine No. 3, into facts and figures and was horrified. To carry out the intended plan by the year 2000 we would have had to spend a minimum of five trillion roubles, militarize the whole country, and bring the Russian people and the hundreds of other peoples of the Soviet Union to utter ruin. And, on top of that, there was the risk of retaliation from the West. Nuclear retaliation, leading perhaps to full-scale war.'

'So Rakitin was spying for the Americans, then?'

'Well, kid,' said Merkulov, taking out his handkerchief and trumpeting into it, 'it all depends what you mean by "spying". Come on, let's get out of here.'

They began making their way to the exit, treading on people's toes and jostling the backs of cursing fans. Wings had just scored their first goal of the match.

'Some day. I've got to have a drink,' said Merkulov. Leaving Sasha to keep his seat, he headed for the buffet.

The beer-stalls at Luzhniki are a legend in their own right. Many Muscovites travel there just to drink some well-kept beer and have a sandwich of fresh-smoked sausage. And no one is too bothered that the beer and sandwiches all come from 'under the counter', and that the lion's share of the rake-off from them lines the pockets of shady middlemen.

Sasha liked the place because he often used to go there with his best friend, Borya Nemirovsky. Borya wasn't around any more. He lived in New York now. Sasha wondered if he still went to hockey matches there.

Merkulov stacked half a dozen bottles of Moskovskoye beer on the table and went back for some sandwiches and beer-mugs. They sipped their first bottle slowly. When they got halfway down, Merkulov pulled a quarter-litre of vodka out of his case and quickly poured its contents into the half-full beer-glasses. Exactly nine minutes later when, according to medical science, alcohol enters the bloodstream, Sasha felt completely smashed. But before the vodka hit him, during the nine sober minutes, Merkulov and he talked business. He repeated his question, and Kostya repeated his answer.

'So Rakitin was a spy, right?'

'Depends how you look at it. In one way, a Soviet citizen can't be a spy. According to article 65 only foreigners are criminally liable for the charge of espionage. If you want to be legalistic, then Rakitin's actions could be classified as state treason. But it's six of one and half a dozen of the other what you call it – in either case they would have shot him for what he did. But there would have to have been an enquiry and a trial before that.'

Some police officers and police voluntary helpers went by. The man in charge, a tall lieutenant-colonel, greeted Merkulov with a nod.

'That's Akulov, head of 135th Luzhniki precinct,' he explained. 'You can't even have a drink in peace! So, you see, Sasha, it's all professional nitpicking what article of the penal code you get him on. It's more correct to ask if Rakitin was a traitor or not. I'd say not – but I'm speaking personally, not professionally. You think that's a contradiction? Our whole life is one long contradiction.

'Rakitin realised something very simple: Doctrine No. 3 meant the ruin of the Soviet people. He tried to prove this by all manner of means, open and covert. First, openly. They called him an anti-party nationalist and practically sacked him. He wanted to appeal to public opinion, but where do you find that? In the kitchen of a communal apartment? Here?' Merkulov looked round the beer-hall where everyone was drinking like there was no tomorrow. ' "A government has to be under the control of the public opinion of its country. . . ." Don't make me laugh!'

Sasha said stiffly: 'I think Lenin once said—'

'What difference does it make what he said? The important thing is that no one does anything, no one controls anything, no one wants to control anything! But Rakitin wanted to. No doubt Podgursky was no ordinary journalist but a spy. That is, a spy-journalist. What's the difference? Rakitin, intent on his million, seeing nothing else for it, decided to appeal to world opinion. Of course, one can question the moral aspect of his actions. But he had swallowed so much shit from the people at the top that. . . .'

Grimacing, Merkulov finished drinking the fiery mixture in his glass, glancing sideways at the sign which read: 'Smoking and bringing-in of spirits strictly forbidden.' He lit a Dymok.

Sasha tried to digest what his boss had said. God, life was getting more complicated by the minute. He felt as if Merkulov had shifted a great burden on to his shoulders. He must either throw it off, refuse to listen further, maybe speak to Parkhomenko – or quietly bear it, like Merkulov had.

The Senior Investigator was looking through the window towards the Lenin Mountains black in the twilight.

'Listen, Kostya,' Sasha said, and stopped short.

'Go on, Sasha. This is between friends now'

'I still don't understand who killed him, and why.'

'Kazakov killed him – or Kramarenko, the hardened criminal. Someone else tried to liquidate Kazakov – the bullet we pulled out of his skull didn't come from one of our weapons.' Merkulov threw his cigarette-end on to the sandwich-plate. 'But that's another story.'

'Do you mind telling it to me?'

'Yes.'

'Was there something else there in the flowerbeds? Kazakov wouldn't give a shit for Rakitin's thoughts on the doctrine, would he?'

Merkulov groaned and rubbed his hand wearily over his forehead.

'God damn it, Sasha. Yes, there was something else. And Kazakov wouldn't give a shit for that, either. He was just a pawn in a very big game. And I don't know what to do with what I've found! In my book, work means achieving a goal, winning or suffering a defeat, taking it on the chin, whatever you like. Not just wringing your hands in despair. I don't want to drag you in deeper, isn't that clear? If they go after you, you might as well jump under a tram. Officially, we're looking for Rakitin's murderers – we've found one, and we'll find the other – and that's an end to it.'

But Sasha could see that it wouldn't be – not for Merkulov.

'So the "Cagey" killed him. Any idiot can see that. They were looking for what you found at Romadin's home and later in the Central Hotel. And now they're on our trail. And it doesn't matter whether I know about these papers or not. But if you still don't want to tell me. . . .' Sasha fell silent because he could see his chief fairly killing himself laughing.

'What did you call them? The "Cagey". Where did you pick that up?'

'I just thought it up myself. I don't see anything funny in it.'

Merkulov stopped laughing, took out a handkerchief and blew long and hard.

'Yes, Sasha, it's shocking, because it doesn't leave any doubt.'

The Palace of Sport roared. The Wings had just equalized.

11

Yuri Vladimirovich Andropov was looking through his speech to the November plenum of the Central Committee.

'The demise of Leonid Ilyich Brezhnev has caused much speculation abroad about the future course of the Communist Party of the Soviet Union, and the Soviet State in international affairs. . . .'

Yegor Ligachev, head of the Secretariat of the Central Committee, came in, grey and shadow-like. He carefully placed on the leather-topped writing desk a memorandum from Savinkin, head of the administrative organs.

Andropov put his own speech to one side and immersed himself in Savinkin's masterpiece.

> According to a special report from Instructor S. A. Yemelyanov, who oversees the Public Prosecutor's Office of the USSR, Comrade M. P. Georgadze's country house has been converted into an unofficial bank, where, for a certain percentage – 6–8 per cent of the capital sum deposited – speculators from Trans-Caucasia deposit their ill-gotten millions of roubles for safe-keeping. . . .
>
> Yuri Vladimirovich, let me remind you of warning signals we have been receiving. Over many years of working with Leonid Ilyich Brezhnev, who exercised no control whatsoever over Mikhail Porfiryevich, the latter granted pardons to and freed from legal responsibility various speculators from Georgia, Armenia and Azerbaijan.
>
> I beg to concur with the opinion of Comrade Yemelyanov that an immediate search of Georgadze's residence be conducted.
>
> N. SAVINKIN

Andropov summoned Instructor Yemelyanov, who ran into the office of the General Secretary three minutes later and stood bolt upright to attention.

'Is it your view that a search should be conducted of the residence of a Secretary to the Supreme Soviet?' asked Andropov, his customarily dry tones masking his excitement.

'I base my opinion, Yuri Vladimirovich, on the opinion

of Investigator Merkulov, who has discovered this information in pursuit of a certain case. Merkulov has my complete confidence – we worked together for many years. And I have studied the evidence closely. Only yesterday a number of black-marketeers took a great quantity of valuables to Georgadze's house. Although—'

Andropov interrupted him. 'What is the case that this investigator is handling?'

'The murders of an executive functionary of the Ministry of Foreign Trade, Rakitin, and a female acquaintance of his. But Georgadze, of course, has nothing to do with the murders. He is only circumstantially implicated; it's just a side-issue that has come to light.'

'Go on.'

'I wanted to say,' said Yemelyanov, picking up where he left off, 'that it will, of course, be a dangerous matter, searching the house of a Secretary to the Supreme Soviet.'

'Dangerous?' asked Andropov again, his eyes behind the lenses of his glasses flashing with indignation, 'what do you mean, dangerous? Isn't it dangerous to keep a bribe-taker and crook in a post like this? A Secretary to the Supreme Soviet, a bribe-taker and a crook. That's what's dangerous! Highly dangerous!

'Let's not bury our heads in the sand, Comrade Yemelyanov. At plenary and other sessions I know we're afraid of speaking out – God forbid that the people, or President Reagan over there, might get us wrong! But in the Central committee we can open our mouths and call a spade a spade. I demand that urgent measures be taken. Tomorrow the Supreme Soviet is starting its seventh session, and I can't permit a crook to be elected to be my right-hand man.'

Andropov got on the hot line to Chebrikov, the head of the KGB.

'Victor Mikhailovich, I have one of my instructors, Yemelyanov, with me now and he has some interesting information about Georgadze. It connects with what you were telling me. I've sanctioned a search of his house. What? No, no. The Prosecutor's Office is handling the case; they can stay with it. You just make a note of it and monitor the operation. I've already put down a motion for the Politburo that in future the Ministry of Internal Affairs and the Public Prosecutor's Office should deal with basic inter-union operations. It's time to relieve your people of internal affairs – plenty to keep you busy in the outside world, after all.

'By the way, remind me, who is handling that operation of yours – what's it called, "Operation Export"? Major-General Kassarin eh? Well, I wish him success. Kassarin – an excellent worker and dedicated to the cause is he? You're right – sounds a fanatic! But just the sort of person we need now. Keep me informed. Goodbye.'

When he had finished talking to Chebrikov, Andropov asked Yemelyanov: 'What did you say was the name of that investigator of yours?'

'Merkulov,' replied Yemelyanov.

'I see. He's not a relative of that Merkulov who was Minister of State Security, shot with Beria in 1953?'

Red blotches appeared on Yemelyanov's cheeks.

'Certainly not, Yuri Vladimirovich! On the contrary. His grandfather and Academician Korolyov launched the Kosmos sputnik that carried Gagarin. . . .'

Andropov smiled thinly. He tore a page from his note-pad, wrote something down, and handed the sheet to Yemelyanov.

The cream-coloured paper with the red Kremlin heading 'General Secretary of the Central Committee of the Communist Party of the Soviet Union' bore just a few words in Andropov's large neat hand:

> To Comrade A. M. Rekunkov
> General Prosecutor of the USSR

Dear Alexandr Mikhailovich,
I sanction a search of M. P. Georgadze's house.

Investigator Merkulov, and the new Prosecutor of Moscow, Yemelyanov, are handling the case. Report to me on the results of the search tomorrow before the session starts.

Yu. Andropov
22 November 1982

Seeing that Yemelyanov still looked stunned, Andropov elaborated.

'Sergei Andreyevich, you've brought a lot of common sense to the Central Committee. Now it's time you had your own patch. Take Malkov's – we'll pension him off. And report to me on the search tomorrow, at a quarter to ten.'

Advancement: short, sharp and in true party fashion.

Yemelyanov left the office with a jaunty step. The General Secretary took up his speech again and continued reading: 'We will always and unfalteringly remain faithful to Leninist norms and principles, which are confirmed in the life of the Party and the State.'

Andropov gave a little laugh. He knew that at this point the audience would probably burst into applause.

12

Without waiting for the end of the second half, they left the Palace of Sport, wandering towards the Yunost Hotel next to which stood the darkened Sportivnaya Metro station. A goods train roared by overhead as they walked under the line that circled Moscow.

With the skill of a professional thief, Merkulov put his hand into Sasha's coat and pulled out the blue packet containing Rakitin's papers. Like lightning his hand vanished into his own breast pocket; even an enemy spy would have had difficulty in registering what had taken place.

In the entrance hall of the Sportivnaya Metro, Merkulov went over to an empty phone-booth. Sasha noticed that he chose one between two other empty booths. Merkulov had asked him for three two-copeck pieces. Three calls, then. One would be to the Moscow CID, to Romanova. The second to the Burdenko Institute. But what about the third? Maybe to Yemelyanov at the Central Committee.

After his brief conversations, Merkulov rejoined Sasha. They put their five-copeck pieces in the automatic Metro barrier and walked down the escalator. There they went their separate ways for the night, Merkulov in the direction of the Park of Culture, and Sasha heading towards Leninsky Prospekt.

'See you soon,' said Merkulov as Sasha's train arrived first. 'Five in the morning at Petrovka. Ring Shura's department and tell her to send a car for you. We've got an important job tomorrow.'

13

When Sasha rang his mother's doorbell, it was way past nine o'clock. Pavel Semyonovich Satin opened the door, his face registering genuine pleasure. Sasha began to make apologies for being so late, but his stepfather just brushed them aside and dragged him through to the dining room. He kissed his mother, who was looking distinctly pale. Her hands were icy as she clasped her son's face between them. He had not seen her for about six months, but noted that she still looked young – small, slender, wearing a girlish sweater.

'Come on, Sasha, put down a penalty drink for being late, and then we'll have something to eat,' said Satin heartily. 'Oh, what am I thinking of? First, let me introduce you to Vasily Vasilyevich Kassarin, a colleague of yours.'

Vasily Vasilyevich got out of his armchair, straight as a ramrod. Without smiling, he pressed Sasha's hand pincer-like.

'Only sort of,' he commented.

'How do you mean, "sort of"?' Sasha asked, confused.

'A sort of colleague.'

What the hell was this? Sasha's head was ringing from the drink, the cold, the lack of food.

The Satins served supper on a low glass-topped table. His mother had never been noted for her cooking, and on the table was the usual Satin assortment of cold delicacies: sturgeon, black caviare, various kinds of sausage.

Sasha smacked a few pieces of sausage and pickled gherkins on to some bread and, egged on by Satin, sank a glass of vodka in one. He could barely catch his breath; it was the strongest brand.

Pavel Semyonovich launched into a diatribe that made sense only to him. Sasha's mother kept jumping up to fetch an ashtray or turn the music up or down. He found himself laughing for no reason at all as the evil mixture of vodka and Luzhniki beer made its presence felt.

Kassarin took no part in the conversation, but Sasha caught his sharp eyes following Mrs Satin's movements. He had a very interesting face, Kassarin. It was lined but boyish, open yet watchful. He had cold green eyes.

Without any pretence at joining in Satin's conversation, Kassarin suddenly addressed his wife.

'Yelena Petrovna, you know Boris Borisovich Turetsky and I were great friends. I'm sure you remember. . . .'

For a fraction of a second, she stood quite still, eyes wide with shock. Then she pressed her hand to her bosom and exclaimed: 'What are you saying, my dear Vasily Vasilyevich? Did you really know Boris? My God, it was such a long time ago. Did you hear how he died? It was terrible, terrible. Tell me what you remember of him.'

Kassarin drained his glass of Cognac, leant back in his armchair and smiled for the first time. Sasha felt his glow of alcoholic well-being begin to evaporate. The moment Kassarin smiled, that good-looking boyish face resembled nothing so much as a rat's. He drew his free hand over the lower part of his face in a curious gesture, as if removing a terrible mask.

Sasha's mother chattered away animatedly to the guest, even recalling that Boris had told her something of their friendship. Well, maybe, she wasn't certain. It was so long ago. . . . But he must certainly be sure to come again, even get both their families together. She would look out some old photographs.

Then she suddenly seemed to remember herself and said that the men must want to talk amongst themselves. She'd go to her own room and leave them in peace.

'Sasha, come in to me later on,' she said with a wistful smile.

Satin kept pouring out lethal combinations of vodka and some liqueur, but Sasha instinctively knew he'd better sober up. He excused himself politely and stumbled off to the lavatory. Two fingers down the throat, cold water on the face, and he felt far more able to cope. But, so far as his 'colleague' was concerned, he'd stay drunk. It was obviously what Kassarin wanted. Who else had given Satin the export-label vodka? Sasha was getting used to acting. First, Lyona Parkhomenko; now a command performance for this mysterious friend of the family.

Kassarin knew just how to impress the wet-behind-the-ears kid Sasha was playing. Without any preliminaries, he just pulled out his identification and introduced himself properly. A major-general in State Security. Some colleague!

Humming a little tune, Satin clumsily withdrew to the kitchen to make some tea according to a 'special Chinese recipe'.

Vasily Vasilyevich looked Sasha steadily in the eye and said: 'Alexander Borisovich, I want to have a confidential

– and at the same time completely official – conversation with you.'

There was a pause to give Sasha time to work that out, then he went on: 'I have already told you I knew your father. We did our postgraduate work at the same time, he in the Economics Faculty, I in the Arts Faculty. I don't praise people lightly, you know, Sasha, but you father was something else.

'We used to meet on Mikhovaya Street or at the Lenin library. We used to discuss Marx, Lenin – and Stalin! – and reflect on socialism. We hammered out the basic truths which were to underlie the foundations of our future life. I can't hide the fact that it wasn't all plain sailing. Boris Borisovich had a challenging, enquiring economist's mind. . . .'

The man sitting opposite in the blue leather armchair, could he really have been a fellow-student of Sasha's father?

'You have to understand, Alexander Borisovich,' Kassarin went on, 'that the struggle in society never died away. It is still going on at this very moment while you and I are drinking Cognac. The world is divided into two hostile camps, red and white, the socialist camp and the imperialist camp. Please, forgive the banalities.

'There can be only one victor in the struggle, of course. Marx said the reds would win, and I believe Marx. But, more than that, I believe our own great Russian – Ulyanov – Lenin, who discovered the remarkable truth: "The dictatorship of the proletariat is power unlimited by any laws, and this power rests on violence." You understand – on violence? Time has simply shifted the emphasis.

'At first, instead of the dictatorship of the proletariat, there was a different concept – the Communist Party. But that concept is just too big, too unwieldy. Now the dictatorship belongs to us, to State Security! We are the party within the Party because we are more organized, more competent that the Party as a whole. The KGB is the vanguard of the Communist Party of the Soviet Union!'

180

Sasha's stepfather's hand appeared round the door but disappeared at the mention of 'KGB'.

'I want this conversation to be in perfectly realistic terms.' Vasily Vasilyevich poured some Cognac, this time only for himself, and made it a pretty decent measure. 'At first I wanted to invite you into my office and have a word with you there, but I then decided that it would be better here. I know your stepfather and, more important, I knew your father. I bear a certain moral responsibility for you. . . .'

Kassarin got to his feet, straightened up and asked suddenly, his penetrating eyes boring into Sasha: 'This is the point – are you with us or against us?'

Sasha got up, too, and said in astonishment: 'I don't understand you, Vasily Vasilyevich. Do you doubt it? The Prosecutor's Office is part of the Party, and so I am with you.'

Kassarin's face darkened.

'The Prosecutor's Office is an appendage. What are your Prosecutor's Office or the Ministry of Justice worth? We created them to rake over the rubbish. I'm talking to you about the KGB, about our new, perfect party, which has at last come to power! Lenin and his party of Bolsheviks conquered Russia. We, the KGB and Andropov, will conquer the whole world!'

Sasha thought at first that he was unhinged, ready for a stint in the Serbsky Psychiatric Institute. He'd seen more than enough inmates from there in forensic psychiatry classes with Professor Bobrova. What had he got into?

Kassarin shook his head as if to clear his thoughts and said in a quite different, down-to-earth voice: 'Maybe I'm not making myself clear. You're not a political theorist, I know, so let's forget the politics. A simple question, then: will you agree to work for the KGB? That is, for me? I'll look after the formalities, don't worry.

'You'll have prospects that you couldn't even dream of working in the Justice Department. We get trips and work abroad, access to real power, valuables. . . . I wanted to take you on right away, but I couldn't – our rules don't permit it. We have to look closely, check cadres at work, and only then invite people to join.

'I've been watching you closely for a long time, examining your work in the special section of Moscow CID. We need intelligent people nowadays. We don't take fools and slobs any more. So what do you say?'

Sasha was at a loss. Parkhomenko this morning, and now a KGB general driving him into a corner. If at the April session of the commission that designated posts to young specialists he'd been offered a job in the KGB, he would have been as happy as a lottery-winner. But the General was practically poaching an employee of the Prosecutor's Office, for some secret purpose known only to him. It smelt rotten somehow.

'What do I have to do?' Sasha queried.

Kassarin smiled fleetingly. The rat-like transformation flickered over his face and was gone again.

'I'm in charge of "Operation Export". Have you heard of it?'

Sasha shrugged his shoulders.

'We're turning the Foreign Trade Ministry inside out, and all trade missions abroad. When Brezhnev's son was running the foreign trade operations he installed some out-and-out villains in our departments. They only bothered about themselves, didn't give a damn for the homeland, or the interests of the people and the State. They manipulated deals with American, Canadian, Japanese and other foreign firms. A lot of money – millions in hard currency – was lost to the Treasury.

'For the time being, we wouldn't want to take over the Rakitin case from the Public Prosecutor, but I have to know all that's going on. It'll be different once this business takes an international turn. When there's some foreign connection, I'll take it on officially.'

'But, Vasily Vasilyevich, why don't you talk to Merkulov direct about all this?'

'Merkulov works only for the Central Committee. He

182

wouldn't want any contact with us. He's already had one conflict with KGB Centre on another matter, and on that occasion the administrative section of the Party supported him, not us. The politics of the situation are complicated. Savinkin and Yemelyanov are afraid of the KGB's power and they'll do all they can to play up the role of the Public Prosecutor's Office of the Soviet Union. I've just received information that Malkov is being removed and Yuri Vladimirovich has confirmed Yemelyanov as new Public Prosecutor of Moscow.'

Sasha couldn't have cared less whom they'd appointed new Prosecutor. He had enough worries of his own.

He tried to imagine what Merkulov would do in his place. Well, first of all, he'd pull out a handkerchief and blow his nose, long and hard. And then he would cough just as long. And then he would give this rat-like creep such a mouthful he'd run off and hide in his stinking hole for ever. An exaggeration, of course; but, all the same, Merkulov would find a way out. Sasha couldn't.

'So what have I got to do exactly. Vasily Vasilyevich?'

'First of all, you've got to say just two words: "I agree." Secondly, sign a statement and, thirdly, answer all my questions truthfully and keep me informed about the investigation of the Rakitin case.'

Sasha took a deep breath.

'I agree.'

Kassarin took a sheet of paper out of the inside pocket of his grey jacket and put it on the edge of the table.

Statement

I, Alexander Borisovich Turetsky, born 1957, native of the city of Moscow, acting in the highest interests of the Soviet State, voluntarily agree to work for the organs of the Soviet State Security and to carry out only the personal instructions of the head of the Third Main Administration 'T' Committee of the KGB of the USSR, Major-General of State Security Comrade V. V. Kassarin. It has been made clear to me that in the event of my divulging state secrets and withholding information of state importance I can be held legally responsible under article 64 of the Criminal Code of the RSFSR, which may involve the ultimate punishment – death by firing squad.

A. TURETSKY
City of Moscow, 22 November 1982

Sasha pulled out his pen and signed his own death warrant – because he intended to 'divulge' the whole thing to Merkulov at the first opportunity. Thirty seconds later he could have been stood against a wall for 'withholding information' when Kassarin asked: 'Have you found the duplicates of Rakitin's papers?'

'No, we haven't.'

Sasha didn't know whether Kassarin believed him or not, but he took the statement, folded it in four and put it back in his inside pocket. Strangely, Sasha felt relieved. He was now firmly in the role of informer and traitor. A double agent, no less. A real James Bond. One of his masters was a KGB general. The other. . . . Was it Merkulov or himself? What did it matter anyway?

Sasha crossed his legs and said matter-of-factly: 'So you're putting me on Merkulov, are you?'

'I wasn't mistaken in you – you're smart,' said Kassarin approvingly. 'That's dead right. Find out what he's up to at any price. I must know any news five minutes before Kolya Savinkin does. If you cope with this assignment, if you can tell me where Rakitin's duplicate papers are and any other matters that come to light, it'll be good for both of us.'

'You'll be made a Hero of the Soviet Union and I'll get the Order of the Red Banner,' Sasha blurted out, surprised at his own insolence. The drink was fighting back. Thanks to it he kept up his impudent act and looked straight into Kassarin's expressionless eyes.

'Not far off the mark.'

'Vasily Vasilyevich, can you give me any guarantee that I won't do myself harm at the Prosecutor's Office.'

'Yes, I can.'

'What?'

'My word of honour. The word of honour of a KGB general.'

Sasha raised his eyebrows.

'Do you need anything more, Alexander Borisovich?' asked Kassarin, an unmistakable undertone to his voice.

Satin came into the room, humming his little dance-tune. He was carrying a tea service and a Kiev cake on a tray.

14

Moscow was quieter than ever on that dank November evening. Even right in the centre of Prospekt Marx, there weren't many pedestrians. A group of foreigners in the foyer of the fashionable Berlin Hotel was arguing with the manager. The grey-haired porter, sheltering from the cold at the back of his booth, was reading the evening paper. The sound of lively music came from the basement restaurant.

It was really noisy down there. The diners were talking animatedly, the waiters were bustling about everywhere, and the famous Heller Jazz Orchestra was blasting out variations of the tune 'Bubliki'.

A party of well-dressed people was eating at the back of the room about ten metres from the ornamental pool and fountain containing live fish. The table was laid for twelve people with fine hors-d'œuvres, bottles of Cognac and vodka. Two well-disciplined waiters tactfully withdrew when a tall thickset man stood up and began to speak. He spoke softly but quite clearly, with a barely noticeable Baltic accent.

At three minutes past ten, a young man in a blue sports coat came into the restaurant, glanced across at the foreigners crowded round the reception desk, slipped the porter something and turned to the right down into the basement.

There was nothing particularly noteworthy about the man. A Muscovite like any other, with fifty roubles in his pocket, had decided to drink a drop of export vodka and eat some sturgeon. No one looked twice at him, and he looked neither to left nor to right. He walked past the orchestra, past the manager, mumbled something to the waiter and then went coolly over to the long table where the party was seated.

He went up very close to a thin red-haired man sitting at the right-hand corner of the table, and touched him on the shoulder. The redhead turned, apparently recognized the new arrival, got up and went with him over to the ornamental pool where an elderly waiter was trying to catch a mirror carp with a net.

The conversation between the two men was brief, lasting no more than about two minutes. The red-haired man shouted something and ran back towards the table, but before he could reach it he collapsed to the floor. The man making the speech turned his head to see who was interrupting him, but suddenly staggered himself, falling on to the table, where his clean-shaven cheek landed in a dish of satsivi garnished with parsley.

No one noticed the soft reports of the two shots, which were drowned out by a roll on the drums and the strident tones of the saxophone and trumpet. The newcomer slipped the long-barrelled gun under his blue sports coat, turned and walked calmly to the exit by the same route as he had arrived. In the hall, he nodded to the grey-haired porter, who was engrossed in reading the accident reports in the paper. He held the door open for a foreign lady, testifying not so much to his good breeding as to his extraordinary self-possession, and then faded into the rainy Moscow night.

The black-moustached Caucasian and his student lady-friend, who were sitting three tables away from the party, froze with their glasses of champagne in their hands. They'd been about to link arms and drink to a closer relationship but never made it.

The red-haired man was killed outright, the tall thickset man was only wounded. When the terrified waiters and guests sat him on a chair he groaned, 'God, it hurts!' and added something else that was not in Russian.

15

Sasha opened the door into the bedroom. His mother was sitting on a chair by a low table on which there was a typewriter with a sheet of paper threaded in it.

She raised her head and whispered: 'Have they gone?'

'Yes,' he answered, for some reason also in a whisper.

His mother jumped up from her chair, opened her wardrobe and pulled out a packet containing nylon tights. She wrenched out the cardboard the pair of tights was displayed on.

'What are you doing, Mother?'

Glued to the back of the cardboard was an envelope. Without a word, his mother slid it quickly into Sasha's inside jacket pocket. Then she put the tights back in the packet and stashed them away in the wardrobe.

'What is this?'

'Sasha, I played the hardest part of my whole life today. I think he believed me. Do you think he believed me?'

'What are you talking about?'

'Don't ask questions; just read that, then do what you like with it. Keep it, or throw it away or, better still, burn it. I think Pavel has come back – I heard the lift. Not another word.'

They could hear him singing outside in the corridor.

'Pavel, be quiet. It's past midnight!'

'Why? Why be quiet? Sasha, come here. Let's have another little drop. There's nothing wrong with going a bit over the top when you've made the acquaintance of someone like him. What a man that Vasily is! A real prince! The way's wide open for you now – you're on the way up, son.'

Satin handed Sasha a glass, but he didn't drink, just placed it carefully back on the table. His stepfather drained his glass, scooped up some caviare with a spoon, ate it, then belched noisily.

'You've had enough, Pavel,' said his wife, clearing the table. 'Go and lie down. I'll make up a bed for Sasha on the divan in the dining room.'

'Yes, sir, your Exce-llency' said Satin with a hiccup. 'See how she orders me about, Sasha? But I still obey. You know how I respect your mother. I don't begrudge her anything. . . .'

'Oh, you don't, eh? She's up banging out something on her typewriter now because she can't get money out of you. And she gave up the theatre because of you – her going on tour didn't suit you, the Othello of the Sports Industry. . . .'

Sasha waited until it was quiet in the apartment and then went to the bathroom. He put down the toilet lid, sat on it and pulled out the envelope.

My only love, my Lena. My son, Sasha. You will never forgive me for what I intend to do to myself. My Lena, my life, you must know one thing, that if I stayed alive it would be worse for you. And our son could never live down his father's shame. I have no proof, so there is only one way – may our son never know the truth.

I ask just one thing: if you hear the name Vasily Kassarin, then run away from him, hide. And hide Sasha. Kassarin is a villain and a murderer. And I've only just discovered the worst of it –

188

Kassarin works for the security organs! I was fool enough to share with him my innermost thoughts, as I would with my own brother. I've just discovered the full horror of it: all of our group from university, committed members of an organisation whose aim was to struggle for the spiritual rejuvenation of Russia, have been arrested. It is all the work of Kassarin, and my doing, too, since I was the unwitting informer. How can I expunge my shame? How can I prove to my friends that there was no intention on my part that they should be arrested, condemned and killed? I see no other way but one.

They're coming for me, too, now. But I'm not afraid of arrest and trial. I fear only the contempt of my friends and of dying in the bitter knowledge that evil is so strong and will go unpunished. Who will avenge me?

Goodbye, my dear ones. Forgive me, if you can. Thank you, Lena, for your love, and for everything.

Your
BORIS

At first Sasha thought it was a bad joke, a piece of cheap fiction like dozens he had read. He kept rereading the letter, twice, three times, ten times, until he finally got the sense of what was written there. His mother had known that this Kassarin was the one his father had written about. And he'd been checking her out: 'We were great friends.'

Sasha looked at the envelope – it was postmarked Archangel, 21 November 1962. Twenty years ago. What an anniversary!

Back in the dining room, he hid the letter away in his jacket then sat on the divan for a long time, his mind a complete blank.

At that moment his mother was probably curled sleepless on the edge of the bed, punishing herself. Her husband had ordered her to hide and to hide their son, and she had brought Kassarin and Sasha together after all those years. He got undressed and crawled under the blanket, but he could not sleep. The ceiling kept flickering with squares of light reflected from the headlights of passing cars. Everything went hazy and began to swim before his eyes. Too much vodka.

Sasha closed his eyes and started a waking dream – a funny clown was playing copper cymbals and whistling some sad-joyful tune. He realised it was not a dream but a recollection. He opened his eyes again. The clown was whistling, and someone next to him was saying: 'Just like before the war!' Had there really been a war? 'Just like before the war, Lena, isn't that right?'

Tum, tum, tee-tum . . . Sasha remembered. He was at the puppet theatre in Sokolniki Park with his mother and father. He was five. They lived on Stromynka Street in those days, close by.

He looked at his watch; it was half-past two. He lit a cigarette but put it out immediately – there was a horrible taste in his mouth. Still two and a half hours to go before he could ring Petrovka.

He got dressed quietly and went outside to stand on the corner of Leninsky Prospekt. A taxi came by about twenty minutes later. He got in and gave the driver Rita's address.

KASSARIN AND OTHERS

1

23 November 1982

Merkulov liked to say that good management meant seeing ahead. He'd worked out a foolproof plan for the surprise search of Georgadze's house. There was no chance of the slightest hitch. He'd foreseen everything, it seemed: the weather, the mood of the great man himself, the number of guards at the house, their degrees of devotion to the boss. . . .

Merkulov even incorporated a special co-efficient which he called 'the chance factor', which meant that each member of the team, including junior officer Turetsky, was authorized to deal with any unexpected eventuality as swiftly and effectively as possible using his own judgement.

It was still completely black, impenetrable night when the CID driver rang Rita's doorbell and told Sasha that his carriage awaited him. By then she'd managed to sober him up with strong black coffee and liver salts. He hadn't felt like sleeping, still less like leaving Rita's apartment. They sat in the kitchen before dawn, talking about his father, Merkulov, Kassarin. . . . Rita's expression was inscrutable, her eyes blank.

Sasha went down to the car. The CID Volga took him through sleeping Moscow from the Frunzenskaya Embankment to Petrovka. After a fifteen-minute conference in Romanova's office, the ops team poured out on to the street and got into two cars.

Moscow was dead. There was not a single pedestrian or car by the Hermitage Garden. A strong wind tore scraps off posters depicting the ugly faces of Muslim Magomayev, Alla Pugacheva and Ludmilla Zykina pasted to round hoardings along Petrovka. It was a real winter wind, cutting and teasing as if trying to say: 'Hang around here long enough, friend, and the frost will get even harder'.

Major Krasnikovsky was at the wheel as the patrol car sped through the silent side-streets.

'I wonder if I turned my kettle off before I left home?' said Merkulov suddenly.

Krasnikovsky glanced briefly at the Investigator sitting next to him.

'Don't worry, Konstantin Dmitriyevich. This operation is going to be a big success. . . .'

Following the first patrol Volga carrying Romanova, Panyushkin and Rex, Merkulov's car turned on to Sadovo-Samotechnaya Street by the Polish trade mission. Here the police car in front turned on its hazard lights and, at full speed, siren wailing, tore off in the direction of the Moscow ring-road, which led directly to the 'village' of the Supreme Soviet. The second car followed closely. A reluctant dawn started to break over Moscow – not an opportune time to rouse the second-in-command of the Soviet people's state and search his house. . . .

Magomayov's baritone voice crackled over the radio, while Krasnikovsky and Potekhin argued themselves hoarse about Georgian cooking. Only Merkulov and Sasha stayed silent.

Sasha wasn't too keyed up about the forthcoming search, and the policemen's views on sulguni and satsivi didn't exactly thrill him, either. He took no interest in Magomayov's singing. There was something preying on his mind, some half-remembered snippet from his childhood, possibly to do with his father. Why did he feel uneasy as though his life depended on remembering it?

What, in fact, did he remember about his father? And what had happened to him? From what his mother always said, Sasha's father had died in a flying accident when he was a small boy. He had finished his postgraduate degree with distinction and was working on a thesis on some important economics project – apparently his proposals would bring about a revolution in the country's planned economy, and lead to a tremendous rise in labour productivity and the production of consumer goods. He went to Archangel to try out his ideas on a newly created state farm, and worked there in the north for six months. He went off to some remote district in connection with his work, flying in a U-2. The accident occurred over the sea; the wreckage of the aircraft, together with the pilot and his only passenger sank without trace, so Sasha had never even visited his father's grave.

Evil, which had figured more than once in his childhood dreams as something diffuse and ephemeral, suddenly assumed tangible form. Evil now had a first name, and a surname, and the rank of general.

At that instant, while his head was full of the man who had destroyed his father, another connection was made. Lyosha, too, had talked about Kassarin! He was the rat-like man who had carried out the search of the Rakitins' apartment.

Kassarin really was a rat – a big cunning monster rat! Funny how you only noticed it when he smiled. Or, perhaps, strange and terrifying. . . . Usually a man, even if he is not good-looking, lights up when he smiles. But this man, handsome in repose, showed the rat-like depths of his character just when he bared his teeth in a would-be friendly smile.

Sasha felt sick. The main thing in the duel with Kassarin was not to do anything stupid, not make any sudden moves. He would be restrained and methodical, tell Merkulov everything and get his advice. . . .

They were approaching Georgadze's country residence. Thirty seconds left before the operation started in earnest.

'I like karsky best of all the shashlyks!' Krasnikovsky was saying.

Sixteen seconds. . . .

'No, Comrade Major, ordinary Caucasian shashlyk is great, much better than karsky,' retorted Potekhin. 'The meat's juicier. . . .'

Eight seconds. . . .

'I'm very fond of spare ribs, especially with tkemali sauce,' Sasha put in distractedly.

Three, two, one!

Georgadze's residence was just what they'd expected. Only part of it was visible from the road: a three-storey building, garish and showy, with fancy ironwork round the balconies and windows, and highly coloured orchids in the mosaic friezes on the façade.

'God, it's monstrous!' exclaimed Romanova, coming over to Merkulov's Volga. They stood in a small circle, waiting for his last-second instructions.

The greater part of the house was shielded by a line of evergreen spruces, very high and unusually thick. Beyond this was a custom-built fence, also very high, made of steel. Georgadze's property seemed excessively large, even for a Soviet Secretary's. The sprawling garden that stretched down to a huge lake was more like a public park.

'Ladies and gentlemen, at one time this house belonged to a filthy capitalist, a merchant called Ryabushinsky,' said the omniscient Krasnikovsky as if he were a tourist guide.

There was a green sentry-box at the main entrance, in imitation of those to be found outside foreign embassies. The security man on duty, a lieutenant from the ninth division in police uniform, came out and walked over to them. He looked like a raven with its feathers ruffled. He was all in black – a black sheepskin coat down to his ankles, black felt boots and galoshes, and a black fur hat with the earflaps down.

'What do you want? You can't come in here. Can't you see you're on government property!' he said in a lazy drawl, and pointed out to them with his black-gloved hand the sign saying 'Government property – entry strictly forbidden'.

Shura Romanova stepped forward. She was in full uniform today, and even had her greatcoat open so you could see her high bosom with all its orders and medals pinned on it, jingling with every step she took.

'I am Lieutenant-Colonel Romanova. I have a package for Comrade Georgadze, an urgent one. Nikolai Anisi- movich Shchelokov has ordered me to hand it over to Mikhail Porfiryevich personally.'

'What did you say your name was?' asked the miserable little lieutenant though they were sure he had heard everything perfectly the first time.

'Romanova, from the Ministry of Internal Affairs,' repeated Shura quite calmly, without any of her custo- mary irritation. 'It's a package from the Minister himself.'

Looking at Romanova – and the rest of them, for that matter – with all the contempt of a military timeserver, the lieutenant strode over to his box, his feet dragging heavily in their felt boots.

In another minute, he would be calling for reinforce- ments. Sasha caught his breath. Shura scraped her booted feet on the ground. Krasnikovsky eased the safety-catch off the gun in his pocket. Potekhin's stomach rumbled loudly – he must have been thinking about shash- lyk in tkemali sauce. Panyushkin swore. Only the bravest of them were totally silent. Rex the Alsatian, and Special Crimes Investigator Merkulov. . . .

The gates were closed. The guards were most probably at the ready by now with their Kalashnikov automatics trained down on the gateway. The Raven was on his way to the telephone. Sasha could not imagine how they would carry out a search under these conditions.

At last Merkulov blew his nose noisily in the pre- arranged signal. Obeying the command, Krasnikovsky, Potekhin and Sasha went up the steps of the entrance porch.

'You can't go there! Come down, right now!' barked the Raven, holding the telephone receiver and the grip of his gun at the same time.

But Shura's gun, pointed straight at his heart, forced him into silence. Merkulov took him from behind and crushed his arms to his sides so hard that he yelled:

'Ah-ah, that hurts. You're breaking my arms, Comr-a-de!'

While Merkulov and Romanova were bending his arms behind his back and tying them, Major Krasnikovsky backed off from the door to the entrance porch, staring intently as if bent on hypnotising it. While they'd been working out the plan, they had learnt that Krasnikovsky had a passion for smashing down doors.

The Major took a few steps back and steadied his left shoulder against the sentry-box behind which Merkulov, Panyushkin and Romanova were bedding the lieutenant down for the night. Potekhin copied Krasnikovsky.

The ex-champion light-heavyweight of the Dynamo sports club half-squatted, stiffened, then put his right shoulder forward.

No one could have foreseen what happened in the next minute – exactly what Merkulov had dubbed 'the chance factor'.

Meeting no resistance, Major Krasnikovsky charged head first through the annexe leading into the grounds of the estate, and met head on with the door – which turned out to be open. Obeying the laws of inertia, the Major's hefty frame described a somersault in the air and the deputy chief of the section went arse-first into the garden on the other side of the fence. By some sleight of hand, Krasnikovsky managed to pull out his gun in mid-air and get off a shot, after which he hung by his trousers from the branches of a tree growing next to the annexe.

The rest of them were inside. Glancing quickly round the premises Sasha was convinced that there was no one there: no security men or police.

Then a half-clothed man came running out of the house, alarmed by the shot. He was probably the head of the guard whom the Raven had intended to phone. Waving a gun high above his head, he screamed hysterically in a Georgian accent: 'Bandits! Don't move. You're surrounded! Drop your guns!'

The Georgian fired and hit a street-lamp. The glass

196

shattered with an incredible din – and a hail of fragments came raining down on the search party's heads, especially Krasnikovsky's who was still dangling from the tree.

The usually phlegmatic Rex had had enough. He barked hysterically and, without waiting for the command, went for the chief guard. The dog moved like greased lightning. Almost simultaneously an inhuman cry echoed round the neighbourhood. Rex had sunk his teeth into the guard's hand and then, once the soldier had dropped his gun, into what forensic scientists term 'the soft tissue of the body situated below the back'.

Two more men came running out of the house. They had managed to get dressed but not to size up the situation. So they started blazing away at poor Rex, who was now dragging their boss back to his handler. The shots struck the earth beside him, and the dog sat on its haunches and howled in fear. Strange – he was a police dog, after all! In the heat of the moment, it seemed that there were two Rexes – one safe and sound next to his handler, the other howling in no man's land. But the second four-legged figure was quickly revealed to be the captain of the guard; in the commotion, his men had shot him in the calf.

Krasnikovsky finally extricated himself from the branches of the tree and rushed over to the main entrance of the villa. He would have burst into the house if he had not tripped over the wounded soldier on his way and measured his Herculean length along the porch beside him.

Everything went quiet. The search party's major and the captain of the guard lay side by side in the porch, battered, wounded and utterly debilitated. But the brains of these two glorious law enforcers were still intact. They had a talk, intoning Andropov's name in various ways, and reaching identical conclusions: both parties were law enforcers. One might have arrived to get Georgadze, the other might have been guarding him, but they were both acting under orders from Comrade Andropov and consequently the firing could stop.

At that moment, from somewhere upstairs in the house, boomed an authoritative voice.

'Captain, what is it? What's the matter? Whatever's going on out there, eh?'

A majestic figure in an ankle-length dressing gown appeared on the porch. Mikhail Porfiryevich Georgadze, in person.

Georgadze was about seventy, but looked younger: tall, lean, with the fine aristocratic features of a Georgian prince, and a mocking expression in his dark eyes.

The search party entered the hall of the house, and suddenly it filled with people. They just appeared from nowhere, milling about and making an incredible noise. Waves of hostility towards the newcomers rolled off them like tear-gas.

As if not noticing the rest of the party, Georgadze was looking at Merkulov, the experienced eye of a senior bureaucrat pinpointing him as the leader of the deputation.

'Well, then,' asked Georgadze, 'what can I do for you?'

'This is a search warrant,' said Merkulov, handing him a piece of paper. All the domestic servants laughed as if on cue – but not Georgadze. He gave the slightest smile and squinted as he examined the warrant. When he had finished reading, he thought hard, looked Merkulov over from head to toe, and let slip the sheet of paper, which glided down on to the carpet.

'I haven't got time for this charade. I'm in a hurry to get to the Kremlin. I'm being re-elected as Secretary to the Praesidium today.'

At that very moment the phone rang. A woman's voice upstairs shouted something in Georgian, and Georgadze went up to the first floor.

Five minutes later the same woman, this time speaking Russian, asked the party to go up to Georgadze's study.

The spacious carpeted room was hung alternately with portraits of Politburo members and pictures by famous artists – Savrasov, Kustodiev, Levitan and Aivazovsky.

There were sculptures by prominent craftsmen and so many books that the room resembled something between a museum and a millionaire's library.

Half-turned away from them, the owner sat in a high-backed armchair behind his expensive desk with the half-dozen telephones on it. His hand was still gripping the red one – the Kremlin hot line – and he was staring into space.

Seating themselves in armchairs around the desk, they saw that Georgadze was not looking into space at all but at the portrait of Andropov hanging over the door. Next to it hung another portrait, that of his immediate predecessor, now deceased, Leonid Brezhnev. The portrait was edged in black crêpe.

'It's not me, it's you he's removing,' said Georgadze slowly to the black-edge portrait. 'Do you hear me, my dear unforgettable friend? Remember what I, Mikhail, said to you? You must not allow that man to get close to you . . . he's bad . . . You didn't listen. He's not a Russian or a Jew or a Georgian, he's an Armenian – the worst kind of traitor!'

Merkulov fixed his eyes on Georgadze. 'Are you unwell, Mikhail Porfiryevich? Shall we call a doctor?'

Taking his hand from the telephone, Georgadze reassured him with a wave.

'Well, unwell, what's the difference? What's it matter to me? I can't go on living now. A Caucasian can't go on living after this kind of disgrace. Georgadze's house searched! How can I look people in the face again?

'Please carry on with the search, if Andropov has sanctioned it. Don't be afraid; we won't shoot. I'll order my people not to. I'll tell you something extraordinary. You will find a million, five million, ten million roubles here: trinkets, jewellery, paintings. . . . It's not mine. You see, people trust me. They bring me things to look after for a time. Is that a crime? The trinkets and paintings come from museums and they'll go back to them when I die.'

Georgadze fell silent. He was breathing heavily and

looked pale, crushed. His hand pressed feebly against his chest.

Sasha thought they should call a doctor and go away without carrying out the search. They called a doctor – then they carried out the search.

They went all over the villa, amazed by what they saw. It was not so much a villa, more a small palace with countless rooms. And they were luxurious despite the pretentious architecture – little towers and turrets and merlons everywhere. They found more than Kustodievs and Aivazovskys on the walls; there were innumerable treasures brought from various storerooms of the Moscow Kremlin, the Hermitage and the Historical Museum: paintings by Rubens, Van Dyck, Rublev, Leonardo da Vinci; gold and silver work by the greatest masters of the Gothic and Renaissance periods; Tsarist dinner services with Nicholas II's crest upon them; precious stones neither emperors nor oil magnates would sneer at.

What they found in the basement, which resembled a medium-sized Soviet savings bank, shook them all – even Rex. There were really untold riches in metal deposit-boxes stacked on metal shelves. They took it in turns to make out the inventory, including in it all obvious valuables, their trembling fingers opening packages carefully tied with silk ribbon of various colours.

To make out the list, they unpacked precious rings, ear-rings, brooches, pendants and necklaces from cotton-wool shrouds, and then put them carefully back to rest.

They also discovered about forty million Soviet roubles, two million in foreign currency, a hundred gold bars, and jewels weighing about eight kilograms, or forty thousand carats of top-quality stones.

Some of them were uncut South African diamonds. . . .

2

After a sleepless night and a hard morning, Sasha slept for about two hours without even dreaming. He was woken at three o'clock by the insistent ringing of the telephone. There was a domestic row going on in the apartment, and no one could be bothered to take the call.

'Yes!' he shouted, running out into the corridor and snatching up the receiver.

'We've got some news,' said Merkulov.

'It had better be good.'

Merkulov cleared his throat.

'I've just been told that Yuri Yurevich Leonovich was killed in a restaurant yesterday. We really fucked things up there. And that's not all.'

'There's more bad news?'

'Georgadze died an hour ago.'

'Died?'

'That's right. This afternoon he was at a session of the Supreme Soviet, and Andropov called him in during an interval. Apparently he wanted an explanation of the "bank" and the search. Georgadze shouted, collapsed, and the doctors pronounced him dead. I'm going to the Central Committee now, waiting for Yemelyanov. We're going in with Savinkin to see Andropov soon.'

Sasha was remembering the look on the old man's face as he stared up at the two portraits.

'I'm going to be out of circulation for today, Sasha,' Merkulov continued, 'at least till this evening. So will you go over to Petrovka now, room 625? The head of the Anti-Corruption Squad, Abrikosov, has taken an interest in the Soya-Serko robbery.

'You'll have two people assigned to you, Pogorelov from CID – he's just back from holiday – and Grechannik from the Anti-Corruption Squad. Grechannik tells me you know each other.'

Sasha certainly did know Zhosef Grechannik. The

showy bigmouth had been a well-known personality in his faculty, running the mass cultural section of the trade union committee, and graduating from Moscow State a year before Sasha. He'd have thought the man would be in the KGB by now.

'Then go over to the Sklifosovsky Institute and question the businessman who was wounded in the restaurant when they shot Leonovich. Then come back to the Prosecutor's Office. I'll be there by evening.'

Sasha shivered like a dog, standing on the icy floor. The loony old women he lived with had left the corridor window wide open for some reason. He went back to bed for a minute to get warm and collect his thoughts. The cold prevented him from concentrating and getting the priorities right. Everything was jumbled up in his head – Rakitin, Kassarin, his father, Leonovich, Georgadze. . . .

He felt quite different from the callow youth worrying about his jeans and impressing Rita only days before.

'Comrade Turetsky, we need your help!' Someone was wailing from outside his room.

Oh, God. He'd better get up and get dressed. He had to go over to Petrovka anyway.

He went out into the corridor. Fat Polina Vasilyevna Korobitsyn was hanging out of the window, exhibiting her violet bloomers. The Vixen – that is, Angelina Garyevna Fox – was wailing hysterically while holding on to Polina's leg. Sasha had some difficulty pulling the fat old woman back in.

The Fox woman had dropped a pan of cutlets out of the window; they were the property of the Korobitsyn sisters, who were determined to reach them from the roof of the neighbouring house. Polina had just been stopped in time. Sasha climbed out of the window. The roof was slippery and steep, about fifteen cutlets strewn over its ice-covered surface. He gathered up whatever was within easy reach – about ten – and scrambled back into the apartment. Gratefully, the old woman gave him tea and some pie.

3

'Yes, yes, dear. I understand everything. So he was playing that part, Alain Delon? Well, that's very interesting.'

Erich Karlovich Abrikosov, the forty-five-year-old head of the Moscow Anti-Corruption Squad, was sitting in his office at Petrovka, talking on the phone. Grechannik and Sasha were waiting patiently for the conversation to end so that they could discuss with the General the forthcoming operations regarding the Soya-Serko case and the others which, as a result of Volin's testimony, had been passed on to the anti-corruption squad.

The whole of Petrovka knew that young Major-General Abrikosov was a notorious womaniser. He frequently spent the night away from home on the pretext of dangerous night-time operations, while actually taking a girlfriend out of town to spend the night at a government villa. Now he was talking to his wife, holding the phone to his ear with his shoulder and studying some papers while he spoke. It took the General's wife another five minutes to finish her account of the film.

'Yes, yes, Nina, all very interesting. No, dear, don't wait dinner for me. I've got a very important job on tonight.'

At last, Abrikosov turned his attention to work.

'There was a shooting yesterday in the old "Savoy". Some speculators fell out over the spoils, it seems. The usual thing. Yuri Leonovich, a very big fish, is dead. I've been after him for a long, long time! Would have had him months ago if it hadn't been for "the other firm".

'But we've still got work to do on the man. We may not have got to the bottom of him alive, but we'll do it now he's dead. I've already rounded up ten of his cronies, speculating in kerchiefs for him and buying up paintings. Butyrki Prison will soon loosen their tongues for them. They'll tell me who Yuri was working for, and who he was trading with. I don't doubt that you, Comrade Prosecutors, together with the KGB, will catch the villain who finally settled his account!'

Sasha mumbled something incoherent and lit a cigarette. Meanwhile Abrikosov embarked on an impassioned monologue. He should have been an actor.

'He was a cautious man. Always used others to do his dirty work. But, then, there you are. The one time he comes to the secondhand shop himself, he's nailed!'

With gleaming boots, and spurs ringing (and what the hell did an Anti-Corruption general need spurs for?), Erich Karlovich strode over the thick Persian carpet, which had been requisitioned during a search of the house of the manager of the Tadzhikistan store. He opened the safe, took out a canvas bag and, grabbing the corners skilfully, turned it upside down. It was a real horn of plenty. A bright shower of precious metals and jewels cascaded on to the desk.

'Well, now, Comrades, let's have a look and see if there are any odds and ends from Soya-Serko's collection here.'

'There is,' Sasha sighed, recognising a bracelet in coloured enamel, a Sinhalese brooch, and a golden statuette of a ballerina.

'Now, then, Comrade Prosecutors,' said Abrikosov in a satisfied voice, virtually snatching back the statuette from Sasha's hands. 'Please note that it wasn't the CID boys who pulled this one off. This is down to me!'

The Anti-Corruption Squad, like the Moscow CID, was housed in Petrovka 38. They shared the same entrance hall and canteen. But on the commemorative plaque in the hall where the names of heroes are etched in gold they were unrepresented. They did not go in for firearms training, unarmed combat and arm-twisting.

These intellectuals of the Ministry of Internal Affairs have a different way of doing things. It's all a matter of the enemy they're dealing with, of course. Their enemy is himself an intellectual. Crude CID tactics won't work with the businessman. Without any knowledge of the Soviet economic system, you can't beat the speculator.

That's why, these days, the Anti-Corruption Squad employed only selected people, almost like the KGB. People with a higher education, like Zhozef Grechannik, now sitting opposite Sasha.

'And how did you come across that collection, Comrade General?' asked Zhozef, turning over the Sinhalese brooch in his hands.

'You can see for yourself what the weather's like. A removal van ran into a high-voltage cable last night. Do you know where? On the former estate of Natalya Goncharova, Pushkin's wife, in Lopasnya, just by Serpukhov.'

The General picked up the report lying in front of him and started to read in a well-modulated voice.

' "As a result of the collision, the doors and the panelling of the van burst open. Cases of goods were thrown in all directions, even over the fence of an old country estate cemetery. Among the packages picked up by us marked 'Made in USSR' were antique jewellery, icons, religious items, paintings, gold and silver coins, ivory articles, silver tea sets, Caucasian coinage and weapons. That is, valuables prohibited from export. . . ." '

Sasha still did not altogether understand how the items from Soya-Serko's collection turned up in the van, but Abrikosov stood up and said: 'Now go over to the Sklifosovsky Institute. You'll have to question that businessman Mazer – a real roasting! I would go with you but I've got to be in ten places at once. Thank Kostya Merkulov for giving us Volin. He's quite a gem, is Volin.

'He's giving us so much evidence about the Hippodrome, the Elisei Food Store and Pavlov of the Sports Committee that we've hardly got time to do all the questioning, inform the security boys, and send in the auditors. . . .'

Abrikosov was off again, but one thought bore in on Sasha. Why Leonovich, the very man they were breaking their necks to get? If he was killed precisely because they wanted him, then someone had pointed the finger. Someone knew that they had unearthed Leonovich. . . .

Sasha felt his ears begin to burn, then his face, neck, and even his hands. It was him. He had pointed the finger at Leonovich when he'd leant on that Soya-Serko bitch and told her to remember Yuri. Well, she had, and served him up with all the trimmings! They had to do something about her, fast!

'Prosecutor you haven't by any chance got a touch of this Asian flu that's about, have you? You're very flushed.'

'No, don't worry. Lack of sleep, that's all,' Sasha said, averting his face. 'And then there was the search this morning. . . .'

'Yes, yes,' said the General with an understanding nod. 'I've been told about the search . . . and about the bereavement we have all suffered.'

4

In front of the main block of the Sklifosovsky Institute, several ambulances were parked randomly. Injured people were brought here from all over Moscow to be patched up and sent home again, or else they were taken out feet first down to the basement.

Now was visiting time, and a crowd of people was trying to get through the narrow side-door. Two police sergeants, instead of opening the wide main doors and thus restoring order in a minute, were pushing people away from the entrance. Grechannik nodded to the policemen, and he and Sasha went into the building through the parting crowd.

A fat man of indeterminate age, dressed in a soft grey suit, stood at the enquiry desk in the hall. When he saw them, he said: 'Pogorelov from Moscow CID. I've been expecting you for some time.'

Pogorelov chose Sasha to take by the arm and lead to the lift. Once inside, he pressed up close and, smelling of garlic and vodka, asked in a whisper: 'Have you received any instructions from "the other firm"?'

Sasha shrugged his shoulders and spoke, like Pogorelov, in a whisper. 'No, none. We've just been sent by Abrikosov. He said to spin things out until he got some more evidence on this businessman.'

'He won't crack,' said Pogorelov hoarsely. 'I spent five hours with him, and you can hear the result.' He drew a puffy hand across his throat. 'I lost my voice and he ain't talking. Not a word. Rashilin's working on him now.'

In the private ward marked 'No unauthorized person', on a bed fitted with a table covered with standard Soviet metal dishes of hospital food, sat a large balding blond man. His left arm was bandaged and hung in a black sling across his chest.

The foreigner did not like hospital food, judging by the untouched dishes. A tall man with horn-rimmed glasses sat next to him on a white chair, an open dossier on his lap.

Captain Rashilin turned out to be an investigator from the Moscow directorate of the KGB, and he was their man in charge of the Leonovich murder and the attempted murder of Mazer himself. As he asked each question, he carefully noted the answers on an interrogation form.

The three of them stood by the window so as not to disturb the KGB man. There was a good view of the Sadovoye ring-road, and the radio goods store over which a neon sign flashed. They did not interfere with the KGB man's conversation with Albert Mazer.

'When did all this happen?'

'I've told you already. About five past ten.'

'Who did you come to the restaurant with? A woman?'

'With some women and some men,' answered Mazer in good Russian with hardly an accent; he obviously did not need an interpreter for the interrogation.

'Give me their names and addresses,' said the KGB captain, already noting something on the form, although the man being interrogated had not even opened his mouth yet.

'I've already answered that question for Mr Pogorelov.'

'We may ask you the same questions, but our work is different. Pogorelov and Moscow CID are looking for the murderers, but we are conducting the investigation. I've already explained Soviet law to you: cases involving foreigners are handled by the organs of state security,' explained Rashilin with robot-like calm. 'Would you please answer me, Mr Mazer?'

'Very well, I repeat! I was with employees of the Chamber of Commerce and the Ministry of Foreign Trade. What do you Russians say? We were "wetting the head" of a new business deal. The minutes of the meeting had been agreed with the management side. Mr Sushkov, the Deputy Minister of Foreign Trade of the USSR, will confirm that.'

Ignoring this point-scoring, Rashilin asked: 'Where were you when the stranger came in?'

'I was at the table. We had been put near the pool with the crucian – no, what do you call them? – the carp.'

'Can you give us a description of the man who did the shooting?'

'No, unfortunately, I can't. I had just proposed a toast to friendship, to mutual understanding, to peace between the West and the Soviet Union—'

'And what about your companions? Do you think they knew him?'

'No, I don't think they did.' The blond man's face twisted momentarily, and he put his fingers to his bad arm. 'Unless Yuri Yurevich, the deceased—'

'Tell me, Mr Mazer, what illegal deals were you and Leonovich involved in?' asked Rashilin brusquely with another penetrating look.

The eyes of the KGB man did not frighten Mazer. He

208

answered without looking away: 'There were no deals with Mr Yuri—'

Captain Rashilin suddenly stopped writing, leant back in his chair wearily, and said: 'Your turn, Comrade Prosecutor!'

He placed his papers in a leatherbound file with the monogram 'To Captain Rashilin from his workmates, on his thirtieth birthday', then stood up, whispered something to Grechannik, and walked briskly out of the ward.

Now it was Sasha's turn. He knew – or, rather, he had a hunch – that the KGB and the Anti-Corruption Squad, either separately or together, were behind this game with Mazer, the rules of which remained unclear to him. While he was putting his papers in order and reflecting on where to start in order to show Grechannik how good he was, Grechannik proved how good *he* was.

He started taking Abrikosov's 'trinkets' out of his modern document-case – the comb, an ivory set of some sort, and other material evidence. Mazer looked at it all without any apparent interest. Grechannik put the collection of valuables on the hospital side-table and proceeded to read aloud the testimony of the van-driver, who alleged that it was none other than Mr Mazer who had entrusted him to smuggle the bag of valuables over the Soviet frontier.

Mazer listened to all this very carefully. After Grechannik banged his folder of reports shut, Mazer stayed silent for a long time. The ward was so quiet, they could hear a pigeon cooing outside on the window-sill.

'I have known Mrs Soya-Serko for several years now,' he began tonelessly. Sasha snatched up his pen and paper and began recording Mazer's evidence, word for word.

'I often visited her magnificent apartment in the Arbat district, where we made agreements about exchanging goods. I met Mr Leonovich only afterwards, introduced by Alla Alexandrovna. That was in Moscow, too, in the autumn of 1979. I had a business – no, commercial – relationship with him. Our operations consisted primarily of my importing into the USSR on several occasions personal items for employees in our embassy here and, in significant quantities, ladies lurex headscarves, artificial fur coats, American denim suits, velvet trousers manufactured in France, video-cassettes, Orient and Seiko watches, and other goods.

'In return, Leonovich prepared consignments of icons, pictures, silver coins, various religious items and antiques for me. I despatched these goods to Europe in our embassy's vans, or resorted to assistance from the Soviet road haulage organisation, Leonovich providing the drivers.

'So far as the diamond comb and the carved ivory set are concerned, I bought them from Mrs Soya-Serko in the Ukraine Hotel at the end of last month. In order to get these valuables through customs you need official documentation saying that they're not particularly valuable, and so on. That's why Leonovich took me to his acquaintance who managed a secondhand store. It was no problem for him to get the documentation. Mrs Soya-Serko waited for us in her Zhiguli outside.'

When Sasha had taken down Mazer's statement, he asked one question.

'Did you know engineer Rakitin of the Ministry of Foreign Trade?'

'What's his first name?' asked Mazer.

'Viktor, Viktor Nikolayevich.'

'No. I didn't know him,' said Mazer firmly.

If only we could fix a lie detector to your skull, damn you, then we'd know if you were telling the truth or not, Sasha thought.

Aloud, he said: 'Mr Mazer, your activities come under article 78 of the criminal code concerning smuggling. The sentence is pretty severe – three to ten years. If you come clean about all your crimes in detail, then in accordance with paragraph 9 of article 38 we might make some sort of deal. . . .'

Mazer looked at Sasha sideways and asked suddenly:

'Are you really a prosecutor? In our country, a young squirt like you couldn't be a clerk.'

Sasha pulled out his leatherbound identification card and waved it under the businessman's nose so that he could see the gold letters: 'Public Prosecutor's Office, USSR'.

Satisfied, Mazer said: 'Then, I have an official statement to make. I must return to my own country immediately, and in return I am prepared to reveal certain secrets to the Prosecutor's Office of the Soviet State, concerning illegal operations by Western firms with officials of your Foreign Trade Ministry – and another government department.'

Sasha's heart nearly stopped beating.

'Mr Mazer, you'll have to give me a bit more to go on.'

Mazer flicked a glance to right and left then looked at Sasha intently. Sasha was about to request Grechannik and Pogorelov to leave when his old friend from college cleared his throat and said smoothly; 'Comrade Turetsky is a Junior Investigator with the Prosecutor's Office, not the Prosecutor himself. In any case, there's a special Prosecutor, Funtov, who deals with foreigners' cases. We wouldn't want you to be misled, Mr Mazer, would we, comrades?'

Sasha dared not open his mouth. What the hell was that bastard Grechannik playing at?

'That changes things,' said Mazer immediately. 'I insist on talking to this Mr Funtov, if the Chief Prosecutor of Moscow can't see me.'

Sasha swallowed his anger. Forcing himself to speak calmly and reasonably, he began explaining to Mazer that according to Lenin himself the Soviet Prosecutor's Office was the only organ of one-man management in the country, and that therefore talking to him was exactly the same as talking to the Chief Public Prosecutor. He explained that Russia did not have one legal system for Kursk and another for Kaluga; there was only one uniform legal system. . . .

Mazer stuck to his guns. 'Will you please fix a meeting for me with your Chief Prosecutor, or at least with this Funtov? When can I see your boss? I can deliver, damn you!'

Painfully, he pulled out some crumpled sheets of paper folded into three from underneath his pillow. He waved them around till everyone had registered them properly and then slipped them back under his pillow, wincing with pain as he did so. Silently, Sasha got him to sign his statement, left Grechannik to arrange some security, hot-footed it back to the Prosecutor's Office, accompanied by a silent Pogorelov. Merkulov would know how to handle this one.

As they entered his office, Merkulov was on the phone, speaking rapidly.

'Are you the doctor on duty? Merkulov here, City Prosecutor's Office. What's the latest on Mazer – yes, OK, the foreigner!'

Closing the double doors behind them, Pogorelov and Sasha stood just inside the room, pools of melting snow forming around their feet.

'What! How do you mean, "in a serious condition"? What goddamn operation – he was brought in with minor wounds, for Christ's sake! You've obviously mixed him up with somebody else. My assistant was just questioning him. . . . When did this happen?'

Merkulov leant wearily against his desk, ignoring the excited voice still jabbering down the line. He replaced the receiver leadenly.

'Looks like we've lost our second lead,' he said impassively. 'They're operating now but there's not a cat in hell's chance of saving him, apparently.'

'How come?' Sasha asked in amazement. Not thirty minutes before Mazer had had a bullet hole or two in him, sure, but he'd been years away from dying. What the hell sort of place was the Sklifosovsky Institute to do this to a reasonably healthy man? Damn it, it wasn't even a psychiatric hospital!

'You haven't let the car go, have you?' said Merkulov to a faintly perspiring Pogorelov.

'No, Comrade Investigator.'

'Then let's go!'

Twenty-five minutes later they were back at the Sklifosovsky Institute, in the corridor outside the operating theatre.

A green-clad surgeon flanked by two nurses stopped in the doorway, removed his mask and said: 'Dead. Never regained consciousness. I did warn you. . . .'

'What went wrong? And no cover-ups, Doc. This is a priority investigation.'

'See for yourselves, gentlemen.' The surgeon turned gracefully on his heel and held open the doors to the theatre.

Mazer was still lying on the operating table. Sasha did not recognise him at first – emaciated, deathly pale face, blue lips, sunken eyes. Merkulov bent forward and sniffed rapidly several times.

'Yes, it was most probably poison,' said the surgeon impassively. 'We think it was hydrocyanic acid, but we'll know precisely tomorrow. The post-mortem, thank God, is still the most precise area of modern medicine.'

A few minutes later, after a quick word with the nurses, orderlies, the doctors and a shame-faced Grechannik, the picture was a little clearer.

Sasha was not the only one to have left Grechannik 'on guard'. He'd received the same order from the KGB captain, Rashilin, who had promised to send his own men along by about nine o'clock. But the Lieutenant's patience had only lasted ten minutes, after which he'd called a nurse to stand in for him and cleared off downstairs to the ground floor to ring up a girlfriend.

The angel of mercy, too, was not the most forbearing and 'slipped off for a minute'. That was enough. Another nurse came into the private ward to give Mazer a pain-killer. She waited while the patient took his medicine and then, according to a ward orderly who happened to be around, the dark-haired woman of around thirty, with sharp clear features and dark deep-set eyes, left the ward and went to the service exit.

When the real nurse returned to the ward, she took one look at the patient, grabbed his wrist and felt for the pulse. . . .

'It looks like heart failure,' she told Grechannik when he came running.

'You stay here and I'll fetch the doctor.'

But a whole swarm of quacks didn't make the slightest difference. Mazer was obviously dying. His statement, intended for the Moscow City Prosecutor, disappeared with the nurse.

Merkulov dialled the emergency number and called out an investigations and operations team from the City Administration of Internal Affairs. He informed 'the other firm' that, whether they liked it or not, this one was down to them. They waited until Investigator Borovik, a long, lugubrious, worm-like individual, arrived and then they left Department No. 1 of the Sklifosovsky Institute.

Merkulov was in a hurry. Madame Soya-Serko's place was about to be turned over, and this time there were to be no cock-ups.

5

Soya-Serko lived in a tinted-glass high-rise block on Taneyevykh Street next to Sivtsev-Vrazhek Lane. On the left was the house of Rossinsky, the father of Soviet aviation, on the right an old manor-house, derelict and boarded up, where once the writer Herzen had lived. Opposite, glistening with fresh paint, was the flimsy-looking house – now a museum – of the composer Taneyev.

Merkulov, Pogorelov, Sasha and two witnesses, a man

and a woman, got out of the police van. Two smartly dressed men passed by on the pavement. One was saying to the other: 'The new boy's taking a tough line – he's got rid of five ministers in a week! And did you hear? Ryzh-kov at our place did himself in, scared of going to gaol. . . .'

What would they be saying once they heard about Operation Export?

From the spacious hallway they took the huge lift up to the ninth floor. Soya-Serko opened the door and frowned in surprise to see Merkulov's warrant.

'A search? Of my apartment? But I'm the one who was robbed!'

Merkulov simply stepped past the lady of the house into the apartment. The look she threw at him would have turned water to ice.

'I'm not having this!' she said, rushing over to the phone. But Merkulov had the receiver already. Giving his name and rank, he requested the operator to block all calls for the next three hours.

Soya-Serko threw herself theatrically into an armchair in the sitting room and picked up the latest copy of *The Literary Gazette*, which bore a portrait of Lenin. She pretended to continue reading.

'Anything interesting in it, ma'am?' asked Pogorelov, glancing over her shoulder.

'I'll say! Do you know what Dostoevsky died of?'

'Old age, I expect.'

Sasha doubted Pogorelov had even heard of Dostoevsky.

'Wrong,' said Soya-Serko with a malicious laugh. 'For your information, the great writer died because of a house search. In 1881 the police came to his neighbour Barrani-kov, a member of the People's Will, to search his apartment. When Fyodor Mikhailovich learnt of it, blood gushed from his mouth and he later died.'

'You're safe with us, ma'am,' said Pogorelov reassuringly.

'Major, skip the history lesson,' interrupted Merkulov. 'We've got work to do.'

Merkulov took off his uniform jacket as well as his topcoat. He checked the waste-pipe in the toilet, felt in the stove, crawled under divans. . . . Beads of sweat appeared on his forehead, and his face was streaked with dust. But he was smiling.

In the extensive library Merkulov assigned Sasha a set of shelves containing the classics, and himself started work on the pre-Revolutionary editions.

The rhythmic chiming of the clock in the sitting room marked another hour. Sasha skimmed through the collected works of Tolstoy, Balzac, Dickens and Thackeray. Unhurriedly, with relish, Merkulov was leafing through *The Institution of Judicial Resolutions, A History of Russian Literature in the Nineteenth Century* and a novel by Charskaya. From time to time, like bibliophiles in a bookshop, they exchanged remarks.

'Look, a first edition of *The Twelve Chairs*.'

'Peanuts! I've got Bryusov's first book of verse here. That really is a rarity.'

Another half-hour of books, stamp-albums, collections of postcards. . . . Soya-Serko was a regular Monte Cristo in skirts. The books were a treasure-house, worth hundreds of thousands of roubles.

At that moment Merkulov said: 'Confabulation time.'

Sasha had never heard the word before, but Merkulov seemed to enjoy pronouncing it loudly, syllable by syllable, to attract everybody's attention.

He succeeded. As if to order, every head turned in his direction. His face remained impassive, but Sasha knew, from the angle of his head, that the boss was going to let himself go again. Which had to mean another breakthrough.

In the language of investigators, this was: 'Inclusion in the report of any important piece of evidence discovered in the physical presence of the accused and witnesses'. The boss was going to make quite sure his discovery was registered by everybody.

Merkulov requested: 'Comrades – and you, too, Alla Alexandrovna – would you please gather round?'

Major Pogorelov, scruffy and perspiring, the male witness, a shaven-headed man in a military-issue shirt, and the woman, a very good-looking snub-nosed blond in a brightly coloured dress, all came over to the shelf by which Investigator Merkulov stood.

'Alla Alexandrovna,' said Merkulov unctuously, 'you are obviously a well-read person. Would you please explain to my assistant what "confabulation" means! Can you?'

'Of course,' answered Alla Alexandrovna, pulling her lace housecoat tighter over her breasts. 'Are you listening, kid? "Confabulation" is a form of mental disorder. It's the presentation as if it is fact of what one merely wishes to be true. OK?'

'OK,' Sasha replied seriously.

'In my opinion the disease is rife among certain comrades – particularly our valiant workers and peasants. It's high time they sorted themselves out, Stalin's been dead for thirty years.'

Merkulov didn't flicker an eyelid.

'Thank you, Alla Alexandrovna, you've a way with words. I'm sure Comrade Turetsky will now remember all his life what "confabulation" is, and won't accept what he simply wishes for as being reality.'

While speaking, Merkulov automatically took the next volume off the shelf. It was the 1913 issue of the journal *Niva*, bound in thick leatherette. As his audience watched intently, Merkulov started leafing through the folder, page by page. Glossy photographs, neat illustrations, long leisurely articles flashed by. This was pre-Revolutionary, uncomprehended Russia.

When he reached the back cover, Merkulov turned the journal upside down. What looked like a pale green postcard fell to the carpet with a slight ringing noise. Sasha bent down and picked up a wafer-thin sheet of metal. The number 100 appeared on each corner. There was some black and white lettering in what could have been English, and in the middle was the handsome oval portrait of a benign-looking old man with a double-pointed beard. Peering close, Sasha was able to read in mirror-image the word 'Franklin'.

Christ Almighty, it was the plate of a hundred-dollar note!

Open-mouthed, he looked at Merkulov, who was still holding the journal in his hands, extending it for everyone to see. There was a recess cut inside the thick back cover, exactly the dimensions of the plate. The Special Crimes Investigator stared into Soya-Serko's dark eyes, which were dilated with terror.

'Where did you get this from, Alla Alexandrovna?'

6

The tobacco smoke in Merkulov's office had to be seen to be believed. The smoke from the Dymoks and Belomors hung in such thick acrid layers that as soon as Sasha came in his eyes started to water and he rushed to open a window. Completely absorbed in their discussion about the deposits of micro-particles in certain fibres, Merkulov and Gryaznov noticed neither his entry nor the open window. He took off his coat, sat at his desk and started to listen, reflecting as he did so that it is only in a detective story that the more unexpected the final solution, the better and more spectacular the read. In the present case it was not like that at all; the solution was coming piecemeal. And the Investigator's task was not to think up some winning move, as some crime writers, who have never seen a real investigation, think; but, rather, not to overlook a single fact or circumstance that real life throws his way, to extricate the rational grains from the huge piles of dung, to analyse them, compile them, take decisions and make deductions. Sasha's prince Merkulov was not fictitious, but a real-life investigator. Instead of thinking up all sorts of weird and wonderful theories, he just worked hard at the job. Not sparing himself. Or others. . . .

Apparently, on Monday, after the hockey match, Merkulov had got hold of Lieutenant-Colonel Bratishka, the deputy head of the Sokolniki district CID. Following instructions, he was in charge of solving the murder in Sokolniki Park. Bratishka showed up for a midnight meeting with Merkulov armed with various skeleton keys. These were to the heavy-duty locks on the apartment on Kotelnicheskaya Embankment where Kazakov-Kramarenko lived.

They didn't bother with a search warrant issued by the Moscow Public Prosecutor. Bratishka was an old hand at violating the Constitution, and Merkulov knew that if they found something worthwhile in Kazakov's apartment they would be covered by article 168 of the judicial code which stated that: 'In instances requiring urgent action, a search may be carried out without the authorization of the Prosecutor, so long as the Prosecutor is informed within the twenty-four hours following the search.'

If they found nothing, why trouble a superior unnecessarily. . . ?

Bratishka dealt with the locks. The enormous residence, consisting of two three-roomed apartments knocked into one, was furnished expensively, but in excruciatingly bad taste: fabric patterned with red poppies the size of footballs on a gold-coloured background covered several luxurious divans. The curtains were wine-coloured, patterned with water-nymphs piping on some improbable-looking instruments. A look at the Czech-made bar in the corner made Merkulov wince. The outward-facing side was upholstered in thick yellow material, patterned with creatures halfway between tadpoles and spermatozoids engaged in some indecent-looking dance.

The table in the dining room was set for six. Kazakov had obviously been expecting company for the Sunday evening meal. The light from the crystal chandelier was reflected in the wine-glasses. Bratishka had a finger or two of English gin from among the battery of imported spirits, and grimaced in disappointment at the weakness of it.

They found nothing of interest in any of the numerous drawers in the secretaire, bedside tables and writing desk. In the bedroom, Bratishka pulled out a large sheet of paper from under the bed, covered in poster-size lettering.

'Double Dutch to me,' he said.

Merkulov took the paper and laughed. 'Our good friend is a man of education and accomplishment. He's been teaching himself English.' Four useful phrases had been rendered into phonetic Russian.

I am sorry.

Do not worry.

Son of a bitch.

Fucking bastard.

Merkulov tried to translate accurately. Bratishka looked on admiringly.

In the music room stood a huge concert Steinway, a Grundig stereo system, a Sony television and an American 'Realistic' radio receiver.

'I just don't believe that the King of the Hippodrome sat here quietly tinkling out an Oginsky polonaise,' said Merkulov. He walked over to the grand piano and swept about twenty ornaments off the top; Bratishka caught a bronze corkscrew in the shape of the Brussels boy and stared at it stupidly.

'Son of a bitch, that's really decadent!'

Merkulov lifted the piano lid and looked inside.

'There don't seem to be any corpses in here, but there are one or two other things. . . .'

He pulled out a battered folder with well-thumbed string fasteners. It contained documents, certificates for Heroes of the Soviet Union and Heroes of Socialist

Labour, passports, deputies' identity cards, Communist Party membership cards, etc., including Comrade Volin's, marked in pencil 'Ten thousand roubles'.

'This will have to be confiscated,' said Merkulov to Bratishka. The Lieutenant-Colonel was silent. 'OK, Comrade Lieutenant-Colonel?'

'I think so,' said Bratishka in a constrained voice.

Merkulov looked enquiringly at the head of Sokolniki district CID. Wheezing asthmatically, Bratishka was slowly leafing through an American *Playboy* calendar. Bony beauties cavorted lasciviously in front of the camera lens, licking their lips and adopting gynaecological positions.

'I'm sure that won't be missed, Comrade Bratishka. But can we get on with the search?'

Still no response. Merkulov gave up and went back to the piano. This time he pulled out what looked like a school reading-book. Inside were velvet 'leaves' covered in small pockets. Inside was a whole collection of orders, medals, insignia. About a hundred were made of precious metals. These toys could fetch really good money on the black market; five thousand for a Hero of the Soviet Union, two and a half thousand for an Order of the Red Banner, a thousand for the Order of Lenin. This collection was in mint condition, each leaf lovingly labelled. One of the pockets in the 'Master of Sport' section was empty. . . .

'Comrade Bratishka could you organize some witnesses, please? We're going to conduct this search by the rule-book,' said Merkulov, trying to sound as businesslike as possible.

To his astonishment, the only answer was 'I wonder how much a policeman earns in America? It's got to be two thousand a month.'

'What?'

'And, if you're my rank, maybe even three.'

'Listen, Lieutenant-Colonel, if you don't go and get some witnesses now, I'm going to tell the KGB you've been seduced by Western propaganda and are planning to defect!' Merkulov could hardly restrain his combined indignation and amusement. Bratishka just chuckled by way of reply, spreading his arms like a child while heading for the door. The fat little man in the police greatcoat was obviously still enthralled by thoughts of the *dolce vita* in the West.

Merkulov was very thirsty. He went into the kitchen, opened the ice-box and took out a bottle of Borzhom water. He drank the ice-cold gassy drink straight out of the bottle, relishing the slight aftertaste of iodine. When he had finished, he noticed that the kitchen was decorated in the very latest fashion, strongly resembling an underground grotto. The grey-green walls still exuded a faint smell of fresh paint.

Bratishka soon came back with two witnesses, the caretaker and his wife. Who else could you get at midnight?

'OK, Lieutenant-Colonel, have the witnesses. . . .' Merkulov didn't finish the sentence, for he saw that Bratishka held in his hands a chequered coat.

His fat face was split by a grin. He seemed to have grown a couple of inches taller.

'I went into my friend Yanko's apartment, the caretaker here. I took a look behind the door and there was this chequered coat on a peg. I asked him where it came from, and Yanko explained. . . .'

'I didn't know Comrade Kazakov,' the swarthy skinny caretaker interrupted. 'I only know he is some kind of bigshot, working in a shop downtown. It must be a good job; he led a very good life. A lot of people said he was a pickpocket, but I could see he was educated. . . .'

On the night of 17 November, Yanko was burning rubbish in the boiler room: rags, paper and other rubbish. About half-past one, while he was resting in his cubbyhole down there, someone came quietly in. Yanko said nothing, but looked through the crack in the partition and saw Kazakov stuffing a big bundle of newspapers into the stove. When he had gone, Yanko pulled the burning parcel out, rolling it on the ground to put out the flames, and undid it. There was a green bag with flaps, the kind you can only buy in the hard-currency shops, and inside was a man's coat, chequered, all rolled up, a black suit, and high brown boots from West Germany. It was a shame to burn good stuff like that, so the caretaker took it all home.

Merkulov pulled the sleeve of the chequered coat closer to him and grunted in satisfaction – there was a clear grey-green stain on the cuff. The investigator took the shade off one of the table lamps and shone the light along the walls of the kitchen grotto for some time. Then he grunted in even greater satisfaction and set about resolutely ruining the modern design by scraping the paint off the artificial granite.

As Merkulov made out a report regarding the discovery and removal of the material evidence, Bratishka followed all the rules of forensic science and packed everything into cellophane bags of various sizes while the Yanko couple perched on the very edge of a plush divan. But, gradually, the caretaker began to feel like the hero of the hour. When the time arrived for him to sign a witness's statement, he was lounging all over the huge poppies and sticking his long skinny legs in their home-made socks and galoshes right into the middle of the room as if he owned the place.

Merkulov sent the material evidence to the forensic department with questions for the scientists to answer.

You had to give modern criminology its due; it had reached mind-boggling heights of efficiency. The experts gave satisfactory answers to at least 140 of Merkulov's questions. Forensics had used emissive spectral analysis on the micro-particles for the purposes of identification, and now Merkulov and Gryaznov were busy classifying the information received according to its degree of importance to the investigation.

Firstly, the experts had found on Kazakov's chequered

coat bits of fibre from Rakitin's coat, from Kupriyanova's suede skirt, not to mention some particles, visible to the naked eye, of paint from the kitchen. Again, the scrapings from the grotto wall also had fibres from the chequered coat on them. So, given that the decoration of the kitchen in Kazakov's apartment had begun on Wednesday (according to statements wrung from a gang of godawful interior designers), on the day of the murder Volodya must have been wearing that chequered coat.

Secondly, the forensic boys took samples from under Kazakov's fingernails and from the top layer of his facial skin where the beard grows. It wasn't difficult to do – the crook was still unconscious. To the delight of the forensic scientists, Kazakov was not overly enamoured of personal hygiene and there was a mass of micro-particles under his nails; brick and soil particles from the scene of the crime at Sokolniki Park; shavings of the wire which strangled Rakitin; fibres from the scarf belonging to the ballet dancer. By the same method they discovered the presence of a gluey substance on Kazakov's facial skin with which he had stuck on his false beard.

Thirdly, the footprints found at the scene of the crime were made by Kazakov's German boots.

Fourthly . . . tenthly . . . forty-fifthly. . . .

'So we can say that we have proved Kazakov-Kramarenko's guilt completely,' concluded Merkulov, and took out of his drawer his grandfather's watch. He set about polishing it with a piece of velvet as if this would take about a hundred years off the life of the damn thing. 'But we haven't got very far with the other man. And, incidentally, there were no signs on Kazakov's jacket of the badge having been pinned on it.'

7

The Forensic Prosecutor, Semyon Semyonovich Moiseyev, was master of his trade and an ex-commander of a tank corps during the Second World War. He had a smashed knee and five medals to remind him of it. Faced with any figure of authority, the war hero became a gibbering wreck, since by birth and passport he was one hundred per cent Jewish. And that meant that as soon as they started cutting back on staff he was the first candidate for the boot, in accordance with the secret instructions regarding further improvement of party cadres.

And so, while Merkulov, Gryaznov and Sasha, summoned by Lyonya Parkhomenko to the forensic department office for a routine pep-talk on the Rakitin case, were sitting the length of a ridiculously long table and listening with only half an ear to the boss's wince-inducing maxims, Semyon Semyonovich was bustling about from cupboard to cupboard, limping more than usual from the activity and doing his best to justify himself for sins he had not committed.

'Sit down, can't you, Semyon Semyonovich?' said Parkhomenko in irritation, and Moiseyev promptly obeyed, sitting down on a handy chair in the farthest corner and mumbling something apologetic – he had something the matter with his teeth as well.

Everyone sighed with relief when Parkhomenko finally called it a day and they were able to get on with something important.

A bulky package of forensic reports had just been delivered express from the All-Union Institute of Science and Research: photographic plates, diagrams, conclusions drawn from the complex medical and ballistic tests, and a box containing handguns, cartridges, cartridge-cases and other ammunition.

The great criminologists of the world looked down from the photographs on the walls: the Frenchman

Alphonse Bertillion with his moustache, the first pro-
ponent of scientific method in criminology; the Austrian
investigator Hans Gross, with his high forehead, author
of *The Criminologist's Handbook*; the brown-haired,
intellectual-looking American Colwin Goddard, out-
standing ballistics expert; and the Russian scientist Yev-
geny Fyodorovich Burinsky, who discovered and put into
general practice the method of colour-separation photography. To judge from their expressions, they perfectly
understood the matter in hand.

With incredible speed, Moiseyev 'set the table' for
seven people, but instead of plates there were four real
handguns and three cardboard replicas, with cartridge-
cases and shells laid alongside like knives and forks. The
forensic expert picked up the three cardboard replicas
and piled them on top of one another, then ranged the
three cartridge-cases and three slightly misshaped bullets
in a neat row, pointing his finger at them, as he spelt out
his conclusions.

'Given that the traces on the bullets extracted from
Kupriyanova's, Leonovich's and Mazer's bodies clearly
reflect in micro-relief the inner wall of the same gun-
barrel, we can conclude that each victim was shot by a
nine-millimetre parabellum Browning. And so gun
number 7 remains unlocated. Number 5 belongs to police
sergeant Zamotayev. The nine-millimetre bullet fired
from this gun lodged in the wooden trim of the railway-car
ceiling. Kazakov was wounded with a 7.65 bullet from a
foreign gun, possibly a Colt.' And Moiseyev pointed at
replica number 5. 'The ballistics tests have established
that Kazakov was not shot from the direction of the front
compartment where the sergeant was, but from the
toilet. . . .'

Moiseyev put the Makarov and the bullet away in a box
and went on:

'Then we have our own home-grown TT, 7.62 calibre,
that's number 3. Well, it's a TT like any other – no
problem – that's the one that fired the three bullets that

226

wounded comrades Gaibov and Nagorny. A loaded 32-calibre Beretta was found on Kazakov, a nice imported little piece, that's number 6. I would advice you, Konstantin Dmitriyevich, to bear these two guns in mind, though in practical terms they don't play any part in the case. . . .' Semyon Semyonovich put the TT and the Beretta to one side and asked: 'What do you say to that, Konstantin Dmitriyevich?'

'Damn all. Everything is as unclear as it was on the day of the first murder.' Merkulov cast an eye over the two remaining replicas on the table. 'So, Alexander Borisovich,' he said, 'we're looking for two handguns: a nine-millimetre parabellum Browning and a Colt 7.65. The Browning killed Kupriyanova and Leonovich and wounded Mazer; the Colt made a hole in Vladimir Georgiyevich Kazakov's head.'

And then Gryaznov piped up.

'By the way, did you find "Lesya"?'

Sasha was about to open his big mouth and tell Slava about their trip to Bolshevo, to Lucian Germanovich Romadin, when he suddenly caught sight of Merkulov's inscrutable expression. He stopped short, biting his tongue and forcing himself to stare with studied carefulness at the portrait of the French scientist Marin Mersenne, who first coined the term 'ballistics' in 1644.

Merkulov calmly replied to Gryaznov: 'Of course we found her, Slava.'

'And?'

'And nothing. She's a girlfriend of Kupriyanova's who brought her some perfume from abroad. Valeria owes her fifteen roubles, but her friend will have a long wait.'

Gryaznov sniggered as only he could, and said: 'I see, Konstantin Dmitriyevich.'

Sasha glanced at Merkulov, but he was already writing something on a sheet of paper. Gryaznov got up from his chair, sticking his cap on the back of his head.

'Well, if you don't need me, Comrade Chief Investigator. . . ?'

'That's OK, Slava. Alexander Borisovich and I are just going over to Lianozovo to see about some auto spares that came through the back door.'

'Well, say "Hi" to everyone, now I've finished my stint for Petrovka,' and Gryaznov saluted and went off.

Moiseyev was tidying up the forensics room. Merkulov beckoned Sasha to him and handed over the piece of paper he had just been writing on.

'Sasha, phone Kupriyanov right away from a call-box. Tell him that Lesya is Alisa Fyodorovna Smityuk, phone number 2187421, and she lives in Ostankino. Save your questions for later.'

Sasha hared downstairs and ran across Novokuznetskaya Street to a row of phone-booths. When he had dialled Kupriyanov's number, he turned to face the pavement and saw, in a box opposite, Police Captain Gryaznov.

8

'Exactly. He rang the Public Prosecutor's Office of the USSR and spoke to the Chief Public Prosecutor. He asked for it all to be put down in writing and said that measures would be taken. . . . I wrote this letter. I'm a deputy, for fuck's sake, not a piece of trash! And I think I did right. How long do we have to put up with this sort of thing? In the middle of Moscow, in broad daylight, thieves can break into an apartment, steal a collection of valuable items, and nobody does a damn thing about it.'

Major Pogorelov stood by the window of his office and, watching the usual hustle and bustle in the street below, listened to the tape-recorded evidence of the famous airman and cosmonaut, Major-General Pavel Popovich. The astronaut's voice was harsh and abrupt. Major Pogorelov's head ached.

For forty-eight hours now Romanova had been enquiring, with ill-concealed sarcasm, as to his progress with the Soya-Serko case. There had been nothing much.

The day before, acting on instructions from Investigator Merkulov, the Major had gone to the cosmonaut's village of Star, next to Kaliningrad outside Moscow, for a heart-to-heart talk with Popovich. He was a big wheel now, Deputy Head of the Cosmonaut Training Centre.

Pavel was a joker – recently he had even had some of his jokes published in the humour page of *The Literary Gazette* – and he was very approachable. A few years before he had been involved in criminal proceedings which Pogorelov had investigated. With Pavel's knowledge, his own Volga was sold by some crooks to some fruit speculators from Transcaucasia ten times, and he, Pavel, was paid a cut for allowing the 'test run'.

Pogorelov pressed the rewind button and started the tape again, listening carefully to the cosmonaut's voice. A sound recording can be more illuminating than a written statement. Written words cannot convey the timbre of the voice, the intonation and the tension of oral speech. A live immediate account is far better than the words of a statement, carefully vetted by an investigator.

'Fuck the police – they're the layabouts of our country. They've done nothing for me. No offence, Pogorelov, I'm talking about the local boys. Instead of dragging those crooks out into the open, they're just covering up for them. Some decent men come to me, Grachev and Solomin – they work in the Chamber of Commerce – and they say to me: "Look, Pasha, someone we all know, Alla Soya-Serko, has had a lot of antiques stolen from her apartment on the Arbat. They haven't hauled anyone in yet. The police don't seem to be looking for the thieves. So then I ask; Why doesn't Alla come and talk to me herself? After all, we know each other. They are a bit put out, say she's busy with one thing or another. . . . Then I rang Sasha Rekunkov. I get some response out of him, and he refers the matter to the City Prosecutor's Office, where the investigators have got more go in them. And they're not as crooked as you lot in the police. No offence, Pogorelov!'

The Major pressed the stop button and began thumbing through the statements of the witnesses whom he had questioned two days before. There was nothing very striking about them at fifteenth sight.

His eyes ran over Soya-Serko's evidence – all the usual sort of evasions: 'I don't know', 'I can't remember', 'I didn't see', 'I didn't hear', 'don't agree'. There was the first contradiction: 'When I realised that our local police in the Leninsky district were not actively looking for the criminals, I approached Pavel Popovich for help. . . .'

Popovich said: 'Some decent guys come to me, Grachev and Solomin.'

Soya-Serko was lying through her teeth. Why? Grachev and Solomin, employees of the Chamber of the Commerce, provided some answers. Pogorelov put on another cassette and listened. Unlike the first voice, this one was measured, even and cultured.

'It's generally accepted that a person is capable of being deceived only in his rose-coloured youth. Well, I got cheated when I was well past thirty. I'd never have believed that Alla Soya-Serko would be capable of such a thing. You see, Comrade Major, to put it frankly, in Soviet life today it isn't done to keep your savings openly. At any moment the Anti-Corruption Squad can ask: "Where did you get this from, dear Comrade Grachev, this pure gold statue?" So Solomin and I, and a few others, went to Alla to have her keep our things in her collection. In your eyes she'd be quite legal and above board – her husband's family had been building up that collection for over a hundred years.

'She agreed, then one fine day she came to us. "Isn't it awful?" she said. "All the valuables have been stolen, yours and mine. In broad daylight some crooks opened the security locks, got into the apartment and took all the antiques."

'Solomin and I thought: Well, they'll find the collection if the CID does its job as it ought to! But a day, a week, a month went by, and the police were really dragging their heels. We asked Alla to write a letter of complaint, and she started dragging her heels, saying there was no point in getting on to the authorities, it got you nowhere.

'I'm afraid Solomin and I were forced to listen in on her telephone conversations. We taped them. It turned out she was selling our things which were supposed to have been stolen from the apartment! We needed to approach someone well known to lean on the police and get the enquiry speeded up, exposing Alla for what she was, so we went to Popovich. . . .'

Pogorelov rang the duty section of the Remand Centre where Soya-Serko was being held and asked for her to be brought from cell 5 to the interrogation room. He put down the receiver and went over to the safe, took out a metal hip-flask and drank some vodka straight from it. Then he munched some nutmeg seeds to disguise the smell of the liquor.

Maybe close acquaintance with a prison cell would have put some sense into that stuck-up bitch's head!

The rusty hinges of the door creaked open, and Alla and the warder came in. The warder put a chit in front of Pogorelov and withdrew silently. Soya-Serko gave the Inspector a blank fish-eyed stare, not even nodding in greeting.

Pogorelov said politely. 'How do you do, Alla Alexandrovna? Please, sit down.'

But Alla Alexandrovna just went on standing there, brown eyes slightly puffy from sleep, staring into space.

Pogorelov went up to her, took her by the shoulders and pushed her down on to the chair bolted to the floor. He went back to his desk and asked: 'So how to you feel, sweetheart?'

Her eyes remained perfectly blank.

'Playing dumb, I see. Well, be our guest – for as long as you wish.'

231

Pogorelov sat down at his desk and stared straight at Alla. She seemed to be looking passively at some nonexistent object hanging in the air before her.

Establishing simulation is not easy. It requires hospitalisation and forensic–psychiatric tests; at least two, sometimes three, months of messing around. Pogorelov was well aware of all this. He cursed under his breath and then began to outline to the prisoner article 38 of the criminal code, concerning a full and frank confession of guilt and other mitigating circumstances. After that, he tried intimidation: he read out all twelve points of article 39, about aggravating circumstances. Soya-Serko's face remained a lifeless mask.

'I hope that you understand what has been said to you, my dear, and that you'll stop playing blind man's buff with socialist law. Tell me who put you up to stealing from your own apartment, who gave you that plate for forging American dollars, and everything else.' Pogorelov waved a fat threatening finger at her. 'For example, how did you manage to poison that foreigner?'

Pogorelov was not expecting an answer, so he was very surprised when Soya-Serko stood up, pulled the lead of the tape recorder out of the wall and hissed straight into his face.

'Forget it, pig! Stick your questions up your arse. If you try to pin anything on me, my boss will get you one dark night, I'm warning you. Now take me back to my cell. Can't you see I'm not going to talk?'

'What a charming turn of phrase, Citizen Soya-Serko,' Pogorelov managed to say. But she was mummy-like once more. At that moment the door opened and the man who shared his office, Captain Gryaznov, came in.

'Valentin, the "lady of the house" wants you!'

Romanova! Pogorelov sped out of the office like a bullet, saying 'Slava, stay with this lady for a bit. I'll be back in a second.'

When the creaking door closed behind the Major, Gryaznov handed Alla Alexandrovna a scrap of cigarette-paper. She looked sidelong at him, then took the note and read it. It consisted of just a few words. Alla laughed, picked up a pen from Pogorelov's desk and wrote something on the same piece of paper. Then, with another laugh, she pressed the note into Gryaznov's palm.

9

Special Crimes Investigator Merkulov was currently engaged on fourteen cases. He was having real problems trying to find time for them all, or at least get some postponement. One of them concerned bribery in the road haulage department of the Moscow Soviet. The time allotted to the enquiry had elapsed, and to get an extension he had to perform, according to the law, 'essential tasks connected with the enquiry'. To which end, he and Sasha had planned a trip to the secondhand auto stores.

Sasha returned to Merkulov's office after making the call to Kupriyanov and wrote his boss a note. 'Phoned. Saw Gryaznov in another booth.' Merkulov struck a match without saying anything, burnt the 'report' and mixed the ashes with the remains of his efforts at planning his schedule.

A young driver came into the office.

'We're off, Comrade Chief.'

Getting hold of a car for official business in the Moscow City Prosecutor's Office was a problem. The top bosses usually grabbed them all first thing in the morning – one of them would have to go to a meeting at the City Committee, another one had to attend the funeral of an old employee of the Prosecutor's Office. Or someone's wife just *had* to have her hair done at the Enchantress salon. Today was Gena's day off, but he had been hanging around in the corridors of the Prosecutor's Office since morning, trying to fiddle a way of having his own Moskvich, which he had brought to work that day, fixed on the side. Luckily for Merkulov, he had turned up just at the right time – in less than a minute Gena was working overtime.

In the log of official journeys that Garik kept, Merkulov wrote: '1300 Lianozovo, secondhand store.' He put a dash in the 'arrived' column, since he wasn't thinking of a return journey.

'Come on, Gena, let's get over to South Port,' said Merkulov as they struggled into Gena's battered 1965 vintage Moskvich.

'You said Lianozovo, Comrade Chief.'

'Yes, but I've just remembered that that black market in Lianozovo operates from four to eight in the morning.'

'South Port it is.'

They were expected. The deputy manager of the spare-parts store, a tall thin Estonian called Svenovich Linno, had a word with his boys and they led Gena through to a treasure-house of autoparts usually inaccessible to mere mortals. Merkulov spoke to Linno in a low voice. The latter opened a back door and shouted something in Estonian. An even thinner and taller man came into the office, and they exchange a few brief words in their own language. Then the deputy manager said in a heavy accent: 'This is my son, Gunnar. He'll take you wherever you want to go, Konstantin Dmitriyevich.'

Gunnar, without the slightest trace of an accent, confirmed this. 'I'll bring my Zhiguli round to the gate.'

Before leaving the garage, Merkulov opened his briefcase and pulled out two battered hats. He pulled one almost over his ears and handed the other one uncertainly to Sasha, asking: 'What size do you take?'

He had no idea and took the shapeless piece of green felt rather reluctantly.

'God, I hope nobody recognises us.'

'That's the point, idiot.'

At that moment the garage doors swung open automatically. Gunnar looked frankly incredulous when the hats registered on him.

Fifteen minutes later, he deposited them at Nizhniye Kotly railway station, where, still sporting the hats, they bought tickets to Rastorguyevo.

Only in the empty compartment of the local train did they dare to draw breath. They both began speaking at once, like close relatives who had not seen each other for years. Putting the hat in his briefcase, Merkulov said: 'You first, Sasha. But keep it short; we've only got twenty-five minutes.'

He told Merkulov about his meeting with Kassarin and his father's letter. Merkulov looked in his direction but not at him, as if at something only he could see. Suddenly, completely unconnected with what Sasha was saying, he asked: 'How are things between you and Rita?'

He could not have admitted to his own mother that he was in love with her, so he was surprised to hear himself saying: 'I . . . she. . . . We're going to be married. What's that got to do with. . . ?'

'Nothing.'

Merkulov blew his nose, turned to the window, and for half a minute looked out at the distant woods they were speeding past. At last, he said softly: 'We are on our way to see an officer in Army Intelligence, General Tsapko – Ippolit Alexeyevich Tsapko, Viktoria Rakitin's father and a marvellous man. I want to nail Kassarin if it's the last thing I do. Rakitin describes all his crimes in detail in his diaries. In detail, but without proof. Kazakov and the other unknown man, in the windcheater, were just hired assassins. Madame Soya-Serko is apparently Kassarin's fancy woman. I very much doubt if Kazakov and Soya-Serko will testify against him.

'Rakitin was working for the Department of Strategic Operations of the KGB and tried many times to get through to Andropov or even Brezhnev. No one believed him, and all his information fell into Kassarin's hands. The fact is that he, as someone participating in foreign operations – flooding the money markets with counterfeit notes, covert activities in raw material exporting countries, and so on – can dispose of millions of roubles and use forged dollars on trips abroad.

'He's got rid of Mazer and Leonovich, he's tried to do the same to Kazakov, and quite possibly Soya-Serko is at risk. As soon as he's sure that we have copies of Rakitin's papers, he'll try to silence us, too. He's already tried to get you in his pocket, and he's having us watched. There are microphones everywhere, and he's using Parkhomenko – even Gryaznov – for his own ends.'

None of it was exactly news to Sasha. Ever since he'd met Kassarin two days before, he'd had the uneasy feeling that his life was suddenly worth far less.

'It's quite possible that I also made a mistake in not passing on Rakitin's papers to the right quarters immediately,' Merkulov continued. 'I was certain, and I still have a faint hope, that we could get together some evidence against the bastard. But I admit, Sasha, I didn't expect the rot to have spread so far. I give you my word that if I don't nail the whole gang of them by the end of the week, then I'll go to Yemelyanov on Monday with the evidence I've got on Kassarin and ask him to take me off the case. Or else I'll accept his offer – which will amount to the same thing.'

'What offer?'

'Deputy Public Prosecutor for the City of Moscow.'

'Great!' Sasha laughed, picturing Parkhomenko's mule-faced reaction to the bombshell that he was Merkulov's subordinate instead of his boss.

'You see, Sasha,' said Merkulov, doing his mind-reading routine, 'there's nothing special in it for me. Just becoming a useless bureaucrat, a part of the party oligarchy, struggling for more power. . . . An investigator's work is to solve crimes, and I like doing my share. The Soviet people, like any other, have a right to be protected from murder, theft or anything else. Imagine – a house catches fire and the owner is a well-known crook. What are we supposed to do: ignore it, let it burn down and endanger others? What if there were kids inside?'

Merkulov looked around, but there was no one else in the compartment.

'I don't like everything about our life, but I'm not about to kick the Soviet system. I'm just a professional, an investigator doing my job of saving kids from a house – and not joining in the wolf-hunt conducted by a lot of running dogs and impotent placemen.'

Sasha felt absurdly flattered. Merkulov was telling him – or maybe himself – things that could get you a nice stretch inside, if not the six o'clock walk. He clearly trusted Sasha one hundred per cent.

If only he could get rid of that weight of worry and unease he seemed to have been carrying around since the hockey stadium.

'Rastorguyevo. Next stop, Lenin Hills,' announced the nasal impersonal voice over the speaker.

They stood up and went to the exit. Sasha saw a pre-Revolutionary landscape through the train windows: imposing merchants' houses, each with its own miniature 'estate' perched on a hilltop, a long wooden flight of steps leading up there from the station.

Merkulov looked at his watch. 'I must get to the hospital to see Lelya today.'

Top secret
To Head of Special Investigations Section
Major-General of State Security
Comrade V. V. Kassarin

Special Report

In the course of today we have continued our surveillance of K. D. Merkulov, Investigator of the Moscow City Public Prosecutor's Office, and his assistant, A. B. Turetsky.

Both of them arrived at the Prosecutor's Office by 9.00 and were in the investigations department before lunch.

At 12.48 Centre received a telephoned report from Captain Gryaznov, stating that

- the Head of Investigations, Parkhomenko, held an operations meeting with the team regarding the search for the murderers;
- Merkulov, Gryaznov, Turetsky and the Forensic Prosecutor Moiseyev carried out an examination of the results of the forensic and other tests;
- Investigator Merkulov informed Gryaznov that he had established that the 'Lesya' in Kupriyanova's notebooks is Citizen Alisa Fyodorovna Smityuk. Alisa Smityuk confirmed to us that she really did sell some Polish cosmetics to her friend Kupriyanova for 15 roubles but had not received the money.

At 13.01 Merkulov and Turetsky set off for Lianozovo in a Moskvich (licence no. MLS 48 33) to the auto spares black market. However, they changed direction *en route* and went to South Port.

At 13.38 Merkulov and others entered an auto plant and soon the vehicle MLS 48 33 was being serviced.

However, Merkulov and Turetsky, by means

of subterfuge, left the premises of the auto plant and went off in an unkown direction. From that moment the surveillance ceased, owing to circumstances for which we were not responsible.

Head of Section 5
Major in State Security
P. SMOLYARCHUK
24 November 1982

10

As they approached the old but still sturdy brick house belonging to Tsapko, Sasha reflected on the way the witnesses to a crime always form the majority of humanity, and the participants the minority. In his eyes, and those of Merkulov, the ex-deputy head of Military Intelligence was clearly a witness, yet to others. . . . In his long years of complex work the Lieutenant-General could not have helped but commit a few crimes. Naturally, in the name of and for the good of the Motherland.

Merkulov looked cautiously round the open door – so they weren't afraid of robbers here. A buxom young woman was busy at the stove. Sasha tried to imagine what she could be to the old general. She certainly was easy on the eye; tall, black-browed, though with a slightly heavy chin and lowish forehead.

'Hello. We're not disturbing you, are we?'

'Oh, it's you! Not at all. Come on in. Ippolit Alexeyevich is upstairs.'

She spoke in a low voice with a distinctive northern accent.

There was a blue lamp on in the room upstairs. The General was sitting at a newly planed table, grey head and mild wrinkled face bent over a handgun marked with a swastika on the sides of the grip. Merkulov drummed his fingers on the glass of the open door. Tsapko started to put his work aside and came over to them.

'Ippolit Alexeyevich,' he said, offering his hand.

General Tsapko looked like a seventy-year-old eagle, stiff-necked and lean, but his yellowish eyes had retained a measure of youthful merriment and curiosity. Life's storms, of which he must have weathered quite a few in his time, had not dimmed his interest in those around him.

'Take a seat. I'll be with you in a moment.'

The General resumed some minuscule adjustments to the gun. Ippolit Alexeyevich's room was not so much a study as a storeroom, a peculiar repository for three different sorts of relic: of Russian orthodoxy, of the Tsarist army, and German trophies from the Second World War. In the corners stood the banners of Tsarist regiments – dragoons, uhlans and cossacks; the walls were studded with icons, and on home-made shelves were ranged fascist insignia seized from Hitler's HQs, original photographs of the leaders of the Third Reich, Hitler, Himmler and Bormann.

'Yes, I'm playing about with the past,' said the General, putting down the gun. 'My assistants in defeated Berlin in 1945, where I set up the spy network for the future West Berlin, said that this once belonged to Himmler himself.

'I have a weakness for weapons and for pathological cases alike. People like Himmler, rather than healthy people, have a kind of heightened subconsciousness, infinite recesses of dark uncontrollable urges. You legal people must know all about that. Freud noted it, too. I have studied the archives of the fascists. Both Hitler and Goebbels had a premonition of their end, you know. No point in your grinning like that, young man; I've had a premonition or two myself. For instance, that you have some taxing questions for me.'

Tsapko turned his chair to sit facing them and looked straight at Merkulov.

'You're Merkulov, aren't you? Lyosha's girl delivered your message. I remember when you used to run around Kratovo stark naked with a potty in your hand yelling "I can sit on it myself! I'm brave! I'm a hero!" And now here you are, investigating Viktor's death. And you're Turetsky, I suppose, the man who's helping him. Is that right?'

They nodded silently.

'What's the matter, young men, have you lost your voices?' said Ippolit Alexeyevich. 'Or don't you know how to talk to me? I may be nearer heaven than earth but I'm quite approachable!

'All right, then, I'll start of my own accord. I suppose you want to know whether I was fond of my son-in-law, Viktor Rakitin, or whether I just treated him as one should a relative. Well, I loved him, and I still do, as one of my own children. . . .'

He carried on speaking clearly, angry with himself as the tears came to his eyes. 'So I'm entirely at your disposal. Go ahead! In Viktor's memory, I'm prepared to speak quite openly.'

'Tell us, Ippolit Alexeyevich,' said Merkulov diffidently, 'why did Viktor die exactly?'

Tsapko stood up, his general's tunic, unbuttoned and without epaulettes, flapping open. Sasha noticed a silver chain glinting beneath. Did the General wear a cross? He paced up and down the spacious study, his spare figure and grey hair appearing and disappearing again round the corner of a high carved tallboy.

'My dear chap, how best to explain?' said Tsapko, his own pensive yellow eyes meeting Merkulov's. 'You heard, of course, that Viktor created problems for himself?'

'Yes, your daughter told us as much.'

'Ah, so you've spoken to Viktoria,' said the General acerbically. 'She must have told you a thing or two! But not everything, I'll be bound, or I don't know my own daughter! My grandson told me something of it, so there we are. I was, apparently, the only person from whom Viktor never concealed a thing. No, I tell a lie, there was one person with whom he was more candid.'

'You mean you know everything about his struggle with the people at the top over Doctrine No. 3?' asked Merkulov carefully.

'Of course!'

Tsapko stopped by the tallboy and opened it. There was a carafe of vodka on the shelf inside, and some neatly sliced pickled gherkins on a plate. With his back to the two men, the General quickly poured himself a glass and drank it. They could see his slightly stooping back twitch once beneath the thin material of his tunic.

'Would you like a drop?' he offered. 'Talya will rustle up a meal presently, so wouldn't you like a glass before lunch?'

'Not just now, thank you.'

The General walked across the study again, his hands in the pockets of his trousers with their scarlet side-stripes.

'I'm still thinking how best to answer your question – why did Viktor die? And do you know what I say in reply, Kostya? Look at me. I always hated military service but I was a soldier all my life. Why? Because everybody said the most important thing in life was love for one's country, selflessness. And in their heart of hearts they were thinking: "It's skilled work, good pay. You don't always have to take orders. One day you can lord it over others. . . ."

'But Viktor wasn't like that. He was true to his ideals all his life. He wanted the work done on his patch – in the Foreign Trade Ministry – to be efficient. The Ministry was a paradigm for the whole Soviet system, and it was just coasting along because of wholesale corruption. The Minister himself, his deputies, the whole apparatus – they were just feathering their own nests, filching everything that wasn't properly accounted for. Nothing is accounted for properly in this country!

'And so when Viktor started fighting corruption he was beaten. You can only fight corruption successfully on one condition – that it's an individual phenomenon. When the whole system is rotten, no amount of fighting is going to help matters.

'Everyone knows that the party apparatus governs the whole system. And this apparatus enjoys numerous privileges, and these privileges are in essence the same as corruption, except that this corruption is legalised by the party apparatus itself. Fighting corruption in a corrupt state is quixotic lunacy. . . .'

Without realising it, the General was describing for Merkulov and Sasha the grim paradox of their investigation.

243

'Ippolit Alexeyevich,' said Merkulov politely, 'please tell us about Kassarin. We are investigators, not members of the Politburo.'

The General sighed heavily and began a flat recitation.

'It was 7 March 1982. An armoured vehicle was travelling along a winding road from Berne to Lucerne. The truck was carrying approximately thirty million dollars, intended for a foreign communist party. Although the sender was the Central Committee of the Communist Party of the Soviet Union, the fiction was that the money belonged to a front organisation, Context.

'The driver and those with him were slow to notice that the narrow road ahead was blocked: a car was parked across it, lights flashing, men in uniform, flagging them down. The driver began to explain that their documents were in order, but he didn't get the chance to finish. Automatic weapons were trained on them from left and right. One of the "policemen" smirked.

' "Take it easy. We don't need any documents. Just open up the doors or hand over the keys."

'The driver swore. The guards next to him kept quiet. Then the "police" used a method that quickly made the driver talk. They dragged the guards from the cab, tied them up and doused them with petrol. A cigarette-lighter was held near them.

' "If you don't give us the combination to open the doors, your friends are going to go up in flames."

'The bags containing the dollars were transferred to the "police" vehicle. The real Swiss police were on the spot twenty-five minutes later, but all trace of the thieves has vanished. . . .

'A year ago the KGB was planning an operation to seize the premises of one of the London companies that store valuables, the object being to destabilise the world market by taking a large quantity of gold out of circulation. The operation was a success. Four robbers got away with three tons of gold bullion and two bags of South African diamonds. They tied up the guards and gagged them, using the same method to extort the keys. Two guards were doused with petrol.

'But the stolen valuables never reached the Soviet exchequer. Kassarin was supposed to be in charge of this operation, but he reported that it had been carried out without his knowledge.

'Viktor insisted on these two cases being investigated, and drew the attention of the men at the top to the fact that Kassarin had been abroad on both occasions and the methods used had been identical. Moreover, one of the field agents who tried to report on the strange behaviour of a certain KGB general was killed in an opportune road accident.

'Another case, in Moscow this time, leading straight to Kassarin, was also hushed up. Through some frontmen, he was negotiating the purchase of a laser gyroscope made by the American firm Honeywell. The Soviet Bank sent the hard currency in batches through various New York banks. One instalment of fifty thousand dollars was mistakenly sent twice. Kassarin signed for it both times. An audit a year later brought this to light, but he wriggled out of it, saying that the second sum was passed on to an intermediary as a bribe.

'And then, quite recently, there was another story. For many years I'd maintained a coded correspondence with an old friend – the last of the Berzin guard, Andrei Yemelyanovich Zotov, familiarly known as Saturn. He was a KGB mole in Western Europe, and in recent years had been working directly for Kassarin. Recently, Saturn died in Zurich. After his death, it was discovered that all the valuables in his safe-deposit box in the Röntgen Bank had disappeared. The value of the stolen goods was put at five million roubles, money intended to maintain spy networks in Austria and Switzerland.

'Zotov was an old man like me. What's more natural than that he should die of a heart attack as the Swiss doctors asserted? But the date of his death coincided with a visit by Kassarin to Austria. Zurich is only a stone's throw away.

'Well, I've chopped some logs for you, Comrade Prosecutors, and your job is to stack them up so they don't fall down again. There's nothing else I can do for you, gentlemen, but you should have a word with Viktor's friend, a KGB colonel called Ponomarev. He knows the score even better than I do. Maybe he can advise you further.'

Sasha had said nothing so far. He found the General an awe-inspiring figure. Even over a typically Russian meal – marinated antonovka apples, pickled saffron milk cap mushrooms, herring and hot potatoes – he did not pay attention to what the retired general was saying so much as to the lively play of expression on his mild scholarly face, the movements of his extraordinarily long hands with their bony fingers, and the colour of his eyes, constantly changing from greyish yellow to emerald green.

They said goodbye to Ippolit Alexeyevich and his young wife at six o'clock, sprinted the last part of the way to the station and squeezed on to a crowded train. Half an hour later they were at Paveletsky Station. Merkulov found himself a moonlighting cab-driver and rushed off to see Lelya in hospital.

Sasha went to the Metro station and headed for home.

Walking along Arbat Square, he breathed in the cold air and contemplated the homegoing crowds. Tonight was going to be great. Tonight he would see Rita.

He crossed Aksakov Lane, stubbed out his cigarette on the pavement and went into the block.

Something hard hit him about the eyes and he reeled back, momentarily winded. Vice-like hands grabbed him by the shoulders, arms, neck. Something peculiar and sweet-tasting was held over his mouth. He fought to gulp in some of the apartment block's air, which reeked of ersatz coffee. Scenes from his past life flashed before his closing eyes – a meeting of the commission that assigned young specialist to their jobs, the silent applause in a huge hall as he stood on the platform of honour for winning the university's unarmed combat championship, his deflowering at the hands of a gymnastics mistress, and then, from far away, the words: 'the following are written with an apostrophe: "who's", "it's", "there's". . . .'

11

Everything around him had subtly altered. The world was bathed in a pink mist which rose up into the sky in a conical shape. Unearthly pink light assailed his shrinking eyes. He felt weightless, bodiless and quite calm. Without surprise he saw an angel bending over him, but its childish face was so full of despair that Sasha could not bear to look at it. He closed his eyes.

The intolerable cold woke him again, and he found himself huddled up, muscles rigid and locked, his throat unnaturally dry. His head rang when he tilted it back. Just above him, beneath a domed ceiling with the paint flaking away, was a naked lightbulb, swinging in the draught. The wall against which he huddled was cracked and mouldy. He turned to one side and saw a little girl of about ten sitting on the filthy cement floor beside him. She, too, was shivering from cold, hugging her knees with her arms and staring at him from round blue eyes.

'Who are you?' he asked.

The child didn't answer, so he yelled: 'Are you deaf or something?'

She was still silent, but a look of dawning comprehension appeared on her strained face. Mother of God! It dawned on Sasha that not the slightest sound had come from his mouth. He tried to cough but clouds of silent breath came out. Mute, he was forced to think logically about what must have happened. He'd been snatched and then dumped in a derelict church. His vocal chords had stopped working because of the cold. Nothing that time and a hot bath wouldn't cure.

247

Maybe I'm deaf, too, he thought in horror. As if to refute that idea, he heard the child say: 'Turetsky, have you lost your voice?'

Summoning all his strength, he rasped in a terrible whisper: 'Who-o-o-o you-u-u?'

'Lida Merkulov.'

He thought he might pass out again but forced himself to lurch to his feet and lean against the slime-covered wall. The building swam crazily before his eyes, and the ceiling was coming down, down. . . .

He turned his face to the wall and vomited convulsively, something foul, green and bitter-tasting. Completely annihilated with shame and pain, he struggled instinctively to purge himself.

At last it was finished. He stood there, hands still resting against the slippery wall. He was covered in sweat and tried to find a handkerchief. His pockets were empty: no wallet, identification or keys.

As if staggering on a rolling deck, feet spread wide, he made it to the door, opened it, and found himself enveloped in thick fog. His foot encountered a snow-covered doorstep. He picked up a frozen handful and rubbed it over his face and hands. He could see Lida's thin little figure behind him, in the narrow strip of light channelled through the open door.

'Are you Konstantin Dmitriyevich's little girl?' he said hoarsely.

'Yes, only he's not my real daddy. But I call him Daddy. We've all agreed now that he'll be my proper daddy,' she said, suddenly talking very fast. 'And my mummy is supposed to come home from hospital today and they won't know where I am.' She was shivering from cold, and her voice was high and faltering. He smelt the sharp smell of petrol coming from her beaver-lamb coat.

'Why do you smell of petrol?' The evil-sounding whisper of the Big Bad Wolf getting ready to gobble up little Red Riding Hood. It was too much for Lida, who started to sob.

'Let's get away from here, Turetsky, quick, before they come back.' She rubbed her streaming nose with the back of one hand. Sasha wiped the tears away with the knitted scarf tied round her fur collar.

'Who are "they"?'

'The ones who kidnapped us.'

Lida started to pull him by the hand into the impenetrable darkness. It made no difference in which direction they travelled – there were no landmarks. Wet branches whipped their faces as they avoided spectral trees that loomed up from nowhere, stumbling over stumps and branches concealed underfoot. Sasha looked back. About fifty yards away their former prison was dimly illuminated, the blank windows like so many empty eye-sockets. Ahead loomed something tall and thorn-studded – a barbed-wire fence! They made their way along it, feeling carefully with their hands. In the distance they could see a light.

The going became easier. They did not hold the barbed wire any more, just hung on to each other. The trees thinned out, and up ahead, beneath the lamplight, they saw a plywood sign.

LISTED BUILDING

RIGHT OF WAY STRICTLY FORBIDDEN

TRESPASSERS WILL BE PROSECUTED

There were broken bottles, dried-up rotten newspapers and old tin cans lying round the lamp-post. An animal, probably a squirrel, flashed through the bushes and up a tree, looking down for an instant before disappearing into the night. God Almighty, where were they?

Sasha picked up an empty bottle and was just able to make out the label: 'Kalininsky Brewery'. They were in Kalininsky region, then? They carried on along the fence. From time to time he bent down to identify scraps of newspaper.

They were all *Pravda*, except for one he did not know. *On the Lenin Path*, organ of the Solnechnogorsky District Committee of the Communist Party of the Soviet Union.

Lida found a school exercise-book belonging to 'a pupil of the 6th grade, School No. 2, Solnechnogorsky. Alfred Slepugin.' So they were in Solnechnogorsky, which was on the 'October' railway line, if Sasha remembered correctly. Where the hell was it?

They walked on and on, for maybe an hour. Suddenly Lida said, 'There's a train,' and pointed ahead with her wet mitten. Sasha did not hear a thing. He was still a little deaf.

Sure enough, they soon came out on to a path that followed the railway track. They walked the sleepers for about twenty minutes, and then waited for about another twenty in the station building for a local train. Sasha had no money to pay for tickets and kept an eye out for the guard all the way; he did not want to land in a police station at this stage.

On the way, Lida tried to revive his powers of speech by using a method of hypnosis known only to her. By the time they reached Moscow an hour later, he was able to emit the odd croak.

It was exactly midnight according to the clock at Leningradsky Station when, having queued for half an hour, they got into a taxi. You would get caught if you tried to use public transport without a ticket at that time of night.

Sasha thought Merkulov would smash the door to pieces in his eagerness to open it.

'Konstantin Dmitriyevich . . . please . . . pay . . . the taxi,' he managed to get out.

Merkulov looked them over with half-crazed eyes, then covered his face with his hands.

LIDA'S STORY

'Mashka Goldshtein's daddy rang about five and told me to come over right away to say goodbye to Mashka as she

250

was going away – only I think that it wasn't Mashka's daddy, that's what I think now, but I didn't think that at the time, and ran straight over there because she's my very best friend, and she told me they were going to go off to America.

'I dashed outside and there was a car there – a Volga, I think – but I didn't see anything because they grabbed me and pushed me into the car and drove me somewhere, and one of the men kept holding my face down hard so I couldn't see anything and we went on and on and I was frightened and I was crying, but he told me not to yell 'cause they weren't going to do anything bad to me, and we came to the woods and it was really dark.

'They carried me into some tumbledown church and Turetsky was sitting there and they kept slapping his face and telling him to stop kidding, but I don't think he was kidding at all and was completely unconscious. Their faces were covered with scarves, and one said to the other one: "Give me————" It was some medical word – ax-ax-menitsi . . . And the other one opened a bag and took out a gre-a-at big needle and they said, "OK, Turetsky, tell us where you and Merkulov put the diaries," and Turetsky shouted real loud but it didn't make any sense, and the big one hit him round the ear and the other one said, "If you. . .". Well, he used bad words, and said: "If you finish him off, then we won't get the information from him."

'And then they gave him another injection and after that he stopped talking and only kept opening his mouth like a pike. Then the tall one brought this big square bottle and poured it over my coat. I think it was petrol or paraffin. And the other one got a lighter and said: "Look, Turetsky, your boss's little girl is going to go up in flames. . . ." '

Merkulov shuddered as if he'd been stung.

'You hear that, Sasha?'

He heard. It reminded him of something else he'd heard very recently. Before his eyes floated the faces of

Hitler, Bormann and something quite ridiculous: Alpine meadows of exceptional beauty surrounded by soaring white-capped mountains.

'. . . And Turetsky kept on opening his mouth but he couldn't get anything out and he couldn't make any sense. And then the tall one said they wouldn't get anything out of him today because they had doped him up too much, and he called the other one a cretin and a rat and said he would set fire to *him*. And then he pulled out his gun and said: "Get in the car, you bastard." '

KASSARIN AND SASHA

1

25 November 1982

Outside the window an early-morning wind had sprung up and now it was a howling gale. Sleep had come only in fits and starts. Sasha had a terrible headache and still felt nauseous. Lida was asleep next to him in her bed, kicking her legs and sobbing in her sleep. In the next room Merkulov and his wife spoke in hurried whispers, their conversation frequently overlaid with Lelya's restrained sobbing. There were some shuffling footsteps and then Merkulov was standing in the doorway, glancing into the room.

'I can't sleep, Kostya,' Sasha croaked.

'In the morning I'll get hold of Ponomarev, Rakitin's friend, come what may. Then it's Kazakov and Soya-Serko. We've no more time. If we don't get rid of Kassarin, he'll get rid of us. We must trick him.'

'Kostya, let me do it. I'll go and see him today. I'll play the dumb innocent till he doesn't know where he is!'

Sasha was pulling on his shirt and jeans already.

'First of all, you're going to the clinic to make sure you're OK. Then come and find me. Ring that girl – what's her name? – Lyosha's girl.'

'Yulya?'

'Yes. But don't do anything by yourself. Be very careful. Keep looking over your shoulder all the time.'

Sasha drank several cups of strong black coffee. Merkulov sat opposite, smoking one cigarette after another. Lelya stood by the gas-stove, her back to them, watching the steam rising from the kettle.

2

Sasha left Merkulov's block and walked along Prospekt Mir towards Rizhsky Station. The weather was foul, and a cold wind cut him to the marrow. The legs of his jeans had not dried out and clung to him clammily. When he had gone about ten blocks in the bitter morning air, the drowsy disoriented sensation began to ebb. Going to the clinic would be so much wasted time.

Sasha quickened his pace decisively. He went down into the Metro at Rizhskaya, changed once at Prospect Mir and Circle Line and then again at Kievskaya to get on the Filyovskaya Line. Normally he avoided the Filyovskaya like poison. Today, he hardly noticed it.

At the Metro entrance he dialled Kassarin's personal number. It was exactly nine o'clock. The receiver was picked up right away and Sasha gave his name. Kassarin sounded surprised at first but soon regained his poise.

'I'll be waiting. A pass will be made ready for you.'

Sasha went up to the third floor of the KGB's cylindrical building. He walked into Kassarin's office unannounced, face grim and uncompromising.

Kassarin froze in surprise, cigarette-lighter in one hand, a crumpled piece of paper in the other. Sasha scowled straight into his face, seemingly blind to the paper and the lighter. He threw himself into a deep armchair opposite the General without waiting to be invited to sit. He crossed one leg casually over the other, immediately noticing a long grass stalk sticking to his jeans leg. He picked it off fastidiously and dropped it into the large cut-glass ashtray under the General's nose.

Kassarin stiffened in outrage at this display of boorishness. He even forgot to burn the paper, crumpling it up mechanically instead and dropping it into the ashtray next to the grass stalk. The lighter was still blazing in his hand. Finally, it burnt his fingers. He snapped it shut and mechanically slid it into the inside pocket of his tunic.

'Would you kindly let me know, Alexander Borisovich,' he said coldly, 'why. . . ?'

But Sasha didn't wait for him to finish. He started talking – or, rather, yelling. He yelled for ten minutes: about his dedication to the cause, the homeland and the Soviet security forces. He was outraged by the behaviour of persons unknown to him – 'I suspect that they were your people!' – who had kidnapped Lida Merkulov and used medieval methods on him to try to gain information. He had expressed his ardent desire to serve Comrade Kassarin personally and he was pretty damn pissed off at the lack of trust shown in him.

Kassarin sat back in his chair and pushed the ashtray with the tantalising piece of paper. He looked straight at Sasha, and it was difficult to say whether he was outraged by such insolence or whether he didn't believe a word of it.

He was no Parkhomenko, of course, to be fobbed off with inane simple-minded reports on the level of 'How I spent my summer at Scout Camp'. But it didn't really matter whether he ultimately believed Sasha or not. He'd have to spend time deciding how to handle the situation – and time was what Merkulov needed.

Finally Sasha wound down.

Kassarin ran his hand over his face and started speaking in a low sincere voice. Sasha could not even hear him properly, perhaps because of the blow to the ear he had received the day before. The General seemed to be speaking eloquently and convincingly. Sasha could see he was watching for a reaction, but he was damned if he knew which one.

Finally it penetrated that Kassarin was saying that the Americans were after Rakitin's papers. He handed Sasha a sheet of paper – an American intelligence report, he said – which they had intercepted at the American embassy and decoded. Sasha read the report attentively and looked suitably concerned.

Kassarin continued that Investigator Merkulov had

taken the Rakitin case at face value, as engineered by the KGB, and was now following it blindly. Sasha expressed profound anxiety and even wiped his forehead with his palm. In fact, his only concern was the piece of paper in the ashtray. Assuring him that the KGB would conduct an enquiry into the circumstances surrounding the kidnapping of Investigator Turetsky and Lida Merkulov, and that all possible measures would be taken to safeguard the lives and well-being of the investigations staff of the Prosecutor's Office and their families, Kassarin rose from his chair.

Mumbling some incoherent words of appreciation, Sasha got clumsily to his feet and knocked over his chair with a crash. He picked it up carefully, before finally tumbling out into the corridor. Undetected, he was holding between his middle and index fingers the scrap of paper from the ashtray.

3

Merkulov met Colonel Ponomarev early in the morning on the Lenin Hills. It was quite chilly, the temperature about zero. Although the strong wind had died down, there was a cold drizzle, and the grey surface of the Moscow River rippled silver beneath the falling rain.

'Valery Sergeyevich?' called Merkulov, addressing a thickset man in a brown leather coat and hat.

'Konstantin Dmitriyevich?' said Ponomarev with a smile, examining the Investigator with bright attentive eyes. 'Sorry I had to drag you all the way out here but it gives us two advantages: one, I am near to home; two, you're a long way from our office.

'I haven't been feeling too good, actually. Lethargic, short of breath, high blood pressure. . . . I haven't been to work for a week. But, more to the point, how are you?'

'Me?' said Merkulov, trying to laugh it off. 'One hundred per cent.'

'H'm,' said Ponomarev doubtfully. 'Surprising in view of our mutual acquaintance Vasily Vasilyevich Kassarin.'

'That's just who I'd like to talk about.'

'Well,' said Ponomarev, 'let's talk.'

'There was a conspiracy against your friend Rakitin, and Kassarin was at the bottom of it. We have to nail him, Valery, and I need your help. It's not a question of going against the KGB, but more of eliminating a personal enemy.'

'Are you sure you've got a watertight case against Kassarin?'

'I think so.'

'Think!'

'Then, let me ask you a question. Did you fall sick the day Rakitin was murdered?'

'Yes, why do you ask?'

'No reason.'

'So you think you know all about Kassarin, his past and what he's up to now?'

'I think so.'

'Have you studied the notes Alexei passed on to you?'

'With great interest and not just those. I've read everything I can on the world raw materials markets. Doctrine No. 3 is a time-bomb, but it's in Kassarin's interests to keep it alive, no matter what.'

'I want to explain to you a little more about the circumstances leading up to Viktor's death,' said Ponomarev, taking Merkulov by the arm and guiding him at a leisurely pace over to a view platform. 'No holds barred, Investigator. Rakitin's statements and all his evidence against Kassarin were examined by the people at House number 14 in Kuntsevo, in room 419 of our "cistern" – that is, by the management board of the KGB. And the result was that a decision was taken to consider Rakitin a person "indulging in unauthorised activity". Which meant that Viktor was as good as dead.

'We have an internal instruction number 47. According to it, a security man has no right to complain to another department over the head of a superior – and Viktor did just that. And not just over one head but ten, right up to the Politburo. Can you imagine how angry our bosses were? The next step after "unauthorised activity" is death. If the board of the KGB makes a decision, our boys arrange a little accident. . . . Or sometimes it's plain murder.'

Merkulov shuddered: 'So Rakitin was officially sentenced to death?'

'No, it didn't come to that. Rakitin's mistake was that he confused two issues. Instead of just talking about the malpractices of one person – Kassarin – and keeping quiet about all the rest, he vented his anger on the management of the Party and the KGB, and only exposed Kassarin afterwards.'

'I still don't get it,' said Merkulov.

They had reached the parapet and were looking out over a splendid panorama of Moscow.

'What don't you get?'

'Even if Viktor Nikolayevich got his tactics wrong, wasn't it clear to everyone that Kassarin was an enemy of the Soviet system?'

'But Kassarin is an excellent worker – a genius even when it comes to intelligence work. The fact that he deals in valuables is neither here nor there. It's lawful! The head of a section in a committee like "T" committee can do what he likes. In theory, of course, there is a directorate head above him, and one of the chairman's deputies. But in practice there's no control over him. Tsinyov and Serebrovsky are his personal friends and may even get a rake-off.

'He's got a "green", a special pass, which gives him the right to take flights to the West: Vienna, Paris, London. He's also got an "all-rounder" – that's another special pass signed by the General Secretary of the Party and the Chairman of the KGB. That really is something! If you have that document, you can do whatever you like in our country. Write out a cheque for a million roubles, or have someone taken out – for reasons of state.'

'I see,' said Merkulov sharply. 'So Kassarin killed Rakitin with the connivance of others, and that's all there is to it. We can't even ask him questions?'

'Not quite. Kassarin may be one of the pillars of Soviet intelligence, and an expert on foreign affairs – you have to be extremely careful with him – but he could still be stood against a wall.'

'How?' Merkulov demanded incredulously. 'You say youself that the board of the KGB heard all Rakitin's evidence and it still hasn't found him guilty. It exonerates him, damn it!'

'There's still one way,' said Colonel Ponomarev with a wry smile. 'When Yuri Vladimirovich was still Chairman of the KGB he brought in a new rule. In order to prevent people just standing bail for each other, and to stop them being afraid of earning the label "unauthorised activity", Andropov gave orders for a special letter-box to be placed in the hall of the main KGB building in Kuntsevo. Any employee of the security organs could go there and drop a letter in. In writing you could say, for example, that your boss, General so-and-so, was an American spy. The box is emptied every hour and the contents placed on Andropov's desk.'

'Fedorchuk's desk now,' corrected Merkulov.

'Chebrikov's desk now! A decree was signed yesterday transferring Fedorchuk to the Ministry of Internal Affairs and confirming Viktor Mikhailovich Chebrikov as the new Chairman of the KGB. Shchelokov and Churbanov have been given the push, thank God. They've done so much damage to party credibility, stolen so much from the State. . . . It's still being decided whether to arrest them or not. So, Konstantin Dmitriyevich, only two people, the Chairman's assistants, have keys to that letter-box. . . .'

'I see,' said Merkulov, looking blindly down. 'You're advising me to use the box?'

'Yes,' nodded Ponomarev. 'If you like, give your letter to me and I'll find a way of posting it.'

'And then what?'

'Then Viktor Mikhailovich will invite you to see him. You'll tell him all about Major-General Kassarin's misdeeds, you'll report on your investigations into Rakitin's murder, and give the full background. I think – in fact, I'm certain – that the security organs will draw certain conclusions. Kassarin will be removed from office, and it's not impossible that the management of the KGB will sanction his arrest and perhaps his trial *in camera*. And so, Konstantin Dmitriyevich, the meek shall inherit the earth.'

'OK,' said Merkulov thoughtfully. 'That's what we'll do, Valery Sergeyevich. When can you deliver my statement for me?'

'Any time. You have my address. *Au revoir*, Konstantin Dmitriyevich.'

4

As the train came into Kutuzovskaya Metro station, Sasha looked at his watch; it was seven minutes past ten. He estimated that if he had gone to the clinic it would have taken about two hours – maybe three with the queuing up, and going into various offices, and waiting for X-rays. So Merkulov would not be expecting him for another two hours. . . . He jumped out of his seat and prised the doors apart as they started to close. On Kutuzovsky Prospekt, he took a cab to Frunzenskaya Embankment.

Rita opened the door, her face pale and haggard.

'Sasha! I looked everywhere for you yesterday. Is everything OK?'

She was wearing a grey knitted hat and a blue coat with a grey beaver collar. Today she looked about fifteen years old. She was holding some aluminium pans that slotted into each other – the kind that well-to-do old-age pensioners on the Arbat – the merited artists and dentists – use to fetch take-away food from the Prague.

'They operated on Zhorka yesterday; he's got something wrong with his knee. You remember Zhorka, the man with the beard at the studio? The food in the district hospital is lousy so I've just cooked him something.'

Rita stopped chattering nervously, put the pans on the floor, went into the sitting room and came back with a telegram in her hand. Sasha read it and all the horror of the previous day descended on him again.

'Flying out Saturday, 27 November. Sergei.'

He felt completely thrown, but Rita took him by the hand and led him to the couch.

'Sasha, it'll work out fine, you'll see. I just couldn't get round to writing to him. Now things will sort themselves out. You think I'm pretty bright, don't you? But I'm very stupid.' Rita spoke softly and slowly, studying her lilac-painted fingernails. 'Sergei came to our college, to the graduation party. He was an adjunct in the Frunze Academy in those days, and I really loved his uniform. Stupid, huh? We danced some silly waltzes together and then he brought me back to this apartment.'

Rita lit a cigarette. Sasha didn't know whether to laugh or to cry, but he was sure of one thing. He loved Rita Shchastlivaya as no one had ever loved her before.

'And then – well, it wasn't that I got any smarter. I just saw that I couldn't go on. We were on opposite sides of the fence. . . .'

'Are you sure you'll be on the same side of the fence as me?' he asked, thinking about Kassarin, Parkhomenko, Gryaznov. Whichever way you looked at it, he was from the same stable as them.

Rita stubbed out her cigarette in the ashtray, put her arms round his neck and said light-heartedly: 'That's irrelevant, because I love you.'

He pressed his lips to hers. The knitted hat slipped

from her head, and her ashen hair cascaded over the green upholstery of the couch.

Outside in the hall, Zhorka's dinner got cold.

While Rita was feeding the insatiable artist, Sasha drove her car round and round the hospital. He was getting the hang of it quite well, but a cyclist who was unaccountably taking the same route at the same speed kept getting in the way. At last he was able to overtake but scraped the door against some shrubs.

Then he drove out on to Lyusinovskaya Street as far as the Danilovsky department store, turned round, surreptitiously stuck out his tongue at a policeman on point duty, and made a few more trips up and down the adjoining streets.

Rita showed up half an hour later. Invincible after his motoring success, Sasha told her what had happened the previous day.

'I'll pick you up at six tonight,' she said in a shaky voice.

5

'I should blast you to Kingdom Come,' Merkulov said when he heard Sasha's account of the morning. 'I told you to get your health checked out, not to stick your neck on the chopping board. Whatever your motives, Sasha, my orders were—' But at that moment Sasha produced his trump card – the note stolen from Kassarin's ashtray.

' "Alla, urgent, where have you hidden Mazer's letter? Yours, V.," ' Merkulov read aloud in a sinister guttural voice. ' "You'll get it when you get me out of this shithouse. Alla." She hasn't lost her sense of humour in detention, I see. And the postman was. . . ?'

'Pogorelov interrogated her yesterday, and then

Gryaznov came in and said the boss wanted him. She didn't apparently.'

Merkulov rubbed his cheeks with his palms as if he had just come in from the cold, and said at last: 'When characters like Parkhomenko go in for this kind of thing, I just take it for granted. But Vyacheslav is basically a good man. It's such a waste, Sasha! As far as your raid on Kassarin goes, then maybe you were right – we need to gain time. But stealing that piece of paper wasn't smart. It wasn't smart at all. Kassarin is on to us again and he's not the forgiving sort.'

Top Secret
To the Head of Special Investigations Section
Major-General of KGB
Comrade V. V. Kassarin

Special Report

Today we were able to record a conversation that took place on the Lenin Hills between Investigator K. D. Merkulov and an employee of the First Main Administration of the KGB of the USSR, V. S. Ponomarev.

Colonel Ponomarev, a friend of the deceased Rakitin, advised Merkulov to seek a personal audience with Colonel-General V. M. Chebrikov. He recommended the use of the letter-box for correspondence addressed personally to the Chairman of the KGB. Merkulov asked Ponomarev to pass on his letter to Comrade Chebrikov in the course of the afternoon.

Today we installed electronic listening devices in the bodywork of the trunk of the Lada, licence no. MKT 1477, belonging to Citizen M. N. Shchastlivaya, and in the Volga, no. M05 8869, assigned to Investigator K. D. Merkulov.

The surveillance showed that the Lada no. MKT 1477 left no. 48 Frunzenskaya Embankment and reached Lyusinovskaya Street at 11.30. For half an hour the car circled Hospital No. 35 and then went to Danilovsky Square going the wrong way up adjoining one-way streets. At 14.30, the Lada returned to its permanent parking place on Frunzenskaya Embankment.

A tape recording is enclosed.

Head of 5th Section
Major of KGB
P. SMOLYARUK
25 November 1982

6

Merkulov looked sternly at Kazakov.

'Tell me about the murder of Rakitin and Kupriyanova.'

'Stupid bastards, they should have known better than to cross him. I played it straight, for Christ's sake, and I got a bullet in the brain. What did they expect?'

Volodya Kazakov was deathly pale, but he sounded in rude good health.

The interrogation was taking place in the Burdenko Institute in the presence of the doctor who had saved him, the eminent surgeon, Solovyov.

The patient spoke in a hoarser voice than normal, his lips parched and cracked, but Merkulov heard every word. He wrote down the suspect's words, omitting the choicer descriptive phrases.

Top Secret

Statement of Interrogation of Suspect
Kramarenko a.k.a. Kazakov

City of Moscow   25 November 1982

On the premises of the Red Banner of Labour Scientific Research Institute of Neurosurgery, named after Academician N. N. Burdenko, in the presence of Professor G. I. Solovyov, Special Crimes Investigator and Judicial Counsellor of the Moscow City Public Prosecutor's Office, K. D. Merkulov, carried out an interrogation of the suspect, Vladimir Georgiyevich Kramarenko (Kazakov), born 1944, non Party-member, Russian nationality, educated to eighth grade, unmarried.

I have been informed that I am suspected of murdering Viktor Rakitin and Valeria Kupriyanova.

signed
VLADIMIR KAZAKOV

Investigator's question: There are three men and three women in these photographs. Tell me, do you recognise any of them?

Answer: Having examined the photos shown to me, I recognise man no. 1 and woman no. 3. The man is Viktor Rakitin, and the woman is Valeria Kupriyanova. Vitalka Shakun and I killed them. Rakitin in Sokolniki Park, Kupriyanova in the Central Hotel.

Question: Under what circumstances did you see these people the first time?

Answer: Before Brezhnev's death, Vasily just told me and Shakun to take a look at our intended victims. He said we have to 'take them out', that is, kill them. Vasily gave us their photos and told us to go to the stage door of the Stanislavsky Theatre after the performance of a ballet. Sure enough, these two came out, arm in arm. We recognised them from the photographs Vasily gave us.

Question: Who is the man you call 'Vasily'?

Answer: 'Vasily' is Vasily Vasilyevich Kassarin, a KGB general. Vitalka Shakun and I were his agents and informers for years. We did whatever he told us.

Question: How did you meet Kassarin?

Answer: When I broke out of gaol ten years ago and came to Moscow. I was really starving. I didn't have anything to live on. I did small jobs just to get by! Mugging, burglary, petty thieving. I had my own patch – the National Hotel. Once I got this smartly dressed man in 'the pipe', the pedestrian walkway under the Manege. I squeezed his throat a bit and took his hard currency. The next day I found out it was some Frenchman, an official from their embassy. He was taken off to hospital. To cut it short, they put me in Lefortovo Prison for mugging a foreigner.

Kassarin – he was a colonel then – let me go when I signed a piece of paper to say I would work for him.

Question: Did you have any personal score to settle with Rakitin or Kupriyanova?

Answer: No, I had no score to settle with them. There was no hostility between us. I didn't know them from Adam.

Question: Then, how do you explain your decision to kill people you didn't know?

Answer: Do you know what Vasily would have done to me? His favourite is to hang someone upside down and pour boiling wax over their balls. No ordinary crook could think of the things that Kassarin knows! I was totally in his power – he knew about all the guys I'd rubbed out – he could just have rung Moscow CID at any time and turned me over to them. He set me up at the Elisei Food Store. I'm just a legman; he's the real boss. All the rake-off from the bookmaking is his. I only take a percentage, one-third. You think all that gold and diamonds I stashed at Georgadze's place are mine? Fat chance! Nearly all of it was Vasily's.

Question: What do you know about Citizen Shakun?

Answer: I know he also used to run errands for Kassarin, and he killed a lot of people for him, too. Vasily got this Vitaly Glebovich Shakun out of some shit, and then used him as a hit-man. Shakun's a crack shot, uses a rapid-fire handgun. He was a Master of Sport for shooting, only he had the title taken away from him because of some court case, and the diploma and medal were kept at the city court. He asked me to get him another medal and I gave him Volin's, which I had in my collection. He used to wear it on his lapel all the time, till he lost it in Sokolniki Park when we strangled Rakitin.

Question: Tell me about the murder of Viktor Nikolayevich Rakitin.

Answer: On 17 November, Kassarin invited me and Shakun to a secret address. It was on Rusakovskaya Street in the block where the department store is. He gave us instructions, how and where to meet this Rakitin and finish him off, and promised us a bonus when we completed the job properly. Ten thousand roubles each. By twelve noon we were at the park, right by the administration building. Rakitin came along and we tracked him. Then they announced over the PA system that the park would be closed temporarily.

Rakitin went to the Prague. We followed him and let him have a drink. When he came out, we were waiting. There was no one around at all, so we just kind of strangled him with the noose. Then we hung him up on the tree, like Kassarin told us to do, so it would look like suicide. . . . We even put four bricks underneath to make it look real.

Question: And how did the murder of Kupriyanova take place?

Answer: After Sokolniki, we went back to the secret address on Rusakovskaya Street – it's next to the Sokolniki Metro station. We sat around there as Vasily told us to. We didn't drink anything; that's not on when we're working. Kassarin came to see us at ten, gave Shakun a parabellum Browning, and took us into town in an official car. On the way he explained what our next job was. He gave us the keys to room 547 in the Central Hotel, told us that we had to find out from this Kupriyanova woman where she and Rakitin had hidden the duplicates of his papers, and then finish her off before we left. Me and

Shakun opened the room and waited until she showed up. We talked to her straight for about ten minutes, worked her over and threatened her. She didn't say anything that made sense. Then I put all her things in the green bag so that it would look like the motive was robbery. I grabbed all her papers, documents and notebooks. Then Shakun fired once. There was no noise; the gun had a silencer. We just went out and down the stairs. Kassarin was waiting for us in the car.

Question: Do you have any suspicions regarding the attempt on your own life?

Answer: I have no doubt that the attempt on my life in the train was organised by General Kassarin. He was afraid that I would squeal on him for sending me and Shakun to kill Rakitin.

Kassarin wanted me dead, so no one would be any wiser about the killings and his other doings. Like the valuables taken to Georgadze's place.

Question: Do you know anything concrete about Kassarin's illegal activities abroad?

Answer: No, he wouldn't tell me. I know he goes abroad a lot, and not just to Bulgaria, Romania, East Germany and Czechoslovakia, but also to Austria, Switzerland, France, West Germany, England – even the USA. He's got a pass that they call an 'all-rounder'. It gives him the right to get on the helicopter on the roof of the KGB building in Kuntsevo and fly to some secret airfield in Golitsyno or Alabino, and from there he can just clear off to Paris for a Sunday and eat at Maxim's. And Kassarin doesn't travel alone. He takes his bosses, or their children, those whose dads are in the Politburo or the Central Committee. And you wouldn't believe the orgies he has! I haven't been abroad with him but I've been to plenty of closed saunas and whorehouses. He has the best women – some new starlet or a new chorus girl at the operetta, Vasily will get them. When he's through with them, it's Tsinyov's or Serebrovsky's turn, then all the others. It's not that he himself is a great womaniser – he just likes to be in charge of it all so that his bosses, even marshals or people from the Central Committee of the Party are subordinate to him.

For example, when they have a 'closed doors day' in some whorehouse like on Prospekt Mir or Kutuzovsky Prospect, then, first, they have to make sure that no outsiders come along and, second, that it's not just whores but the wives of executive functionaries that are invited along to do the honours. Otherwise he's not interested.

Question: Do you know Citizen Alla Alexandrovna Soya-Serko?

Answer: Yes, I know Alla Soya-Serko: she's Kassarin's mistress and an old friend of his. It was through her that Kassarin did his business with me and with Yuri Leonovich, one of the men who Kassarin went shares with when they brought in valuables from the West, or sent them there.

Question: When did you see Soya-Serko last?

Answer: The last time I saw Alla was on Sunday, 21 November. She came to my box at the Hippodrome and gave me an order from Vasily. She said I was to take all the goods, mine and Kassarin's valuables, to Georgadze's country house right away. She said that the Moscow CID had got Volin and that he wouldn't hold out long.

At this point, in view of the serious condition of the interviewee Kramarenko (Kazakov) the interrogation was terminated.

The evidence here recorded has been read to me and is a correct verbatim record.

VLADIMIR KRAMARENKO-KAZAKOV
(signature)

I hereby confirm that the record of the evidence given by the patient Kramarenko is correct.

Professor Solovyov
(signature)

The interrogation was conducted by investigator

K. D. Merkulov
(signature)

7

'Grachev is an excellent worker! So is Solomin!'

The section manager of the all-Union Chamber of Commerce, Professor of Economics Medvedev, smiled reassuringly as he sat Shura Romanova in a soft armchair. 'I've been working here for twenty-three years now, and I've never known better workers; that's all I can say.'

Romanova was with Professor Medvedev in his office at the subsidiary of the Chamber of Commerce in Sokolniki; the room was light and had contemporary furnishings. They sat in armchairs upholstered in imitation grey leather. There was a mountain of publications on the magazine-table in front of them, from *The British Ally* to *Time* magazine. On the window-ledge stood a row of well-tended pot-plants – flowers and creepers – and the bookcase behind the desk was full of thick files containing scientific works and abstracts, the arcane titles of which were completely wasted on Lieutenant-Colonel Romanova.

'Would you like to know what Grachev and Solomin's jobs are? What special aptitudes they possess? But you didn't tell me what this is all about.'

'Didn't I?' said Romanova innocently. 'We have received information that these two men, together with an attractive woman, have been forging banknotes.'

'That can't be true. It must be a mistake.' Medvedev spread dry little hands. 'I don't believe it.'

'Strange.' Romanova shook her head. 'I was told the opposite – that you were in on it, too.'

Professor Medvedev's face changed subtly. His sharp beak-like nose broadened as his nostrils flared.

'Very amusing. I understand perfectly well what you're up to. It's what my son calls the secret service mystique: the thrill of the chase, tracker dogs, cocked guns, setting traps. But I don't know anything about forged money.'

He squared his puny shoulders. Evidently Section Manager Medvedev possessed not just a sharp mind but also a strong character. He was not going to be easy to crack.

'If I had to summarize what I know about Interpreter Grachev and Senior Chemist Solomin, then I would say that I have never met such talented professionals or such decent people. They work hard, bringing great benefits to the State. In addition, Grachev is a polyglot. He knows twelve languages and is very keen on music: Tchaikovsky, Shostakovich, Brahms. Solomin is a connoisseur of the fine arts. . . .'

Romanova stared at Medvedev expressionlessly.

'Grachev does have one shortcoming, though,' he went on. 'He is needlessly prolix for these days. He should have been born in the last century!'

Romanova seemed to come to life.

'I don't understand you, Professor Medvedev. You said that in the performance of your duties you had almost no contact with these employees, yet now you're talking of their love for Brahms, antiques. . . . Maybe you're on the prolix side, too, Professor!'

And Romanova proceeded to take some photographs out of her shopping bag. There were a lot of them, and they were of excellent quality. They depicted one naked Professor of Economics, in the society of some naked ladies. And some naked men. In poses that could have come from a skinflick.

The Professor stared at the photographs wordlessly. Romanova crossed one leg over the other and pulled the hem of her uniform skirt a little higher.

'Wouldn't you like to know how I came by them? Prospekt Mir, the building on the corner by the Botanical Gardens Metro station. The Apartment of Madame Lessner. Seventh floor. Ring twice. Do you know it?

'My boys have been working on that whorehouse for some time now. We've had concealed cameras in there for more than two months. If you answer all my questions precisely, you'll have all these photographs and films, plus a guarantee that no one will ever know about your visits to Madame Lessner's brothel – neither your wife nor your Party Committee. So are we going to be coy with one another, or are you willing to do a deal?'

Medvedev answered resignedly: 'I'll trade.'

He locked the office door before beginning his story.

Apparently, Grachev and Solomin were naturals, prodigiously gifted. They made plates for manufacturing hundred-dollar and hundred-rouble notes. For six months they passed off their counterfeit money to foreigners and Soviet citizens, and also to the Soviet trade network, but then they were caught and put in Lefortovo Prison. There they did a deal with the security organs, carrying on work as before, but this time for the KGB. After three years' detention they were freed and put on Medvedev's staff, but still working covertly 'for the organs'.

To avoid any misunderstanding on Lieutenant-Colonel Romanova's part, Professor Medvedev was quick to declare that he considered it, and always would consider it, his duty as a Bolshevik always to rebuff any attacks on the Party or its programmes. He warmly approved of the idea of destabilising Western society, which meant supporting the KGB plan for flooding leading Western countries with forged currency.

With the help of Grachev and Solomin, the top-secret workshop number 10 in the Goznak plant went into production. The results of the work were not slow to be seen: in the United States, Canada, France and West Germany one could see economic collapse – or so-called recession.

But little by little, thousand by thousand, Grachev and Solomin started removing dollars secretly from the Gosznak plant and palming them off on foreign tourists again. They bought themselves a country house each, a car each, started investing in antiques. . . . And then they had their first skirmish with the Anti-Corruption Squad. The boys from Abrikosov's pernicious department got to wondering about them.

At that time Solomin got to know the brown-eyed Alla Soya-Serko, a young antiques connoisseur. They agreed she would register their valuables as her own property, and keep them and the hundred-dollar plate at her place. Two years went by and then *bang!* Alla's antiques were stolen.

Medvedev urged his men to turn their attention to the lady herself. By following her, and bugging her phone, they found out that Soya-Serko had bribed two housebreakers to remove the whole collection from her apartment. Alla started to sell it discreetly, mainly abroad. Grachev and Solomin were incensed, wanted to bring in the police. Medvedev warned them off on the grounds that if the enquiry turned to Alla it would certainly get them, too. And maybe their powerful connections would stand back. That's the way it turned out, of course.

'And do you know Rakitin from the Ministry of Foreign Trade?'

'Viktor Nikolayevich? Who doesn't? I saw him about ten days ago, in secret workshop number 10. . . .'

8

26 November 1982

Merkulov was banging something out on his battered old typewriter when Sasha entered the room. He was scowling ferociously at the noise from the next room where the television set was on at full volume. Some third-year students sent over to Petrovka for procedures training were in there playing around.

Sasha recognised Merkulov's fixed stare: he didn't even have time to bang on the wall and tell the kids to be quiet. Sasha went next door and interrupted a training film *Killed in the Line of Duty*. He sent all the students on a practical to Moiseyev's laboratory so that they could familiarize themselves with the latest achievements in our motherland's criminology.

When he returned, Merkulov was smiling. No point in asking why – if he wanted to, he'd say.

Sasha began catching up on the most recent statements from the witnesses interrogated, which a motorcycle courier had brought over from Moscow CID.

'Read this!' grunted Merkulov suddenly. 'I have to go and see Yemelyanov, at half-ten.' He handed over the fourth copy of the document he had just typed.

At that moment the phone buzzed like a gnat. Funny, they seemed to have changed the phone since yesterday. The old one had a clearer tone.

'Yes, Sergei Andreyevich. . . . Yes, I'm on my way.'

Merkulov stood up behind his desk and began to gather up his papers.

Sasha immersed himself in the report while Merkulov went along the corridor to Yemelyanov's office.

Resolution
(Regarding the summoning of an accused person)

City of Moscow   26 November 1982

I, K. D. Merkulov, Special Crimes Investigator of the Moscow Prosecutor's Office, Judicial Counsellor, having examined the evidence in the case arising from the discovery of the bodies of Citizen V. N. Rakitin and V. S. Kupriyanova
HAVE ESTABLISHED:
As head of the special investigation section of the third Main Administration 'T' committee (scientific and technical strategic investigations) of the KGB of the USSR, and having at his disposal considerable autonomous power as well as handling credits for the purchase of Western technology and the sale of strategic raw materials, V. V. Kassarin has systematically enriched himself at the expense of the Soviet State and has made financial profits for himself and for other persons occupying especially responsible posts in the Communist Party and the Soviet State.

Between 1975 and 1982, V. V. Kassarin misappropriated for his own use approximately 6 (six) million roubles.

Fearing exposure by the staff of the Ministry of Foreign Trade, the HQ of Military Intelligence of the USSR and the KGB of the USSR, Independently or with the aid of his subordinates and agents, he carried out a series of assassinations, including that of A. E. Zotov, Yu. Yu. Leonovich, A. Mazer, V. S. Kupriyanova and V. N. Rakitin.

To enact his criminal designs he enlisted the

276

services of his agents Vladimir Kazakov-Kramarenko and Vitaly Shakun, who were dependent on him for work and in other ways, and for whom he provided the necessary information, shelter and weapons.

On 17 November, Kazakov and Shakun, at Kassarin's instigation, attacked citizen V. N. Rakitin in Sokolniki Park and strangled him with a wire noose, stealing his briefcase containing secret documents, samples of counterfeit foreign currency, and notes proving Kassarin's culpability of carrying out crimes against the State; they then tried to disguise the crime as suicide.

On the evening of the same day they entered the Central Hotel, subjected V. S. Kupriyanova to torture and then killed her with a Browning handgun.

Fearing that Kazakov-Kramarenko would expose him, Kassarin charged one of his agents, as yet unidentified, to kill Kramarenko. On the night of 21 to 22 November, in a compartment of the Moscow–Novorossiisk express, an unknown person shot Kazakov-Kramarenko with a 7.65 Colt. The wounds that Kazakov–Kramarenko sustained are officially described as 'grave' and 'likely to endanger life'.

Additionally, fearing exposure by Yu. Yu. Leonovich and a foreign citizen Albert Mazer, partners in his mercenary crimes, Kassarin charged his long-standing agent Vitaly Shakun to kill them. On the evening of 22 November 1982, in the Berlin Restaurant, Shakun killed Leonovich and wounded Mazer with shots from a parabellum Browning.

Moreover, Citizen A. A. Soya-Serko, a partner in his many crimes, carrying out Kassarin's wishes, on 23 November entered the Sklifosovsky Emergencies Institute and, in the guise of a member of the nursing staff, administered poison to A. Mazer as a result of which he died.

In view of the above, and invoking articles 143 and 144 of the Criminal Code of the RSFSR
I HAVE RESOLVED:
To bring to justice Citizen Vasily Vasilyevich Kassarin, charging him under articles 102 paragraph '3' (premeditated murder), 17–102 paragraphs 'b', 'c', 'e', 'f', 'l' (complicity in premeditated murder), 93–1 (exceptionally large-scale embezzlement), 88 part 2 (speculation in hard currency on an exceptionally large scale), 170 part 2 (abuse of one's official position), 172 part 2 (accepting bribes).

> Special Crimes Investigator of the
> Moscow Public Prosecutor's Office
> Judicial Counsellor
> KONSTANTIN MERKULOV

Sasha waited for Merkulov in a state of extreme tension. He wanted to ask some questions this time, damn it! But when Merkulov finally came back he was not as cheerful as before and immediately started hammering away at the typewriter like a demented woodpecker. He addressed an envelope, placed a report in it, counted out twenty roubles for a taxi and told Sasha to go over to Ponomarev on Universitetsky Prospekt right away.

The return journey took just over an hour.

At two o'clock, when he came back, Merkulov and he began to chain smoke, wondering if the note in the box would settle things once and for all.

9

They were starting to tidy Merkulov's desk, filing away textbooks and witnesses' statements, and getting ready to place the remaining two copies of the report in the safe, when the phone rang. Sasha answered it.

'This is the assistant to Colonel-General Chebrikov, the Chairman of the KGB. Viktor Mikhailovich would like to talk to Comrade Merkulov, Special Crimes Investigator.'

Merkulov had already picked up the other receiver. He listened silently for a minute, and then thanked Chebrikov and hung up.

'Sasha, Chebrikov's car is coming to pick us up now. He's going to see us at a safe house where he meets his personal agents. I'll get all the material – you collect your thoughts!' Then Merkulov flew out of the office.

Damn! Rita was picking him up at a quarter to six outside the entrance to the Prosecutor's Office.

Merkulov cannoned into the office, sorting out a pile of papers. Rakitin's notes! Where the hell had they been? He must have hidden them in the Prosecutor's Office all along. Merkulov scooted out again. Sasha peeked into the corridor and saw the Forensic Office door close carefully behind Merkulov. So Merkulov was hiding life-threatening evidence in Semyon Semyonovich Moiseyev's number 2 strongbox, together with pieces of skull, flattened bullets and hypodermic syringes that had once contained quick-acting poison. There was a sort of logic to it, he supposed.

Merkulov was hardly back in the office when Garik peered round the door.

'A car's here for you, Konstantin Dmitriyevich!

Sasha tried to tell him but, damn him, he was already pounding down the stairs.

'I can't go, Kostya!' Sasha shouted down the stairwell. 'Why not?'

'Personal reasons.'

Merkulov turned round, pushed open the door, and they both saw Rita, running along on the other side of the street, waving hello.

The young fresh-faced driver of the black limousine obligingly opened the car doors. Merkulov pointed. 'This lady is coming with us, too.' The driver shrugged indifferently – what was it to him? – and sat behind the wheel. Merkulov sat in front, Rita and Sasha behind.

'Rita, I'll try to let Sasha go as soon as possible.'

'It doesn't matter. I can wait, Kostya.'

Sasha took her hand in his.

The driver hadn't fully braked before Merkulov was jumping out of the car, clutching his battered old briefcase. Sasha briefly registered that the villa ahead looked very dark, but Merkulov was already striding towards it. Lights shone faintly behind a row of nearby pine-trees.

Sasha darted after him. Surely something was horribly wrong. . . .

'Sa-a-sh-a-a!' screamed Rita.

He turned around, straight into a different time-scale. When he tried to remember the sequence of events, it was different every time – like looking into a child's kaleidoscope, trying to identify the pattern you remember from last time. . . .

He was running back to Rita and his foot felt like lead. His head was hammering like crazy, and he was running, running, but there was no way he could reach her. Another few steps, another, another. . . . Half a step and she'd be safe in his arms. He seemed to freeze in mid-air as Rita put her arms around the trunk of a pine-tree and slowly slid to the ground.

And then, for the first time, he realised that the pounding all around him was automatic fire. He began falling fast from an incredible height. It lasted a very long time. There was Rita's bag, lying open right beneath him, and her bunch of keys to one side. Then everything went dark. . . .

He lay immobile on the ground, pressing his cheek to Rita's cold face and clawing convulsively at the frozen earth. There was no room for life in the frozen hellish world he found himself in.

Then he saw the luminous dial of his wristwatch. Twenty-one minutes past six. He struggled to his knees and looked around.

A few feet away from him, slumped against a tree, sat Merkulov. His eyes were closed and instead of a mouth there was a gaping black hole. His clenched fingers still gripped the torn-off handle of his briefcase.

They hadn't been expecting Rita. The man with the gun hadn't seen her at first, but she saw him. She screamed, 'Sa-a-sh-a-a'.

Unseen, the man with the gun sprayed bullets in the direction of the noise, then all around. He'd got Sasha in the shoulder or the forearm; he couldn't lift his hand.

Merkulov was dead. Rita's grey eyes were cold and hard as glass.

The pain was unbearable. Sasha threw back his head and howled.

Secret

Telephone Report

In accordance with secret instruction no. 24 of 5 August 1971 regarding the immediate reporting to the Prosecutor of Moscow of all violent deaths in Greater Moscow, I report:

On 24 November of this year Junior Investigator of the Moscow Public Prosecutor's Office Alexander Turetsky and the daughter of Special Crimes Investigator K. Merkulov, a minor named Lida, were abducted and tortured.

In connection with this, secret orders were issued by you to the head of Moscow CID of Moscow City Executive Committee, introducing urgent measures to safeguard members of the investigation team working on the murder of V. N. Rakitin.

To carry out your orders of 25 and 26 November 1982, a squad from the second section of the Moscow CID, consisting of Captain Potekhin and Lieutenant Lazarov, was guarding the investigation team.

On 26 November at the end of the working day at a quarter to six a Volga, registration no. M05 1012, arrived to collect Merkulov and Turetsky. Together with the forensic expert M. N. Shchastlivaya, they got in the car and left Moscow City Public Prosecutor's Office. Potekhin and Lazarov followed them in a Volga, no. MKTs 3939.

As the patrol was not supposed to make its present known, the police car followed the Volga M05 1012 at a distance of 30–40 metres. The car turned off the Sadovoye ring-road and went along Leninsky Prospekt. At the end of this road it turned left and approached its destination (Later we discovered that this building is designated for operational purposes by KGB Centre.)

The police officers were not expecting danger, thinking that the investigations team was engaged in its appointed business and was carrying out an urgent task connected with the investigation. However, at 18.20 an attack was carried out on the employees of the Prosecutor's Office: persons unknown opened fire on them with automatic weapons as soon as they left the car.

As a result of the attack, the forensic expert M. N. Shchastlivaya was killed on the spot, Comrades Merkulov and Turetsky were wounded. Having snatched the briefcase with the documents from Merkulov, the driver of the Volga M05 1012 disappeared from the scene of the crime, together with the machine-gunner (or gunners). We have taken measures to apprehend them, but we have been unable to catch up with them. A search has been mounted through the various traffic departments.

K. D. Merkulov, who has been seriously wounded, and A. B. Turetsky, whose wounds are not critical, have been taken to the Gagarin District Hospital in Moscow.

An operations team from the Gagarin District Committee of Internal Affairs went to the scene of the incident, and then an investigations team from the Public Prosecutor's Office and the City Committee of Internal Affairs, Moscow City Executive Committee. After an examination of the scene of the incident was conducted, the body of citizen M. N. Shchastlivaya was taken to the morgue of the City Hospital No. 1.

For the present, the second section of the Moscow CID has mounted a search for the murderers of Citizen Shchastlivaya.

In view of the fact that the present case of premeditated murder is under investigation by the Prosecutor's Office, I strongly request you to instruct the head of the investigations department of the Moscow City Public Prosecutor's Office, Senior Judicial Counsellor Comrade L. V. Parkhomenko, to assign a qualified investigator to this case.

Head of second section of the Moscow CID
City Committee of Internal Affairs of
Moscow City Executive Committee
A. ROMANOVA
City of Moscow, 26 November 1982
19 hrs, 27 mins

10

Sasha did not want to think, to see or to hear. He just wanted to lay his head on the table and die.

He struck his bandaged arm on the edge of the table. For a moment that helped to focus the pain somewhere a little more bearable.

Time became compressed, just one solid wall of pain.

He answered phone calls, rang one or two people himself, took painkillers and drank chicken broth on the orders of Irka Frolovskaya, the visiting niece.

But it wasn't him; it couldn't be. Sasha was still staring into Rita's glassy eyes, pressing her ice-cold cheek and howling like a wolf from unbearable, searing pain.

Dear Zhora,

We have buried Rita without you. I can't believe it's really true that we'll never see her again. You asked us to tell you in detail what happened, but some things are better not written in letters.

There were a lot of people at the funeral, both from City Hospital No. 1 and from Petrovka 38. Sergei Ivanovich Shchastlivy flew in from Afghanistan yesterday.

Rita's boyfriend, Sasha, that kid of an investigator, was wounded in the arm, and the other investigator is in a bad way. Apparently, Sasha sat with him all morning today, and they told him not to hope.

We all went to Vostryakovo – Valka Nikulin and Senya and your artist pals, even Inka Nikulina. You were the only one who wasn't there. You wouldn't believe all the flowers. My Mr David Drapkin was very kind and brought an enormous bouquet of roses, but his appearance really shocked everyone at the cemetery – he was wearing a shabby old coat and scruffy jeans, and driving that fabulous Ford. Do you remember how Rita always dreamt of a ride in that Ford?

We all went to my place in the Ford, all of us squeezed in. Senya Shteinbock had to ride in the truck, and he was so squeezed up there like a ram's horn that even Sasha smiled. David had bought all sorts of stuff in the hard-currency shop, so we were able to say goodbye to Rita in style. And, of course, everyone got really drunk – especially Sasha and David. Sasha cried all evening afterwards, but that's a good thing. He needs to cry himself out.

In the end I put them both on my bed. David is still sleeping now, in his filthy old scarf. You wouldn't think his father owns a huge law practice in New York.

I'm just sitting here on my own, bawling. It's a terrible thing, burying people who were close to you. It's so terrible, Zhora. Rita was only twenty-eight. It shouldn't have happened.

A big kiss on that horrible beard. I hope your knee is better soon, and I'll visit in a few days.

ALYONA

11

Sasha sat at Merkulov's desk. With an inhuman effort of will he tried to force himself not to think about Rita's death. Yet there were moments when he was ready to get up, burst in on Semyon Semyonovich in the Forensic Office and grab a gun. He wanted to shoot Kassarin himself. He needed to avenge Rita, his father, Kostya, himself. . . .

He had arrived at work half an hour earlier, and it was like being away from home for ten years and returning to find that people had given up on him. They whistled up some looks and questions, though. Maybe they were going to make a hero out of him.

The enquiries department at Hospital No. 11 was engaged for fifteen minutes. Finally an elderly voice answered.

'Merkulov, Konstantin Dmitriyevich? Ward 12. His temperature is 39.2; he's in a serious but stable condition.'

All Saturday and Sunday his temperature had been 40, and he was in a critical condition. Oh, God, God, don't let Merkulov die. . . .

'Are you there, Alexander Borisovich?'

He noticed the light of the intercom flashing desperately. 'The Prosecutor of Moscow, Comrade Yemelyanov, is calling you about the Rakitin case. Please bring your files.'

Parkhomenko was sitting in Yemelyanov's office, hanging on his new chief's every word. Tapping his pencil on the desk, the Prosecutor of Moscow said, with no preamble: 'Comrade Merkulov's mistake – and yours too, Comrade Turetsky – was that your trip to Comrade Chebrikov was not cleared with us.' He gestured to himself and his colleague.

Parkhomenko nodded his head sagely. Although Sasha wasn't about to start arguing the toss about 'uncleared actions', Sergei Andreyevich Yemelyanov protested: 'No, Alexander Borisovich, I don't intend to discuss now who was right and who was wrong – all the more so given the losses suffered. But we have to go on working, fulfilling our duty to the people, the Party and the government.'

He stretched out his hand, and Sasha put two bulky files into his fleshy palm. 'Today is the last of the ten days that the Central Committee gave us to discover the murderers. Your team handled its task excellently. Today I shall report to the Central Committee on the solving of the murder. But, as I understand it, the Rakitin case has spawned a good dozen associated cases, and there's a great deal of work ahead. . . .'

Yemelyanov jumped up from his armchair and walked round the office with small steps, his hands behind his back. 'There are two paths open to us. The first is by far the easier and the more pleasant: to farm out – I mean *refer* – these cases to the relevant departments of the Ministry of Internal Affairs, the Anti-Corruption Squad and the KGB. But politically – politically! – we ought to conclude this case ourselves. We, the Public Prosecutor's Office, which in the mind of our General Secretary, Comrade Andropov, must become the focal point of investigative authority in the country.'

The introductory part of the Moscow Public Prosecutor's speech was concluded, and he sat down in his armchair again.

'Unfortunately, Comrade Merkulov can't resume his duties for some time. Incidentally, I have been informed that we need have no fear for Konstantin Dmitryevich's life now. I suggest that we assign the Forensic Prosecutor, Comrade Moiseyev, to your investigation team. You, Alexander Borisovich, will temporarily become Senior Investigator. What do you say? Can you handle it?'

Sasha answered unequivocally: 'Yes.'

By 1.45 he was working in his new capacity, as head of the

investigation team engaged on the Rakitin and Kupriya-nova murders. Only there was no team to speak of since Semyon Semyonovich attended a clinic for some treatment on Mondays and would not show up until after dinner and the second member of the team, Captain Gryaznov, had not arrived for work, for reasons unknown, according to Romanova.

Sasha was typing out a resolution announcing a local search for Vitaly Shakun. His photograph lay on the desk – round-faced, tow-haired, a broad nose, bright, slightly bulging eyes. An ordinary face. A murderer's face.

He continued tapping away with one finger. Under article 90 of the Criminal Code, the ten-day time-limit for detaining the large number of suspects was running out. When it did, they had to be charged, released, or have their circumstances alleviated – maybe by getting them to sign a statement saying they would not leave town. The list was endless – Volin, Lukashevich, Frolov – plus another five or six people from Volin's black-market business and the Leonovich–Mazer shady deals.

The head of the remand prison had been driving every-one up the wall with his phone calls. Damn legalistically minded character. Sasha would just have to pound out these resolutions and let him have them. He was working furiously when he heard a stick tapping along the corri-dor. Semyon Semyonovich had returned.

Sasha picked up the case notes and went to his office to give him the job of collating the circumstantial evidence against Shakun – footprints, particles – just as with Kazakov-Kramarenko. It must all be ready for when the second murderer was caught.

Yemelyanov had said: 'I shall report the solution of the murder.' And it was as if no one by the name of 'Kassarin' existed on the face of the earth. As if the Moscow Pros-ecutor had never seen, with his own eyes, the documents incriminating a KGB general. As if there had never been a false summons to a meeting with Chebrikov. As if Special Crimes Investigator Merkulov had gone on a joyride without his superiors' permission, and for that must pay a high price unavenged.

It was a struggle between life and death, a wolf-hunt, but no one knew which was the hunter and which the beast, dripping blood. . . .

Semyon Semyonovich opened the safe and took out a quarter-bottle of vodka. He poured out two little glassfuls and said: 'Let's drink, Alexander Borisovich, to Margarita Nikolayevna. God rest her soul.'

Sasha took a sip and looked longingly at the bunch of keys to the safe. They were swinging like a pendulum, beating out a rhythm on the safe-door. Behind that door were Rakitin's duplicate papers.

Merkulov's attempt to expose Kassarin had not come off, just as Rakitin's operation in Sokolniki Park had not come off. Kazakov-Kramarenko's testimony against Kassarin on its own meant nothing – it would just be regarded as the slanders of a long-standing criminal – all the evidence about Kassarin's criminal activities abroad would be seen as so much window-dressing. He would blame the murders on American intelligence; the capitalists had been hunting for the secret doctrine, and that was all there was to it.

But there was one question whirling deep in Sasha's subconscious, slipping and sliding and evading his grasp. Suddenly it broke through. *Why did Kassarin want those papers at any price? What was he afraid of?*

He could have picked off the investigators at any time but he wanted the papers.

Merkulov had said when they were in the compartment of the local train that Rakitin wanted 'publicity' for Kassarin, and he was obviously dead scared of such publicity in the West. That would be the end. No one could cover up that.

Sasha looked at Moiseyev's safe again. He knew what he was going to do. With Rita gone, he had nothing to lose.

But back in his office his heart was pounding as he took

a volume of some old case from the shelf and rang Moiseyev.

'Semyon Semyonovich, Leonid Vasilyevich wants you right away,' he chirped into the receiver in imitation of Garik, then rushed headlong out of the office, walking into the Forensic Office as naturally as could be with the file under his arm.

'Alexander Borisovich,' said Moiseyev fussing around, 'just sit here on your own for a bit. I don't think I'll be long.'

What he was doing was highly irregular, but so what? He went quickly over to the safe. Moiseyev, in his anxiety, had left the keys still dangling from the lock. Sasha searched the shelves. Under a bundle of newspapers, he felt a piece of rough oilcloth. He pulled the thick packet of papers out of it and replaced them with the old case notes.

A disappointed Semyon Semyonovich came limping back. Some idiot had been playing a joke on him. The old Forensic Expert ignored the evidence of his own eyes – Sasha's beet-red face and shaking hands.

'Seventeen hundred hours precisely,' answered the 'dial the time' service. He was counting the minutes to the end of the working day. His watch seemed to be getting slower and slower, so he kept dialling every fifteen minutes.

Suddenly, there was an incomprehensible din in the corridor outside. Someone was swearing loudly. Sasha went over to the door, which burst open to him together with a foul smell of vodka-laden breath. Captain Gryaznov toppled into the room, dropping into a chair with a grunt and leaning back dizzily.

'I'll get him, Sasha. I'll get that rat and his bitch. . . . I could strangle them with my bare hands for what they did to little Rita. And Kostya, my friend. . . .'

Gryaznov and the chair crashed backwards. Sasha tried to pull him on to the divan, but he fought back; he wanted to stay on the floor in the small space between the cupboard and the edge of the divan.

Sasha ran off to enlist Moiseyev's help, locking the door behind him. Semyon Semyonovich had chemicals in his lab for every contingency. A minute later they were massaging the Captain's temples, pouring something into his mouth, and waving ammonium chloride under his nose.

'Don't you find, Alexander Borisovich,' said Moiseyev, 'that this spectacle coincides with the well-known supposition that "Man" has a proud ring to it.'

He did not. But he felt sorry for Gryzanov and knew pretty well what he must be going through. When he had calmed down, Gryaznov lay on the divan, his thin ungainly legs dangling off it, still in their fashionable boots, toes pointing inwards like a child's. Semyon Semyonovich hobbled off to organise some transport to take Gryaznov home. Sasha locked the door and put down the safety-latch so that no one could unlock it from outside. Then he listened to the Captain's confession.

They had bought him because of a two-bit misdemeanour. Someone had seen him drunk while on duty on 7 November at a government establishment. Count number one. While heavily intoxicated, he was telling anti-Soviet jokes. Count number two. Three, and worst of all, he had been caught at the Sandunovsky public baths by a district committee team out hunting for violators of labour discipline, while he and some other men from Moscow CID were calmly drinking beer in a private room there during working hours.

Kassarin called him in and said he would have all the charges dropped if he would work for the KGB. Slava had a spirit of adventure and at first even liked the idea of checking up on his own boss, Merkulov. Later he realised there was something crooked about the whole business, but by then it was too late. . . .

Moiseyev came back with Gena and all three of them pushed Gryaznov into the driver's car, shielding him from the bosses' eyes.

It was five to six.

Sasha sat on a lavatory seat. It was a bit banal but the best he could think of. He waited until he footsteps and conversation in the corridor outside had died away. He listened to office doors slamming, and keys turning in locks, for about thirty or forty minutes, then he emerged from his retreat and walked the length of the corridor both ways, checking all the doors. There was nobody about. He took the screwdriver he had ready and unscrewed the metal hinges from the padlocked glass-fronted cupboard, he took out the key to the forensic office and screwed the hinges back in place.

In Moiseyev's room, without putting on a light, bumping into some instruments in the gloom, he pulled down the blackout curtains and then turned on the table lamp. He set up a tripod and fixed a Zenith camera in place. The lab also had some special reproduction apparatus, but he was not sure how to use it and unwilling to take a risk. He switched on four arc lights, set the aperture at 5.6 and the exposure at 1/125 of a second – the standard settings for the best results.

He had to fix the objects to be photographed to the wall. Only then did he realise that not once had he examined the Rakitin 'originals'. He just hadn't been interested in them. He knew that they contained the notorious 'Doctrine No. 3', Rakitin's notes on Kassarin's nefarious activities and some documents relating to them. Sasha was interested in only one thing – sending the papers abroad and getting his revenge on Kassarin. He had very little time. David Drapkin was flying to America the next day and he must – he *had* to – help. After that, Kassarin could do what he liked.

Sasha looked at his watch. He'd been cutting it fine to finish here and find David Drapkin. It was ten past seven already.

The 'originals' consisted of a hundred and six neatly cyclostyled pages, twenty-two from a 'Chief Raw Materials Export' note pad covered with Rakitin's large handwriting, a few foreign invoices in German, French and

English, copies of bank cheques, bills in Russian, and about a dozen documents he could not understand. Two printed sheets or four notepad sheets per frame made fifty-nine altogether. Ten or twelve more for the rest should do the trick. Two rolls of film. Half an hour's work.

Sasha fixed the first two sheets to the wall.

LENIN DOCTRINE NO. 3
(A Plan for implementing a world-wide communist programme of national creation)

Proceeding from the basic tasks contained in the historical work of V. I. Lenin, 'The Future Tasks of Soviet Power', and from the programme of the Communist Party of the Soviet Union received at the 22nd Congress of the Communist Party of the Soviet Union and the Declaration of the Moscow Conference (Moscow, November 1978) – the Communist Party of the Soviet Union calls upon all states and peoples to embark resolutely on the path of adherence to a policy of peace, of détente. . . .

Sasha did not bother to read any more of these pages and guessed the Americans wouldn't bother, either. He pinned up the next page.

. . . that the doctrine worked out by V. I. Lenin whereby the complete destruction of capitalism and the complete victory of the socialist system will be realised in practice by the year 2000. . . .

Boring. Then the next ones.

He clicked through several pages of pure demagogy – and then there was something more interesting.

. . . in developing the plan one notes the following politico-military options open to socialism for

295

its seizure of the countries of the capitalist bloc. . . .

He quickly skimmed through a few pages before filming them. He was surprised that Rakitin and then Merkulov should have taken all this nonsense seriously. They were supposed to be grown men yet they were afraid of. . . .

The next part was headed: 'Competition between the two economic systems of socialism and capitalism.' Sasha photographed ten pages without even looking at the text, and realised he had used up the first roll of film. It was already ten to eight. If he went on studying this stuff, he wouldn't be through before midnight. He finished photographing the rest of the doctrine in a quarter of an hour. While he was putting the pages back in order, he read one of them.

Thanks to the successful activities of 'T' committee of the KGB of the USSR, we have at present been able to bring to the USSR the blueprints of the French fighter plane, the FI Mirage, the laser gyroscope made by the American firm Honeywell, and a lot else. . . .

Exploiting the internal contradictions between the USA and her partners – Japan, Canada, Great Britain and others – widening the radius of isolation the USA finds itself in. . . .

To create a policy of economic pressure on the USA by using the unlimited resources of raw materials in the USSR and the countries of Comecon (at present the USSR exercises control over 40% of the world's oil, 60% of its diamonds, copper 70%, nickel 60%, bauxite 90%).

By 1995 the USA must be deprived of, in the first instance, steel, titanium, nickel, chrome and aluminium – essential elements in the manufacture of aircraft and submarines, and also of vital strategic resources, especially resources for the production of nuclear energy.

Someone was coming down the corridor! Sasha froze. A woman's voice was singing tunelessly. Hell! He'd completely forgotten the Prosecutor's Office cleaning woman.

She was called Serafima Ivanovna, and the staff were more afraid of her than they were of Parkhomenko, though they had something in common – Serafima was a professional informer, too. She swept floors of an evening in at least four different organisations and that was why she showed up so late at the Prosecutor's Office. Her cleaning was sketchy, to put it mildly, but her earnings equalled the monthly salary of the Head of the Investigations Section.

Sasha put the papers in a cupboard quickly, turned out the light, and bent double inside Semyon Semyonovich's cupboard.

As expected, Serafima did not stay long in the Forensic Office – or, for that matter, anywhere in the building. Stretching his muscles after half an hour or so, Sasha continued his espionage.

Kassarin's service record came next, and other personal information. Sasha completed the work by nine o'clock. He tidied up Moiseyev's office, put Rakitin's papers in his own safe, left the building by the boiler room exit and hailed a cab in the next street.

12

Irka Frolovskaya was sitting in the kitchen, chewing sunflower seeds. Richard, the Alsatian that belonged to her aunt, was lying at her feet.

Irka Frolovskaya's parents were in a state of constant

marital warfare so she spent any time she had off from studying at the conservatory in her aunt's communal apartment, where Klavdia Petrovna kept an old piano.

'Irka,' Sasha hissed, and she jumped readily off her stool. He beckoned her into his room. 'Please, will you help me?'

'Shurik, you know I'd be glad to.'

'Sh, not so loud. Here's a telephone number. Memorize it.'

Her lips moved and she screwed up her cat's eyes.

'Got it.'

'Now go to the corner of Sivtsev Vrazhek Lane. There's a call-box there. Make sure no one can hear you. Ask for David. Tell him that I've asked you to phone him, and that I have to meet him tonight. Understand? Tonight!'

Irka put Richard on a lead and obediently strode to the door, putting on her shabby old coat as she went.

She came back about fifteen minutes later. No one was answering David's phone. When Sasha asked her if she had noticed any suspicious-looking people in the street, Irka unexpectedly replied: 'Yes, I did. There were two of them standing in the churchyard.'

'What made you suspicious of them?'

'Richard growled at them. He knows all the people round here.'

'Did you see a car?'

'No, but I'll go and have a look if you like.'

'Later. What about David!'

'Maybe he's taken his girl to a movie.'

'Who?'

'This David of yours.'

'How did you know he had a girl?'

'Just a supposition.' Irka had entered into her role of detective. 'How's your arm, Shurik?'

'My arm? Oh, OK. Hurts of course, but it's OK,' he answered automatically, trying to recall something. David and Alyona speaking English at Rita's funeral. What had they said? 'Till tomorrow'? No, not that.

Tomorrow he was flying off. He said: 'See you later.' Then they said something else – he couldn't remember what.

Then Alyona said in Russian, 'I'll take you to the airport,' and David said, 'I'll drive myself there. You can drive back.'

'What's up, Shurik?'

'Don't you see – he's at Alyona's! I'm a fool.'

'At who's?'

'It doesn't matter.' He opened his writing desk. Next to Rita's photograh was the bunch of keys to her car. He didn't know how on that day, Friday, they had ended up in his pocket. Probably the boys from work had put them there.

'Irka, we're still in business. Get Richard and take him for a walk. I'll climb out of the window and cross over to Malo-Afanasyevsky Street on the roofs. You wait on the corner. If you see those two men, try to stop them – let Richard loose on them or something. I've got to get a 39 bus and get away.'

'Who are they?'

'They killed Rita.'

Irka pulled Richard's lead and started downstairs.

It was *them* or, rather, *him*. Sasha did not know his name and he hadn't seen his face, but he was certain that it was *him*, the murderer. A black Volga was parked outside the apartment block. Sasha sat on the roof of the house on the corner and waited for a trolley-bus to come round the bend.

He went over to the car and bent down to speak to someone inside. At that second, the bus appeared. Irka saw it as well, because she immediately shortened the distance between herself and *them*.

As always at the terminal, the bus waited a long time. Sasha's legs had gone numb and his heart was thumping. The bus-driver got behind the wheel and opened the door. Sasha jumped. He fought his way through the folding doors as they closed.

Richard was barking wildly as the bus slowly turned on to Bolsoi Afanasyevsky Street. Sasha looked out of the back window. Richard was stopping *him* from getting into the car; Irka had let go of his lead and was flapping around in simulated horror. And then Sasha saw *his* face. It was Vitaly Shakun.

He leapt out of the bus at the Vakhtangov Theatre and ran headlong over to the other side of the Arbat, dashing into the entrance hall of some apartment block. The black Volga was coming from the direction of Arbat Square breaking the speed limit. The bus was heading at full speed along the deserted Arbat towards Smolenskaya Embankment. Through a narrow crack in the door he saw the Volga draw alongside it somewhere by Plotnikov Lane. He left the apartment block and turned into Staro-Konyushny Street, weaving his way through the side-streets of the Arbat until he reached Kropotkinskaya Metro station.

He took Rita's Lada out of the carpark like a thief, gradually gathering speed, then went diagonally across night-time Moscow – towards Sokolniki Park and the Bogorodsky highway.

They caught up with him at a place where an unnamed road debouches to the right from the Bogorodsky highway. It was no more than a kilometre to Alyona's road – if he could just make it!

Sasha looked into the mirror repeatedly. The yellow points of the headlights were getting inexorably closer. He gripped the steering wheel until his hands hurt and put his foot down as far as it would go. The speedometer jumped up to 140 kilometres an hour. The car was almost out of control. He could not cope with the steering, and kept thinking of the stony drop to the side.

A few seconds later, it was clear he couldn't outstrip them. He slowed down. The reflection of their headlights in the driving mirror dazzled him. He clawed at the door-handle. Pushing his right foot down on the brake with all his strength, he kicked open the driver's door with his left.

300

He did not hear the screech of brakes or the spine-jarring crash, but his head felt loosened from his body under the impact. He was sent flying, skidding over the wet concrete surface of the road. The black bonnet of the Volga concertina'd into the boot of the Lada with a terrible crunch, then reared up.

Sasha collided with a post at the side of the road and screamed with pain. A second later he forgot everything as Kassarin's contorted face loomed above him.

'Where are the documents?' he hissed. He looked more like a jackal than a rat. And he was pointing an elongated handgun straight as Sasha's forehead.

Sasha lay back, beaten, immobile, impotent, waiting for his brains to be blown out.

At that moment there was a crashing and tinkling of broken glass, as if a Christmas-tree had fallen over. The windscreen of the Volga, which by some miracle had stayed in place till then, had suddenly shattered into a thousand pieces. Kassarin gave a start, turned his head in surprise for a split second – and Sasha kicked him in the knees with all the force and skill a battered expert in unarmed combat could muster.

Kassarin folded up but managed to shoot, wide to one side, and by then Sasha was on him. But he kept firing, without aiming, the shots striking something metallic. The air filled with the strong smell of petrol. Sasha pushed him away, chopping at his hand and giving him a karate punch to the throat. Head thrown back, Kassarin fell on to the bonnet of the Volga.

Sasha caught his breath and checked that the films were still all right. The two cassettes were safe and sound, stuck firmly in the pockets of his jeans. He looked inside the Volga. Shakun sat there, his face covered in blood. Sasha pulled the gun from Kassarin's limp hand and threw it down the embankment. Then he put his ear to Kassarin's chest. He was still alive.

Sasha got into the Lada, turned the key in the ignition and put his foot down hard. The engine roared, accompanied by a strange loud knocking. Sasha let in the clutch, put her in first gear, and pressed on the accelerator again. Something in the Lada screeched painfully, but it got going, reeling and sagging to the right side, the silencer obviously shattered.

Sasha managed to get as far as the turn off to Alyona's street, then braked and looked back. At first he thought he was mistaken, that he was only imagining it, but then he realised that the yellow headlights were not in one place but were slowly moving, faster and faster still. He speeded up.

Then the sky around him suddenly exploded and shattered. He stopped and jumped out of the car: instead of the yellow headlights on the road there was a blazing ball of fire, crackling and sizzling as it emitted long blue flames.

Sasha ran to save Kassarin, to save the man who had killed Rita. He dashed for the blazing car. Maybe there was still time, maybe he could make it. . . .

Tears cascaded down his cheeks, and he hated himself for them. He was ready to throw himself into that blaze out of hatred for his own weakness, but he pitied Kassarin his manner of dying.

Sasha stood next to the fiery grave and felt nothing more than desperate pity. He could hear an unseen stream flowing close by. He was utterly alone. Everything – all that was beautiful and terrible, good and evil – had passed him by, reached its own conclusion. Only dull irrevocable pain was left.

He took out the film cassettes, exposed them, unwound the black film and threw it on the funeral pyre.

It flared up and disappeared before it touched the flames.

EPILOGUE

Lelya raised Merkulov's head carefully, straightened his pillows and started to feed her husband with something she had cooked at home. He glanced at Sasha in embarrassment but obediently opened his mouth.

Sasha took five sweet-smelling Moroccan oranges from his briefcase and put them on the hospital table. Lida promptly began juggling with them, occasionally dropping the bright-coloured fruit on the floor and rolling it under the bed.

He kept the opened briefcase on his knees, undecided. Inside was the previous day's edition of *Red Star*, on the fourth page of which was an article edged in black.

On 30 November, in the execution of his official duties, in the 48th year of his life, member of the Communist Party of the Soviet Union and Executive of the KGB, Vasily Vasilyevich Kassarin, died. By a decree of the Praesidium of the Supreme Soviet of the USSR, for his accomplishment of a government assignment – the exposure of crimes committed by an entrenched group of felons based in the Ministry of Foreign Trade – V. V. Kassarin has been posthumously awarded the military rank of Lieutenant-General of State Security. . . '

He should tell Merkulov all that happened on that terrible night in Sokolniki. But now yet; not now.

Sasha snapped the locks on his briefcase shut, put it on

the floor and said: 'I'm to stay in the City Prosecutor's Office, in your team.'

Merkulov smiled with his eyes; while Lelya, showing herself well versed in the bureaucracy, asked: 'Does that mean that you've been given your certification ahead of time, Sasha?'

'Well, yes. Kind of.'

Lida had lost interest in the oranges. She hopped on one leg over to the window and yelled: 'Oh, look at all the snow that's fallen. It's horrible!'

Sasha went over to the window. A cold crimson sun hung over the white-blanketed grounds of the hospital.

Winter had come to Moscow.